Door in the Sky

Carol Lynn Stewart

Hard Shell Word Factory

Carol Lynn Stewart

ISBN: 0-7599-0051-5
Trade Paperback
Published February 2002

© 2000 Carol Lynn Stewart
Ebook ISBN: 1-58200-560-5
Published November 2000

Hard Shell Word Factory
PO Box 161
Amherst Jct. WI 54407
books@hardshell.com
http://www.hardshell.com
Cover art © 2000 Dirk A. Wolf

There are so many people to thank.
I could not have written this without the loving
support of Christopher and Daniel Stewart,
Keith and Ginny Mattison,
and the help of my readers;
Kathryn Crabtree,
Marty Wofford, Madeline Archer, Karen Stewart,
Karen Rice, and Susan Williams.

I also want to thank the members of Paul Cohen's Writers Workshop,
with thanks to Jane Cullinan and Anne Friedman.

A special thanks goes to the late Diogenes Angelakos
and Ruth Tobey of the Electrical Engineering
and Computer Science Department at Berkley,
who gave me the time necessary to finish the first draft.

Finally, my fondest thanks goes to my Editor, Christine
and to Mary Z. Wolf,
Publisher of Hard Shell Word Factory.

Chapter 1

THE NIGHTMARE woke her, jolted her into awareness. Maríana de Reuilles sat up in her bed and pulled the blankets to her chin, clenching the heavy woolen fabric so tightly her hands tingled. When her heart slowed and she could breathe without wheezing, she listened for Alys, her nursemaid. All she could hear was a gentle snoring.

Good. This time, she had not screamed. Usually when she had the nightmare, she cried out in her sleep and Alys awakened. The priests had told Alys to plaster Maríana's chest with garlic paste when she had the dream. The smelly paste sat ready in a pot on the shelf. It did not matter to Alys that the garlic had grown mold; the priests told her to plaster her lady's chest and so she would.

Maríana put on her shoes and drew a woolen mantle over her gown. She could not risk slipping back to sleep, to the nightmare. There was one place where she could prove to herself that she was not afraid, that it had only been a dream. Meadow rushes were strewn across their chamber's worn stone floor, but she still felt the chill of granite through the shoes' thin leather soles.

She listened at the entrance to their chamber. No sound came from above where her father's guards patrolled the tower ramparts. She crept down the curving staircase, her hand trailing along coarse and jagged stones. Torches set along the staircase wall were guttering. Someone would be along soon to replenish them. No time to waste.

At the bottom of the stairs, she pushed aside the bolt that sealed the massive door, cringing at the creaking howl of iron against wood. She waited a moment longer, listened again, and heard only the rustling whisper of torch flames. Slipping through the doorway, she emerged into the moon-washed shadows of the inner bailey.

The night was old. Perhaps only a short while till dawn. She noted the position of the moon and morning star, then looked back at the brooding hulk of the tower behind her. It was the donjon, the oldest structure of the château fortress. It should be locked until sunrise, but she couldn't lock it from out here. She could only pray she got back before anyone noticed.

It was a small thing, surely, leaving the door unlocked so close to dawn. In her thirteen years, she had never witnessed a real battle, though her father and his vassals fought for the King of Navarre and the squires continually practiced their battle skills. She stopped on the top step, her foot tracing the smooth, worn surface at the center of the next step.

Rumors from Toulouse spoke of siege and death.

There was always a war somewhere. Anyway, Reuilles-le-château had stood for five hundred years and she heard that even the priests were blessing the war in Toulouse. She drew her mantle more tightly against the early morning chill and raced across the uneven stone surface of the inner bailey, past the stables, around the corner of the wooden pens that housed cows and pigs, and finally to the low stone wall that enclosed the château garden. Her mother's garden.

THE WALL stretched one hundred paces on either side of the garden's entrance. The back of the garden was bordered by the outer wall that surrounded the entire fortress, although trees within the garden obscured this. She peered into the tree shadows. People told her this garden was haunted. No one would go there before the sun peeked over the horizon.

She squared her shoulders and walked past the row of hawthorn trees that stood in solemn and holy guardianship of the entrance. She could see no more than their shapes now, but she knew these trees, knew the shade of their trunks was the gray of cold hearth ashes, knew that the early spring flowers just starting to appear among their leaves were the pink of a baby's ear.

This was her mother's garden, after all. What could harm her? She came there often enough in daylight. She followed a twisting path toward the garden's center. Along the way, she greeted every plant she could name, squinting at their silhouettes in the dim moonlight. She curtseyed to the spike-leafed henbane; waved at the feathery meadowsweet, nearly as high as her shoulder; smiled at the barberry, flowering now, the scarlet berries would come later. Dropping to her knees, she ran her fingers along the soft leaves of eyebright, while she breathed in the carrot fragrance of caraway, newly budding, and the earth spice tang of mugwort, now blooming.

Alys had told Maríana that her mother knew all the names, all the uses of the plants that grew there. But Maríana could barely remember her mother, Thérèse, Baroness de Reuilles, daughter of Iranzu Jakintza. Thérèse from Canigou, mountain that could not be climbed. Thérèse, who had paced the worn stone floor of their bedchamber, thick braids of her ebony hair hanging down below her waist, swinging in time to her restless motion.

Thérèse, who had disappeared when Maríana was hardly more than a baby.

Maríana shuddered. She was only delaying, avoiding what she knew she must do. She had been kneeling too long in front of the eyebright. Her legs and feet were prickling and the damp ground made a wet blotch across the middle of her skirt. It was time to face her fears. She stood and brushed bits of earth and moss off her gown, then continued down the path to the center of the garden.

To the pool that had no bottom.

As she moved past flowering bushes and silvery birch that arched in a graceful curve over beds of prepared earth, she clutched her mantle to still the shaking of her arms. The pond was not large — in daylight it was easy to see the opposite bank and would take little time for a strong swimmer to cross it. Yet no one would go into it. They would draw water from it for the garden, yes; they would dip a bucket into it and use the water to rinse off the sweat of work during the hottest part of summer. But swim in it? They would not even drink from it.

Last year a young boy, just barely old enough to leave his mother's breast, had wandered into its icy embrace. Her father's men had used their tall oak staffs and long branches to sweep into the waters, leaning as far over the edge of their sturdy wood and bark boat as they dared. She had watched from the shore, had seen the grief and resignation upon the mother's face. The boy's body was never found.

Such water must have power, great power. Her steps slowed. She smelled it now, the chill, green fragrance of floating weeds, and could see the scaly burdock bushes that hugged its banks. It was darker here — a mourning blackness swallowing all hope. The flowering brush and birches formed a thick stand around the edge of the pool. Clouds had danced across the moon and were lingering there. Her eyes strained to catch a glimpse of the surface. Until the moon emerged, the pool was hidden. If she was not careful, her feet would take her straight into the water.

She dropped to the ground and reached out to feel through the thicket of burdock for the pool's edge, thrusting her hands into the tangled mass to find the earth. The wind was rising and leaves shivered above her head. If she could find the surface of the water, she could dip her fingers in and anoint her brow, her shoulders, her chest with it. The château priest had told her to do this, to make the sign of the cross upon her body with water from the bottomless pool. Only last week she had crept out to the garden before the donjon door was locked. It had been daylight then. She had knelt at the edge of the pool, quivering when the frigid water trickled down her forehead, between her breasts. Blessed Mary, mother of God, deliver me. But the nightmare still came.

Well, she was here again and she had better find the water. Then she could leave the murky shadows, leave the rustling and grieving sighs of voices with nothing human in them. She could go back to her chamber and draw the blankets up around her face and pray for the nightmares to cease. Maybe this time it would work. She dug her hands deeper into the brush and leaned forward.

Her fingers touched something smooth and warm, something that trembled. She snatched her hand away and bit back a yelp as the brush before her parted. A shape emerged and loomed over her. Strong hands grabbed her arms from behind. She was lifted up off the ground and held there, dangling.

"Not a ghost." A voice spoke close by her left ear. "A girl!" The accent was cultured, but clipped, with a nasal quality that was unlike speech from Navarre. This one was from the north, Paris, maybe. But the voice held a grating whine. She knew this voice, yet when the hands upon her arms pinched, the name fled. She turned toward the speaker and struggled to see his face, her heart tripping and fluttering in her throat.

"How can you tell?" The figure in front pulled free of the burdock, branches snapping and cloth ripping. "I cannot see beyond my nose." His voice was breathless, had he been running?

"My hands can tell," the first speaker said. His fingers caught in her hair and then followed the line of her back, while his other hand still held her arm in a tight grasp. Were they bandits? She had heard of rebel knights who had taken to the road, but how had these men gotten across the lake and over the high walls surrounding the château fortress without the guard spotting them?

"Well, let's move her back onto the path so we can see her better." Another voice spoke from her right side. Three of them, then. No one knew she was here. If she screamed, would anyone come?

The man who held her pulled her away from the pool. When they reached the path, clouds bid the moon farewell and its silver light touched the trees, the bushes, the ground, and her captors. She squinted at their faces, and her body sagged in relief.

"Whoa! Is she fainting?"

She stared at the long nose of Jean-Pierre Rhomboid, the unruly curls of Arnaut Vaillancourt, the straight black hair and thoughtful gaze of Richard de la Guerche. Three of her father's squires — boys, not men. Not bandits. "What are you doing here?" she demanded, shaking her arm free of Arnaut's grasp.

"What are we doing here?" Arnaut recaptured her arm, his fingers digging into her skin. "I might ask you that! Don't you know that this garden is haunted?" He leaned forward. His breath moved strands of her hair. The honeyed scent of mead tickled her nose.

"This is my mother's garden." Her heart started tripping again.

"So you say." Mocking laughter ran beneath his words. "Will she come out of the bushes to scold me?"

Richard stepped forward and placed a hand on Arnaut's arm. "Enough, Vaillancourt. You were the first to reach the pool — you have won your dare. Leave the girl alone."

But Arnaut tightened his grip on her. Bile rose in the back of her throat and outrage stiffened her back. She shook her arm again and slammed her heel on Arnaut's foot. He fell back. Richard's hand stopped him from tumbling into the bushes.

"Yes! Leave me alone," she said. "All of you must leave. This is my mother's garden and my father's château."

"Wait!" Arnaut shrugged off Richard's hand. "I know you — the girl who lives in the donjon!" He leaned toward her. "If Baron Louis-Philippe de Reuilles is your father," he said, "then why don't you live with the rest of the family in the palais instead of in the donjon?"

"That is my father's concern," she countered, meeting his eyes steadily. His words brought hollow anguish into her chest, but she would not show any of them her sorrow. Lifting her chin, she stared back at him.

Arnaut laughed and took her face between his hands. "I think you are lying," he whispered, then, "I think we will throw you in the pool!" His voice rose to a shout as he released her face and grabbed her by the waist, lifting her into the air and starting back toward the bottomless pool.

"No!" She shook so hard her protest was no more than a squeak. Bushes passed in a blur.

Jean-Pierre said, "No, Vaillancourt..." But Arnaut was already ahead of them, nearly to the edge, now.

"Well, what do you think? Will you float? Will you sink?" He held her close and spoke into her ear. "If you float, what does that make you? A demon?" The still surface of the water glimmered through twisted branches.

"My father will have you whipped," she said, twisting her head and grabbing at his tunic with her teeth. "Let me down!"

"Ha!" He lifted her higher and swung her from side to side. "So you say."

She could not seem to catch her breath, and the taste of acid coated her mouth. If he threw her in, she would join the small boy at the bottom. But who would cry for her? She lifted her feet to her chest and threw her weight back. He stumbled and crashed to the ground, pulling her with him.

"Bloody bitch!" he roared.

She rolled away from him and leaped up, sprinting toward the path. The moonlit space beyond the thicket of birch beckoned, but her feet took her directly into one of the other boys who caught and held her fast.

"Enough of this jest, Arnaut." It was Richard. She knew his voice now, remembered its timbre, darkly rich. He held her face crushed against his chest. She could smell the evening meal of roast goose and bread custard on his shirt. "The girl is terrified, and we must get back to our quarters before Guillaume finds that we have gone out."

Arnaut cursed at the mud on his breeches. "Vascone! Just like her mother," he grumbled, then "Jakintza whore." His voice dropped so low that she was not sure of his words. "Why don't you join your mother? We can arrange..." The last words were bitten off.

"Quiet," Jean-Pierre whispered, then, "We will meet you back at the stables."

"We can't leave him here with a Jakintza!" Arnaut said.

"Come on, will you!" Jean-Pierre again.

Her back stiffened again, but she stayed where she was, listening to Arnaut's grumbling complaints and their footsteps fading away.

"They're gone." Richard's voice rumbled in his chest.

She lifted her head.

"Really, you can let go now." There was an undertone of laughter in his voice, but she did not mind. His laughter did not mock. He released her and she backed away.

"He wouldn't have thrown you in, you know."

The sky was pale gray. He was visible now, the faint gleam of his teeth and his brown-black eyes, the smooth line of his black hair as it fell forward over his face and the motion of his head as he shook it back. She knew the exact shade of his hair in the sun, a warm black that shines deep burgundy in the light. His eyes were also warm, the color of dark old wood that had been polished and rubbed to a fine sheen, with an amber glow.

Her fingers twisted in her mantle and she pulled it forward to cover the damp spot on her skirt. "He has pulled my hair often enough. Tripped me, too." And called her Jakintza whore.

Richard shook his head and started down the path toward the entrance. "Well," he looked back, "that is Arnaut. He dared us to come here in the dark." His shoulders lifted. "What were you doing out here, anyway?"

Her throat closed and she fought to make her speech even. "A nightmare."

He stopped, turning to face her. "Indeed! What did you dream?"

Could she tell him? Would he mock her, too? But he had never laughed at her. Richard stood watching her, not speaking, not moving. Drawing in a shuddering breath, she spoke, "I dreamed my mother left her grave and came to my chamber. She was trailing dirt and ooze and mud. I could see the marks from her feet on the floor. Weeds from the pool were hanging everywhere on her body — from her neck, from her fingers, from her legs." Maríana wrapped her arms around her middle and continued softly, "She reached out for me, to hug me. I left my bed and ran to her, but when I got close all her skin and muscles sagged and peeled away from her face and skull."

"A horrible dream!" His hand rose and nearly touched her. "But why come out here?"

"I am not sure. The same dream has come to me often. Every time I have it I feel drawn to come here. To prove I am not afraid," she mumbled the last words. This was the first time she had ventured to the pond in the dark. But she was not afraid. She had come out here, hadn't she?

"Well, anyone would be frightened by that dream." Richard looked away, toward the edge of the garden where birds in the hawthorn trees were starting to awaken, their trilling making the leaves shudder.

"You don't understand! I would give anything to see my mother again, anything. But in the dream I push her away. I reject her." It was not fear that drove her to the garden. Not fear.

He watched her in silence again. "It was a dream," he finally said. "Father Gregory says we have no control over what we do in dreams."

A strangled laugh broke into a sob. "He also says that God speaks to us in dreams." She rubbed at her eyes and walked away from him toward the entrance. "If that is so, then what is God trying to say to me?"

"Perhaps your dream was the result of the onions at supper last night?" He had reached her side. His eyes glimmered in the growing light and crinkled at the corners.

"You have been talking to Alys. The priests make her put garlic on me to stop the nightmares." Her voice was steady now, as they walked past the hawthorn trees.

"Well, this is where I must leave you," Richard gestured toward the stables, where Guillaume, her father's seneschal, was struggling to open the enormous wooden doors. Arnaut and Jean-Pierre were leaning out of the upper window, the squire's quarters, and waving at Richard. But Richard turned his back to them, facing her. "I may have something that will help stop your nightmares." He fumbled with the pouch attached to his belt. "Ah! Here it is."

A small stone lay in the center of his palm. He took her hand and closed her fingers around it.

"It is a bloodstone. My mother found it for me years ago when I had nightmares."

She glanced up at him. "You?"

His cheeks turned pink. "It was years ago. I was just a baby. Here, I will show you what to do with it." He took the stone from her and grasped it tightly in his left hand. "You hold it like this when you go to sleep." He returned the stone to her and she held it up to her face. It had bands of red against a dark green and was warm from his touch.

"I will use this," she said. "How can I thank you?"

For a moment, he did not speak. The honking of hungry geese and the grunting of pigs from the pens around the corner tickled her ears. Alys would be waking; she must get back. But she waited, watching his face.

"Do you still have lessons?" Richard asked.

"What?" Looking at the curve of his cheekbones had set her dreaming. "Lessons?"

"Lessons. With your grandmother." He stared down at his feet.

"Oh. Well, yes, we still read together. She will not allow me to be dependent on priests to keep château records. But how did you know about my lessons?"

He smiled. "I saw you with her on the steps of the donjon. You were reading something. She was listening."

His brown eyes tilted above high cheekbones. The intent regard made her face warm. "Yes. *Songs of Raimbaut d'Orange*. A gift from minstrels who passed through here." She looked up. "But why do you ask?"

"I do not know how to read, and, well..." his voice trailed off and he looked over his shoulder to where Guillaume spoke to the squires, who now formed a line between the stables and the livestock pens.

"You would like to learn," she finished for him.

He turned to her, but backed away, toward the squires.

"You could come to the donjon later — Grandmother comes to my chamber every morning." She raised her voice to reach his ears as he backed away. "I could ask her."

He lifted his hand and was gone, joining the jostling crowd.

GUILLAUME marched up and down, scowling at his charges. She watched the good-natured shoving and teasing among the squires until a piercing horn sounded from the crown of the donjon. Allowing herself one final glance across the yard to where Richard now huddled with the other squires, she skipped across the cobbled surface of the inner bailey all the way to the donjon. She stopped at its base and stared upward.

The donjon soared into the leaden sky. It was the tallest building of the château. The mountain Irati loomed behind it. Slopes covered by dense woods of pine and beech marched down to the back walls of the château.

Since the time of Charlemagne, the donjon had stood guard over the fortunes of the de Reuilles, an unrelenting reminder of the danger that marches with power. The donjon used to house the entire de Reuilles family, their servants, guards, knights and squires. Now only the lesser servants and tower guard slept on moldy straw and rag mattresses in the five chambers that opened onto the winding central staircase.

She put her back toward the donjon and faced the graceful palais her grandfather had constructed to house the de Reuilles family and visiting knights. Where the donjon brooded, its thick walls jutting into the sky, the palais danced. The elegant lines of its arched doors and windows proclaimed that a fine and ancient family resided inside. The de Reuilles lived in perfect comfort there. Mattresses were stuffed with crushed rosemary and meadow rushes. Floors were smooth river stone in the great hall and polished wood in the upper chambers. Windows were covered with rich tapestries that servants could push aside so that the soft air of summer would fill the hall. Johanna, Maríana's grandmother, Geneviéve, her aunt, and Louis-Philippe, her father, all lived in the palais. Every de Reuilles except Maríana.

She turned back toward the donjon and the work she knew waited: the half-finished tapestry of the de Reuilles crest, the tangled threads of her attempts at embroidery, the slim volume of troubadour songs. She felt the weight of the bloodstone and ran her fingers along its smooth surface. Would Richard truly share her lessons? May the blessed Virgin grant her this wish, at least. She bowed her head to the watchtower guard, who stood scratching his head while he examined the doors and muttered, "Unlocked." She fought to keep her face solemn while she mounted the stairs, but before she could push past him, another voice outside called her name.

"MARÍANA!" Johanna de Reuilles was slowly crossing the inner bailey.

"Grandmother!" Maríana flew down the steps and ran to Johanna's side, taking her arm.

"Did I see you with that young page from la Guerche this morning?"

Nobody could keep anything from Johanna. "I was just talking to him, grandmother. And he is a squire, now." How could she convince Johanna to allow Richard to share her lessons? "He gave me this stone to chase away my nightmares." She opened her hand and Johanna peered at the bloodstone.

"What sorcery is this?" Johanna grumbled, touching the stone. Maríana waited while Johanna pursed her lips and her forehead creased.

"Well," Johanna finally said. "I suppose if it helps..." Her words stopped when an angry voice echoed across the bailey.

"Wait for me, you bastard!"

A knight was running across the courtyard. Ducks and geese scattered as he plowed through them. Maríana froze. The knight chased her father. She stood, transfixed, hands clutching the folds of her gown as her father moved toward her in an easy loping stride. No matter how many times she saw him, she could do little more than stare.

Louis-Philippe de Reuilles stood at least a full head taller than most men, his body powerful, yet slender with height. Thick chestnut hair swept his shoulders and his skin was flawless. His eyes were a startling blue-green, deeply set beneath straight black brows and fringed by a velvet brush of lashes as dark as pitch. He was dressed for riding, his right hand impatiently tapping his left with the gloves he used. Indigo breeches clung to his legs and his long shirt was covered with light chain mail that glowed softly in the gray light.

He glared at the knight, who had reached him and had taken his arm.

She felt a hand tugging her and glanced away from her father to see Johanna motioning for her to follow.

"But he may come this way..." A lump formed in the back of Maríana's throat. She rubbed at her eyes. No crying! Her father, above everyone else, would not see her tears.

"Now is not the time, my dear." Johanna's mouth looked pinched and sour. "He is in a mood this morning." She turned toward the donjon, but Maríana stood watching her father, her teeth set and hands clenched. Ducks and geese that the knight had set in motion now brushed past her, their wing-tips grazing her legs in delicate strokes.

Her father bent toward the knight and scowled, then shook off the knight's hand and turned, walking purposefully away, his stride taking him directly toward her. She looked back over her shoulder and saw Guillaume standing by the main gate, gesturing to Arnaut as the young squire secured a heavy saddle to a fine Arabian gray stallion. Her father was going to the main gate where his horse was waiting. She was in his way.

She shifted her weight, standing firmly in the path her father was taking. He continued toward her, his eyes upon the ground, hand absently tapping his gloves against his thigh as he walked. Closer now. His expression was blank, eyes shuttered, turned upon some inner landscape. He had nearly reached her. Curling her hands even tighter, she felt the rasp of her nails against her flesh. She drew a breath. "Father?" Her voice was harsh.

Two paces from her, he halted, raising his head. A line formed between his brows and his mouth twitched. But his eyes looked directly into hers.

She could not speak now; her tongue felt thick and clumsy. But she held her body still and met his stare.

He looked down first. He pulled his gloves on, deliberately working the fingers over his knuckles. "Move aside," he said, his voice commanding, but a low murmur. He finished drawing on his gloves, staring at his right hand as he flexed it. Then his gaze raised and bored into her. "Girl."

She straightened her back and stared into his face, but his eyes were shuttered once more, no longer seeing her.

"I have no wish to humiliate you," his voice was still hushed, "but if you do not move aside..."

"Yes. Father." She dropped her arms to her side and drew her skirt out, dipping halfway to the ground and backing toward the donjon in a graceful curtsey that took her out of her father's path. Then she stood there, head bowed, hands clasped demurely below her waist, her spine rigid and her knuckles white. She would give him no reason to humiliate her. But she had made him speak to her. It was several heartbeats before her father moved on his way. Her head still bowed, she watched his progress across the inner bailey, through the arch and the outer bailey to the main gate. A small triumph, but she treasured it, counting the words he had spoken to her. Seventeen. In her thirteen years, he had spoken but forty words to her.

He mounted his dancing Arabian gray, swinging his long leg easily over the horse's back and pulling himself into the saddle in one fluid motion. Arnaut held the bridle and gave her father the reins. Richard handed her father his sword and stepped back while Louis-Philippe slid it into the sheath fastened to his saddle. The yawning gate arched over them and beyond, the fields of Reuilles-le-château formed a golden ripple down to the lake that separated château from town.

The knight who had chased her father was already mounted on his destrier, a glossy red-brown war horse with thick muscles and broad chest. He had turned his horse to the open doors and was riding through. Louis-Philippe drew his reins up, fighting the tossing head of the gray, and glanced back toward the donjon, where she stood. One glance only, but he found her. Then he was through the gate in a brisk gallop.

She stood there looking out through the gate at the fields until she could no longer see the riders. He had looked back. His eyes had sought her. She lifted her face to the donjon and smiled.

Chapter 2

THREE MONTHS had passed since Richard gave Maríana his charm against nightmares. The bloodstone was tucked away under her pillow, now, but she held it clutched in her left hand every night. And every night passed quietly, even when she woke in the morning to find the stone on the floor or hidden deep within the covers.

The same three months had brought Richard to their chamber every day with scraps of cloth, pots of blackberry ink, and tail feathers of geese. Johanna made him copy all the letters of the alphabet four times before she allowed him to see the fragile volume of troubadour songs. When she had first put it into his hands he simply sat on the edge of his stool and stared at it. Maríana had said, "Why don't you open it?"

His teeth had flashed in a quick smile, but he did not speak or move until Johanna reached over and turned the first page. Then he gave a long sigh.

From that moment, whenever Richard came to the chamber, he went directly to the "Songs of Raimbaut d'Orange." He always bowed to Maríana and Johanna when he had to leave, but the entire time he was in the chamber with them, his nose was buried in the book of songs. The only words he spoke were to Johanna and then only to ask her about a word he could not read.

MARÍANA bent over the tapestry, struggling with the precious needle that defied her efforts to draw it through fine woolen fabric. It was early summer and her hands were sweating, even though it was cooler in the donjon than outside the walls. She caught the thread in her teeth and gnawed on it, jumping when she heard footsteps on the tower stairs. Their door stood open. Anyone could enter without warning. A fluttering started in her belly. Spitting the thread stuck between her teeth into her hand, she raised her head to the door.

Her aunt Geneviéve's ample frame filled the doorway. Geneviéve stepped heavily into the chamber. Her plump face smiled. Her weight obscured the de Reuilles features, but she carried her body proudly and her eyes were the same thickly fringed blue-green as Louis-Philippe's. She hugged a large pitcher against her chest and three cups hung from her fingers.

"Maríana, Mama," she said. "I am joining you today." She set the cups on the table, pushing Johanna's lace frame aside and pouring a thick liquid from the pitcher into the cups.

"You are always welcome, daughter." Johanna rescued her lace and placed it upon the bed behind her. "Since you visit us so seldom... .

Geneviéve waved her hand. "But look what I have brought you! Gifts from my bees." She held a cup she had filled underneath Johanna's nose.

"Zythus! I thought it was too early." Johanna raised the cup to her mouth and tipped her head back.

"It is too early for this year. This is the remainder of my last harvest." Geneviéve motioned to Maríana. "Come, girl. You can share with Alys." She poured another cup and placed it between Alys and Maríana.

"What is it?" Maríana peered into the cup and sniffed at it. "It smells of spice!" She moved the cup around in a circle. "And it is heavy."

"It is spiced honey." Geneviéve settled her behind on a stool and held her own cup under her nose, breathing deeply. "Fermented for months in a closed vessel with the blossoms of dandelions, lavender, and Mary's gold." She sipped at it and smacked her lips. "The thin liquid on the top we drain off every month for bochet. Surely you have let her have bochet, Mama?"

Johanna nodded, wiping her mouth on her sleeve. "Everyone has bochet."

"It is not as strong as zythus," Geneviéve agreed. "But the bottom where it is richest is what I bring you today."

Maríana tasted the syrupy drink, dipping her tongue into the cup. She looked up to see Geneviéve filling Johanna's cup again.

"Zythus. Well," Johanna's eyes narrowed as she held her cup in her lap and leaned back against the bed. "What do you want, Geneviéve?"

Geneviéve shrugged, then turned to Maríana. "They tell me that your nightmares have stopped."

Maríana handed her cup to Alys. She had only taken a mouthful, but her head already felt lighter and the chamber had taken on a dreamy clarity. "Squire de la Guerche gave me a charm."

Geneviéve leaned forward. "Did you really go into the garden at night?"

"That was months ago." Maríana gave a wary glance at Johanna, but her grandmother had not seemed to notice what she said. Johanna's eyes were closed, her head bowed.

"All the way to the pool?"

Maríana started. "Who told you?"

Geneviéve waved her hand, a smile making deep creases in her cheeks. She opened her mouth to speak but Johanna abruptly straightened her back and glared at Maríana.

"You did not go into the water, did you?" Johanna asked.

Maríana shook her head, but Geneviéve spoke.

"Oh, mother. You don't believe those tales, do you?" She placed her cup on the table and rubbed her reddened nose. "The water is cold, of course, but the pool is quite safe for people who can swim. After all, Thérèse swam in it every night."

"What?" Maríana's hands knitted together in her lap.

"Well, she couldn't just doff her gown and swim in the lake, could she? After all, they fish at night in Reuilles-la-ville. The whole town would have been looking on her."

Maríana forced her hands to relax. "Maybe that is why Arnaut said I was like my mother." Her words were soft, but Johanna answered.

"You have her eyes. Dark green. I had never seen such color in eyes until I met her." Johanna raised the cup and drained it. An ember fell to the base of the hearth and the fire flared. Johanna's eyes were distant, the edges crinkled with age. She ran her forefinger across the rim of her cup.

"I first saw her when he returned. He had just come back from Damascus, my Louis-Philippe. I never knew why he had gone in the first place. He was not part of the crusade that year." Johanna leaned her head back against the bed. "It was his twentieth summer. He was bored and looking for trouble. I was not paying attention. I suppose his friend Bernart had something to do with it. Bernart was always going somewhere." The bones showed under her skin, sharp edges pushing against soft wrinkled flesh. "Louis-Philippe did not return to us until three years later."

Geneviéve took her cup and raised the pitcher, but Johanna shook her head.

"When he came back he was surrounded by Moors in turbans and flowing robes. All he said to me was 'God's greetings' and then he swept his Moors up the mountain Irati to build that monstrous structure... and some other things here in the château."

"But his mountain palace is beautiful!" Geneviéve cried.

"It should never have been built. He didn't even bring his wife to me! Thérèse came to me herself, to the great hall in the palais. I knew she was from the mountains, the daughter of a Vascone, a Basque." Johanna's eyes gleamed. "They work the land, but call themselves nobles. Nobles by birth," she huffed. "She was not afraid, though. She looked directly into my eyes and told me I would have to find a place for her in the château. Or she would take my grandchild to her valley in the mountains."

"That was I?" Maríana breathed. She did not want her grandmother to stop.

Johanna stared at her. "I knew she was expecting, of course. I could smell her. Pregnant women always smell a bit like babies, a little sour. I asked her how I could be certain that it was my grandchild she carried."

Maríana flinched away from her grandmother's slate stare. "What did she say?"

Johanna did not speak for several moments. Then she closed her eyes. "Nothing. She said nothing." A long sigh shuddered through her body. "But I put her in the tower and gave her Alys."

Maríana's hands twisted the skirt of her gown. A dragging thump outside their door signaled the change of the tower guard. She heard the steady scrape of his sword against the stone of the outer wall, his heavy step.

"Mother," Geneviéve leaned toward Johanna, "That is exactly why I came here today. This situation," she waved at the walls, the bed, the table and stools, "simply cannot continue. Oh, I know it is not my place to chastise my brother." She shook her head at Johanna's raised brow. "Yes, he took me in after Charles was killed, and I am grateful. But he ignores the girl. This cannot go on forever." Her lips set. "There has always been talk among the servants. And the squires torment her."

Maríana held her hands in tight fists next to her belly. "Father spoke to me."

Geneviéve turned to her. "When?"

Maríana stared into her lap.

"I thought so." Geneviéve reached out to Johanna. "Mother, we must both see him."

"Which squires?" Johanna asked.

"It does not matter." Maríana held a hand out to Geneviéve and shook her head in a silent plea.

"Nonsense. What happened?" Johanna looked from Geneviéve to Maríana.

Maríana drew back in alarm as Geneviéve's hand snaked toward her and pulled her skirt above her knee.

"Here." Geneviéve's mouth set in a grim line. "You can see what happened."

Maríana pushed at her aunt's hand, but she heard the sharp intake of breath as Johanna rose and moved to her side. Johanna touched the angry red blotches stretching from Maríana's knee to her ankle. Just below her knee, her skin had blistered in painful bubbles that had oozed at first, and later bled. Now her leg was a mass of crusting scabs and tender pink skin where the scabs had rubbed off.

Maríana ducked her head and yanked her skirt out of her aunt's hands, dropping it once more to her feet.

"I was clumsy and spilled the wax," she muttered. "That is what happened." She looked over at Alys, but Alys would not meet her eyes.

"You mean someone threw it at you. It went right through your gown, didn't it? You can't get that type of burn in a spill." Geneviéve turned to Johanna. "Louis-Philippe has to acknowledge her. Until he does, this kind of thing will keep happening."

Johanna's eyelids had dropped over her eyes so they were slits of blue-gray. "I have not been able to move him in all these years. What makes you think that I will have any success now?"

"This is not like him. I am shocked that he does not acknowledge her, even though she is a daughter, not a son." Geneviéve fell silent.

Maríana stared at her grandmother. Her jaw ached from biting back her words. Yes, tell us! Why does he ignore his only daughter?

"Well, I am sure has reason for what he does," Geneviéve said.

"Yes," Johanna said, "There are reasons."

"But there have been whispers recently, about Ib..." Geneviéve's words broke off. "Well, we will talk later."

Johanna clasped her hands before herself. "Later," she agreed. "But there is something I can do about this now. I will take this matter to Guillaume. He will deal with..."

"No!" Maríana fell to her knees before Johanna and grabbed her hands. "Don't say anything. It is nothing, really. I have almost healed." If her grandmother said anything, then they would know how they had hurt her. Their scorn, she could bear. But not their pity.

"Silly girl." Johanna brushed back a lock of Maríana's hair. "Thérèse was the same. She would not let me intervene."

"Then you won't say anything?" Maríana stared into her grandmother's face.

Johanna did not speak for several moments. Her eyes were opaque, measuring. "No," she replied. "I cannot let this pass." She shook her finger at Maríana. "Your mother was a grown woman. What she did was her own affair. But you are my granddaughter. I will not allow them to bully you."

"There, now." Geneviéve reached out and patted Maríana's arm. "Things will be better for you after this."

"So you say," Maríana whispered as she watched her grandmother leave. The early summer heat and the hearth fire had brought a moist sheen to Geneviéve's skin. But Maríana shivered.

Chapter 3

RICHARD STOOD in the palais's great hall, watching Louis-Philippe de Reuilles read the message he had just handed to him. Golden light from the enormous hearth glinted off the planes of the Baron's face. Voices echoed around the cavernous hall. The palais was filled with a company of monks who were passing through Reuilles-la-ville on their way to St. James de Compostella. They were the last of the pilgrims who would come through Reuilles-la-ville this year. The final moon of summer came next week; already wind from the south — the bochorno — was scattering leaves and fraying tempers.

Johanna had ordered château butchers to slaughter three pigs. These now turned on great spits over the central hearth, the fat sizzling and sending its heavy scent into the air. Monks were everywhere. They crowded onto planks pulled up to the seven tables set around the hall's perimeter, milled about in its open center, their feet shuffling stalks of dried lavender and rushes carpeting the stone floor, or stood in groups conversing in hushed voices on the broad staircase leading to the palais's second floor.

One of this company had sought Richard and given him the message, saying, "This is for de la Guerche's son." Richard passed the message to Baron de Reuilles when he saw the tangle of lines spreading across the parchment it was written upon. He could now read and write well enough to jot down words to the songs that were always dancing in his head, but this message was beyond his ability to decipher.

Louis-Philippe slowly read the words scrawled in an unsteady hand on stained vellum. "It says your father has the wasting sickness. They are asking you to return."

Richard held his breath. Hearing the words spoken so baldly chilled him. "When can I leave?" he asked.

Louis-Philippe gripped his shoulders. "Bernart will accompany you. You can go at first light tomorrow." He waved his hand and a page from Béarn trotted over to them. "Gather some bread and meat into a sack for Squire de la Guerche," he told the boy, then caught him by the arm as he started to dash away. "And some ale," Louis-Philippe added.

THE WASTING sickness meant death, didn't it? It had taken a fortnight for him to travel from la Guerche to Navarre. What if his father died before he got home? Richard halted at the edge of the stables. His mind had been turning the Baron's words over and over. Now, he heard the sound that had jolted him out of his thoughts, heard again a muffled thump.

He listened. Horses moved restlessly. Then the rustle of cloth, another dull thud and a smothered pleading drew him forward, into the stables.

Richard stopped where he was, dropping the sack of meat, bread and ale he carried In the gloom, shapes huddled around a body lying still upon the ground. Hair spilled around the body's head. Richard silently unsheathed his knife and glanced around the empty bailey. No help there, he must confront them himself.

"Get up!" One of the shapes spoke. It was Arnaut, his voice cracking as he grabbed the shoulders of the person lying there, shaking her.

"Why did you hit her?" The other shape asked, his voice shaking as he grabbed Arnaut by the arm. Jean-Pierre!

"She would not say it!" Arnaut spoke hoarsely. "All I wanted was for her to say it." He leaned over the body again.

"Say what?" Richard sheathed his knife. "What trouble have you gotten yourself into now?" He looked down at the girl who lay between them, at the fine-boned face, the tilted eyebrows, the tumble of auburn hair.

"You bastards!" he shouted. He thrust Arnaut away and dropped to his knees next to Maríana. He put one hand underneath her nose to feel her breath and the other on her chest. "What have you done?"

"She told Guillaume about the wax," Arnaut said, his face surly and aggrieved. "She told him!"

The air surrounding Richard seemed to curdle. His mouth moved soundlessly, then he found his voice. "I think you have killed her," he whispered.

"No!" Arnaut leaned over Maríana again, seizing her shoulders and shouting into her face. "Wake up!" His spittle marked her skin. "See!" He placed his fingers lightly on her throat. "Her heart beats in her neck."

Jean-Pierre put a hand on his arm. "Leave it, Arnaut. Let's get Father Gregory."

"No! We will get Jacques the healer. I will look for him," Richard said, then froze. Maríana's eyes blinked open all at once, rimmed in white.

"What?" Arnaut turned his head from Richard to Jean-Pierre. Maríana had lain beneath him, arms still and limp at her side. But now her hands shot up and locked around his neck, her knuckles growing white as her fingers dug into his skin. Arnaut uttered a single, choked cry, tearing at Maríana's hands, striving to pull them away from their grip on his throat. His skin darkened and mottled.

Richard grabbed her right hand and pried at her fingers. He looked over to Jean-Pierre, who knelt there, eyes wide.

"Rhomboid!" Richard said. "Help me here."

Jean-Pierre's hands fluttered around, nearly touching her fingers. When he brushed against her, his face drained of color. "She is like stone! What sort of creature is she?" He moved back.

Richard pulled another of her fingers loose and jumped at the hiss of air rushing into Arnaut's lungs. "Hold on, Vaillancourt," he said, then, "Blessed Mother of God!" when the fingers he had freed clamped hold again.

"Maríana," he strove to keep his voice steady, "you must stop this. Damn!" he shouted when Arnaut convulsed. "Gelditu!"

Maríana released Arnaut and her arms flew outward. Richard stumbled back. Jean-Pierre scuttled away from her left arm when it grazed his leg. Arnaut fell on his bottom and sat holding his throat and wheezing.

"Maríana." Richard struggled to his feet and took her by the arms, pulling her up beside him. "Can you walk? I will help you to the palais." Her eyes were open but he thought she was not seeing him. "Can you hear me?"

"No! Don't take her away." Arnaut had risen also and stood there swaying. "Guillaume gave me extra duty-only me!" He rubbed his throat and his voice sounded raspy. "How did he know I threw the wax if she did not tell him?"

"Leave it, Arnaut," Jean Pierre took his friend's arm. His hands shook so his shaking was jiggling Arnaut. "Let's go."

"I warned her what would happen if she told anyone," Arnaut glared at Maríana and shuffled forward toward her, pulling Jean-Pierre with him.

"How do you know that she told them?" Richard asked, his hands chafing Maríana's arms while she stood unresponsive at his side. "I told you not to hurt her. She has never harmed you, has she?" Arnaut's lip curled in a snarl. Richard sighed and looked away. "Anyone who was there could have told and just about everyone knew about it." He kneaded the skin on her arms. Soft, she was soft. But her skin felt cold to his touch.

Arnaut's puzzlement gave way to comprehension. Rage consumed his features. "Is that it? You want her for yourself?" His lips stretched across his teeth. "Well, why not? She has lost her senses. You could take her right here! We won't say anything. She is mad. Just like her mother." His gaze fixed upon Richard, he grabbed Maríana's gown at the neck, then yanked it toward him. "See for yourself!"

Maríana's gown split and tore. Fury boiled in Richard's belly. He swung his right arm back to strike Arnaut.

Three words stopped him. Words that issued from no human throat.

Words that dropped Arnaut to his knees, his hands digging into his ears, that drove Jean-Pierre back several paces, his arms windmilling in his effort to stay on his feet; words that forced Richard's arms to fall limply to his side.

Then silence. Maríana stood where he had left her. Her extended hands cradled a shifting light that writhed between her palms.

Arnaut lifted his hands from his ears and his eyes bulged as he looked upon the light that danced around Maríana's hands. Richard tried to move but his limbs would not obey his will.

Maríana stood there, her face impassive and severe. She appeared to look into the shifting beam that bent and twisted within her curved hands. It glowed green-gold, its luminous strands throwing the planes of her face into a trembling play of light and shadow.

Richard felt himself drawn to it, deeper into the pattern it formed. Sweat beaded his brow. The pattern was pulling him into the center of the glow, where a dark spot widened, a door was opening... .

He blinked fiercely and forced tears to blur his eyes. Then he clamped his lids down and forced his body to wilt, to pitch forward.

He fell to the ground, his arms unfreezing just enough to stop a bruising blow when he hit the cobbles, and lay there panting. Then he glanced up to where Arnaut and Jean-Pierre still stood. Arnaut's face had grown slack. He was drooling. But Jean-Pierre was still fighting the pattern, his face rigid with fear.

Richard crawled to Maríana, using the glow from the light pattern as his bearing, but keeping his eyes unfocused. He could not risk being drawn into it again. When he was next to her, close enough to smell the rosemary and lavender bag she wore at her waist, he put his arms around her legs and drew her slowly down toward him.

Her body resisted at first, then succumbed to his insistent pressure. He risked a quick glance at her hands to see that she still held the pattern. Keeping his eyes unfocused, he reached up and pushed her hair back from her ear. Then he said, "Maríana. Close the door. Send it back."

She did not respond.

"Maríana. This is Richard. You must send it back now." He felt a shudder course through her body as her lungs sucked in the night air. Then words.

"Richard? But what is..." She looked upon the glowing green-gold form that floated in front of her, no longer in her hands. She reached for it.

He grabbed her hands and repeated. "Send it back. You must tell it to go back."

She met his eyes. Her body curled around her middle, her hands pulling her torn gown over her breasts. Then she turned toward the glimmering light. It was larger now and he was sure it was trying to form words.

"Go back," she said. "Go away. Begone!" She turned to him. "It is still there."

"Damn!" He put his head against her shoulder, fighting the pull of the light. "Can you look into it?"

"Of course, but..."

"Then look at it." But how to send it away? "Look for a dark spot inside it."

He held his breath until he heard her speak. "I see it."

"That is the door. You need to close it." He felt her reach out again. "No! Don't touch it." He paused. How had he broken her grip on Arnaut? "Tell it in Basque."

"What?" Her voice was breathless now. Was it drawing her in?

"Just do it!"

He felt her body shudder again, then uncoil, her back straightening and her chin raising. She seemed to inhale forever, but it could only have been the space of ten heartbeats before he heard her scream, "Aldegin!"

From the corner of his eye, Richard saw the shifting light fold in on itself, curling into nothingness like a burning piece of parchment. A burst of light brighter than the sun lit the night sky. Thunder bellowed, echoing around the bailey. At the same moment, wind slammed into them, tearing wooden slats away from the livestock pens and sending these crashing against the chapel, the stables, the donjon. One piece scraped his arm as it hurtled past; he shouted and grabbed at his torn sleeve. He had to get Maríana to safety. Screams rose above the roaring of the wind and the doors to the great hall of the palais flung open, but bits of ice now pelted him, and the path to the palais was blocked by a cart that tumbled end over end across the stones of the inner bailey. He pulled Maríana away from the stables, his hand holding her head tucked down, while he grabbed his sack of provisions with the other hand and fled with her toward the garden. He did not look back to see where Arnaut and Jean-Pierre had gone.

The long stone wall that surrounded the garden lay ahead. His arm looped around Maríana, Richard passed through the gate. Outside, the hawthorn trees' branches bent before the force of the wind, but inside the gate it was still. He stopped in surprise, but Maríana tugged at his arm. "This way," she said. They ran along the path that led to the pool. Shouts echoed over the roar of the wind outside the garden. She pushed a strand of blackberries aside, then ducked and crawled between the bushes.

"Where are you going?" He dropped to the ground and pushed in behind her, the sack he carried catching on thorns.

She sat huddled on the earth, her arms crossed over her chest, fingers smoothing the tear in her gown. There was room for him to sit across from her in the space between the bushes. The pool shimmered behind her. They must be right at its edge.

"How bad is the rip in your gown?" he asked, tugging at his sack until he got it all the way into the space where she sat.

She shook her head and her hands dropped to her lap. "I cannot repair it."

He averted his eyes from the creamy skin that showed through her bodice. The ground was soft with pine needles, but no pines stood around them. "Did you bring these in?" He grasped some needles in his hand and held them up.

"No." Her face turned away. "This place was already here when I was little."

The howl of the wind had faded to a whisper and the shouting voices were far away now, but there would still be people in the bailey picking up debris. He shrugged his arms out of his shirt.

"Here." He held out his shirt. She stared at it, then at him. "You will need it in order to get back to your chamber."

"But you..."

"I will be warm enough." He tried to drape it around her shoulders, but she held her arms across her chest. "You can wrap it around you." He held the shirt out to her until she took it from his hands. "Do you want to go back now?"

"You can go back if you want to." She slid her arms into the sleeves and held the garment around her. His heart quickened at the sight of the shirt, warm from his body, enveloping her.

"Do you want to tell me what happened?" He saw her start, then she raised her eyes from her fingers to his face.

"Arnaut was angry," she said. "He grabbed me when I came out of the chapel and pulled me with him to the stables." She spoke softly. Richard had to lean forward to hear. "Jean-Pierre was there and they both, they both..." She bit her lower lip. "Arnaut wanted me to say I was like my mother, so I told him that. Then he wanted me to say that I had told Guillaume about the wax. But I did not tell Guillaume, so I would not say it." Her jaw set, but he could see her hands trembling. "I would not say it."

"Was there anyone around? Did anyone see what they did to you?"

At first, she did not speak. Light from the stars trembled upon the surface of the pond. A muscle in his thigh jumped and he moved his leg to ease the cramp. "There were servants and other squires in the bailey, going to the great hall," she finally said. "I called out for help."

"But no one would come," he finished for her.

She nodded, her fingers still running over the material of his shirt. "He pushed me down." She looked up at him with her quiet, luminous gaze. "That is all I remember until you said my name."

"Well." No need to speak of the rest of it now. He lifted the sack and dug his hands into it. "You have not eaten, have you? Are you hungry? Your father gave me bread and meat." He brought out hunks of bread and a large joint wrapped in fresh leaves. "And ale!" He divided the meal in two.

He finished eating first and sat watching her while she ate. He had watched her for a long time, now, from his place in the stables, the inner and outer bailey, the fields outside the walls. Maríana was a puzzle. He saw the squires teasing her, of course. But they teased all the girls. Most of the girls joined in the game. It was all in fun, wasn't it? Yet she never joined in the game, never fought back. She bore it in silence.

Her silences touched him, how she could be so still and at the same time so alive and aware. The way the light loved her face, kissing the finely sculpted bones. Her lustrous skin. How her dark green eyes looked into him. Every minute in her chamber, under her grandmother's eye, he was aware of her. When he looked up from the book Johanna had allowed him to read, it was to see her face, the tiny curve at the corner of her mouth, her clear and radiant eyes.

She was looking at him now. "What was that?" she asked.

He shook himself. "What?"

"The light." She leaned forward. "You must know what it was — you knew how to get rid of it."

"I am not sure, but I am from Brittany and we keep the old ways there." He saw her brows lift. "The old rituals, like buttering the leaves the morning of May eve, so our butter will always be sweet."

A small dimple on the left side of her mouth deepened. "We give cream and honey to the lamia, the mermaids, so our fishing goes well." Her face grew solemn again. "But we are not talking of such small things. What would the light have done if we had not banished it?"

"You banished it, not me. I have heard of such things at home." He raised his hands and spread his fingers, flexed the stiffness out of them. "We were lucky, I guess."

She wrapped his shirt more tightly around her and said, "You can go back. I want to stay here until dawn."

"I should go back." He crossed his arms over his bare chest. "Your father will have me flogged if I stay here with you all night like this." What if Arnaut and Jean-Pierre came here? "And your reputation..."

"No." Her hand on his arm stopped his words. His skin warmed under her fingers, a warmth that spread to his belly. "My father does not notice what I do," she continued. "I have no place here. No place to lose." Her voice was even, but her words touched a place deep inside him. She lifted her hand and he shivered.

"I will stay with you." He bunched the sack into a small pillow and placed it at her side. "Why don't you try to sleep? The ground is dry."

"What will you do?" She did not move.

"I will sit over here." He leaned into the trunk of the bush behind him, ignoring the scratch of branches against his bare skin, then pulled his knife out of the sheath on his belt. "You can take this." He turned it so the blade was in his hand and offered the handle to her.

"Why?" She still did not move.

He placed the knife on the ground between them. "In case I fall asleep and Arnaut comes here. Or in case you feel you may need to defend your honor."

She slid to the ground and burrowed her head into the sack pillow. "Thank you, Richard."

He shifted his weight until he found the least thorny spot and closed his eyes. A heavy warmth spread throughout his body, starting somewhere below his belly and flowing outward in tingling waves. His eyes kept opening. He found himself looking at her motionless figure curled on top of the pine needles. He waited until he saw the gentle rise and fall of her side, the rhythm of sleep. Then he leaned his head back against the bush.

SHE STOOD at the edge of the pool. The water was still and black, mirroring the murky sky above — no stars, just endless depths of oily blackness. She could see her reflection. Bending her head, she tried to make out her features but the water moved, ripples spreading out from the center. Something was trying to get out.

Her heart raced but her feet remained frozen to the ground. A thing made of weeds and mud rose from the water, sprouting a head and arms. Ears and hair formed from the dripping strands of drowned plants. A mouth and nose took shape, but the eyes were hollow. It shuddered, reaching out and touching the surface of the water. She could not turn away; stood and looked at it while it patted the water. Then it whimpered and raised liquid hands up to the space where its eyes should have been. Underneath the gentle trickle of water from the weeds, she could hear a tune. The thing was trying to sing.

"Where is my baby? Where is my little one? How far must I go? The moon pales, the sun rises." The words were half-sung and half-sighed and all the time the thing gave a shaking inhalation as if breathing hurt.

Maríana could smell the carpet of pine needles, the muted, green fragrance of the blackberry bushes, the remains of the pork joint she and Richard had shared. There was something familiar about the tune. The sound painted a picture of gentle hands and curling black hair, of a soft shoulder where she lay her head. Comfort, safety... "Mother?" she wondered aloud.

The thing straightened with an exclamation and turned its eyeless face to her.

"No!" she screamed. "You are not my mother! Go away!"

The thing floated across the surface of the pool until its fingers touched her face with the chill of the grave.

She threw her arms up and screamed again. Richard was standing over her. His hands were dripping and his eyes twitched.

"What?" She was laying on the ground. Surely she had been standing, hadn't she?

"You were dreaming. I tried shaking you." He helped her to her feet. "When I could not wake you I splashed you with water."

She held out her empty left hand. "I did not have my bloodstone." A dream, then.

"What?" He glanced at her hand. "Oh." A quick smile showed his teeth. His bottom front teeth overlapped a little, a small boy's crooked teeth, but he was almost a man. "I think we can go back now without anyone seeing us." He lifted his head to the sky. "The moon just set, so we still have an hour till dawn."

"The donjon will be locked." Her skin tingled under his touch. She leaned toward him, but he dropped her hand.

"Then I will take you there. You can wait on the steps until the guard unlocks it." He dropped to the ground and pushed through the branches to the path.

"What about your shirt?" She crawled after him.

He straightened his back and shrugged. "I have others." He took her arm. "You should tell your grandmother what happened, though."

"I cannot tell her everything." She looked down at his hand on her arm. Now warmth spread in a delicious ache from her belly to her toes.

"No," he agreed. "Not about the light. But do tell her about Arnaut."

"So he can do something even worse? No! He will not get the best of me!"

He lifted her chin so that she had to look into his face. She looked into his warm brown eyes, tilted upward in an almond curve. There was a small white scar at the corner of his broad mouth.

"So stubborn." His eyes danced and laughter lay beneath his words. "But we cannot let this pass. Arnaut should be stopped. And I know how to deal with him."

THE INNER bailey was deserted. Richard swallowed when he saw the devastation the wind had brought. Dead geese were stacked at the corner of the livestock pen, the wooden fence that circled the goose hutch was piled in a heap. He escorted Maríana to the donjon steps and left her there, huddled at its base. Then he marched across the inner bailey to the chapel. He must see Father Gregory first, then Arnaut and Jean-Pierre. His shoulders slumped. In less than an hour he would be on his way back to Brittany to see if his father lived or died.

He remembered riding with his father's seneschal, riding off to Reuilles-le-château. He had been only ten years old and his heart sang at the thought of traveling to Navarre, to serve as page, and then later as squire. His mother and father had come out to watch him leave. Baroness de la Guerche held his baby sister in her arms; his father stood rigidly beside her, his hands gripping his sword hilt. But when Richard's eyes caught his, his father had raised his hand in a proud salute.

Well, first task now. He would have enough time for such memories on the journey home. His hand grasped the chapel door and he pulled it open, pausing to kneel and draw the cross on his forehead and shoulders. He offered a prayer for forgiveness, for entering God's house without a shirt, and rose to his feet. There was a soft glow down at the altar and hushed voices.

"The girl is a witch," he heard Jean-Pierre say, then he saw Arnaut standing beside him. Good. This would save time.

He strode across the rough stone floor to the altar where Father Gregory stood with Arnaut and Jean-Pierre.

"Here he is." Father Gregory's mouth twitched as he saw Richard's bare chest. "Richard de la Guerche, do you know anything about this?"

"I just saw the wreckage out there." Richard shook his head. "The bochorno is bad this year, eh?"

Jean-Pierre's face paled. "Now you!" he said. "First Arnaut will say nothing about the girl and now..."

Richard glanced over to Arnaut. He stared at Richard and his eyes quivered. There was a plea there somewhere in his face. Richard smiled, then turned to Father Gregory. "What girl?" he asked, smoothing his face of expression.

"I see." Father Gregory waved his hands. "Out. All of you." He glared at Jean-Pierre. "And no more waking me in the middle of the night with stories."

OUTSIDE THE chapel, Jean-Pierre stormed away, his back stiff and arms swinging. Arnaut plucked at Richard's hand. Richard turned to him and folded his arms across his chest.

"You won't say anything, will you?" Arnaut pleaded.

Richard looked down and studied his feet. "Will you leave her alone?"

Arnaut jumped. "I will not go near her." He glanced over his shoulder to where Maríana sat and he flinched. "I just want to forget this ever happened."

"Well." Richard considered. "If you keep Jean-Pierre from her."

Arnaut's face sagged. "That won't be difficult. He didn't want to join me in this anyway." He watched Jean-Pierre's retreating back. "No one will listen to him if we stick to our stories."

Richard clapped him on the arms. "Then we will see that we do." He looked over to the donjon where the guard had just opened the door and held his breath until he saw that Maríana slipped inside without incident. On the other side, Bernart loped toward him from the palais.

"Make ready, de la Guerche," Bernart said. "We leave within the hour."

Chapter 4

GOLDEN SUN blazed out of a cloudless sky. Maríana sat with Alys and
Geneviéve on squat stools set at the base of the donjon steps. Bundles of
bright material and ribbons in gold and rose, scarlet and indigo, lay upon
old quilts Geneviéve had placed on the cobbles. Maríana's fifteenth
birthday had come and gone, and now Jeanne, dressmaker for Reuilles-
le-château, measured the length of Maríana's arm with a red cord. A
circle of servants' children surrounded them, watching Jeanne poke and
prod at Maríana, kept just out of reaching distance of the precious fabric
by Geneviéve's bulk and Alys's sharp eye.

"Pick the green," Geneviéve said. "It is your first midsummer fête,
so make the most of it."

A little bird fluttered in Maríana's belly. It was midsummer and at
the feast of the rowan moon, the first full moon of summer, she would sit
at the family table. Her father would present her to his knights and
vassals, to the King of Navarre. For the first time, she would be there.

She had swallowed her pride and gone to her grandmother after
Arnaut and Jean-Pierre attacked her, as Richard had asked. Her hands
had opened the shirt Richard had given her, showed Johanna the bodice
that Arnaut had split from neck to waist. Johanna had paled, then taken
Maríana by the arm and pulled her across the inner bailey and up the
steps to the palais. Maríana could still see her father's shock when
Johanna dragged her into the great hall and stopped in front of his chair.

"Do you see what they did to your daughter?" Johanna's voice had
sliced through the morning chatter in the hall. "Your squires!"

Of course, he had wanted to know which squires, and of course,
Maríana had sealed her lips into a thin line. It was enough that she had to
endure the stares of her father's villeins when Johanna thrust her in front
of her father. Maríana now turned and looked at the pile of fabric that
gleamed on the stones. Only her father had seen the damage Arnaut and
Jean-Pierre had done. Johanna had seen to that, keeping Richard's shirt
wrapped around Maríana until they were directly in front of Louis-
Philippe. Louis-Philippe had called in Guillaume and several moments of
whispering and troubled glances toward her sealed the fate of Arnaut and
Jean-Pierre. They were sent home in disgrace the next day.

After that, her father visited her in her chamber in the tower —
Johanna had insisted on this. Three times in the two years since Arnaut
and Jean-Pierre had been sent away, he had come and talked to her.
About little things, really. How she was progressing with her embroidery,

what new songs she had learned. All the time his eyes would dart to the doorway, but he never left until Johanna stood. And now he would present her to the King.

"It is my first fête, yes. But Armand always let me watch from the roof of the donjon," Maríana said, turning her head again to the spill of silk and fine spun wool. "I could hear the minstrels." She lifted her arm and Jeanne drew the cord around her waist. "He let me dance up there."

"Not the same thing, I assure you." Geneviéve fingered a length of emerald silk shot with gold thread. "This will set off your hair." She held the fabric up to Maríana's face and Maríana shivered as the silk brushed her skin. The fine silk felt as soft as a kitten's tail.

"It is only five days until the fête," Maríana said, standing when Jeanne pulled her hands up. "This will never be ready in time."

"Come with me." Geneviéve heaved her bulk up off the stool. "We have work to do."

EARLY ON the morning of the festival, Maríana stood with Geneviéve in the palais kitchen. She had been allowed to enter the kitchen for the past six months, but her throat still quivered with excitement when she walked inside. Pages and kitchen maids scurried across the granite floor and cooks thumped dough and sliced meat on tables set the length of the room. The kitchen ran underneath the great hall, its doors opening out onto the inner bailey, facing the tower. A narrow staircase climbed to the hall above.

Geneviéve leaned over a steaming pot of drunken chicken stew. "The day before the feast we give them only salted bread crusts to make them thirsty. Next, wine — they get very drunk, you see!" Her face was ruddy and shining. "But that is what makes this so good." She dropped the ladle into its holder and moved on to the next kettle. "When your father introduces you, what will you say?"

Maríana wiped her hands against her apron. "I curtsey, and I say nothing."

Geneviéve deftly lifted an iron lid with quilted gloves, her plump arms bulging. "We expect offers after this evening," she said. "Offers for your hand."

Maríana looked down. Richard had not returned to Reuilles-le-château.

"You must aim higher, Maríana. Richard is a fine young man, but la Guerche is small and too near to Anjou. Some day Anjou will swallow it up." Geneviéve shrugged. "He wrote to you, at least."

Maríana touched the small scrap of vellum she kept in the leather pouch on her belt. She had memorized the words he carefully blocked out for her. *Maríana, my father is well. I hope your nightmares have ended. Keep the bloodstone and remember me. R.* No more nightmares. But her dreams were filled with aching longing. She almost preferred the nightmares.

Geneviéve regarded her solemnly. "Mama is of the Capet line, daughter of the old King Louis," here she dimpled, "not legitimately, of course, but of the blood. She expects more for you than la Guerche."

TRESTLE TABLES sat outside the walls. The evening held the promise of a clear, starry night and full moon in the sign of the sea goat, auspicious for a midsummer festival.

Maríana walked from table to table, listening to the blaring of krumhorn and shawm, trying to stifle her cough. That afternoon she had coughed so hard she could not catch her breath. Alys had clucked and felt her forehead, then warmed some mead for her to drink. Now she was sucking on mint leaves. Nothing was going to stop her from being present at this festival!

The sun dipped behind the mountain Irati, its red-gold rays gilding the thick stand of beech and maple that stood on either side of the road leading down to the lake. Dense forest swept all the way to where marsh lands lay with drowned trees jutting out of still and mossy waters, where foot paths disappeared. She leaned on a table and looked across the blue-black lake to Reuilles-la-ville. The walled town held aloof from the merriment around her, but the blinking light of torches dotted the tops of watchtowers there.

Her fingers smoothed the silken expanse of her emerald skirt and then shook it so the fabric caressed her legs. Jeanne had edged the sleeves and neck with dark blue. Maríana glanced around the throng milling around on the open field. No one else here had such a gown. A lady from Béarn stared at her, then leaned over and whispered into the ear of her companion. Maríana returned the woman's glance and smiled, then moved away without speaking. When the crowd closed the space between them so she could no longer see the woman, Maríana stopped. This was her moment, this evening. No one would spoil it.

She raised her head as shawm and singer joined in the greeting song and saw Louis-Philippe, resplendent in polished chain mail and the de Reuilles colors of indigo and white. Geneviéve was at his side, but moved away when several of his knights approached. She motioned for Maríana to come forward.

THE NIGHT of the feast passed in a blur. Maríana watched as dishes of tasty delicacies were presented for Louis-Philippe's approval by his head squire, and then, after approval, were served, first to their table, and then to the other tables. Servants ran from table to table replenishing the wine as both high and lowborn men and women flirted outrageously over the single goblet they shared between them.

"It is customary for each pair of man and woman to share a goblet," Geneviéve whispered, "and few of these pairs are married." She grinned at Maríana's frown. "You know the trouvérè song — married couples cannot truly love? Well it is true, you know." Then she pointed with her chin at a portly knight dressed in burgundy robes. "Béarn is here at our table. Bernart de Bazas you already know." Bernart was leaning over and nuzzling the ear of Lady Béarn. Geneviéve licked her fingers and peered at the head of the table where Louis-Philippe and Johanna sat. "Ah, he came!" She dimpled at Maríana's start of surprise. "Thibaut is here."

The King of Navarre! Maríana tried not to stare at him. Instead, she glanced at the basket sitting on their table. From time to time her father and the other lords and ladies present tossed bits of bread and meat inside it. "What are they doing?" she whispered in her aunt's ear.

"They take those over to the poor in Reuilles-la-ville after the feast." Geneviéve pointed to baskets set on every table. "See, all of us have one."

Louis-Philippe stood and raised his hands; minstrels lifted pipes and krumhorns in a rousing chorus while drummers pounded out a frantic beat. All eyes shifted to Louis-Philippe, who took his mother's hand and pulled her up beside him. Johanna spoke, but Maríana's eyes were on her father and she missed her grandmother's opening words.

"By the grace of God and all His saints, Ysabel of Gréves in La Touraine will marry my son Louis-Philippe," Johanna said. Applause greeted her words.

Maríana swallowed. Ysabel?

"You are hereby all invited to the wedding, next year on August eve, here at Reuilles-le-château." Johanna raised her hand, then sat.

"What?" Maríana's dinner rumbled in her belly. Her throat felt tight. "Geneviéve?"

"Curious," Geneviéve said. "Why now?" She leaned toward Maríana and whispered, "Do not feel badly, my dear."

Then she settled back in her chair. "I knew nothing of this." Her eyes grew opaque. "It is news to me, too."

There was no time to hear anything more. Maríana's father motioned for her to rise and come to stand beside him. Her mouth suddenly went dry as she moved to his side and she started coughing again. She had hoped to be equal to the occasion and not dishonor the de Reuilles name, but she quailed before all those flat, curious eyes. She looked up and saw her father's face crease into a smile. He took her hand. His felt cool and dry, but it trembled a little. He glanced down at her and she felt the pressure of his fingers. Then he lifted her arm.

"My daughter Maríana," he said, his voice sailing over the crowd. The minstrels sounded their instruments again, but this time, all eyes went to Thibaut of Navarre.

The King of Navarre rose from his seat and graciously nodded to her. A cheer rippled through the air. Maríana felt the pressure of her father's fingers on her hand again before he released it. She dipped in a curtsey and Thibaut's bearded mouth quirked. Louis-Philippe vigorously clapped his hands and the minstrels started a circle dance.

People leaped off the benches and streamed toward the clearing where circles were forming. For a moment, she did not move from where she stood. Ysabel. She searched for Johanna, but her grandmother was already swallowed by the crowd. Who was this Ysabel? Would her father tell her? She spotted the black and silver wave of his hair and pushed through the throng toward him.

He was not joining the dancers. She saw him skirt the edges of the gathering, then duck down, slipping away into the stand of trees surrounding the clearing. She marked where he had entered the forest and stared at the people nearest him when he slipped away. None of them had been watching, their eyes were on the dancers cavorting on the green. She drifted around the boundaries of the crowd and stopped at the edge of the clearing, peering into the lowering gloom of close maple, beech and pine. Bears and wolves lived there. Her hands gathered the silky fall of her skirt, then released it, smoothing the wrinkles she had made.

She looked back at the dancers. Should she join them, whirling under the stars? Her gaze darted back to the forest. Deep black shadows stretched beneath branches that moved. She looked down at the gleam of her emerald gown. This was her first feast, her first dance. She should stay and meet the fine people who had traveled here to enjoy the hospitality of Reuilles-le-château. Yet she could not keep her eyes from the forest shadows, where her father had gone. Her feet kept edging toward the trees. Heart pounding in her ears, she turned and entered the woods.

There was motion among the trees. She waited until her eyes matched the shadow play of starlight through branches. Her father's chain mail was there, glimmering in the distance. The sound of branches snapping and muffled exclamations told her where he was. Drawing her skirt up and holding it close to her body, she trod across deadfall and piles of pine cones. Up ahead, she could see him step out into the open where moonlight gleamed on the metal of his light armor, of his sword. She followed and found a path.

He had not heard her. She could see him toiling up the rock-strewn path that stretched before her, a track that climbed into the lower reaches of the mountain Irati. What would she say when she reached him? Biting her lip, she clambered along the path toward Irati, fighting to control the coughing that seemed to bubble up from the back of her throat. The wind sighed though pine branches. Owl wings beat in whispering thunder. Small creatures scuffled in the brush. Her father had his sword; she had nothing. The climb seemed to go on forever, but finally the path leveled off.

She had never been up there before. The pathway through the back arm of Irati was forbidden to nearly all who lived at the château, this much she knew. The only servants her father allowed to go up there never spoke about what they saw. Her heart pounded from exertion and fear and there was a cold spot in the pit of her belly that would not go away, but she continued following him, taking care not to be seen or heard. She hurried to catch up so she would not lose sight of him as he strode around a bend in the path where oak trees leaned across the track. When she turned the corner behind him, she stopped.

For a moment, she could not move. In the clearing, a palace stood dreaming under moonlight. It was small, no more than three rooms could fit inside, and its white stone walls were smooth and rounded, not rough and square like the walls of the tower. Fronted by a courtyard with a bubbling fountain, its arched doorways and the blue-gold tile patterns visible in the golden torch light from within were unlike anything she had ever seen before. The heavens curved above it, swimming with stars and crowned by a full moon. Her father marched to the door and entered, then Maríana crept closer and knelt beneath one of the windows.

On either side of the door, amber light poured out of two windows whose shutters were thrown open to the warm summer night. There were tapestries on the walls inside; abstract, repeating patterns of red and orange and deep blue. Metal lamps sprouted golden flames and thick rugs covered the floors. Pillows in every hue of the rainbow lay in piles scattered across the room. Her father paced from one side of the chamber to the other, talking to a figure she could not see. She raised her head above the sill and held her hand over her mouth.

A woman dressed in an indigo silken gown lounged upon the pillows. She was garbed in the fashion of the east; a gold belt encircled her waist and bracelets graced her slender arms. Long, thick black hair fell in a wave below her shoulders. Her eyes were also pools of darkness, depth upon depth, and she looked at Louis-Philippe with an expression of sad amusement.

"I did what my mother asked," Louis-Philippe was saying. "I presented her to Thibaut. Soon she will be married and away from here."

The woman murmured something that Maríana could not quite hear, but whatever was said affected Louis-Philippe. He groaned and sat upon one of the larger pillows, burying his head in his hands.

"I have no choice," he said through his fingers. "I cannot honor that agreement." He broke off and lowered his hands, looking in the direction of the woman. "You know this, you were there! Thérèse had plans for her, yes, but she thought it best that Maríana never know me." His mouth made a thin line. "My mother forced me to acknowledge her, but at least

I can try to follow the spirit of Thérèse's wishes."

The woman must have spoken again. Her father blanched, then his voice lowered to a rumble. She moved closer.

"Once I tried to resolve what divided us and, well, you know better than anyone what came of that." He buried his face in his hands again.

Maríana leaned on the window sill now. She could see her father and also the woman, her face still and remote. Then the woman looked at the window and her eyes widened.

Maríana dropped below the sill and held her breath. Maybe the woman had not really seen her. But a male voice cried out. She heard the scrape of her father's sword as he vaulted over the window sill.

She huddled against the wall, arms across her face. Her father stood in front of her, sword held ready, blade pointing at her. "Who are you? Why have you come up here?" he demanded, then, "Maríana?"

She lowered her arms and looked up into her father's stricken face. He opened his mouth to speak, then closed it, then opened it again. His hand moved toward her and halted above her head. She reached up to touch him, but he snatched his hand away, making a fist. His chest rose and fell rapidly as he stood there before her.

Then he turned and ran.

She stared after him, tears blurring the courtyard, the fountain. A form at the window cast a shadow upon the stones where she crouched. The woman was beckoning her to come inside.

She walked slowly into the palace. Was this real? Would it disappear? The woman pointed to a pillow and motioned for her to sit. Maríana ran her fingers lightly over the smooth texture of the fabric. It was real. She looked into the woman's face and saw that her black hair was threaded with silver. A quiver took her breath. She knew this face. Somewhere, she had seen it. Well, she would not show that she was afraid! She lifted her chin and blinked her tears away.

"Maríana." A deep, resonant voice caressed her name. "Don't worry about your father. He has done this sort of thing before; he will return."

"I am so pleased to finally meet you face to face, although I was there when you were born. You really are so much like your mother." There were unimaginable depths of pain in the voice that spoke those words, in the dark eyes that regarded her.

"I am Ibrahim," he said.

Chapter 5

"HERETICS!" The shattered treble of Geffroy de la Guerche's yell shook the tapestry hanging behind his chair. "All of them. No son of mine will marry a girl from such a family."

"Yet, you sent me there to serve as page." Richard stood before his father, back locked, as he had stood for the entire morning while Baron de la Guerche railed. Thin sunlight glazed the rush-strewn granite floor of the empty hall. Sounds of the morning drifted through wide doors flung open to the day; a mother's sharp reprimand, followed by a child's wailing complaint, the clank and slosh of milk buckets set upon the stones of the inner bailey, laughter that swelled, then dwindled. All the servants had slipped out of the hall when his father started the tirade. He was glad his mother and sister were still in the ladies bower. "You let me stay to squire for Baron de Reuilles."

Richard had no illusions about the position of his family. La Guerche was small, perilously close to Anjou. So far, its modest size and the King had kept it safe from the Angevins. His father had married well; Richard's mother had brought a handsome dowry to swell the coffers of la Guerche. But, they needed more than a dowry now. They needed an alliance with an old family, a marriage that brought lands.

He stifled the words he longed to say. De Reuilles was an ancient family, with ample lands bestowed by Charlemagne. Yet it was not what Maríana would bring to la Guerche that had compelled him to finally approach his father with his request for Geffroy's paternal blessing and approval.

"Have you been listening? When I sent you there I did not know of the girl's mother Thérèse," Geffroy repeated the words he had stated all morning. "Jean-Pierre Rhomboid brought this tale to his father, and then to me. You are my only son. When you returned the year before last..." Geffroy's voice splintered into a long, racking cough.

Richard poured watered ale into a silver cup, his eyes downcast, while his father wheezed. Geffroy did not like anyone to notice. "The de Reuilles are as Christian as any of the barons." This, at least, was true. As far as he knew. "I have not heard this story Jean-Pierre told you." He handed the vessel to his father and sent a silent prayer for God to forgive the way he had just bent the truth. "Baron de Reuilles and his family are as Christian as you or me." He had not heard the exact story Jean-Pierre told his father, but he could guess what Jean-Pierre had said. The four years he spent at Reuilles-le-château, he had heard whispers about the de Reuilles and Maríana's mother. They said that the dead Baroness de Reuilles lived at the bottom of the pool in her garden, that she arose from its depths when the moon swelled full. That she dressed in a turban and ate the eyes of babies. Geffroy bent over the cup, shoulders jerking with each cough. Richard had not repeated the tales of Baroness de Reuilles.

He knew the truth in his heart. The de Reuilles were fine and noble. What others said did not concern him.

Geffroy straightened and glared at Richard over the rim of his cup. "You have never defied me before, boy." He gulped the ale and shuddered. "The girl must have witched you."

"Maríana."

"Eh?" Geffroy wiped his mouth. His breath squeezed out in a tortured rattle.

"Her name, father." Richard lifted the pitcher of ale again. "She is Maríana de Reuilles." Ale streamed in a golden splash. Silence pressed into the hall. He looked up at his father's gaunt face.

Three years ago, an alliance with the de Reuilles would have been welcomed. Three years ago, his father had been a strong and vigorous man. But a fever had stolen Geffroy's prowess, blighting his once-proud bearing. Now Baron de la Guerche huddled inside layers of wool and struggled with every breath. Still, his father found enough air to rant when it pleased him. Not that much pleased Geffroy anymore.

When Richard returned to la Guerche, he had feared to find his mother and sister crying over his father's grave. Instead, he found them standing behind a withered stranger who spoke to him in his father's voice. Geffroy had greeted him with gladness and a spark of the love and proud regard that Richard remembered had washed across his face, although it quickly extinguished. Surely pain had transformed his father into a suspicious and querulous old man who spent endless hours on his knees in the family chapel. Richard had been certain that his father would once again become the patient and virile man he had been, yet the weeks passed and there was no change.

When his father had become ill, the business of running the château had fallen to his mother. Marguerite de la Guerche saw to the dispensing of justice and oversaw the collection of tenant's payments. She even rode out with Geffroy's vassals in their search for bandits who had been attacking friars crossing de la Guerche lands.

Baroness de la Guerche had proved an able châteleine; Geffroy could not fault her management of la Guerche. No one could. But Geffroy had drawn away from his wife. He ordered Richard to work closely with the seneschal to prepare him to command la Guerche and refused to allow Richard to complete his knight's training at Reuilles-le-château. Instead, he sent Richard to nearby Anjou for three months to complete the final tests of combat that earned Richard his sword. When he knelt before the Count of Anjou, Richard was content. As a knight, he could offer his sword to his liege. He had heard there was fighting in Toulouse and throughout the south. Near Navarre.

But his father had called him back to la Guerche. Since then, it had been Richard who saw to the routing of bandits that plagued the borders of la Guerche, Richard who managed the day to day tasks of running the barony. Every week he sat in the great hall listening to tales of discontent and grief; a miller complaining about the pricing of grain, a merchant disputing the dispensation of his new bride's dowry. He had given judgment, solved these troubles. There had been no new attacks on the people of de la Guerche for the past year, but when he approached his father with his desire to return to Reuilles-le-château, Geffroy mumbled an incoherent rant about witches and glowered.

Priests had convinced Geffroy that sorcery caused the illness that seized his breath and roughened his voice. Richard gritted his teeth as his father bent and spat a stream of thick mucous into a brass bowl at his side. His desire to return to Reuilles-le-château was a battle that must be fought with careful words. He loved his father, but he would have Maríana as his wife. His father must be made to see... .

"Richard." The voice behind him was hushed and gentle, yet it stilled the words he wanted to fling at his father. He turned and waited in silence while his mother drifted across the floor. Marguerite de la Guerche, who knew the secrets of the long barrows that dotted the fields, who had traveled among the shining ones in the invisible world and told the tales of these travels to her only son. She reached Geffroy's side, ran her hands over his chest and across his forehead. His father shrugged off her touch, but she captured his hand and held it, then faced Richard.

"You were only a boy when you knew Maríana." He bit his tongue and remained silent as his mother stared into him. Her eyes were perpetually shadowed now. "The years have changed you. She must have changed, too." A deep furrow marked the space between his mother's brows. When had she grown so weary? Upon his return to la Guerche, he had only noticed the dusting of white over her midnight hair. He had been so glad that his father lived, then after he came back from Anjou, so busy with running la Guerche that he had failed to note his mother's despair.

"Nothing will change the way I feel about Maríana." He had counted on his mother's support to convince his father that the match with Maríana was good for la Guerche. "I love her, mother." But she stood before him, next to Geffroy, holding his father's hand.

"You are still needed here." A grim pulling of her lips mocked the broad smile that he remembered. "Until your father is healed." Geffroy startled, his mother laid a finger across his father's lips. Geffroy subsided.

"I could go to Assisi for you." Stories of miracles at the church of Francis di Bernardone had swept up from the south and entered the hall of la Guerche in trembling whispers. "They say prayers offered at Assisi work miracles." Reuilles-la-ville lay on the route to Assisi. His hands curled into fists as he watched his mother's eyes widen. She leaned forward. His father pulled her back.

A sharp intake of breath, then the lines drawn on his mother's face settled, hardened. Her fingers dug into his father's hand. "Assisi."

"I will not let you go that far away. I need you here," Geffroy said. He patted Marguerite's hand and she bowed her head and leaned into Geffroy's shoulder.

The texture of his mother's sorrow coated the air. He forced his own hands to unclench. There would be no help from her and he could not burden her with his own misery. But he would not give up. Someday his father would throw off the mantle of illness he had wrapped about him. He would make his father understand. He must. Richard bowed his head and backed away, but his father's voice stopped him.

"There is another match."

He froze.

"It is with Bourdeilles. The girl is young yet — you need not wed her for another three years — but the match is good. She will bring the income from her own lands her father is giving as part of her dowry. Bourdeilles is a large holding and Beatrice is the only daughter..."

Richard saw his father's mouth continue to move, but did not hear the rest of Geffroy's speech. Frost settled along the rim of his heart, formed wintry spikes that drove into his chest. He looked away, caught only one word in three. Finally, the hall was silent. He looked back to see his father leaning away, eyes closed, but his mother watched him. Despair painted a bleak web that trembled from her lips to the fingers clutching his father's hand. He lowered his head and focused on the train of her gown.

Another match. Beatrice? He had never heard the name. Stale rushes clung to the edges of his mother's skirt, where it pooled on the floor. What could he say? "Repairs to the north gate are going well." He made a quick bow and strode toward the open doors.

"Richard." A whisper.

He stopped, but did not turn. Silence lapped at the corners of the hall; the stillness burned his ears. Finally, his mother spoke.

"I am sorry."

THE SEA never changed. It drew him with its crashing pulse, its dark scent of fish and floating weed. Richard had missed the sea, had almost forgotten the peace it brought him. He dropped his palfrey's reins and stood at the edge, where restless water met the land.

He had tried to forget Mariana. His mother was right, he and Mariana had only been children. How could he have loved her? He had been too young for such a love. Yet, he remembered everything about her. When she had run from Arnaut and Jean-Pierre, her heart had fluttered against his chest, he remembered this. It was odd, how he had thought that he held a butterfly in his arms when Maríana collided with him and he felt the tripping of her heart. Yet when Arnaut insulted her, her back had straightened, formed an iron rod underneath his hands.

He held up his last stone, a red-streaked, green bloodstone, much like the stone he had given Maríana so long ago. He could still smell the earth from which it had been torn. It turned in his hand, fitted snugly against his palm. For the past week, he had clutched the bloodstone in his hand each night. Held it close. But it was not nightmares that plagued his sleep. He stood gripping the bloodstone while the sun slipped toward the drowned cities that lay just beyond the shore.

Maríana had come to him. For three months now, nearly every night. No one knew this and he would not tell anyone. Certainly not his father, who would haul him before the priests. Not even his mother, who would at least understand these things.

At first, Maríana had appeared standing at the side of his bed. He had not realized he was dreaming: he thought she was really in the room with him. It had been nearly three years since he had last seen her. He sat up and she disappeared. The next night she was there again. Why was she silent? If it was really a dream, why did she stand so far away? He wanted her closer.

THE NEXT time she appeared, he took her hand. It was solid, pliant and warm. Richard was startled; he almost let it drop. How long he had sat there, holding her hand, he did not know. Just before she disappeared, he had felt the pressure of her answering squeeze.

After that, he had sought her every night. At times, his dreams were ordinary — small things he had done during the day, riding his palfrey Baldur, teasing his sister. When Maríana did not come to him, he awoke cross and empty, and snarled at everyone all day. When she did appear, the air shimmered and life filled him.

She never said anything. Not ever. But gradually, he pulled her closer, and closer still, until she lay beside him on his bed. For many nights, he was content to lie with her pressed close against him, tracing the bones of her face with his forefinger, spreading her dense auburn hair across the bare skin of his chest. When she lay beside him, her eyes were always closed. At first, he was sad. He wanted her to speak, to look at him. Later, when the throbbing in his groin was more than he could bear, he was glad she did not open her eyes to witness how much he wanted her.

It was the wanting that drove him to cast her out of his dreams. He had tried to kiss her, but she drew away and then disappeared. Three days passed before she appeared again, and another three before she would again allow him to coax her to lie beside him. There she lay, night after night, as he stroked her hair and told himself that this was enough. He filled his head with minor business of the château, the price of oats, a new design for a wagon wheel, anything that would cool the pounding surge of his blood.

Nothing worked. His yearning was driving him mad. If she would not have him, this dream Maríana, he must banish her. He could force her, that was true. Yet he would not dishonor her. Even in his dreams, he would not do this. The next time she came to him, he said his farewells, tried to explain to her why he could not have her visit his dreams. She said nothing, but would not release his hand when he tried to pull away. She had shivered so much that he drew her into his arms and lay next to her, his loins heavy and aching, till morning.

That day, he stole a bloodstone from his mother's chamber and took it to the long barrow that lay between la Guerche and the sea. He buried the stone at the center of the barrow, among the bones of a great warrior. His own mother had taught him this — a warrior's grave always increased the power of magic. That night, he retrieved the stone and held it nestled in the palm of his hand when he went to sleep.

Maríana did not appear. He had barred her from his dreams. His empty arms ached. He could not seem to catch his breath.

It was this that sent him to his father, asking for permission to wed. If he could no longer hold his beloved in his dreams, he must have her, in truth, as his wife. With his father's blessing, Maríana would be his wife.

If only his father had given this blessing.

A single spray hit the rocky shore and sent its streamers across his face. He flinched back and hefted the bloodstone, tossing it from hand to hand. It would be four years before he would be expected to marry Beatrice. Gulls screamed a warning as he trod closer to the breakers. Four years. A long time until he would belong to another. The bloodstone was shiny from the rubbing of his fingers. Would Maríana return if he did not use it? Could he bear to have her next to him? Froth kissed the toes of his boots. Could he bear to never see her again?

He flipped the stone from his right hand to his left one more time, then let it fly and watched as it made a hurtling arc into the froth of breaking waves. His horse stood where he had left it, waiting patiently while he had hurled stone after stone into the sea. He jumped onto the horse's bare back, blinking his eyes until the sting settled deep into his chest. Then he dug in his heels and turned toward la Guerche.

Chapter 6

SHE KNEW him; she was sure of this. Ibrahim handed Maríana a steaming cup of manzanilla that he had boiled over a lamp and strained through cloth. She accepted the earthen cup and wrapped her hands around the sides. Who was he, this Ibrahim? She searched her memory for where she could have seen him, but the kohl outlining his eyes, the gown that clung to his slender form defeated her. He should look ridiculous wearing that gown. But he did not. He was beautiful.

Ibrahim shook his long, silver-laced black hair back over his shoulders, his golden earrings jangling with a delicate, slithering chime. Then he folded his legs underneath him and sat opposite her. "I have known your father a long time. I knew him before you were born."

She looked into her cup, watching bits of leaves that escaped Ibrahim's cloth swirling around as the steam moistened her upper lip. "You look familiar." She raised her eyes.

"You have seen me," he stirred his drink with his little finger, "but not like this." He stretched out his right arm and rattled his bracelets.

She could not take her eyes away from his face. When he turned to jingle his bracelets she saw a woman sitting opposite her, but when he lowered his face to drink from his cup, she saw a man again. It was making her dizzy. "Did my father build this place for you?"

He did not answer at first. His head swiveled around. She followed his eyes, seeing the clean white walls, the repeating patterns of the tapestries that graced them with undulating forms in scarlet and gold and deep blue, the low wooden chest that stood at the back. "No," he said, looking at her again. "Not for me, but he lets me stay here sometimes."

She drew in her breath and coughed. He reached toward her, then stopped when she backed away. "Are you ill?"

She shook her head. "It is nothing. Why are you dressed like that?" How did he know her mother?

One black brow rose. "You mean, why the costume? It is my penance." He lifted his cup and drank deeply.

"Did my father leave here because of me? I mean, I know I was not allowed to come up here." Her voice quivered and she stared down at her cup. A feathery touch told her he had leaned forward. His fingers caressed her cheek. Looking up, she saw flecks of gold swimming in his eyes.

"He often does this, petite. Every time he comes to me up here, he goes back to the chapel and spends the rest of the night on his belly in front of the altar." The man regarded her, his face still and grave. "He has never been able to face his nature."

She felt her cheeks grow hot. "But if he is, if he is..." She could not find the words.

"A lover of men?"

Maríana gripped the cup and gulped the cooling liquid. Her eyes raised to stare unblinkingly at him. "How can he marry? And what does that make me?"

"His daughter." Ibrahim's voice was wry but his eyes were warm. "This," he touched his earrings, his bracelets, his gown, "must go away. Louis-Philippe thought this costume would fool people." Frown lines formed at the corners of his mouth and across his forehead.

"Grandmother said my father is to marry Ysabel de Gréves." There! What would he say to that?

He shifted his weight, setting the bangles and necklaces gracing his arms and neck jingling. "And so he shall. We have been careless, you see." He waved his hand at her when she jumped. "Oh, most in the château do not know that the secret woman your father visits is me."

"Then why change things now?" She was not sure about this woman-man. She knew his face, of that she was sure, yet she could not place him. When she thought of him and her father together, she shuddered. But she found herself drawn to him, to the way he listened to her.

"Who can say why change happens? Perhaps because he and Johanna would both like to see a male heir in place." Ibrahim lifted his chin. "Perhaps because the Church has turned its eye this way."

"The Church?"

"Didn't you know?" His lips curled now in a smile. "It is a sin, what we do. Father Gregory can no longer ignore it. But everyone here would stand to lose if the Inquisition comes." He leaned forward when she could not suppress a shiver. "Oh, you would probably survive. They usually spare daughters, especially if they are pretty and young. It is much easier to hold a claim when you have married one of the family."

"The Inquisition." She looked at the bits of leaves in the bottom of her cup and puzzled over the aroma and pungent flavor. Manzanilla and something else she did not recognize, something that gave her the taste of bitter earth in her mouth. "I have heard rumors. Stories of Toulouse."

"Do you know of the Cathars?"

Her hands were sweating, the sides of her cup slick with moisture. She placed it upon the floor and shook her head.

"The Cathars are Christians," he said, "but they do not accept the established Church and they do not revere the Pope." He paused and his eyes closed. "Rome launched a crusade against them. A man called de Montfort fought for the Church and seized many châteaux larger and richer than your father's holdings. He gave the daughters of the rightful owners to northern lords." A sigh rippled through his frame and his eyes opened. "And even though de Montfort died, that slaughter is still not finished."

Silence now. She straightened her back and waited. If this Ibrahim thought to intimidate her with his silence, she would make him reconsider. She could be silent, too.

"Geneviéve was the wife of a Cathar knight," he finally said.

She startled, then licked her lips. Her mouth was dry and her tongue rasped. She shifted her weight and blinked when the walls slid to the left. Turning her head, she watched the walls slide back to her right. "What?"

"Do not be alarmed." He waved his hand again. "Her husband died long ago. No one has forgotten, but we do not think they will come for her." He bowed his head in a graceful nod. "After your father has married, he should be safe as well."

"How did my mother die?" Her voice was not her own. It rang out into the room and echoed off the walls. Her head spun for a moment, then cleared. "You knew my father before I was born." She leaned forward and the room circled again. "No one will tell me! How did my mother die?"

He stared at her in haunted anguish. She sagged toward the floor, pressed her hands against it, but could not find the strength to stop from slipping down. He took her arms and steadied her. "I am sorry, petite. That is something I cannot tell you. I gave my word."

The walls of the room now made slow arcs around her head. "Ibrahim! What did you put in my drink?" she tried to ask, but her tongue had grown thick and sticky, the words would not form properly. As she pitched forward in a panic, she felt him catch her in strong arms and lower her gently onto the pillows. She felt his hands cradling her head and his gentle kiss on her hair. Then she sank into oblivion.

"LAVENDER," Ibrahim whispered, laughing softly. "You got that from the garden and bathed in lavender before the festival, didn't you?" he said to the now slumbering girl. He checked the pulse beating steadily in her neck and listened to her chest. Some congestion. No matter, that was soon remedied. He would pick some white horehound for her. Bittersweet, colt's foot and lady's mantle would be good too. An infusion of these would soon set her right.

He stroked her hands. He had waited so long for this, to see her up close after all the years of watching her from afar. When she was a baby he had been able to visit and hold her. Later, he had gone away to Montpelier. When he returned, Johanna and Louis-Philippe told him to keep his distance.

"But for those green eyes and fair skin, you could have been mine," he whispered in her ear. "My daughter."

The liquid trill of the nightingale flowed into the room. He shook himself. It was getting late and he needed to move quickly or else the plan he had just set in motion would be lost. He pulled off the gown and jewelry, except for a gold chain with a small key that remained around his neck. Then with meticulous care, he folded and put away each item of clothing and placed the rest of the jewelry in a box. He locked all in a low chest against the wall using the small key on the chain around his neck.

Good bye, secret woman. He strode over to another, larger chest next to the windows. Opening the chest, he pulled out a tunic, breeches and hose all worked into the livery of the de Reuilles, and a leather belt with a compact pouch attached to it. For the past nine years he had worked as the gardener and healer of the château, his special knowledge of plants earning him the elevated status of master on a par with the master of the hounds. Most of the palais servants knew him as "Jacques." He tied his long hair back and slipped into the tunic, breeches and hose. Then he pulled a length of cloth out from underneath other tunics in the chest.

She would be safe there until he returned. Striding outside to the fountain, he splashed his face and vigorously scrubbed kohl and flour off, wiping the last traces away with the corner of the cloth he had brought out with him. Finally, he moved to a quiet section of the fountain where the water formed a still pool and stood looking at his face in the moonlit mirror. Hello, Jacques! He saluted the face in the water, then walked out of the courtyard into the night without looking back.

LOUIS-PHILIPPE was snoring. As Ibrahim moved through the entrance to the chapel, he was greeted by the rumbling dissonance that echoed off the walls. He walked over to where Louis-Philippe lay on his stomach in front of the altar and tapped him on the shoulder.

"Louis-Philippe," he whispered. "You never could stay awake, could you?"

Louis-Philippe grunted and rolled over, groaning. "What is the hour, Ibrahim? I must be getting back." Then he looked around in confusion. "Where am I?"

Ibrahim poured water into a chalice and handed it to Louis-Philippe. "We are in the chapel, my lord, and here I am known as Jacques."

Louis-Philippe looked at the water, then set the chalice down, rubbing his knuckles across his eyes. "This is holy water," he said.

Ibrahim shrugged. "So much the better."

Louis-Philippe covered his face with his hands. "Maríana," he groaned. "Where is she?"

Ibrahim waited until Louis-Philippe looked up and he stared into his eyes. "Louis-Philippe," he said. "She stays with me."

Louis-Philippe grabbed the edge of the altar and lurched to his feet. "What?" he cried out.

"She is with me," Ibrahim repeated. "Remember your promise to Thérèse and me."

Louis-Philippe sank back to his knees. "You can't be serious! You can't hold me to that!" he sputtered.

"You watch me," Ibrahim said. His voice was iron; he would not be moved.

"I will not let you have her for your... experiment!" Louis-Philippe continued as though Ibrahim had not spoken. "It is out of the question!"

"I will have her. A year is what you promised and a year is what I will have."

Louis-Philippe set his jaw. "I received offers of marriage for her last night." His hand made a fist. "Even before I presented her to Thibaut. Two offers."

Ibrahim watched the small muscle at Louis-Philippe's temple jump. "Were these good matches?"

Louis-Philippe looked into his lap. Torches hissed quietly in their sconces. "No," he finally said. "But there will be others." He glared. "You cannot have her."

"But I will." Ibrahim brought his face close to Louis-Philippe so that there could be no mistaking what he said. "Or I will tell her what happened to her mother."

"No!" Louis-Philippe paled.

"I would do that," Ibrahim said, settling back on his heels.

"But why? Why do you want her?" Louis-Philippe rubbed his eyes vigorously.

Ibrahim regarded him for a moment. So many years, so much love, yet so little understanding. "You never could comprehend how rare her mother was," he said. "For hundreds of years, perhaps even thousands, these people have worked to refine their abilities, passing down the gifts and the training to each generation. I will not let that die. It was my promise to Maríana's mother, and your promise too, if you remember." He rose to go.

Louis-Philippe stayed where he sat. "You know what this means," he said. "Ysabel will not be here until next year."

"Just as well we end this now. I was becoming weary of the bangles." And it would be safer. "We decided on this last summer, or have you forgotten?" Ibrahim could still remember the angry words, the anguished pleading. They had argued for months. But Louis-Philippe had finally agreed.

"I will miss you," Louis-Philippe said, his voice echoing around the chapel. "And I will miss the bangles," he added with a flash of humor, but his eyes shone with moisture.

"So, my friend, we will see each other but not meet again." Ibrahim nodded and turned to the door. Stopping briefly, he said over his shoulder, "Do you tell Johanna or do I?"

"She is my mother. It is my place to tell her. I am sure she will be thrilled that you are to be a man all of the time again and that we will no longer... meet... but she will not like losing Maríana."

"Johanna will not lose her. She will never lose her. Tell your mother that," Ibrahim said as he walked out the door. Now, where was the white horehound? Oh, yes, down by the pond. He walked quietly among the servants, greeting those he knew and smiling at the children who were starting to awaken now. In the garden, he tweaked a branch here and pulled a weed there. He had two servants to help him in the garden and one of them, Yves, was ready for Ibrahim to give him more responsibility.

His days would be free for Maríana. He strode easily around the interlaced curves of the garden, locating bittersweet, colt's foot and lady's mantle, harvesting them with a small crescent-shaped blade that was polished to a brilliant sheen, and black as midnight.

After instructing Yves on his duties for the next two weeks, Ibrahim wrote a quick note to Johanna outlining his plans for Maríana and sent Yves off to give her the note.

Johanna could be trusted to take care of any details concerning the move of Jacques the gardener and Maríana, daughter of the Baron, to Louis-Philippe's Saracen palace. It would cause speculation, of course, but the servants were used to Louis-Philippe's caprices. He had asked Johanna to send Geneviéve as chaperon for Maríana. It would not do to have the devout and superstitious Alys up there with them, not with what he planned to do-but Geneviéve, that old heretic, she would enjoy herself.

MARÍANA opened her eyes and then closed them again tightly against brilliant sunshine pouring though large, unshuttered windows. She moved her aching head from side to side on the silken pillow. Someone entered the room; soft footsteps brushed across the rugs. Opening her eyes again, just a little, she looked up through dark lashes.

"Have some water. It will help." A velvety, deep voice spoke.

She opened her eyes more and saw a graceful, slender — beautiful — man. His high cheekbones and smooth golden skin spoke of the south, where the sun burned down on the desert. He touched a memory within her, but she could not retrieve it. She watched as he deftly arranged blood oranges, succulent blackberries, peaches still covered with downy fuzz, sliced apricots glistening with dew, and warm bread, the steam of baking still rising from the broken crust, on a brass tray. Then he poured clear water into a deep blue cup and handed it to her.

"Who are you?" she asked, and was astounded when he suddenly laughed. He stopped laughing when she held her head.

"I am Jacques," he said. "Please drink this. It will make you feel better."

She sipped the water, tasting the bite of ice. Pond water? Her eyes widened. "Ibrahim! But how did you... you look so different!" She gazed up at him, tall and handsome in his livery. Even now she was not sure if it was he.

The corners of his mouth lifted. "I am glad to see that my disguise was so effective. But you will never see it again." He walked over to where a kettle of water was boiling, took it off the fire and poured the steaming water through a cloth filled with the heads and petals of flowers. A tangle of green stems showed through the fabric.

"So the secret woman is gone forever?" she asked after she drained the rest of her cup. "But I have seen you. In the garden, I think. Not up close, just in the distance."

"I tend the garden and the people of the château know me as Jacques." He settled himself on the divan and picked out some blackberries. "I have brought us some breakfast. It would be good if you would eat." He motioned toward the tray on the table.

"Jacques the healer? Of course! You gave a salve to Alys when I burned my leg. I knew I had seen you before." She leaned forward gingerly and picked out a piece of warm, fragrant bread and one ripe peach. "But how did you know that I like these?" she asked, coughing as she settled back on her pillows.

Ibrahim shrugged. "I have been watching you for years. It was not difficult. As Jacques I could go just about anywhere in the château, although I always stay in the background." He popped a handful of blackberries into his mouth.

Birdsong entered with the sun, curling around the edges of the room. The hushed whisper of water continually spilling in the fountain outside soothed her. But Alys would wonder where she was. And Johanna would be coming to her chamber soon. She tried to stand, then fell back when her legs folded. "What did you give me last night? You did not need to make me sleep to keep me here, you know. You only needed to ask. I would have stayed." Her head still felt stuffed with cobwebs.

He swallowed the blackberries whole. She saw his throat working. Then he put his hands on either side of his face and leaned on his knees. "Just balm and meadowsweet," he finally said. "I couldn't take the chance that you would leave. I had waited too long already, and I knew I had to move quickly or your father would have you married off and away from the château. He has already received two offers, you see." His hands lifted when she recoiled. "He has not accepted them... yet."

"What would you have done if I had not come up here?" she asked, watching his face. If he had told her the truth about his relationship with her father, he loved men, not women. Why did he want her?

"I would have followed you." He shrugged. "Wherever you went. There is always use for a gardener and, as Jacques, I am known even outside of the de Reuilles territory."

"Why, Ibrahim?" She watched him again. "What do you want with me?" He was wrestling with some thought. His forehead creased and the lines around his mouth deepened. Then he leaned back and slapped his knees.

"I have written down my story," he said. "I wrote it for you, Maríana — I have it here for you to read." He got up from the low divan and walked over to a chest. Opening it, he removed a book, several pages of parchment bound together with leather dyed the color of rich red wine. He handed the book to her, but held onto her hands before she could open it. "I must warn you," he said. "It is not a pretty story. You may find out much more than you care to know."

Ibrahim's hands felt moist and warm. The book was a heavy weight on her lap. She could smell its pages, musty vellum and sour ink. "I want to know," she said.

His face relaxed into a smile. "The first few pages are in Arabic. But the story you want to know is in your language." He stood, holding the breakfast tray. "Why don't you stay here today? I have some tasks I still need to complete down there, but I will be back before dark and Geneviéve will be up here before midday."

She sat with her hands on the book. The cover was rough and smooth at the same time. A flower pattern was engraved in the leather, four petals curving.

"Over there is a cup filled with an infusion of white horehound... and some other things." His hands were full. He pointed with his chin and smiled wryly as she regarded it with suspicion. "Don't worry, it will not make you sleep, but it may help your congestion." He put the tray down, pounded his chest a moment and coughed, then, after sketching a graceful salaam, he strode out of the chamber, leaving her holding the book.

Johanna would be worried. But Ibrahim had said Geneviéve would be coming up to the palace, didn't he? Surely she could stay here a while. Long enough to read his story. She ran her fingers over the leather cover of Ibrahim's book and hesitated before opening it. Long enough to see if her mother lay within the pages.

When she finally opened it, the strange letters danced across the pages. She wondered if the spoken language was as beautiful as the writing. Then she found the place where she could read what was written. An elegant hand, clear and bold. Ibrahim.

Chapter 7

I AM IBRAHIM Al'Khaldun, youngest son of the merchant Nazir

Al'Khaldun of Alexandria. The story I tell you now is of three people, myself and two of my most cherished friends. What you may think of us, I cannot say, but I commit our story to this paper to ease the anguish in my heart. I know that I put myself and others in danger by writing my story, but if I am careful, I trust that no harm will come. Perhaps in the writing, some of the ache within me will cease.

My family followed the teachings of the Prophet, peace and blessings be upon him, but they also worshiped Isis, as our ancestors have for thousands of years. They gave me to the temple of Isis at birth and I was raised there to serve the Goddess. I performed all of my duties — divination, worship, ritual — and learned all that they could teach me, but I hungered for more! In every ceremony, every ritual, the truth reached for me even as I strained to see it, to touch it. The priests and priestesses, the acolytes, the worshipers all followed the teachings without ever wondering what was behind the words, the actions, the songs. They told me to forget my questions. Why wonder about things that no one can ever know? But me, I was born wondering.

The world is so large and incredible. Surely I could find the truth I sought there! We had maps in the temple, maps that showed the great inland sea and the lands that surrounded it. I wanted to travel and see other lands, other peoples. I wanted to see how they lived, to know what they believed, hear what they could teach me.

"Who made all this?" I could see myself asking them. "Have you seen this Being some call Allah, or Jehovah, or Artemis, or Isis, or Jesus?" Maybe they could tell me how I could see this Being too. And if I could, maybe I could get the answers I sought, the answers that would still the longing from all the questions I held inside me.

But they would not let me travel. They told me I was needed there to serve Isis. And to divine the future for the wealthy of our city.

What can I tell you about my city? Alexandria is brown and ochre; sand and earth walls, so many shades of brown, from palest shell to darkest mud. And the people are brown! The brilliance of the sun bakes everything, you see. We are all tempered in its furnace. But the glorious blue of the river! Of course, when you come close to it that blue is more brown, too, but from my window in the temple it glowed sapphire. I spent many hours hanging out of my window, smelling the air, the scent of camels and dust, of sweat and cumin. The river beckoned to me. But they told me I could not go, so I went back to the halls of the temple and gave obeisance to Isis.

Please do not think that I do not love the Great Mother. Whatever we call Her, Isis, Diana, Athena, or Mary, She is real. This I know. I have felt a shadow of Her presence hovering around the edges of our rituals. But Allah, Jehovah, Jesus, Ra... They are also real. This I know!

I once met in secret with some dervishes from the land far to the east. They told me about a group of masters who cultivated the spread of knowledge and ideas much as a gardener would cultivate a grove of pomegranates, weeding and seeding, pruning and planting. What they told me was so strange that I became dizzy. Yet the truth was shining so brightly in their faces that I came back the next night for more revelations, only to find that all of them had disappeared! I searched and searched and could not find them anywhere.

I returned to the temple. It was the festival of Nut, the sky Goddess, and our high priestess needed me to drink the milk of adder tooth to call down the heavens. I was Sheb, consort of Nut, earth forever straining toward sky. The acolytes prepared me, fed me the sacred drink of venom, lifted me on the dais to the roof of our temple. Then they all settled down to wait while the drink burned in my veins. Magic takes time, you see. Nut must be wooed from Her station above the earth, enticed to come down and share her wisdom. It was my job to call Her, to offer my heart and my body for Her pleasure. In return, She always gave me words and images that I would commit to memory, using my temple training to keep the thread of my awareness firmly rooted, so the drink could not lure me out of my body. These images were for my temple, not for me alone. But this time I was selfish. My heart cried out for the freedom to search for truth. I pleaded with Her. "Nut!" I cried. "Take me away from here! Help me find my destiny."

Ah, how I have lived to regret what I have said and done.

A month later my prayer was answered. My father brought two visitors from the north to see me. Iranzu was tall and swarthy, with long black hair flecked with white. He wore the robes of a monk, a deep rusty brown wool with a cowl that framed his face. A great oak staff rested in his broad, capable hands. I liked him instantly, but his daughter frightened me.

Thérèse was younger than me but her eyes were ancient, the kind of eyes that have seen too much. Her features were almost Greek with her high, strong brow and large green eyes. My father had once given the temple a statue of the Greek Goddess Artemis and when I first saw Thérèse I thought I was seeing Artemis come to life. Her hair was as black as her father's, though not touched by age, and it fell in unbound waves down to her waist.

She took my hands when we first met, and told me her name. When she touched me, I felt such a wave of desire that I nearly collapsed. What was happening to me? She was beautiful, but I had loved women before, many as lovely as she. Although marriage was forbidden to temple initiates many of us had lovers who could be termed "wives." At the time I met Thérèse I had thought myself deeply in love with a woman whose name I do not even remember now. When Thérèse dropped my hands, I backed away and tried to order my thoughts. I was so stunned by her touch that I nearly lost the sense of what my father was telling me.

"Iranzu has asked me to find a companion to accompany him and his daughter to Byzantium," he said, watching me carefully. "I have sent a message to our cousin Justin in Constantinople. We want you to travel with them." He turned to Iranzu, who was standing beside him, and placed a hand upon his shoulder. "They can speak our language, but it would be better if one of our family accompanies them." My father was gazing at me again, assessing my reaction.

Here it was, the chance to start my search! "Me?" I could feel my heart beating. "When do we leave?" I asked him.

WE SAILED on the Al'Bediah at the rising of the sun. The Al'Bediah was a fine large dhow with three strong sails, a swift vessel that would take us to Constantinople. It was my first time out to sea, and although I had sailed on the Nile many times, I spent the first day hanging over the side depositing my meals into the sparkling waters. The next day I was able to respond to simple questions. By the third day I was nearly myself again.

When I was ill, Thérèse watched me from the deck. I felt her eyes on me, but whenever I looked up she was gazing the other way. My face burned with humiliation. From my station at the side of the dhow I saw her stride the decks, laughing and joking with the crew. Their expressions shifted from disapproval to grudging admiration to adoration as she helped them swab the deck, climb the mast, trim the sails into the wind. Her skin turned golden in the sun; her green eyes flashed from underneath her brush of dark lashes in an emerald glow. I tried to ignore her, but when I recovered from the motion of the waves she came to stand before me.

"Your father told us you are an initiate of the temple," she said, her eyes pinning me with the single-minded glare of a hawk. I could not look away, but I would not speak. Had I not seen her easy familiarity with the crew? What kind of creature was she? The women I knew were soft, the doe-eyed concubines of the temple, my giggling sisters. They did not stare at me with the direct eyes of a man. She straightened her back and continued, "Please tell me what you can. I want to know."

I leaned against the side of the dhow and watched her in silence. How long we both stood there like this I do not know. My eyes traveled over her high cheekbones, her burnished skin, her raven hair floating in the breeze that now blew off the water, bringing the chill of sea foam. She stood there before me, her eyes assessing my form as well. Then the breeze lifted her hair again and swept her body. The skin on her arms pebbled with the cold and she shivered — an infinitesimal quiver, that she instantly suppressed — but I saw it. That tiny shiver. I was undone.

"I will tell you what I can," I said, and removing my cloak, I drew it around her so quickly that she could not refuse me. Her eyes widened but her hands pulled the cloak firmly against her side.

"May the blessings of Allah be upon you always," she said, inclining her head. "Now, what can you tell me?"

She had so many questions! She wanted to know everything about my life at the temple and I was happy to tell her all I could. You must understand that there were many rules governing our life in the temple and I could not divulge everything we did there. Still, I found enough to tell her so that she would continue to sit with me at the side of the dhow, the breeze sending her hair across her high brow. Once I leaned forward toward her and the wind blew between us; her hair touched my face ever so gently, intoxicating me.

"Tell me of the catamites," she demanded. "I want to know everything about the sacred men and women who mate with the gods."

"I would not know about them," I told her. "I have never mated with a god." This was true enough, but I knew what she meant and could not stop the blush from staining my cheeks. I knew very well what the temple catamites did, as all dedicated to Isis must serve their time in this way, loving both men and women in the sacred rituals that draw the fertile energy to the land. I made no apologies for this to myself, but I did not want her to know, did not want to see her recoil if she did not understand. Noting my discomfiture, she turned to look out over the waves. She was silent for the rest of that day.

Then it was my turn. "Where is the valley your family inhabits? How did they come to be there? My father told me Iranzu said you could speak with your mind! How can you do this?"

She held up her hands and her teeth gleamed as her lips parted in a smile. "One question at a time, please. Our valley is in the north between Navarre and Béarn. My family came there many, many years ago, after our home across the western sea was destroyed." She looked out across the water and her brow wrinkled. "All the Jakintzas have some ability to speak with their minds. I was born knowing how to send my thoughts to others, how to sense certain things, and my father has trained me to bring these abilities under the control of my will." Her forehead smoothed and she leaned against the railing. "But I have not yet ascended to our sacred cave to commune with the Guardian."

I had to ask her. "Does your Guardian look like Isis?" I held up a picture I had traced from a tomb painting of Isis, her wings spreading out from her shoulders.

She did not even look at the picture. "Some call Her Jainkosa, the Goddess," she murmured. "Her face is the face of all women, just as the God's face is the face of all men." Leaning forward, she took my hands. "They fulfill themselves through us. As we seek to become better and better, to know ourselves and to grow in wisdom and devotion, the gods become manifest."

I was trembling, and she noticed. She dropped my hands and looked down into her lap. The sun had traveled its full course and was now a huge orange and red circle sitting at the edge of the sea. A gentle warmth embraced me where its light touched my arms, but the wind was rising again. I ached to touch her, yet I could not bring myself to lift my hand. She spoke again, her eyes still lowered. "Over the years my family has forgotten our original home. Our traditions have been blurred by the world, but still, most generations have had a woman ascend to the cave and commune with the Guardian through the sacred stone." She turned toward the deck, away from me.

"What is this stone?" I was glad she had moved. I was having difficulty masking my feelings.

"No one knows for sure, but our legends say it fell from the sky." Her eyes grew distant. "There is a song we sing about the first ones, the first of our family to come to our valley." She hummed a melancholy tune, then softly sang words to the melody, "Who are we here in this fair place, these mountains, this small valley? What happened to the others we left behind?" She closed her eyes and her voice soared up to battle with the noise of the steady wind that filled our sails. "We are the shining ones, we are the people of the morning star. Our home is no more, our home is no more." The tune she sang haunted me, and when she sang I could almost hear the echo of other voices singing with her.

She fell silent and a tear slipped down her cheek, a tear she swiftly dashed away with the back of her hand, but I had seen it. Now my arms ached to hold her, to take her into my embrace and kiss the tear away. She had given me no sign that she would welcome my touch so I remained where I was. I tried to keep a proper distance from her, especially at night.

In fact, I spent a lot of time pacing the decks at night, from fore to aft, around and around. Thérèse curled up next to her father at the front of the dhow every evening. When I walked past them, I could see the dark brush of her lashes fanned out against her cheek, her tumble of ebony hair. So strong, I thought, she tries to be so strong. But that little shiver, that single tear! I bedded down with the crew at the back, but even though we were separated by the length of the dhow I found her presence more and more disturbing. The ache had spread now to my chest, my belly.

I must tell you here that I consider my appetites normal. I had enjoyed warm and fulfilling liaisons with many women, and men, too, when I served as catamite in the temple. I had never lacked physical love, and I had never worried about it. But now I found myself close to a woman I wanted more than any other I had ever known and I could do nothing but grit my teeth and pace the deck to tire myself so that I could ignore the ache of wanting and fall asleep.

Even so, I visited her in my dreams and awoke many times with a cry, feeling my seed spilling into my robe. The crew found this all very amusing, especially when they watched me washing my robe out in the mornings after these passionate dreams. I told Iranzu that the washing of the robe was part of temple practice. His mouth twitched, but he did not say anything. What Thérèse thought I did not know.

All journeys must end, and ours did soon, when the Al'Bediah entered the harbor at Constantinople. Byzantium! I leaned on the railing at the side of the dhow and squinted at the wharf. Where Alexandria was all shades of brown, Constantinople shone in white and blue. A cluster of buildings hugged the curve of the harbor, their white walls washed with palest blue, the water answering their cool shadows with fathomless indigo. When our vessel approached the mooring, I could see the blue wash was really a layer of grime that settled on everything, walls, doors, roofs. But where are the spires? I thought. Where is the graceful blue curve of the Sophia? All I could see was a wharf like any other, teeming with folk buying and selling, unloading and loading. I searched the quay for the banner of the Khaldun family and ordered the street urchins to back away while I helped Iranzu and Thérèse off the deck of the dhow and onto the pier.

"There it is!" I waved my arms to signal the Khaldun wagon. The driver urged his horses to pull the wooden cart over to where we waited. I had the crew load Iranzu and Thérèse's chests onto the back, and tossed rosewater sweets I had brought from home into the crowd of children that blocked our path. While they scurried to catch what I had thrown we rode off into the city.

Although he was a Christian, my cousin's home was built in the Moorish fashion, with tall stone walls in blinding white facing the street and the living area inside surrounding a central courtyard. Lush fig and pomegranate trees graced the court, placed in huge clay tubs on the mosaic tiles that formed the floor. A graceful fountain spilled clear water into a large pool at the center of the court.

An entire wing of the house was sectioned off for my cousin's sisters. He had four unmarried sisters he supported, two were older than he and the other two were younger. The eldest acted much as the chatelaine of the household, making sure that the essential function of running her brother's home was carried out to perfection. I watched as she and Thérèse appraised each other and held my breath until my cousin's eldest sister nodded her head, as if to say "You'll do," and the two women embraced. The rest of the sisters spent most of their time in their quarters. They had eyed me with interest until Justin informed them that I was their cousin. Then their eyes had shifted to Iranzu, who played the gallant but elusive stranger for several days until they gave up trying to snare him.

The minute I had completed my duty to my father, seeing Iranzu and Thérèse settled into the home of my cousin, I made my way back to the harbor and wandered around, breathing in the atmosphere and observing the people. Perhaps here I could find the answers I was seeking! But first I sought and found women to serve my need. I returned to my cousin's home drained, but not satisfied, and the minute I saw Thérèse again the ache of wanting her filled my body. It was hopeless.

Iranzu and Thérèse came to me the next morning. "There is a group of dervishes we wish to see," Iranzu said, his hands deftly pouring boiling tea out of the slender neck of Justin's metal jug. "They dance and howl and God answers their questions. You will take us there?" His voice lifted in question.

I folded my arms across my chest. I knew where these dervishes resided, the eastern section of the harbor where thieves and bandits reined. "I will take you." I turned my face away from Thérèse's glare. "But women cannot go there. It is too dangerous," I added as she scowled at me.

Iranzu leaned back on the divan and cradled his steaming cup in his hands. "I see," was all he said and I marched off to my chamber to make ready for our journey. When I returned to the courtyard, it was empty.

They had gone without me.

I waited all day for them to come back, pacing the tiles of the courtyard, dropping to the seat surrounding the fountain, making my hands into knots and gritting my teeth. I would have followed them, but they had taken the cart and horses. It was too far to walk. They would be back before I reached them.

At sunset they marched into the courtyard. Justin's sisters had prepared a fine meal of ground chicken and pine nuts wrapped in a thin dough, spiced with nutmeg. I sat at the table when Iranzu and Thérèse entered the courtyard. "We did not find the dervishes," Iranzu said. Then nobody spoke, the entire meal passed in silence and the sisters eyed us with alarm when they came in to clear away our dishes. I had eaten everything on my plate, but tasted nothing.

Finally, I slammed my cup on the table. "Very well," I stated, "I will take you both." I could see the gleam of Thérèse's eyes though mine were turned on Iranzu. "But your daughter must go in disguise." It was I who demanded that she darken her skin, cover her hair and bind her breasts, dressing like a boy so that we could travel more easily into the dark corners of the city. Ah, had I only known then the trouble this would cause!

THE WHEEL of the year turned to the time of the wolf moon; Thérèse called this time "Txirringa Erreketa," the fire-wheel. It was during the

circle of the lion, and high summer had given way to cooler nights, yet
the days were still hot. Most evenings Thérèse and I played chess in the
center of the courtyard while Iranzu dozed nearby.

I had grown used to the ache within me, the melancholy despair of
loving a woman who treated me only as a friend. I turned to the songs of
the troubadours for my solace. Iranzu was teaching me songs of the
traveling minstrels so I could learn the langue d'oc. I humored him at
first, then eagerly learned all I could when I found these songs reflected
the anguish I felt. I sang a chanson of Raimbaut D'Orange one evening,
watching the golden light from the torches play across Thérèse's
cheekbones and glint off the ebony sheen of her hair. The end of the song
I write for you here:

"Lady, my heart is your slave, sweeten my torment. Help me, God!
What can I do?"

She applauded and smiled. "Ibrahim, your voice is astounding! But
how did you learn the songs so fast?"

My face grew warm. I had memorized the songs to give voice to my
longing, but conversing in the language still eluded me. I was about to
tell her this when Iranzu snored himself awake and abruptly signaled for
us to be still. I could hear a quick inhalation from Thérèse. Then I saw
her close her eyes and listen, her body motionless.

I could hear nothing but the murmuring of the doves and the
tinkling of the fountain. The moon had ridden high enough to shine into
the courtyard, and late evening stars hung in the deep blue arc above us.
Justin had told us that the citizens of Constantinople still had problems
with stragglers from the crusades in the center of the city. Some of these
knights had come to free the holy land and then had developed a taste for
life in the east. From time to time they would become drunk and would
forget that Constantinople was a Christian city. They would invade stores
and houses looking for Saracens. But none had ever come this far before.
My cousin had left that morning to receive a shipment of grain and had
not yet returned. The sisters were in their quarters. I was in charge.

Thérèse's eyes were open and locked with her father's now. I
always found their silent communication unnerving, so I stood and
stretched, the bones of my spine cracking. Iranzu's hand reached for his
staff, yet his eyes were still fixed upon his daughter. All was still, but the
air trembled. "What is wrong?" I asked.

That very moment a crash from outside and the screams of the
Khaldun sisters sliced the air. I looked around for my cousin's guards
and could find no one. Iranzu was already arming himself with his staff. I
ran after him as he made his way to the sisters' rooms. Weapons were no
good in my hands. I had taken the oath never to bring harm to another.
Still, I followed him.

Christian knights! I could smell them — a mixture of sour wine and unwashed bodies — even before I reached the room. Stopping at the entrance, I gazed in horror at three knights dressed in breeches and stained leather shirts. The eldest Khaldun sister was pummeling one while the other two knights were weaving around, brandishing their swords and shouting at the sisters. I turned to Iranzu, who was collapsing with mirth.

"What are they saying?" I asked him.

He could barely talk, but managed to sputter, "They think this is a harem." He wiped his eyes. "They say they are here to rescue the women."

Then Iranzu straightened and his voice boomed out into the room. I could not understand what he was saying at the time, but he later told me that he was informing the unfortunate knights that this was a Christian household and these women were sisters. The faces of the knights sagged. One, at least, had the grace to try to apologize. Iranzu glanced over at me and translated as the knight bowed and spoke.

"He says he is Bernart de Bazas. They were told there was a harem here by some wretch down at the harbor, would we please forgive them?"

The third knight slid down beside him and Bernart looked helplessly at us.

"Very well," I said. "I will help you carry him out to the fountain." I matched my words with action, since Bernart clearly could not understand me, grabbing one arm while he took the other and we dragged the collapsed knight out into the courtyard.

"Iranzu! This one I am carrying is a giraffe! Look at those long legs," I remarked as Iranzu followed us with the other knight he had rescued from the eldest sister. Iranzu's knight stumbled forward toward me as I handed the knight I was dragging into the courtyard over to Thérèse.

"My name is Raoul," he told me in my own language. Then he loomed over the knight I had helped drag out to the fountain. "Damn, I'm sorry, Louis-Philippe!" he said to him in his own tongue. I was so pleased that I could actually understand Raoul that I dropped the arm of the knight Louis-Philippe and watched it hit the tiles. "That guide lied to me," Raoul was saying. He looked over at me as Thérèse dunked the head of the one he called Louis-Philippe into the water of the pool. "It is his birthday," Raoul told me in Arabic again, then he also collapsed, his head making a hollow sound on the tiles. I winced.

"Iranzu!" I took Raoul under the arms to pull him over to one of the four divans around the perimeter. Iranzu was already occupied with Bernart, who had also fainted. I managed to slide Raoul next to Bernart and shove a pillow beneath his head. Then I turned back to see how Thérèse was faring with Louis-Philippe, the giraffe.

My heart stopped.

She was sitting at the edge of the fountain cradling the head of this Louis-Philippe in her lap. His uncommonly long legs were sprawled, one resting on the ledge of the fountain, the other on the tile floor of the courtyard. He stank of wine and garlic. Yet Thérèse was brushing his long wet chestnut hair away from his face and studying his countenance with wonder. "Who are you?" she whispered, over and over. "Who are you?"

I STAYED in the courtyard all night with the three drunken knights. Iranzu had discovered Justin's guards outside. It seems that the knights had overpowered them and tied them up. I found this hard to believe, and made a mental note to tell Justin I suspected bribery.

While the knights slept, I studied the profile of Louis-Philippe. I had to admit that he was very handsome, but then so am I! I vowed to win Thérèse's heart for myself. As dawn was breaking and the sky was turning a delicate gray, Louis-Philippe groaned. I filled a skin with water and poured it over his head.

He sputtered and lunged forward, then he clapped his hands to his forehead and groaned even louder. "What happened?" he asked.

Even I could understand that, but I could not answer him in his own language, so I spoke in my own. "Infidel!" I cried, "you have invaded the home of a fine citizen of this city." I folded my arms and frowned down upon him. "A thousand curses on you and your family!" My curses are not something to be taken lightly, as my training in the temple lends power to my words. Again, how I have lived to regret what I have said and done!

He observed me through his fingers, then astonished me by replying, "I beg your indulgence, sir. My companions and I were mistaken."

How he got to his feet, I will never know. His skin became so pale I expected him to pitch over any moment. Yet he pulled himself up to his considerable height and looked down at me.

"If you will please tell me the damage I will make reparations."

His Arabic was not perfect, but good enough so I could not pretend to misunderstand. Still, I just stood and glared at him. His eyes widened as he saw someone behind me.

"So you are awake," Thérèse said. "Good. I will heat some water for tea." She walked close by him on her way to the kitchens.

"Tea," Louis-Philippe muttered, looking even more gray-faced. Then he turned back to me.

His eyes were the most amazing shade of blue-green — as if sunlight on the waters of the inland sea had somehow been captured and given life in his gaze. I continued to glower, hoping that he would disappear.

"Sir," he mumbled. "I regret..."

He stopped as his incredible eyes focused upon me. His face became very still but his eyes moved as he regarded me and he reached out a hand, his fingers brushing a lock of my unruly hair back from my forehead. I stood my ground. Such expressions, I had seen before, and my heart leaped in gladness. This one would never love a woman. Thérèse would be mine!

"Why don't you try to drink this?" Thérèse's voice came from behind me.

Louis-Philippe ran his hand back through his thick chestnut hair and then gracefully extended his other hand for the lovely blue and white cup Thérèse was offering him. "Thank you," he said. Then he smiled.

I looked at Thérèse's face as she too saw the miracle of that smile. Louis-Philippe was without a doubt the most beautiful man I had ever seen, and from the softening of Thérèse's mouth and the glisten in her eyes, it was clear that he was her heart's desire.

My poor darling, I thought. Such heartache he will cause you! At that moment Bernart and Raoul both stirred and Thérèse reluctantly left Louis-Philippe to tend to them.

"What are you doing here in Constantinople?" I did not care what he answered, but I wanted to engage him in conversation so that he would not speak to Thérèse.

He lowered himself to the divan. "We are on a quest," he stated.

My heart sank. Thérèse's head swiveled around. "What?" she asked.

He made a regal gesture. "A quest for a piece of the true cross."

The next several hours we sat around Louis-Philippe and the other knights, listening to the tale they wove, the stories of their adventures in Jerusalem, in Damascus, even in Egypt. Iranzu and Thérèse translated, first for me, and then for the Khaldun sisters, and even for Justin, who joined us late in the afternoon. The sisters had served us a breakfast of figs and grapes and spicy meat wrapped in thin pastry. Later, they brought us a substantial lunch of boiled eggs nestled in a delicious mixture of hearty grain flavored with cinnamon, cumin and saffron. Finally, at the soft hour when the heat of the day was fading, the knights completed their story and we all sat in silence for a moment.

"A good tale," Justin said, stroking his beard. "Where are you staying?"

Louis-Philippe shrugged. "Our tents are set up in the eastern section of the city."

Justin pulled at his beard some more and eyed his younger sisters, who were giggling and watching the knights with interest. He spread his hands. "Why don't you stay here?" he asked the three knights.

Bernart and Raoul both looked to Louis-Philippe, who seemed lost in thought. He collected himself and his eyes darted to me. "We would be honored." He stood and bowed.

I had not missed the look he had given me, and ground my teeth in frustration. Thérèse said nothing, but her eyes were shining.

At that moment Justin sent the sisters away to prepare our dinner. "Good!" he exclaimed as his sisters scampered off. He leaned forward. "I happen to know of a man in Konya," his eyes twinkled, "who I have heard knows where one may find a piece of the true cross."

AND SO our journeys began. We discovered that Louis-Philippe was a baron of a château and had accumulated considerable wealth during his travels, so our group was well provisioned. When Iranzu, the knights and I gathered outside the walls of Justin's home to start our travels, a slight boy with a blue turban ran toward us.

"Away!" Louis-Philippe shouted, waving at the boy as he ran up to our horses.

The boy came close to Louis-Philippe and bowed and grinned at him, looking up with Thérèse's green eyes. Louis-Philippe's face was stern, then his eyes widened in recognition. His face grew quite still, yet his eyes moved over her form and he leaned forward to touch her cheek.

I clutched the reins of my horse. The change in his face when he really saw her tingled my spine. I resolved to stay close to them.

We went to Konya. What we saw there and what we learned could make a long tale in itself. It is sufficient to say that we did not find a piece of the true cross.

No, I must say more. I promised myself that my tale would be honest. There were two incidents during this quest that sealed our fate.

The first happened on the way to Konya. We had been riding for several days and had seen no one. In fact, I wondered if we would ever reach our goal. We had become tired and fretful, and were not on guard for danger. Louis-Philippe was riding out in front, with Thérèse close behind him. From time to time, he would point to something in the barren landscape and laugh. I could not understand what he was saying, but Thérèse would always turn her face up to him, her lips parted into an adoring smile and her eyes glimmering. I could see all of this because I rode right next to her — I would not leave them alone together!

As I recall, they had been quiet for some time and I was all but dozing on my mount. Yawning, I leaned back in my saddle, an act which they later told me must have saved my life. The rush of air from a lance as it hurtled past my throat nearly pushed me off my horse. It missed me by less than the width of a finger and missed hitting Thérèse by the length of my forearm.

Thérèse immediately dropped from her horse and yanked the reins, wheeling it around, shouting for me to do the same, to put the horses between our bodies and the bandits who were visible now. I slid awkwardly to the ground and watched as one of our donkeys was struck in the leg. It bolted, screaming in pain, dragging the lance across the scrub. It was all I could do to keep my horse from following it. I looked around to see where our attackers had gone and watched in awe as Louis-Philippe bore down on a bandit who was clothed entirely in black. This bandit was brandishing a wicked looking curved sword with one hand and a large knife with the other. Louis-Philippe did not swerve as the man swung his sword around and rode toward him. I held my breath and tried to close my eyes. "Good-bye my rival," I whispered.

But my eyes would not close. I was aware of Thérèse's muffled inhalation when she saw what would happen. Louis-Philippe's face was before me. His features were set and impassive, as if he were made of stone, not rushing forward to certain death. I watched him ride toward the bandit, closer and closer. At the last possible moment before he reached the man, Louis-Philippe dropped gracefully to the side of his mount, hanging over the edge, holding his sword with both hands. The curved sword of the bandit passed harmlessly through the air over him, but Louis-Philippe's razor-sharp sword was swinging upward at the same time and removed the man's arm. Shock took the man's face as he saw his arm fly away from his body and then his strangled yell stopped when Louis-Philippe straightened in his saddle and swung his sword around, taking off the man's head. I could not look as his head flew off his body, but I heard it hit the ground. My eyes were still riveted to Louis-Philippe. He had drawn his mount up and was coolly surveying the area.

Bernart and Raoul were fighting three of the bandits, yelling and clashing swords with them. Iranzu was trying to unseat one of the bandits with his long staff. Louis-Philippe charged over to his friends, raising his sword and swinging it in a circle above his head. Blood was flying off it all around him. "How can he do that?" I asked Thérèse. I knew how heavy that sword was, I had lifted it myself once to hand it to him. His face was still impassive and cold as he expertly urged his mount to the side of Raoul, who was taking the worst from two bandits.

The bandit Louis-Philippe chose to kill never knew what happened to him. Louis-Philippe's damascene blade made a clean arc and swept this man's head off his body, also, just as it had done to the other. The two bandits who were left wheeled their mounts around and rode away, closely pursued by Bernart and Louis-Philippe. Thérèse was already at Raoul's side, helping him dismount. She had ripped the turban from her head and was holding it against his shoulder to stop the flow of blood that had already soaked the ground around his horse.

THE MOON was rising when Louis-Philippe and Bernart returned. Louis-Philippe dismounted easily and was using an old tunic to clean blood and bits of flesh off his sword. I went over to him.

"Did you get them?" I asked. His face went perfectly blank, then animation returned and he held his sword up to the torch light.

"Of course we did," he said. "If we had not killed them, they would have brought others."

"How do you know that?" I asked.

His forehead wrinkled, then his face cleared and he grinned. "I do not know it, my friend," he said. "But we could not take the chance." He became engrossed in scrubbing his sword again. I watched his ears grow first pink, then red. Was he embarrassed?

"Why did you swing your sword around your head?" I asked him.

Louis-Philippe scratched under his chin. "When did I do that?" he asked.

"Never mind," I answered. "But thank you anyway."

"For what?" He was clearly perplexed.

I felt an odd thrill. He had just saved our lives and it was nothing to him. It was what he expected of himself.

I must say here that the idea of violence often made me ill. Indeed, as I stood before him while he cleaned his sword, I found myself wondering if the men he had killed had families. I wondered if their mothers would cry for them. And yet a quivering ache was born deep inside of me. This is what he did best, this man, I thought. He did it without malice, without thinking, even. He is a killing machine, I thought. And within me bloomed the flower of desire. I wanted to experience his strength, the cool reserve he showed while he was fighting.

I wanted to make him quiver inside, too. I wanted him to tremble with desire for me.

Turning away, I walked over to where Iranzu was rubbing down the sweating horses. "This will never do!" I told myself, "and yet..." I kept my distance from Louis-Philippe that night.

THE SECOND incident took place in Konya. I had not forgotten my own quest for knowledge, and sought the great teacher Baha-od-Din Walad. He granted audience.

"Have you seen the face of God?" I asked him. "What is the nature of God? Why are we here? Why is there suffering?"

He sat silently through all my questions, nodding now and then. When my questions were all asked, he still sat there without speaking. The silence became profound. He motioned for me to come closer. I moved toward him and he bent to whisper in my ear.

"I want you to talk to my son," he said. "You must go to see Djalal-od-Din."

I was angry, but I bowed and left him.

I was sitting in my tent fuming about my meeting with Baha-od-Din when a stranger asked if he could enter. I spoke my assent and a boy pushed aside the cloth covering the entrance. He sat before me.

"My father has said you need to see me," he told me. His eyes were the large and liquid eyes of a deer.

A boy, I thought. I felt insulted, but was polite. I asked him the same questions I had asked his father while he sat there before me, nodding his head and gazing at his hands.

When I finished his eyes looked right into my heart. I could not move. Something buried inside me, something ancient, shifted and writhed. A bell sounded deep within my being. Truth spread out in a vast wave, flooding my senses, demanding to be seen, touched, heard, tasted — an immense, uncompromising love. I was myself and yet not myself; suddenly very wise and large and looking upon my life and the lives of others with loving amusement.

It was too much, this truth. I shied away and the flood gates closed. Yet a small, glowing piece stayed behind, warming my heart.

"You have a great dhawq, a great desire for God," Djalal-od-Din said. "Your search is your path. Why are you so afraid?" He reached out and took my hands now. "Your search will lead you to the door of secrets. In the act of seeking you will find the answers you want." He dropped my hands and gestured at the walls of the tent, the carpet on the floor, the gentle beams of sunlight streaming through the doorway. "The answers you seek are all around you. Do you not see?"

Djalal-od-Din still held me with his eyes. "Within you, what you are seeking and the seeker... these are one and the same." He stood in one graceful movement. "Ibrahim," his voice caressed my name. "I am a seeker, too." And he left the tent so quietly that I hardly knew he was gone.

As I write this I know I cannot even begin to convey what happened when he spoke to me. How can I put into words that which cannot be written? Ibn Arabi could have told you with his songs. But I am no poet. All I can say is that my life was never the same afterward. I could never look at anything in the same way again. Was I made holy? I think not, and as you read further you will see that my actions were not those of an holy being. But something changed for me then, changed forever. My search became my life.

We soon left Konya and spent the winter in Constantinople. Thérèse watched Louis-Philippe and I closely watched the two of them. By spring, Iranzu announced that he and Thérèse were returning to their home. We thanked my cousin for his hospitality and I congratulated myself. Soon I would have Thérèse to myself again.

As we prepared to leave, Louis-Philippe took Iranzu aside and they talked for some time. I grew nervous. Finally, Iranzu announced that the three knights would accompany us back to Navarre. "With such an escort we can travel overland without fear of attack." While Iranzu was telling us this, Louis-Philippe stood at his side. But Louis-Philippe's eyes were focused upon me.

Thérèse had abandoned her street urchin garments and now dressed in her flowing gown, with her hair unbound. I watched her hair curl and lift in the breeze, wanting to bury my hands in it. My fingertips ached and the yearning in my loins throbbed. She rode beside Iranzu most of the way, although I saw her looking back at Louis-Philippe. It hurt me to look at her expression, so hopeless! I could not avoid seeing her, though. You see, Louis-Philippe rode beside me.

He had decided to teach me the langue d'oc as we rode. I sang the "Songs of Raimbaut d'Orange" to him and he helped me put together phrases that conveyed meaning, rather than the simple words I had strung together haphazardly in order to communicate. The months we traveled together enabled me to acquire the language. Finally I could understand and converse, and although I was not fluent, I could be understood.

At one point I asked him how he had learned to fight. He looked puzzled for a moment, then his ears grew pink and he turned his face away.

"I am the only son of baron. If I had been born a serf or even a second son I may not have learned the art of battle. I was sent to squire for the Viscount of Béarn," he told me. "All of us learned to fight on the fields. We fought each other at first, then we fought for our lord."

"I have heard of your customs," I said. "So you fought for this viscount?"

He laughed and faced me. "There was a disagreement between the Viscount of Béarn and the King of Navarre. I fought well but on the losing side." Now he lifted his tunic and showed me his scars — an ugly, puckered slash across his belly, and a crooked line down his back. "The dispute was settled and I now owe fealty to the king." He urged his horse forward.

As we traveled further, he pointed out features in the landscape that resembled animals or people and he laughed in delight. The curve of a rock that looked like a pregnant sow, a cluster of bushes that looked like a bunch of monks defecating on the ground, the ragged edge of a gully that looked like huge lumps of turds — all of these strange things he saw in the earth around us. I noted that he mostly saw images of animals or food or bodily waste. Where most men, if they saw anything at all, would see sexual images all around, he did not. He was curiously innocent. I found myself both touched and disturbed by this.

OUR JOURNEY drew to an end. We were outside of Roncesvalles, which was six days ride from his château. You know Navarre. Where

Alexandria bakes gold and brown under the sun and Constantinople ripples in blue, Navarre broods under inconstant sky and cloud; deep forest and soaring peaks. The mountains closed around us in a tight, green-black embrace. I must say here that Thérèse and I were the only members of our company who had our own tents, Thérèse because she was the only woman, and me because I refused to share a tent with men who had not seen soap and water for years. As I recall, on this evening Thérèse retired to her tent early. Louis-Philippe had obtained an earthen jug full of the very fresh and fragrant wine of the region, and he brought it to my tent. I motioned for him to sit across from me on the carpet. We toasted each other and drank the wine out of silver cups he had obtained somewhere during his travels.

"Not bad, not bad," I said, watching how his eyes avoided mine. He looked at the walls of the tent, at the carpet, at his feet.

"Followers of Mohammed cannot drink," he said, wiping his mouth.

I nodded. "Allah will forgive me," I said. "I am of the Temple of Isis."

Finally, he cleared his throat and said, "Raoul has told me a strange tale he heard about the temple — where you lived in Egypt."

I waited.

"He said that the initiates there loved men and women in some kind of ritual."

"The catamites," I said. "Yes."

He squirmed, then drained his cup of wine and quickly poured another. "Would they do this for someone... someone who wanted a certain kind of experience?" His eyes met mine now.

"What do you mean, my friend?"

In answer he put his cup down and reached out to me, his fingers stroking the skin on my chest and moving slowly down to my belly. My body responded as he must have known it would. I was so frustrated from wanting Thérèse that the slightest touch would excite me, and, once aroused, my need was urgent. "No." I started to reject him even then, but he moved forward and took my head in his hands. I felt the strength of his embrace, his power. He pulled me to him and my will dissolved.

I had wanted to shatter his reserve, his self-composure. Well, I had done that now. He trembled so much that he had difficulty removing his breeches. He started to caress me everywhere with one hand while he groped behind us with his other hand, seeking the candle.

"Why put it out?" I asked.

"No lights," he said, his voice thick and heavy. "We must not have any light." His fingers found the wick and he snuffed it out. He truly was a novice. Once I removed my clothes his touch was clumsy. His need was too great. He pulled me down on the carpet and shuddered with a groan that sounded from deep within him.

I showed him what could be done between two men.

Afterward he sat up and continued to tremble. I reached out for him, now.

"What is wrong?"

"I am doomed," he said, his voice muffled by his hands held over his face.

"What?"

"I have had many women, many!" he said. "My friends out there are even jealous of me." His voice took on the jocular intonation of Bernart. "The women, they always come to Louis-Philippe, eh?" Now his voice grew quiet. "But there was always something missing, something not quite..." He could not find the words.

After a long silence he continued, "When I was a boy there were two cousins — both men — who loved each other as you and I have." He spoke quickly. I could see his chest rising and falling in the dim light. "They tried to hide their love but someone discovered their secret and told the priest." I could hear him search around in the darkness for his clothing. "They burned them alive. I saw them burn." He pulled his breeches on, grabbed his tunic and lunged for the entrance to the tent. When he got the flap open, he turned back to me. "You must tell no one about this! Promise!" He waited at the entrance.

"Who would I tell, my friend?" I said. "And why?"

That seemed good enough for him. "This will never happen again," he said. Then he slipped out into the night.

I sat for a moment in a daze. "If you felt this way then why did you do it?" I asked the air. "And why did I?" I should have gone after him but I did not. I felt stupid and belittled, and lay in the dark for a while hating him but I could not hate him for long. If it was true that where he lives they burn people for what we did, then he must surely have suffered from such a long denial of his own nature. I stayed in my tent and slept.

IN THE morning I crawled out of my blankets and made my way to the water trough just outside of Thérèse's tent. We had replenished it yesterday with the clear cold water that flowed off the mountains. I was splashing this over my face and neck when the flap to her tent opened and Louis-Philippe stumbled out. His breeches were unlaced and his tunic was thrown across his shoulders. I watched him stop and pull his tunic over his head, sliding his arms into the sleeves, while my mind refused to believe what I was seeing.

He went to my Thérèse, I thought. He went from my tent to the tent of my beloved. I doubled over as a cramping pain seared my gut and remained bent for a moment, gasping and waiting for it to pass. When I straightened, he was walking away.

I sprinted after him and launched myself at his legs, knocking him over. If he had been expecting this I would never have been able to bring him down. As it was, he soon recovered and had me on the ground, his hands closed around my throat. His skin paled when he recognized me and he released his hold. I slid out from under him and rolled away, using the momentum of this action to leap to my feet. My eyes glared my hatred at him.

He made a gesture toward me. "Ibrahim, I..."

I would not listen, turned on my heel and strode to Thérèse's tent, entering it without even thinking of what I was doing.

She was sitting in a tangle of blankets, holding her sides with her arms and rocking back and forth. Her eyes were red from crying and tears still glistened on her cheeks.

"Has he hurt you?" I asked. My voice was harsh in the stillness inside the tent.

She looked up at me and gave a little laugh that turned into a sob.

"I have hurt myself," she finally said. "Oh, I knew his nature. I have known for a long time. But I thought I could change him. I thought I could make him love me." Her lips twisted in scorn. "I saw the way he looked at you. I knew that he would never love a woman, but my heart could not accept that." She pounded the ground. "I will not accept that!"

Her hands covered her face and she shuddered. "He came into my tent last night looking so lost, so bewildered. 'What is wrong?' I asked him. He could not tell me. I held my arms out to him and he came to me and loved me." She dropped her hands and her eyes glinted up at me. "But while he was with me he whispered your name." Her voice broke. "Over and over, while his hands and his body were loving me he whispered: 'Ibrahim. Ibrahim.'" Her hands gripped the blankets. She looked so forlorn that I went to her and took her into my arms. I murmured the things parents say to children who are hurt, while she buried her face in my chest and sobbed.

"It will pass," I told her. "You will feel differently later. Just wait and see." I had never been this close to her before, never held her before. The scent of jasmine drifted from her hair. Her body curved into mine so naturally I felt that I had come home. This was where I belonged. In the dim light with her soft body in my arms I felt an edge of the wave that Djalal-od-Din had loosed within me rise and wash over my being. I could see her clearly then, her stubborn determination, the tragic beauty of her strength. She would not bend. But now she trembled against my chest. "Beloved," I whispered. Then I could not stop myself. I lifted her face and covered her mouth with mine. She responded, opened to me as her lips parted and she moved into my embrace. Paradise! But she pulled away.

I closed my eyes and tried to master my breathing, tried to still the tremors that shook me now. The familiar dull ache that had throbbed through my body welled up inside with such fury that it was all I could do to bite back a cry. I sealed my lips and shuddered. But her hands touched my face.

"Ibrahim?" I opened my eyes to see her pulling her gown over her head and tossing it aside. There she sat, naked and glorious among the blankets.

She held her arms out to me. "Ibrahim, my dear friend," she said, tears spilling out of her eyes again. "Please. Come and love me."

I needed nothing more than this. Oh, I knew she wanted me at that moment to chase away her despair. But it was enough for me. And though I wanted her so badly that I feared I would burst the moment I entered her, I was skilled in the arts of love. Louis-Philippe was not — didn't I know this from his bumbling performance with me? I gave Thérèse such pleasure that her entire body shivered and she cried out.

Still, as I held her later, she sobbed.

"I am sorry, my friend," she said. "I cannot stop loving him."

I stroked her hair until she slept. Then I dressed and went to find Louis-Philippe.

"I will marry her," he told me when I confronted him.

I laughed. "Even I know that marriages among your people are arranged to unite noble families, and Thérèse is not of your kind," I scoffed. "Tell me another lie!"

"Nevertheless, I will marry her." He looked directly into my eyes without flinching, with the same look of cool reserve and calculation he showed before he killed the bandits.

In the end, Thérèse and Louis-Philippe went into Roncesvalles and found a priest. Iranzu and Bernart were with them. I remained in our camp and drank the rest of the wine Louis-Philippe had left behind in my tent.

So he did marry her. And that way he made certain that I would remain with him. He knew I would not let her go alone to his château. He knew I would not be parted from her.

As we entered the outer court of his château, I urged my mount forward to ride next to Thérèse. "Are you well?" I asked her. Her eyes were shadowed and she was pale. She looked at me for a moment.

"I am as you see me, Ibrahim," she said. Then she reached out and brushed a lock of my hair away from my eyes. Her expression softened. "There is a carving in one of the caves that eat into the mountains surrounding our valley." She took my hand. "It is on the ceiling so it is hard to see at first, but if you look you can see three serpents so closely entwined that you can hardly tell where one ends and the others begin." She settled back on her horse, dropping my hand, and her eyes turned to where Louis-Philippe stood, at the base of a tower that reared into the lowering sky.

Chapter 8

MARÍANA turned the page and drew in her breath. "Mama." Tears blurred her vision as her fingers reverently touched the faded sketch of a woman with curling black hair, her head bent and eyes gazing in adoration at a chubby baby held in her arms. A drawing of the same repeating tile pattern that graced the borders of the palace windows surrounded the portrait. She rifled through the rest of the book, seeing the flowing dance of lines she had found in the beginning. She could not read this. Cradling the book in her hands, she squeezed her eyes shut. Her tears made soft threads of moisture on her cheeks.

The clank of dishes and crockery, muffled clatter of leather shoes across the thick rugs, whisper of fabric against the low table opened her eyes. Geneviéve was there, her skirts rustling against her legs as she moved around the table.

"Hungry, are you?" Geneviéve asked.

Maríana rubbed the tears from her face and looked up. The sky was darkening outside. Geneviéve had lit several candles and was bustling around a table she was setting with goblets and platters. "Come and help me," she said.

Maríana jumped up to help her aunt, but had to catch herself as the walls started to spin and she felt the stab of a thousand needles attack her legs. Rubbing her left leg vigorously, she hobbled over to the table, setting places for three.

"You have been there on the pillows for most of the day," Geneviéve said. "I left you alone to finish reading. Didn't make much sense to disturb you."

"Thank you." Maríana moved the goblets aimlessly around on the table. "Have you read it?"

"Of course not! It is for you. Anyway, I don't need to, do I? Your mother told me enough. I know the story very well." Geneviéve took her hand and led her through the back of the chamber into a small room. A hearth filled one wall. Over the fire crackling within, a three-legged iron stand held a kettle; an entire chicken was spitted and roasting next to it.

"Not very big," Geneviéve remarked. "But it will do for the three of us." She removed the chicken with a wooden spear and placed it upon a trencher.

In the main chamber, the muted tapping of feet across the Saracen rug pushed Maríana toward the hearth. She was not ready for this, did not want to see him.

"Ah, here he is." Geneviéve straightened her back and beamed at the man who entered. "Hello Ibrahim, or is it Jacques for good, now?" He favored her with an engaging smile and ran his finger over the crispy chicken skin, licking the fat that dribbled down.

"Excellent as usual," he said. "I am still Ibrahim here."

Maríana could not meet his eyes. His words had brought her mother to life, but his brutal honesty had stolen her voice. There was so much she still wanted to know, so much she wanted to ask.

She could not find the words.

Geneviéve turned to her. "We have an agreement with your father. You and I will stay up here with Ibrahim for a year." She uncovered the kettle, her hands encased in a thick cloth. Steam arose from a soup of cabbage and onion. "Next midsummer, you and I must return to the main part of the château." She handed the cloth to Ibrahim and he carried the soup kettle into the main chamber.

THROUGHOUT the meal, Maríana kept her eyes fixed upon her plate. Across the table, she could see Ibrahim's square hands; heard his low, resonant voice as he spoke to Geneviéve. Once she raised her eyes when her aunt asked if she wanted more chicken and caught Ibrahim watching her. His gold-brown eyes were sad, yet he smiled.

Geneviéve laughed. "I don't know about you, but I intend to enjoy every minute up here away from the palais and that musty old donjon!"

Ibrahim moved his left hand; his fingers curled, then extended. She looked up at his face. He was nodding at her aunt.

Geneviéve gave a tremendous yawn. "Well, to bed for me." She waddled off to the tiny chamber next to the kitchen, where she had shown Maríana the large straw pallet they would share.

The whisper of Ibrahim's steady breath filled the room. An ember fell in the kitchen hearth, its momentary glow entering the larger chamber before it faded. The door stood open to the night and she could hear the fountain murmuring.

"Writing this was a risk I had to take." He held the book and turned the pages. "I could have left things out, I suppose. But I owed it to her."

"You left out the most important part." She leaned back in her chair.

His body shuddered and lines formed around his eyes. He looked down at the table, his hands clutching the book. "I would tell you," he finally said, his voice a low rumble, "but I promised your father and I will not break my word."

"Very well." He had loved her mother. That would have to be enough. "How did you get Grandmother to allow me to stay up here?"

"Johanna likes me," he said. "She always has."

"And what is this agreement Geneviéve was talking about?"

Maríana met his eyes. "What will we do here?"

Ibrahim's face relaxed and he placed the book on the table. He poured more of the sweet clear wine into his goblet. "I promised your mother to teach you as much as I could about her way of life." He lifted the goblet and regarded her over the rim. "And perhaps also of mine."

"What kinds of things would you teach me?" She held her breath. He knew Egypt, had seen Byzantium! He had known her mother. Through him she could, too.

He smiled warmly, set his wine down, and, standing, drew her to her feet. He led her out the doorway, his arm around her shoulders. Water spilled and gurgled in the fountain. Light from metal lamps spilled out into the courtyard. He pointed to a bright diamond scattering of stars, dancing across the deep velvet blue of summer sky. "That bright one there is Jupiter." His fingers traced a line from Jupiter to a cluster of winking stars. "Draco, the dragon."

Her heart trembled in her throat. "How did they get there? What are they?" She turned to see his eyes reflecting the starlight, soft upon his face.

"I will tell you."

MARÍANA pushed her hair back. Sweat made tracks down her temples and beaded on her cheeks. She counted the tiny sprigs of rosemary she had just planted and sorted through the pile of seedlings at her side. The sun had ridden the sky and now hung in a golden orb just above the crest of Irati. The rest would wait until morning. She gathered rosemary and earth into her hemp bag and tied it closed, then reached over to the pond and sprinkled the bag with water to keep the seedlings from drying. Rising to her feet, she brushed at mud and leaves clinging to her skirt and climbed onto the stone seat Ibrahim had recently placed next to the pond, turning her eyes away from Yves and his scythe. Ibrahim had ordered him to pull out the blackberry bush where she and Richard had taken shelter.

Wiping her hands on her skirt, she lifted two books Ibrahim had given her. De Materia Medica was written in large block letters on the cover of one; the other was inscribed with the same flower petal symbol that graced his journal.

"What does Dioscorides have to say?" Ibrahim sat beside her.

"I could not find his section on rosemary." At that moment, Yves ripped the blackberry bushes from the earth. The books slipped from her fingers as she cringed and looked away, out over the pond.

"Why does this distress you? The bushes were too close to the water — their roots are rotting." Ibrahim retrieved one of her books.

"I used to go inside them." She still could not watch. "They remind me of someone." Leaning down, she lifted the other book and opened it.

Her mother's hand, neat and small, underlined a tidy drawing of the straight stalks and dark seeds of fennel. "When did she make this?" Every time she touched her mother's book her chest warmed, yet her throat clogged with tears. She wiped her cheeks and forced herself to continue turning the pages.

His eyes were on the bushes. "What?" He glanced at the book. "Oh, before you were born." He gestured and Yves stopped pulling at the branches. "These blackberries remind you of someone?"

She nodded, eyes on the careful lines, the precise letters. "Two years ago Arnaut and Jean-Pierre knocked me down. Richard helped me get away from them." Would he disapprove? "We came here to the pond." Glancing sideways she could only see his profile. His face was expressionless, eyes hooded.

"Knocked you down?"

"I hit my head when I fell." She watched Yves stripping the leaves. "They were sent home for doing that." Her lips twisted in memory. "Grandmother insisted." She closed Thérèse's book. "But I want to ask you about something that happened that night."

He motioned for silence. "That is enough for now," he told Yves. "Go back for your dinner. You can finish tomorrow." He waited in silence until Yves was out of sight.

"You must be careful about speaking of such things here," he said. Hooves clattered on the stones of the bailey. Birdsong ebbed and flowed. He leaned toward her, whispered, "What happened?"

"I am not sure even now. I was unconscious, then suddenly awoke. A light floated in front of me, a light that moved." Her fingers described the pattern in the air. "It was like two snakes writhing. Inside the light was a dark spot. Richard said it was a door." She bit off a cry as Ibrahim grabbed her wrist.

"Ibrahim! What..." His eyes were distant, face very still. But there was sweat upon his brow. She had never seen him sweat before.

"A moment." Golden light from the setting sun warmed his features, but his skull showed underneath his skin; his cheekbones made a sharp edge from ears to nose. He released her wrist and sat back.

"What was it?" She cradled her wrist in her hand.

He collected himself, shook his head as a dog coming out of water will, then his eyes warmed and he reached for her wrist again. As his fingers gently rubbed the bruise he had made, he said, "I am sorry, petite." He paused, rotating her hand. "I was remembering something your mother told me, something about the reason they had to leave their home in the west." He placed her wrist on his knee and held his palms over it. "Many years ago, someone in her family opened a door." His hands were dry. "He was unprepared; something came through."

"Richard told me to close it." She watched his hands. Her wrist was warming, tingling.

"And did you?" His eyes closed. The warmth in her wrist spread out, moved up her arm.

"I must have, but when it closed a great wind blew the fowl pen apart." He opened his eyes and took his hands away from her wrist. She held it up. "Oh!" The pain was gone now, the bruise fading to yellow.

"I remember that wind. So de la Guerche took you to the garden, eh?"

She was still examining her skin. "What?" Looking up, she saw his grin.

"Enough!" He stood and pulled her to her feet, then placed the books in the pouch at his waist. "I came here to show you something." He started walking down the path. "We will need to do this before the sun is gone." He led her farther into the garden, past beech and apricot, past beds of fennel, coriander and basil.

"There are two ways out of the château." He had taken her all the way to the back, where ash and hawthorn crowded against the thick stones of the outer wall. A creeping saffron rose climbed the granite blocks.

"The south gate and the east gate?" she asked. He shook his head, lifting a section of the mat of roses.

"I will show you the secret ways out," he said as they ducked beneath the green and ocher curtain. An iron trellis supported the roses. Steps led down to a stout wooden lattice gate.

"This is your key," Ibrahim pulled a large metal key out of his pouch. It gleamed faintly in the chill shadows. "I have one, and your father and Guillaume each have one also." He fit the key into the lock and turned it. The hinges screamed as he eased the door open. "We will have to butter these," he remarked, then motioned for her to follow.

She entered a stone tunnel. Moss coated the damp walls; the air was clammy. Twenty paces took her to its end, where another gate, this one made of iron strips, stood. It smelled of water and blood. He placed the key in the lock and opened it. She held her breath and pushed through.

"This is only a way out, there is no way back in through here." He followed her outside where a thicket of vines covered the entrance. "The gate locks itself behind you — we put a drop bolt in the latch." He pushed her forward. She ducked under the vines. Through straggling thorn bushes, ahead lay the path to Ibrahim's palace.

"If you ever need to come to me in secret, you can take this path." He murmured beside her. "Though this gate is not as secret as the other." The pale fading of twilight was giving way to intense blue, edged with purple. "I must show you the other gate later, when there are fewer people in the donjon," he said. "It goes through a series of caves in Irati itself and comes out behind the palace." She picked her way through the thorns and started climbing. "Only your father, myself and Guillaume know of that one."

"And now me," she said, looking up at his face through blue shadows of the falling night.

His teeth gleamed. "And now you."

SLEEP ELUDED her. Maríana turned over and shifted her legs, wiggling so much that Geneviéve spoke sharply. Dust rising from the straw mattress tickled her nose. It was the eve of St. Agnes, the very end of January, when young women everywhere — from France to the Languedoc, from Brittany to Navarre — would place apples under their pillows, to dream of their future husbands.

Maríana had saved her apple from autumn harvest, wrapping it in wool treated with beeswax. It had dried well; there was little mold. The skin had wrinkled into velvety folds. She placed it under the side of her pillow that faced away from Geneviéve. Her aunt did not need to know she sought to discover the identity of her future husband. Other offers for her had come since the summer festival, but Ibrahim had seen that each offer was carefully considered, and just as carefully rejected. She knew none of the men who had asked for her. It was the alliance with de Reuilles they sought; she would have no say in who her father chose. No one questioned this; why should she?

She stroked the skin of the apple under her pillow. Richard had not written again, but Geneviéve said she had not heard he was wed. He could still come for her, couldn't he? He was there in her dreams so often, holding her in his arms. Surely he would be there tonight on St. Agnes's Eve. The texture of the apple was so like his skin, smooth and curved, giving way slightly under the pressure of her fingers.

It was his face she remembered best-his quiet gaze, the way his brown-black eyes tilted at the corners, the fine bones, the tiny white scar at the side of his mouth. She moved her feet and Geneviéve grumbled.

Maríana sighed. It was surely close to dawn. Too late. She would have to wait another year. Her head turned toward the wall. She closed her eyes.

And found herself standing in the great hall of the palais. How did she get there? Johanna and her aunt had taken her inside the great hall only twice before. It seemed like late evening, or perhaps early morning. Light from the fire in the gigantic hearth bathed the walls in gold and crimson. The hall was filled with guests sleeping on the benches, the tables, in bedrolls upon the floor. So many guests in winter? When had they arrived? She moved toward the staircase, keeping her steps as quiet as she could. Perhaps she could stay in Johanna's room for the night. She was so tired and the snow was too deep to trudge back to the donjon. It was the eve of St. Agnes, after all. Her feet stopped by the staircase.

What was it about St. Agnes's Eve? The donjon, surely she was not there anymore, was she? There was something wrong here, but her thoughts would not march together.

A man stood next to the staircase, his back to her. He was dressed in russet and the green of deep forest. Golden brown hair fell in a straight line to his shoulders. What region wore russet and green? A sword hung from the scabbard on his belt. A knight. A friend? No one would admit an armed enemy to the hall. He was not there a moment ago; when had he come in?

He faced the tapestry of the de Reuilles mermaid; his frame straight and powerful, full of repressed fury and barely controlled anguish. Strength radiated from every line of his form, as concretely as it would from a hurtling lance or a tensely drawn bow. She glanced around the hall. There were many close at hand, even though they were asleep. She was safe.

The knight relaxed suddenly, expelling his indrawn breath forcefully, his shoulders dropping. Her vision wavered. He had just left a fortress, this knight. She saw its walls rising from an immense and barren cliff. Something smoked at its base. How did she know this-had she climbed into his mind? She tried to speak words of comfort, but her lips could not shape the sounds. He started to turn; she saw the curve of his cheek, the glint of blue eyes.

Someone was shaking her arm. "Maríana! Come now, slug-a-bed." Her aunt's voice echoed. The man in front of her, the staircase, the hall, all shattered. She looked up into Geneviéve's face, felt the bulge of the apple under her pillow. Tears prickled in her eyes. It was not Richard there in her St. Agnes's Eve dream. Not Richard.

MARÍANA stepped from their tiny bedchamber to the outer room, her fingers caught in the tangle of her hair, forming braids. "What?" The odor of earth and moss greeted her. Bags of dried plants filled the room, stacked against the walls, sitting on the rugs. The pillows were heaped upon Ibrahim's garment chest. Ibrahim himself was sitting in the middle of the floor, sorting through a hemp sack. Measuring scales and metal pots surrounded him. A stone mortar and pestle stood to his right. He waved toward the kitchen without raising his head.

"Geneviéve has bread and cheese ready for you. When you have eaten, you will help me here." When she did not move he looked up. "Yves brought these up in a cart this morning. I usually wait until later in the spring to do this, but I received word yesterday that we will have visitors soon," his hands spread out, encompassing the jumble of plants and implements, "visitors who will need our medicines." He went back to his sorting. "They should be here today. We must make ready."

LATE THAT afternoon, Maríana rubbed her eyes. One of the lamps was sending an acrid smoke into the chamber. The oil must have turned. She retrieved a metal paddle and snuffed out the flame. Two other lamps sent out their light and the hearth cast a steady glow in the kitchen. They did not need this one.

She stretched her arms and rotated her head, feeling muscles tighten and spine crack. She had gone through all the sacks of plants Yves had brought. Her belly rumbled; she glanced toward the kitchen. Maybe she could stop now and join Geneviéve there. But Ibrahim was still in the center of the floor, his fingers deftly braiding what looked like a bulging white rope. She could not leave while he still worked.

Now he turned away from the packets of dried herbs, mosses and tree bark they had ground and mixed and blended. He rose easily from where he had crouched for hours and moved to the back of the chamber. "I want you to make a carrying pack for the herb mixtures we have created today. It should be made out of this cloth." Pushing pillows aside, he pulled a heavy dark gray material out of his low chest, shaking it out so that it formed one large piece. "It should have a strap to go over your shoulder and the thread you use must be treated with bees' wax."

When she took the material from his hands, he said, "Now, what would you give someone who had a chest ailment?"

She looked at the packets of plants spread out on the floor. "Parsley for congestion," she picked out packets of the leafy green fragments, "mallow for inflammation of the chest, and a diluted infusion of glovewort for pain and pressure in the chest."

She continued until she had chosen a packet or packets for every ailment he specified. All warmth in the palace came from the kitchen hearth. The shutters sealed snow and frigid air out, but her breath still made white clouds in the central chamber.

Someone pounded on the door. Ibrahim leaped to his feet, striding toward the door and throwing it open to the lemon white of late afternoon sun upon snow.

"Old friend!" he cried, throwing his arms around a large figure standing there, encased in layers of wool and holding a staff. Behind this figure a shorter one hung back from the door, swathed in a cape, with a black scarf wound around the face.

Maríana rose to her feet as the two entered the chamber and Ibrahim closed the door on winter. The larger figure emerged from his wool. A full gray beard hung to his waist and his hazel eyes were framed by the deep creases of age. The other figure stood back from him. Cold gray-green eyes stared out at her from over the black scarf.

Ibrahim clapped his hands. "Geneviéve!" he called to the kitchen. "Iranzu is here!"

"What?" Maríana's heart started hammering. "Grandfather?"

Ibrahim took her hands as Geneviéve emerged from the kitchen, beaming. "Iranzu," he said again, pulling Maríana to the old man. "Here is your granddaughter," he turned to the other figure, who was pulling down the scarf that encircled her face, "and this is?"

"Thérèse's other daughter." She spoke to Ibrahim but her frozen eyes were upon Maríana, "Leila."

A BUTTERY gleam filled the doorway of their bedchamber. Grandfather Jakintza and Ibrahim had not retired, but their voices were so low Maríana could not make out their words. The young woman who called herself Leila was a rigid shape beside her. All through their evening meal she had glared at Maríana. When it grew late, and Iranzu told her she must bed down with Geneviéve and Maríana, Leila had flushed a deep crimson. But she said nothing, and she was here, now.

"Are you asleep?" Maríana whispered.

"If I was, I would not be now." Leila's voice was quiet, but acid.

Maríana ground her teeth. Try again. "Why do you hate me?"

"Why shouldn't I? Mother stayed with you, didn't she?" Leila's voice sounded harsh, but the last words quivered and she shifted her body to turn away.

Maríana grabbed Leila's hand and held it before she could turn over. The girl struggled briefly, but a grunt from Geneviéve stilled her. "No, she didn't," Maríana whispered when Leila stopped struggling. "She did not stay with me." Maríana saw Leila blink twice, then Leila's mouth became a thin line and her fingers clamped down on Maríana's hand.

The bones in her hand slid and ground as Leila increased the pressure, squeezing and digging her nails in. But Maríana would not let her sister turn away. "She... left... me, too," she said, each word bit off as the bones in her hand crunched.

Leila released her grip. Maríana caught her breath, stopped the whimper that threatened to slip out. She did not let go of Leila's hand. Then something touched her in a place she could not name. The skin above her navel grew warm and an image blossomed before her eyes. She could see the rearing slopes of a narrow valley, feel her throat clog with pride and sorrow. The image and feelings disappeared abruptly and she turned toward Leila.

"Damn!" Leila said. "I didn't mean to do that, I didn't want to help you." There were tears on Leila's cheeks now. She dashed them away with her free hand and sniffed.

"Help me?" The slopes rose before her again. Now new feelings roiled in her belly; resentment and a grudging curiosity. "Where is that?" Feelings and image shut off more slowly this time.

"He must have told you — the Egyptian, Ibrahim." Leila gritted her teeth.

"Told me what?" Now Maríana saw a stone house with a steep roof. A mountain reared up into the sky directly behind it.

"Don't play with me!" Leila turned her head, eyes narrowed. "You must know why we came! Why else would you touch me?"

Maríana released her hand. "There, I am not touching you now." She rubbed the hand Leila had crushed. The images and feelings vanished. She flexed her fingers slowly, one by one. "You didn't have to do that," she said, and turned on her side, away from her half sister.

The straw mattress shifted. Leila had risen on her elbow. "You are right." Her voice was flat, resigned. "Grandfather said I had to help you, so I will."

Maríana sealed her lips and did not move. Her hand was swelling; she could feel her heart beating in her fingertips. An arm pressed her shoulder, not to turn her, just firm pressure resting there.

"Very well," Leila said.

And Thérèse was there before Maríana, young and smiling, black braids streaming back over her shoulders, hands thrust into a washtub. The stone house stood behind her, its door thrown open. Her arms were bare; it must be summer. Now she was in front of her mother, looking up into her face, as if she were there next to her.

"This is not my memory." Leila's voice cut across the image. She lifted her arm and the scene disappeared at once. "I suppose it is Adelie's — my aunt's." She moved her arm and dust rose from the straw. "I was only a baby when Mama left."

Maríana sat up. Her sister was propped on her elbow, ignoring Geneviéve's snort. Light from the outer chamber revealed Leila's face. It was as stern as before, but her eyes no longer bored into Maríana. "No wonder you hate me," Maríana said. "You never knew her at all."

Leila's eyes dropped, but her shoulder lifted in a lopsided shrug. "My aunt told me about her. I know enough." She looked up again. Leila reached out her hand and her lips twitched when Maríana backed away. "All the Jakintzas can do what I just did," she said. "When you start, you must be touching, but once you have learned, you won't need to touch anymore." Leila sat up and crossed her legs, facing Maríana and placing her hand, palm up, in her lap. Geneviéve muttered, then her breathing deepened.

Maríana sat clutching her injured hand against her chest, staring at Leila's open palm. "You will teach me this?" Maríana asked.

"I won't hurt you again — I promise. Give me your hand. I can heal it." Leila's voice broke off at Maríana's stare. "Oh, I will not lie. I do not like you. I never will. But I will keep my promise to Grandfather." She reached for Maríana's hand. "Come now, let me heal you. Or you can squeeze my hand."

To see inside another, know memories, know feelings. Maríana turned her head toward the door, where she could hear the muted voices of Ibrahim and her grandfather. Ibrahim could not teach her this.

"Well." Leila started to close her hand. "Perhaps you are not a Jakintza, after all."

Maríana extended her injured hand and placed it firmly in her sister's palm.

IT WAS THE eve of the hawthorn moon. Ibrahim had sent Geneviéve down to the palais. As winter gave way, the air grew softer. Four moons until Maríana must return to the château. Only four.

She loaded herb and root packets into the bag she had sewn. Every week Ibrahim accompanied her to Reuilles-la-ville and they joined Iranzu and Leila in the square, offering healing gifts to the people there. Whenever the flat boat took them back across the lake, she averted her eyes from the walls of Reuilles-le-château and, with Ibrahim, climbed the Irati path all the way to the palace. Sometimes squires fought in the fields outside the château walls. She searched crowd for black hair that glinted red in the sun, but Richard was never there. He was a knight by now, surely.

She was replenishing her supply of plants, roots, bark and mosses for the next journey to Reuilles-la-ville. Leila told her that she and her grandfather had arrived soon after the midsummer festival last year. They came down from their valley high in the mountain Canigou to see her, but they could not approach until Ibrahim summoned them and he did not send for them until he deemed her ready. Ibrahim gathered the pillows and piled them on top of the low chest.

"Is Yves bringing more plants?" she asked.

He vigorously swept the floor with his willow broom. "We must create a space for our work, here." He disappeared into the kitchen, then returned carrying a tray filled with objects. Cups, a knife, candles and plants all rested there. A quilted robe with stars sewn onto a silvery blue was thrown over his shoulder. Placing the tray on the floor, he went to the windows and sealed the shutters. He pulled the door shut and dropped the iron bolt into place. Now the only light came from a metal lamp and the kitchen hearth's fire. The corners of the room disappeared into shadows.

She heard footsteps in the kitchen and Iranzu stepped into the central chamber.

He was garbed in a black robe, with the hood pulled up around his face. Behind him, Leila carried a bowl filled with water. A scarlet gown clothed her, the sleeves fitted to her arms, and her black hair fell in a single braid down her back. She nodded to Maríana, but her eyes were cold. Placing the bowl on the floor, she backed away from Ibrahim, standing opposite Iranzu.

"The back door is locked, now." Iranzu's voice was hushed.

Ibrahim nodded, then lifted a figure made of twisted vines off the tray. Dried leaves were still attached in the form of a skirt. He beckoned to Maríana. "This is the maiden," he said, placing the figure on a low stool he had set upon the freshly swept floor. "You will learn how to make your own later — if you decide to travel to your mother's village. This one is old." He paused, stroking it, his face still and reflective. "Usually a new one is made every year at Txirringa Erreketa, the festival of the wolf moon, but you were not ready for this at that time last year." He shrugged his arms into his robe and fastened it at his waist.

"Why am I ready now?" Maríana asked, turning her head when Leila snorted.

"Maybe you will never be ready." Leila had folded her arms, but her eyes were fixed upon her feet.

Iranzu touched Leila's shoulder. "I think it is best that you go now, before we start. You will only hinder us if you cannot let go of your anger."

"Well!" Leila whirled around, glaring at Maríana, then stomped back through the kitchen. Iranzu followed her.

"It is difficult for Leila," Ibrahim shook his head. "She is the elder daughter..." He stopped speaking when Iranzu returned.

"Why did our mother leave her?" Maríana's fingers touched the crumpled leaves and vines that formed the maiden, her eyes lowered. She ached for her sister, but Leila's anger did set her teeth on edge.

"Leila's father was already wed. He is a merchant in Béarn, now, but at the time we knew him, he was a troubadour." Iranzu lit a stick of dried juniper. "Thérèse was very young. She left Leila with Adelie, and came with me to Egypt."

"You know what happened after that!" Ibrahim's eyes flashed as he carried five candles over to her. "Here. I will teach you how to make your own someday," he said, showing her the blue, green, red, orange and white candles he held. "These are made of beeswax and tallow. The scent comes from herbs that you put into the molds as the candles form. The wicks are made from hemp."

Maríana held a candle up to the light of the lamp. The color came from purple-blue flecks of lavender embedded in its shaft. Ibrahim placed the others in a rough circle around her, then looked into the black bowl filled with water that Leila had brought. He adjusted the candles and smiled at Maríana's raised brows. "We must have them aligned with the four directions," he said. He took the candle she held and placed it in the middle, then ignited all of them. Their smoke was blue and fragrant with pine and mugwort, lavender and thyme.

"This was your mother's." Motioning for Maríana to turn around,

Iranzu lifted her heavy auburn hair. The touch of metal chilled her skin.
A silver crescent moon on its side suspended from a sturdy silver chain;
the horns of the moon faced upward. She ran her fingers over the surface.
A four-armed design was carved into the metal. "It is the symbol of
wholeness." Iranzu patted her hand and smiled sadly. "You should wear
this. Your mother did. Until..." He looked down at his feet, then
smoothed her hair back. "You can hide it underneath your gown like
this." He slipped it beneath the neck of her gown and the moon symbol
disappeared.

"I cannot initiate you." Ibrahim placed the knife and cup on the
chair next to the vine maiden. "For that you must go to your mother's
village on the mountain."

"How would they initiate me?" The metal of her mother's necklace
warmed.

Ibrahim turned to her, then looked away. "For women, they have a
rite of initiation where a man calls down the energy of the Lord of the
hawthorn, and the woman initiate calls the energy of the Lady. The two
of them couple inside the circle."

"What!" Mariana stared. He was not jesting. "Grandfather! Is this
true?" Iranzu nodded. "Who would the man be?" she asked.

Ibrahim drew a deep breath. "As I understand it, a man of the
woman's choosing."

She shook her head. "This is very different from what Father
Gregory teaches."

Ibrahim took her hands. "It is not Christian," he agreed. "I will
teach you what I can of your mother's way of life, and of mine, but you
must decide whether you will follow the way of your mother — and me
— or the way of your father." He looked deeply into her eyes. "Once we
have completed this ritual, you will be able to heal with your hands
alone. But you must promise me that you will use your plants and herbs
to heal, not your hands. Unless there is no other way."

"Why?"

"Even using a physician's tools is dangerous. There are many who
hold that cures can only be obtained through prayer."

"But is that different from using your hands?"

His eyes crinkled at the corners. "Mariana. Just believe me when I
tell you it is dangerous! Only use your hands when it is absolutely
necessary, and make sure that you protect yourself by saying that it was
prayers that did the healing." He dropped her hands and drew a long
wand fashioned from a rowan tree out of his blue robes. "Now, we want
you to draw a circle. Start here at the east and move around the outside of
the candles, following the direction the sun takes as it crosses the
heavens."

She took the wand and moved to the eastern candle.

"East is breath." Ibrahim spoke from the center of the circle. She felt his eyes on her as she paced the distance across the floor.

She was now nearly to the south candle, moving past Iranzu. Ibrahim cleared his throat, saying, "South is heat." Was the air quivering? She glanced back. "Keep drawing the space between the worlds," Ibrahim commanded. The air outside of the circle started to thicken into a clear vapor, boiling and churning around the boundary she drew.

"West is blood." Now breathing hurt. Her eyes could not seem to focus. She held onto the rowan branch and forced her feet to carry her to the north candle.

"North is body — going back to the earth." Didn't they notice her slowing steps? She could barely see now, yet the east candle was vivid, a beacon. She shuffled her feet toward it to close the circle, the rowan wand now hanging from her fingertips, dragging on the floor. When she reached it, a curtain of white dropped over her eyes.

She was flying, soaring at an immense height. Dark vistas of tree-covered mountains opened below her. Lakes gleamed in a lightening dawn sky, turning pale salmon as the sun's rays extended fingers of light over the horizon. Hills, mountains and meadows passed in a blur below her.

She raised her eyes to the sky. The dizzying spectacle rushing beneath her tugged and wrenched. Air twisted in a pearl and pink translucence, breathing and alive. She lifted her eyes higher. A large pool of light suspended in the brightening sky lay ahead. A frame bound it, weaving interlace patterns, like the patterns of light she had held between her hands so long ago. Letters formed across its surface. As she drew closer, the pool of brightness swung inward, as a door would, revealing the deep blue of an early evening sky, swimming with stars, beckoning. She was almost upon it.

"Don't go through it." Iranzu's voice shattered the vision. Pieces of radiance fell around her, flaring before they vanished. She lay on the floor, her head on Ibrahim's lap. The candles still burned.

Ibrahim took her hands. "You have opened it, but you must not go through." His fingers rubbed the life back into her numb flesh.

"What would happen?" She wanted to pass through it, beyond to where the universe awaited. "If I went through it, what would it do?"

His hands stilled. "Your body would die."

"Then why open it at all? Why did you send me there?" She struggled to sit but a weakness had taken her limbs.

"I merely prepared you. You went there on your own. After this, you will be able to open the space between the worlds." He drew her up and held her against his chest. "But you will not ever open the door."

"Then I am an initiate?"

Ibrahim shook his head again. "I told you I cannot initiate you. You are like a daughter to me. But Iranzu can give you the Law that guides the Jakintzas."

Iranzu still stood near the south candle. He waited in silence until she nodded.

"You must know this," Iranzu started, "That you hold in your heart the love of all things in the world, for all that lives and breathes, every rock and stone, every creature above and below the water, the very earth on which we stand — all serve the Guardian." He was reciting, his voice rose and fell. Other voices shadowed his words, but there was no one else there.

"That you walk the path between the worlds seeing both light and shadow on either side."

"And that you honor your gifts and the gifts of others." The last words were whispered.

Maríana stared at the smoking candles, the glimmering boundary of the circle. Outside was all she had known, the rules that governed her life. The lamb of God. Mary and the saints. Johanna. Her father. Being pushed away and hidden in the tower, the target of squires.

Richard.

Ibrahim watched her. Iranzu bowed his head.

"You need not discard everything, Maríana," Ibrahim said. "Your mother was as at home in the chapel as she was in the circle. She always told me that there were many paths, but they all lead to the same goal." He lifted her hand to his lips and his touch warmed her skin. "It is all baraka, all spirit."

Then she need not give up Richard. When he came to her, she did not have to turn away from him.

"There is more." The words were whispered. She could not tell now whether it was Ibrahim or her grandfather who spoke. "If you were ever caught, ever accused and imprisoned, we would not be able to help you." Iranzu's face was remote, cold.

She stared at her grandfather. "Why not?" They would not even help their own? What kind of people were they? "Grandmother Johanna would help me if I were in trouble. Why would you not help?"

"We cannot," Iranzu said, raising his hands. "It was part of our pact with the Guardian."

"Pact." Her fingers dug into Ibrahim's arm. She would not let Ibrahim refuse to answer. Not this time. "Like a pact with a daemon?"

"No." Iranzu's eyes warmed. "But one of our ancestors opened the Door and let loose an affliction upon the earth. We were saved, but we paid a price for what we are, for what we did."

"Did you know that I nearly let something through the Door years ago?" She leaned forward and peered at her grandfather through the gray-blue tendrils of smoke.

Iranzu nodded. "Ibrahim told us." His finger made a peculiar gesture upon the air, a short jab upward and two lines below. "You have been prepared — you will not be able to do this now."

"So!" She leaped to her feet. "This is why you have prepared me? So I cannot let anything through the Door to save me? So I must leave everything I know, become someone even more hated than I was?" She glared at them. "You take me into danger, into heresy, teaching me all these things and leave me with nothing to defend myself?"

Ibrahim had paled, but Iranzu was laughing. "I told you Thérèse was in her somewhere," he said to the younger man.

Ibrahim's mouth tightened. "Maríana," he said, "do you think that any of us are safe?" He reached for her. "We are all of us in the same danger, using our gifts in this world." His hands dropped when she did not move toward him. "I have chosen this way, you know this. It is now your choice. You can go back to being what you were, but I warn you! Once your feet have trod this path, everything else in your life will pale."

Iranzu gestured and Ibrahim subsided. Then Iranzu stepped forward to Maríana and grasped both her hands. "If you wish," he whispered, "I can make it as if all this had never been. You could go back to being exactly as you were."

He was touching her. The wall of pines reared up before her, crowned with mountain mist. A large stone house snuggled at the mountain's base. Abruptly, the vision disappeared. "No." She withdrew her hands and shivered. "Ibrahim was right." A glance Ibrahim's way caught the gleam of his smile. "The damage is already done, I cannot go back to what I was." She lifted her chin. "It is too late."

"Then welcome, granddaughter." Iranzu still held back from her, his face shadowed and unsure.

She bowed her head and stepped back from both men. Yes, she would follow this path, walk in her mother's footsteps. Wherever it led, she would follow.

Chapter 9

MARÍANA climbed the stairs to Johanna's chamber, carrying roses she had picked, emblems of love and greeting, in large bunches in her arms. They were burgundy and palest yellow, apricot and dusty pink, ivory and mauve and golden amber. It was just after dawn the week following midsummer, one year since she had begun her training with Ibrahim, and two days after Louis-Philippe told her to move her things into the palais. She was certain Ibrahim had goaded him into it, but that did not matter. She even asked for a chamber facing the donjon, so the first sight she had every morning was its forbidding walls. No, she would never forget. But she was here, now.

The wedding of Louis-Philippe and Ysabel was still a month away, scheduled for the last day of July. The entire château buzzed with the excitement of preparation. Father Gregory had the château servants making hundreds of candles for the chapel, where the ceremony would take place. All the women were embroidering the banners that would hang in the great hall.

Maríana buried her face in the fragrant roses she had picked to honor the impending arrival of her new stepmother, Ysabel de Gréves. She had heard that Ysabel loved roses above any other flower, so much that her favorite sweet was the honey-covered rose petals which were so favored in the French court.

Her grandmother would have first choice among the roses, then she would place the rest in the chamber they had prepared for Ysabel. At Johanna's door, she heard voices inside, so she knocked and waited, her arms overflowing with the blossoms.

The door swung open to reveal Alys. "Maríana!" she exclaimed. "Look at what you have!" She backed away from the door, allowing Maríana entry. As Maríana went through the door, someone inside uttered a muffled cry.

Johanna clapped her hands in delight. "Granddaughter! Bring those closer. Ysabel!" She turned to a woman standing off to the side. "Look what Louis-Philippe's daughter has brought for you."

Ysabel was short, with a round face. She was all shades of brown-light chestnut hair, brown eyes, sallow skin-and wore a gown the rich red-brown color of the earth.

Maríana curtsied. Something unpleasant shone from her soon-to-be stepmother's eyes. But Ysabel smiled warmly enough.

"So, this is Louis-Philippe's daughter," she said, taking Maríana's hands in her own and gazing at her. Then Ysabel dropped Maríana's hands and turned to the young man who stood at her side. He was not as tall as Louis-Philippe, but his arms and legs were well-muscled and the sword he wore was obviously heavy and would take great strength to wield. His hair fell below his shoulders in a straight mane of black. A harp carved into the shape of a dragon rested at his feet. He stood in shadow; she could not see his face. Then he leaned toward her and his hair fell across his eyes. Shaking it back, his teeth showed in a grin, his brown eyes looked directly into Maríana's.

"Well," he said. "Maríana." A voice that warmed, deep and rich.

"Richard!" Her knees wobbled; her heart raced. "But your father, how is he?" she added quickly when she saw a glint in Ysabel's eyes. What were they to each other?

"He is well, but my family still needed me," he said. Ysabel moved closer to him and he glanced over at her. "However," he bowed gallantly, "you see I did finally return to Reuilles-le-château!"

"I am glad." Maríana took his hands in hers and tried to still the trembling in her fingers, disguising it with a squeeze. Ysabel cleared her throat and Maríana pulled away. But Richard's hands remained where they were for a moment longer and a warmth unfurled below Maríana's heart. "You have a harp now?" Maríana asked, feeling the pulse ripple in her neck. Ysabel's eyes were shifting from her to Richard and back again.

He started to reply but Ysabel placed a hand upon his arm and said, "We have been traveling for weeks, Baroness dowager." Her eyes were on Richard. He closed his mouth and a muscle in his cheek jumped. "Could Louis-Philippe's daughter see me to my room?"

"I myself will show you to the room we have prepared, Ysabel." Johanna gave Ysabel a thin smile. "Maríana, you must show Richard to the knights' chamber."

Ysabel opened her mouth to speak, but Richard had already left her side, hefting his harp to his shoulder and stepping easily over to where Maríana stood.

The years had brought changes. His chest had broadened and somewhere, someone had slashed his forehead — there was a thin white scar from his hairline through his left eyebrow.

Maríana turned to leave the room. Behind her, Ysabel spoke, "I must send my maid back. My mother has need of her." Ysabel's voice had lightened. She was every inch the lady now.

Johanna said, "We will provide you with all you require, of course."

Then the door closed and Richard was walking beside her. He carried his harp easily atop his shoulder and his sword swung with his step. She stole glances at him when she thought he could not see her looking; his eyes were fixed straight ahead. What could she say to him?

He had gone away still a boy and returned a man, his boyhood
slenderness had filled out into powerful muscles, his finely chiseled face
now had the bones of a warrior. "You will find the knights' chamber an
improvement over your squire's quarters in the stable." There. She
stopped at the chamber entrance and pointed at the row of beds that
marched along the south wall. "You have your choice now," she said,
backing away. "Later, there will be so many arriving for the wedding we
will need to send guests over to the donjon."

He faced her, regarding her solemnly. His eyes were as she
remembered, a warm brown, the outer corners tilted. Her face grew hot
under his stare and she clasped her hands together to keep them still.
"Well, you know where the hall is."

He did not speak, but his eyes devoured her.

"Perhaps you could play for us later." She dropped into a curtsey
and left, forcing her feet to move smoothly, to not run. When she reached
the end of the corridor, she glanced back. He stood motionless, his harp
on his shoulder, his eyes on her. She raised her hand and slipped around
the corner, finally allowing her feet to flee.

He did not follow.

THE GARDEN again. Richard paused at the entrance in front of the
hawthorns. After Maríana had shown him to the knights' room, he had
dropped his harp and sword on the nearest bed and washed the dust of the
road off his face, using a bowl and pitcher he found on a small table
nearby. Then he descended the central stairs into the great hall, searching
it for a slight figure with flowing auburn hair. But Maríana was not there.
Nor did he find her in the kitchen below. When she had stood before him,
he could not take his eyes from her, but he had found no words to speak.

Now, he leaned against the hawthorn's smooth gray bark and stared
into the garden. When they were squires together, Arnaut and Jean-Pierre
had tried to frighten him with tales of ghosts and drowned children. It
was true that no one would go there after dark. Richard remembered
telling Maríana that Arnaut challenged them to go past the hawthorn trees
after light had left the sky, but he had lied. His own dare had brought
them all to the garden that night when Maríana knelt at the pool. He had
hid among the burdock, sure that she was the ghost Arnaut had warned
him about. When she had touched him, he nearly yelled.

Just now in the palais, in front of her grandmother, in front of the
future Baroness de Reuilles, he had almost pulled Maríana into his arms.
He entered the garden, into the cool shadows. How could he have
thought this trip would cure him, that seeing her again would end the
nights when he awakened with the scent of her skin on him and the
weight of her hair on his chest, with the longing that made him cry out
when his dream faded.

He had even volunteered to escort Ysabel to Navarre, sure that when he saw Maríana, she would be like any other girl, not the way he remembered her. He gritted his teeth. He hated Ysabel de Gréves-her incessant chatter, her meddling, her possessive touch. How could he have believed that seeing Maríana again would lay to rest his yearning?

He raised his eyes and his heart stilled.

Maríana knelt, pulling weeds out of the patch of field violets. He stood there, barely breathing, while he watched her fingers dipping and rising in a rhythm. She had plaited her hair into two braids. One lay along her back. The other hung over her shoulder, swinging in time with the motion of her hands. Johanna had told him that Maríana lived in the palais, now. He had felt a warm gladness — she was out of the tower. Then the door had opened and there she stood, arms overflowing with roses. His pulse had quickened. He had bitten back a cry, but Ysabel noted it. That woman.

He dropped to his knees. "Maríana."

She looked up, then leaned back on her heels. The hair at her temples curled around her forehead. He wanted to pull her over to him and taste her. But her dark green eyes were regarding him, measuring. Then the corners of her mouth lifted in a smile and she reached out to touch the scar through his eyebrow. "How did you do this?"

He shrugged, then stood and reached out his hand, help her to her feet. "Someone insulted my sister." Her hand was damp, but he did not mind. "I took exception to it. He looked worse than me, afterward," he assured her, delighting in her laughter and shining eyes.

He could not help it. He took both her hands and pulled her to him, savoring the clean lines of her face, smelling her sun-warmed skin. His whole body ached; he longed to take her in his arms. She watched him, her eyes still laughing, yet the shadow of hurt showed there, too. He tipped his face down to hers, but the sound of voices made him raise his head and look over his shoulder. Johanna and Ysabel. They were at the entrance, but would be upon him and Maríana soon. He dropped Maríana's hands and stepped back, close enough to touch her again, but within the bounds of propriety.

Ysabel immediately went up to Richard and took his arm, turning toward Maríana. "Richard was my dear protector," she said, her fingers firmly gripping him. "I am so glad he accompanied me to Reuilles-le-château." She looked up at Richard. "You simply must stay for my wedding."

Richard gently tried to extricate himself from her grasp, but Ysabel refused to release his arm. With a sly glance at his hands, she said, "You must tell Beatrice of Bourdeilles that she must wait a little longer for her husband-to-be to arrive!" Blast the woman! Now she was watching Maríana's face.

Maríana stilled and her skin paled, but she said, "Why should she wait?" Her dark green eyes stared into Ysabel's. "Bourdeilles is closer to Navarre than to la Guerche."

Didn't Maríana care? Had he misread the signs? Richard squelched his start of surprise, but he was sure Ysabel had felt him jump. Her hand dropped from his arm and she stepped next to Johanna, staring back at Maríana, who met her eyes in silence.

Richard felt his jaw tighten. "My wedding is not for another two years yet. I am on my way to..."

"Yes, yes!" Ysabel waved him off, her voice sighing in boredom as she dropped her eyes and took Johanna's arm. "You are going to Assisi to burn a candle to thank God for the health of your father at that church of Francis di Bernardone."

Richard backed away from her and muttered, "Among other things." He turned to Maríana again. She was still pale. He reached out but his fingers only grazed her arm. He could not touch her now. Now that she knew.

He dropped his hand.

YSABEL MOVED farther into the garden next to Johanna. That was a disappointing reaction from the girl. She had hoped for sorrow or even anger at the news of Richard's impending wedding to another and was dissatisfied with the outcome of her little game. Richard and Maríana were standing so close in the garden, and earlier the girl had actually taken his hands! But when she revealed what she knew all Maríana had done was stare at her. Ysabel sighed, listening to Johanna's chatter, then her thoughts turned to Richard himself. At least now she knew he had not told Maríana about Beatrice. She savored Richard's reaction to her game. Oh, now, that was perfect! He was furious with her.

Ysabel looked back at the two of them. Richard was earnestly discussing some flowers or something else equally dull. So that was why he spurned all her advances and would not even flirt. He was in love with that girl.

She quickly stifled her stab of jealousy. Her, jealous? Certainly not. Songs had been written about her, after all! Her thoughts turned again to her intended husband as she listened with half an ear to Johanna prattling on about this servant and that servant. Servants! All they were good for is fetching and carrying. Not much better than animals.

She turned her face toward Johanna and widened her eyes, the best she could manage at this moment to express interest, then looked back at Richard. "They say Louis-Philippe is very handsome," she mused. "Too bad he could not come to fetch me himself. Hard to think of anyone more comely than this young one, though." Johanna glanced at Richard and smiled, then pointed at the edge of a bed of flowering herbs, saying something about a physician. Ysabel kept glancing at Richard while pretending to listen.

She had enjoyed teasing Richard on the way to Basse Navarre. Others accompanied them, so she had been unable to take him to her bed — it would not do for idle gossip to be spread about the new Baroness, of course. Not that she was chaste at home, far from it! But she had been discreet enough to keep speculations about her chastity to a minimum. At least she had been able to embarrass the poor boy, wearing her most close fitting gowns when she was around him, leaning over and touching his strong arms constantly during the long ride down to Basse Navarre.

She smiled at the memory of Richard blushing and gnashing his teeth whenever she leaned toward him. But her reverie was shattered when she saw a man striding toward them through the gardens. "Now, look there!" she said to Johanna. "He cuts a fine figure." Her memories of Richard were discarded. "Just look at how tall he is!"

The man wore a leather hauberk and a tunic embroidered with the colors of silver, indigo and sea-green. He pulled off his visor as he came toward them. Ysabel grabbed Johanna's arm at the same time she heard her say: "Louis-Philippe! How delightful, you have returned. Come and meet Ysabel."

Ysabel's fingers dug into Johanna's arm. Her friends had said he was handsome. But the man was a god! Adonis, Apollo! Her head spun and her legs turned to water as Louis-Philippe smiled engagingly. He wiped his sweating brow with his glove, pushing back his damp black hair that, she noticed, was laced with the smallest dusting of silver at the temples.

Gallantly, he raised her hand to his lips, kissing it with gusto. "Ysabel," he said. "I regret I could not come to Brittany to accompany you to your new home. I was engaged in the service of the King of Navarre. Please accept my sincere apology and my welcome to Reuilles-le-château."

Ysabel recovered and smiled her sweetest smile, turning her face up to look at him. All the intrigues and games she had been planning for Maríana and Richard were forgotten as she walked toward the palais beside her intended husband. How can I wait till August eve, she thought in dismay. I want him in my bed right now! She looked at Johanna. No help there. That one would watch her like a hawk. She sighed. It was going to be a long month.

MARÍANA held her body still, face lowered, enduring the wrenching pain that spread from her belly to just below her heart. Before Ysabel and her grandmother left them, she felt a light touch on her arm. Richard stood beside her, but beyond a few words remarking on the violets, he had said nothing since Ysabel and Johanna walked away. She had not

seen her father enter the garden, but she had heard his voice and had
glanced up to see him leaving, Ysabel hanging onto his arm.

Now Richard was speaking again. "Can we stay out here a bit
longer? I would like to see the blackberry bushes by the pond where we
went after... well."

"They are no longer there." Her voice sounded far away. She would
have to do better. "The roots became rotten. Ib... Jacques had them torn
out." Good. She could speak again. Now, could she look at him?

She made herself look up and her own anguish dwindled to a dull
ache. His face was white, his eyes, stunned. A muscle jumped in his
cheek as he clenched his teeth, but all he said was, "The bushes are
gone?"

She touched his arm and he flinched. "There is a seat where they
used to be." Could she make her feet move? "We can go there." Her feet
shuffled at first, but she was walking. She did not look behind her to see
if he followed.

Chapter 10

YSABEL OPENED her eyes and raised her body up on her elbows. Why was she still in her gown? The wedding last night had been everything she had thought it should be. All Louis-Philippe's vassals attended. And such a feast! She would have to let out her clothes if they ate like that again. She had even danced with the King of Navarre. Of course, he could not hold a candle to Louis of France, but, nevertheless, he was a king.

Louis-Philippe lay beside her. What had they done last night? Her memory might slip from time to time, but she could not forget something like her first night with such a man. She reached under the bed and found her needle still in place. A puzzle. The last thing she remembered was lighting the candles and lying on the bed, awaiting him. They had forgone the traditional carrying chairs, where the married couple were carried to their bedchamber in two chairs and placed into bed by the vassals. Louis-Philippe had not wanted that. She ran her nails across the fabric of the sheets. He had kissed her on the forehead and said he would be back soon. Not soon enough, apparently, since her needle was still in place.

Surely he wanted her! She had been courted by many, although, until now, only young Henri had won her heart. She had agreed to this marriage when it became clear that Henri would not come back for her. And she had waited such a long time. Well, the baron was here beside her, wasn't he? She stretched out next to Louis-Philippe, running her hands gently down the skin of his naked back, shivering as her fingers encountered a long, jagged scar running the length of his back. She sighed as she remembered Henri's arms around her. Then she yelped and snatched her hands away from Louis-Philippe.

They could not consummate the marriage in the light of day. She needed darkness so she could prick her finger to provide the blood that proved she was pure. Easing out of the bed, she wrapped her robe around her and tiptoed from chamber.

The next night she was prepared. She stripped all her gowns off and lay naked and ready under the soft sheets. Again he came in very late, after she was asleep, and again she had to leave the chamber before he did so that he would not find out she was not the virgin she had claimed to be.

After a month of this, she was determined to find out where he went when he stayed out so late. She questioned all the servants. None of the dolts would say anything, but the dressmaker, Jeanne, told her in a whisper that he went up to his palace where Jacques the gardener lived.

Men and their drinking chums! She had plenty of experience with this problem — her father and brothers were the same way. Well. She would see this fellow for herself.

The path was steep and rocks tripped her feet. She was sure that a blister was starting on her toe. She was watching the uneven ground so she would not stumble and so she did not notice she had arrived until she saw blue and white tiles under her feet.

She raised her head and her mouth dropped open. There was a fountain and a graceful white palace, complete with arched windows and door. Johanna had told her that Louis-Philippe had been to Byzantium, but not that he had brought some of it back with him. She strode up to the door and rapped sharply on it, then tried the handle. Locked. She would have to try something else.

YSABEL BACKED Louis-Philippe into a corner of the upper corridor leading to the knights' room. It was just after the evening meal, but few were about on the second floor. Most still loitered in the great hall, playing dice. She had made sure that the games would be offered this evening to clear the upper chambers and had followed Louis-Philippe when he climbed the stairs. His eyes lit up in surprise when he saw her, but got even wider when she slipped her hand beneath his shirt and pressed against him. He did not move to kiss her; he just stood there while her fingers teased his chest. A flicker of something dark and red trembled within her breast.

"We will be husband and wife tonight," she said, her voice barely under control. "Or I will seek an annulment tomorrow." She felt him quiver. Then he lifted her chin and seized her mouth with his.

After a long moment, he said, "Lead the way."

YSABEL KICKED the bed again. She had already thrown the chamber pot. It lay in smelly pieces on the floor.

He could not do it! She had not noticed his lack of arousal. He had kissed her with enough fervor, but when she was ready for a deeper embrace, he could not give it.

At first, she had been simply stunned. He had sat on the edge of the bed, his head in his hands. He had said nothing, but had looked so woebegone, she had even patted him on the back to soothe him. Then he had kissed her on the side of her mouth and told her he was going out to clear his head. She had grabbed the chamber pot and it had sailed after him, but he had already closed the door. No one had come running to see what had happened. She could tell them it had slipped. Tomorrow.

He went out. Where would he go? Her back straightened. Then she slipped out of the bed and pulled on an old gown, covering it with a dark mantle. As she made her way through the great hall, she practiced her story for the night watch. She would tell him she was going to see her husband. He had passed this way earlier, had he not? Oh, no, she did not need a page or squire to accompany her. What could happen to her with her lord out there? Open the gate. It had only been a short while since Louis-Philippe left. Well, she would join him at his palace. Then they would see.

SHE DID NOT need to go so far. The blackness of the night, the stony slope, the scuffling of beasts in the brush, none of these disturbed her on her climb to the palace.

They were outside, both of them. She heard their voices before she reached the spot where the path turned, so she moved into the oaks that clustered in a thick stand around the clearing's edge. Louis-Philippe sat upon the ledge that surrounded the fountain, and the other... .

She had seen him in the garden with Maríana. He did not carry himself like a servant. Two torches burned golden on either side of the palace door and light from inside spilled out into the courtyard. The harsh light threw the two men's faces into stark relief. The gardener was almost as handsome, in his own way, as her Louis-Philippe. She crouched down behind the tree closest to the clearing, held her breath and listened.

"I think it is age, my friend," the gardener was saying in an amused voice. "I would not worry if I were you. It will come in time." He patted Louis-Philippe on the shoulder, then he also sat on the ledge.

Louis-Philippe mumbled through his hands so that Ysabel had to strain to understand him. "It has never happened to me before, as you well know!"

The gardener shrugged. "She is a desirable woman," he said. "You are a lucky man."

Ysabel nodded her head. Now, this fellow really knew what he was saying!

"That is just it." Louis-Philippe leaned forward. "She is a woman." He waved his hands. "I am not like you, Ibrahim Al'Khaldun. I don't think I can handle both."

Ibrahim? Who was this Ibrahim? Ysabel had been told his name was Jacques.

"You managed before. You will manage again. Anyway, why not use your imagination?" Ibrahim smiled and crossed his arms.

"You mean imagine she is someone else?" Louis-Philippe asked.

She bristled. How dare he!

"In the dark, who can say? She could be anyone." Ibrahim was still smiling.

"You know there has been only one for me," Louis-Philippe said, now very serious.

"I am sorry, but that is over now and cannot begin again. Off with you, now, you rascal! Do your duty!" Ibrahim patted Louis-Philippe on the back, pushing him toward the path, but the baron foiled him and grabbed Ibrahim in a close embrace.

Ysabel covered her mouth to stifle her shout.

"What was that?" Ibrahim asked, pushing Louis-Philippe away.

She ran blindly from the grove of oaks. Her feet took her deeper into the forest. She kept running, plunging into the blackness, struggling to still the acid in her stomach from heaving out of her. She stopped when the ground fell away into a ravine, held onto a pine branch, her breath whistling in and out.

"I don't see anything," Louis-Philippe spoke in the distance. "There are marmots this time of year."

The other, Ibrahim, said, "That was not a marmot." He did not sound close. They had not followed her.

Louis-Philippe spoke again. "Thank you, ami. I believe I will take your advice." Footsteps rang on the tiles of the courtyard, then she heard the tromp of feet upon the path. The sounds were coming closer. In her flight, she must have run toward the path.

She held her breath while Louis-Philippe strode by where she huddled among the trees. Thirty heartbeats after he passed, Ysabel finally gave way to the urge to retch. She vomited until she became dizzy. Moving away from the steaming puddle she had made, she put her hands up to her hot face. She stayed there moaning, then started to shake in anger.

He would pay for this. She hugged her arms close to her body and rocked back and forth. Ibrahim would pay. No one would take what was hers. And Louis-Philippe was hers.

She stood, balancing for a moment on shaking legs. Then she stumbled back in the general direction of the château walls. After some time, she found herself outside the east gate. She made her face smile and greeted the watchman as if nothing had happened. Finally, she slipped safely into the great hall.

As she climbed the stairs to her room, she kept seeing the two of them together. What would she do if Louis-Philippe was in her room? She still wanted him.

Louis-Philippe was sound asleep in the bed. Had it taken her that long to return to the château? She dressed quickly into her sleeping gown and, blowing out the candles, climbed into bed beside him. She almost touched him, but the red and black rage again choked her.

She turned over and faced the wall. Ibrahim must suffer. She would find a wise woman. Then she would see what could be done.

IT WAS EASY for Ysabel to get passage across the narrow lake. Two enterprising men from Reuilles-la-ville had a thriving business taking people back and forth in their boat. She wanted to keep the château servants out of this, so she went alone, dressed in a plain black gown and gray cloak. Once in the town, she wandered the twisting, narrow streets for hours looking for the old woman Jeanne had told her about. Utarilla was her name, but the people Ysabel asked had babbled at her in a language she had never heard before. Finally, just when she was ready to give up, she discovered a dirty child crouching in the street. She gave him a small piece of gold, said "Mother Utarilla" in a loud voice, and he led her directly to the old woman.

Ysabel frowned as she looked into Mother Utarilla's face. Jeanne had not jested when she said "old woman." All of Utarilla's teeth were gone, she was bedridden, and her arms were so thin they looked like sticks. Yet her eyes were alert and full of canny intelligence.

Ysabel seated herself and came to the point immediately. "I want to rid myself of an enemy."

Utarilla cackled. "Many ways to do that," she said. "The knife, the poison, the charms, the manikin." She drew her shawl tighter around her bony shoulders.

"It will have to be something that cannot be traced to me," Ysabel said in distaste, glancing around the dank chamber where the old woman lived. It was little better than the dungeon of the donjon. "I do not want to kill him, just make him suffer enough so he will leave."

Utarilla frowned and her lips puckered. "Why do you want to get rid of this man?"

What to say? Well, she never expected to see this old woman again, nor had she given her real name. "Because he has twisted my lover and stolen his love from me."

"Why not a charm to gain your lover's heart again? That is much easier and safer."

"I want revenge." Ysabel heard her voice grow hard. Something streaked with red boiled up in her throat and she swallowed it back. "I want him to hurt as he has hurt me."

Utarilla sighed. "That will cost."

"I can pay," Ysabel sniffed.

"That too, of course," Utarilla said, "but that was not what I meant." She seemed to be weighing something, then leaned forward in the bed. "Can you memorize what I tell you?"

Memorize? "Yes, I can, but..."

"Then listen well." Utarilla leaned back again, her mouth working silently, then she said, "You must get some hair, some fingernails and even blood if you can. Blood is best if you can get it. Then you must write the man's name on a slip of paper or cloth. It must be his true name."

Ysabel nodded, staring at the old woman. She would remember this.

"You must make a doll out of cloth. Inside the doll's body you must sew the fingernails, something with his blood on it, some of his hair, and the paper or cloth with his name." Utarilla coughed and smacked her lips. "Then you must wear this mannikin next to your body day and night."

"Yes, yes!" Ysabel said impatiently. "Go on."

"For nine months."

"What!"

Utarilla's face split into a huge grin. "It will be no good if you do not. At the end of nine months you must take it to a priest to be baptized."

Ysabel's face went numb. A priest?

"I can give you the name of one who will do it," Utarilla continued, "although that will cost you, too."

Ysabel gritted her teeth. "I tell you I can pay." She would do anything.

"And pay you will, in more ways than one."

"What do you mean by that?"

"Don't you know the Law, woman?" Utarilla's eyes caught the glow of her meager hearth fire in a scarlet glimmer. "If you go down this path there will be no going back. When you wear the mannikin, it will demand its own price."

Ysabel moved uneasily on her seat. "How?" Wasn't it enough to have to wear it for nine months?

"It will talk to you, for one thing. For another, it often makes the spell-caster ill."

"How ill, old woman?" Well, she could bear that. She smoothed her gown and drew open her bag of coins.

"Ill enough," Utarilla said. "Ill enough. Like having a baby."

"Well," Ysabel said. "What must I do after it is baptized?"

"Stick needles into it, whatever you want your enemy to feel. You can make him go away, if you are brave enough to let him know you have the mannikin." Uatrilla's voice was reedy. "But if you keep the mannikin, he will eventually die."

"No, I will not tell him! And be burned? Do you think I am stupid? I will find another way to make him leave, but I want him to suffer. I will destroy it before he dies. I am no killer." Well, she wasn't, was she? "How much do I pay?"

"Let me see your bag," Utarilla said.

Ysabel looked at the coins in her bag. The old woman swiftly reached over and grabbed it, emptying it out on the bed. "What are you doing?" Ysabel exclaimed, reaching for the bag.

Utarilla looked for a long time at the coins spilled out on her bed. "This could buy my grandson a fine horse and cart," she said. For a moment it looked like she would send Ysabel away-she turned her face to the side and closed her eyes. Then she took four coins and handed the rest back to Ysabel. "Now go," she said.

IT WAS HIGH autumn. Ibrahim was preparing the herb beds for the long winter that would come. Ysabel followed him every day, taking her book of prayers and sitting on a stone seat next to the pond. When he worked, he often placed his mantle there. While he was turned away, she picked the long black and silver strands off his mantle until she had an entire lock of his shiny hair.

Getting fingernail clippings and blood posed another problem. She had already sewn the doll to use for the mannikin and hidden it in her cabinet. She had left its belly standing open, waiting to collect all she needed to make the spell. Every time she looked at it she felt a twinge of something that might have been guilt. It looked like a man who had been disemboweled. She finally had Jeanne cut the fingernails of all the servants, telling Johanna this was what they did with servants in Gréves. The nails were neatly packaged in tiny pouches, little bags that Ysabel labeled and placed in her cabinet. She might want to do this again if anyone else crossed her. She shoved the packet labeled "Jacques" next to the doll, after she had used her knife to score out "Jacques" and her quill to write over it "Ibrahim."

Now, blood.

IBRAHIM BENT over the bed of rosemary Maríana had planted the year before. He was clipping them back and saving the clippings to dry later so Johanna could use them to season winter meals. He glanced over to the pond seat. Ysabel had been there when he arrived. She did not seem to be doing anything; she carried no embroidery frame, nor the book of prayer she usually held. She just sat there, still as the stone she rested upon. From time to time he felt her eyes upon him. He reached into branches he had not yet cut, then drew his breath through his teeth and held his hand up, looking in surprise at the blood streaming from a cut in his middle finger.

Ysabel swooped down on him, her sleeve ready to staunch the blood. She had worn her oldest gown just for this moment. She had thought he would never get to that patch, the branch where she had tied the piece of broken dagger her brother had given her only last year.

Ibrahim's eyes widened, but he allowed her to hold her sleeve against his finger until the blood stopped flowing.

"See." He held up his hand. "It is nothing, but thank you." He smiled warmly at her. Something moved inside her throat. She turned her face away and walked over to the rosemary patch while he sat holding his hand.

He watched her now; she must hurry. She knew just where she had placed the broken metal, but made a show of inspecting the rosemary, deftly removing it, shielding what she was doing with her body so that Ibrahim could not see. Then she turned to him. "Shall I call the physician for you?" Johanna had mentioned that the château had its own physician. Her lips caught on her teeth. She had been smiling too long. Why was he staring at her?

"There is no need," was all he said.

She gathered her skirts, the metal piece tucked in her hand, and hurried out of the garden.

EVERYTHING was ready. Ysabel tore the strip of bloodied sleeve off her gown and wrapped the hair and nail clippings inside. She wrote the word "Ibrahim" on the outside of the cloth and stuffed all of it inside the mannikin. Then she got out the halter-pouch she had made and wiggled into it.

What she would do if Louis-Philippe ever wanted to come to her bed she did not know. He had not pursued the matter after the first time he had tried and failed. He slept in his own chamber now and had not come to hers since that night. In fact, she thought he looked relieved that she did not press him about it. She would have to go without love for the time the mannikin rested in its pouch against her skin, but it would be worth it to see Ibrahim suffer. It would be worth it.

When she was finished and the mannikin was snug against her belly, she looked at herself in the polished silver mirror on her wall. Good, it really did not show underneath her gown. She would have to forego baths, only washing up in the basin for the nine months it would remain, but that would be no problem, even though the de Reuilles bathed more often than anyone she had ever known.

She looked at her face in the polished surface and smiled. "Nine months," she said. "Nine months."

Chapter 11

ANTOINE Jakintza's breath sent plumes of white into the chilled night sky. For the hundredth time, he mentally counted the money he would receive from this venture and, for the hundredth time, he knew it was not enough. No amount would ever be enough for what he had been asked to do.

Montsegur. The fortress of the heretics rose in majestic agony above him. Earlier, he had seen the faint glow from torches at the pinnacle, where the fortress reached upward in a defiant, jagged edge. He had heard voices, the sound rising and falling on the frigid air that curled around the sheer walls of the mountain fortress.

But now, it was silent.

THIS MISERY had started when Henri de Bauçais, nephew of Johanna de Reuilles, had sent knights to the town under the mountain, Reuilles-la-ville, to ask for Basque "volunteers" to come to Montsegur.

"Come with us," they had said. "We have gold for you now, and more when the fortress falls."

Antoine had stared at their beardless faces. These knights wore red tunics slashed by a white cross. "What do the Pope's men want with me?" he had asked in their language, watching their faces for the haughty disdain he felt sure he would see when they heard his accent.

"De Bauçais needs you," one of the knights had said. Antoine could see no change in his face. "We have a mountain for you to climb, a ridge behind Montsegur, the fortress of the Cathar heretics. We must secure this ridge to move another siege engine into place. We heard you were the best climber."

"Cathars, eh?" Antoine had looked at his wife, Cecile. Two of their children played beside her; the third made her belly gently curve. He could almost see the sign he would place over the bakery he would buy with the money the knights offered to give him. He could almost smell the fine bread baking there, almost see Cecile growing plump with the food he could provide, almost see his children in fine clothing.

"Who are these Cathars?" He knew the Cathars were Christian. Why would the Pope's men want to fight them?

The knight had adjusted his leather bag and the sound of coins clinking together could be heard. "What does it matter?" When Antoine did not reply, he said, "They are heretics. That is all you need to know."

Christian heretics. Now, they were fighting each other. Antoine looked around the crowded chamber, the tiny house he called home. Antoine's bakery had a nice sound. Maybe a larger house, too. After all, the Guardian never said anything about helping Christians fight their own.

He looked back at the knight, who stood in studied indifference by the door. The man gripped the leather bag too tightly. Something was not right. Antoine almost said *no*, then his eyes fell upon Cecile. Her hands were curled protectively across her belly. Iranzu and Leila could watch over his family while he was gone. How long could it take to climb this ridge?

He had taken the gold and come to Montsegur.

ANTOINE blew on his hands and stamped his feet against the cold. At least the siege engine catapults had been silent today. It was Christmas Eve, after all! Those bloody French bastards could not pound away at the fortress forever, could they? They usually stopped the battering before the middle of the night, although recently they had been continuing the bombardment throughout day and night.

"Kaixo, Antoine!" He heard the Basque greeting from Pierre Brounnan before he saw the hulking figure approaching him. Pierre was from Reuilles-la-ville. He had taken the knights' gold, too.

Antoine knew both he and Pierre avoided looking at the siege engine that squatted beside them. The lever that released the catapult was loosened now, but both had seen what it could do to the walls above. Antoine did not want to think about the people inside the walls. Demolishing walls was one thing, but setting this thing upon people... he had heard children's voices up there.

"You have night watch, too?" Antoine blew on his hands again.

Pierre spread his arms. "Such a fine night. How could I refuse?"

Antoine snorted. "Night watch is better than manning this thing." He jerked his head toward the siege engine.

Pierre had started to reply when the sound of pebbles tumbling down the sheer eastern face of the mountain stopped him.

Antoine examined the sheer wall of Montsegur. It was only the height of twenty men, but impossible to climb. He released the breath he had been holding and turned to his friend.

Pierre pointed to the fortress's far corner. There the drop was at least the height of a hundred men, but Antoine saw dark shapes descending from the fortress walls. It looked like they were carrying something.

"They seem to know what they are doing," Antoine remarked, watching the climbers. He could barely see the rope they were using. But it seemed sturdy.

"Do we notice them this time?" Pierre's voice brought Antoine's attention back to the sputtering fire.

Antoine tossed more sticks on the embers and spread his hands above the growing flames. "No." His voice was quiet, but hard. "The pope's men lied to us. Why should we do any more than we must to help them?" The knights had promised more gold when the ledge was secured, but when Antoine had gone to the paymaster, the man had refused him.

"No one leaves until the fortress falls," the paymaster had told him.

Now Antoine glanced back over his shoulder. Good. The climbers were half way down.

"We should work on our stories, my friend." Pierre said, looking toward the command tent. "If they are caught down below, Bauçais will want to know how they got past us."

"Lucky for us Bauçais sleeps heavily. He is a decent man. We could tell him we fell asleep. He would believe us," Antoine replied.

The descending men disappeared. Antoine sat with toes reaching toward their tiny fire. Christmas eve. The forest smelled of snow on pine branches. Twigs in the fire popped and moisture underneath the flames hissed. The Christ child was born on a night like this. Now His followers pounded each other with stone and iron, with wood and flames. The Guardian would never ask Her people to kill each other, would She? Antoine had no answer for this; he stretched his stiff body and threw his head back in a jaw-breaking yawn.

"Wait." Pierre had turned toward the fortress. He stood. "Something is wrong."

Another figure was climbing down the fortress wall. This one was in trouble. The rope swung out from the side. The climber slid down, feet flailing in the air. Antoine grabbed Pierre's arm. He saw the climber lose his grasp on the rope, but the climber did not scream. He heard a series of sickening thuds, then silence. Antoine still held Pierre's arm. His knuckles were white. He released his hold and listened.

"He did not fall all the way," Antoine murmured, glancing at the command tent. Silence there, too. Very well. He leaned down, gathering ropes that sat beside the siege engine.

"What are you doing?"

"Someone is hurt down there. We have to go down and get him up," Antoine whispered, but his voice was fierce.

"You go ahead. I am not risking my life to climb down there and rescue some fool of a Cathar who decided to do a little night climb," Pierre grumbled.

"Risk your life? Ha! What about the time you climbed the face of the 'Lady's Breast' at home to impress my Cecile?" Antoine wound the rope around his arm. "This is a walk through the meadow compared to that climb!"

He secured the rope around the post next to the siege engine and stared at Pierre. "Will you join me?"

Pierre shrugged. "Climb, then."

Antoine inched down the sheer face, halting often to listen, straining his ears for the soft, rasping sound that would lead them to the climber-the sound of breathing. Pierre followed closely. Far below, the faint light of a torch from the village that hugged the base of the mountain winked at him. The village night watch was posted, then. He counted knots he had tied into the rope, each measuring the height of a man. Twenty knots, now thirty. The slope bulged outward, then receded until both he and Pierre hung anxiously from the ropes. Finally, Antoine felt the mountain wall beneath his feet again. He nodded to Pierre.

He thought he heard bubbles popping, a gurgling. What was that? He leaned out from the side, holding firmly on his rope, and saw the climber. The twisted body was stuck between two rocks. Antoine gave a low whistle, gazing into the abyss.

"This is what stopped him." he pointed to the jagged teeth of the rocks. The climber had come to rest on top of the lower, but the upper had claimed a piece of his body. His right arm reached above his head at an impossible angle. "Broken, for sure," Antoine said, then moved closer. "Blessed Mother!" He waved Pierre back, but his friend did not heed him.

"Is he dead?"

Pierre swallowed; Antoine heard his friend's throat working. "If you are going to lose your dinner, do it now," he said. He stopped next to the twisted form. The woman's breath was warm on his face. "No, she is not dead," he answered. "She is still alive."

Pierre shuddered. "It is a woman?"

Her injuries were terrible. Even in the dark, Antoine could see many wet places where broken bones had pushed through the skin of her arms and legs, through the wool gown and leggings she wore. The whole side of her face had been shattered, and blood poured steadily from her mouth. Her teeth showed through her torn cheek.

Pierre moaned. "Will she wake up?" he asked. "I hope she will not."

"I do not know. She is bleeding a lot from the mouth, so she will not live very long." Antoine shifted his weight. Maybe if he took her shoulders while Pierre took her feet, they could move her.

"How do you know that?" Pierre's voice sounded muffled.

Antoine looked up at his friend. "I have seen this before. When they bleed this much from the mouth they do not last."

The woman's eyes opened She breathed in with a bubbling sound and tried to speak. Her eyes were rimmed with white, and quivered.

"Do not speak and do not move." Antoine whispered to her in the language of the region, the langue d'oc. "We will try to help you. I am Antoine and he is Pierre."

Panic left her face. She looked from Antoine to Pierre, who hung onto the mountain and stared upon her with undisguised horror. Her lips spread in a faint, lopsided smile. The left side of her face would not move.

"I am Diana," she said, just as she would if they had met in the marketplace rather than hanging on the side of a mountain. The injury to her face muted and slurred her speech, but her voice sounded calm. "I know you cannot help me; you must not worry. You must leave me here, but I would like you to stay until I am gone."

She looked at Antoine, who was regarding her silently. "I am not in pain. I cannot move or feel my body, but I know I am grievously wounded and do not have long. There is something I must pass on to you for safekeeping." Her accent sounded refined, even through the distortion from her injuries, finer than the accents of the knights above in the command tent.

Antoine shook his head and waved his free hand, clinging to his rope with the other, but she pinned him with her gaze.

"You must take it," she said. "It is a package wrapped in silk inside a sling under my cloak."

"How do you know we are not with the French King's army? Would you have whatever this thing is — this thing you want to give to us — fall into their hands?"

"I know you are here with the French." Her eyes closed briefly, then opened again. "But the thing I carry cannot choose wrongly. It is not for me to say who it chooses, if you are with the French then so be it. I can see your hearts are good, and I think you will keep it safe." She looked at him a few heartbeats longer and then Antoine slipped his hand under her cloak and felt around her torso, trying to jostle her as little as possible. He finally pulled out a bulky package wrapped in silk, as she had told him it would be. Her face relaxed.

"Good," she said, then coughed. More blood trickled out of her mouth, the coppery, salty warm smell of it hanging in the still air around them.

Pierre swallowed, his throat making a dry, clicking sound. "Blessed Mother," he whispered.

She looked at him and one side of her mouth stretched into a faint smile again. "Do not worry. I received the consolamentum — our kiss of peace — before I left Montsegur." She looked again to Antoine. "Please keep what is in the package. It has passed to you now."

Antoine saluted her as he would a soldier. Her eyes brightened a moment, then blood spurted from her mouth, soaking her clothes and staining the snow. Her eyes glazed.

When he tried to free her head from the rock, Antoine felt a slender chain around her neck give way. He caught it before it fell down the mountainside. Pierre was at her feet, pulling them free from the rock cleft. Antoine slipped the chain into his mantle with the package she had given him.

"They will be able to see this blood in the morning, my friend," he told Pierre. "We had better start working on our story now."

"But I thought we were taking her to Bauçais." Pierre was wrapping her cloak around her broken body.

"No," Antoine decided. "He would only burn her, then they would ask us if she carried anything." He touched the package inside his mantle. A curious tingling moved from his fingers up his arm and to his chest, settling in a warm glow around his heart. He looked up at the sky. They had time yet until dawn. He peered at the path they had cleared to allow the French to take the ridge. "We will take her below," he said, "and bury her."

HE CARRIED her body cradled against his chest, in a loose halter of ropes crossing his back. She was a little thing, really. Pierre walked behind him, doing his best to clear the traces of their journey. When the slope grew steeper, they took turns climbing and handing her down. Time had no meaning now, there was only the narrow, treacherous path to the valley below.

When they reached the base, they both crouched and breathed, the air pumping out of their lungs in white plumes. The torch of the night watch shone through pines and scrub. Antoine tied Diana's body to his back. The two men skirted the village, running silently, and into the forest that stretched out into the distance toward Navarre, toward home. Antoine carried Diana's body deep into the forest, placing her between the roots of a long-needled pine. There was little snow under the trees here, but they had left their footsteps on the ground behind the houses.

"Pierre," he whispered, "Take some deadfall branches and clear our tracks."

Pierre nodded and melted into the tree shadows. Antoine turned toward the dead Cathar, Diana. "I must bury you here." He spoke to her still form, gazing through night shadows at oak and ash, at scrub pine and hawthorn. "It is near the village, so you will be among Christians. Not Cathars. At least, I don't think they are Cathars. But this is the best I can do." He cleared a space between the tree roots and sank into the layers of needles. "You know, my family would consider this a holy place-these trees, the nearness of the mountain." He searched for sharp rocks, found three with good, flat sides that fit in the palm of his hand. Then he attacked the frozen earth. "So you will have both the Christ and the Guardian to watch over you."

Pierre rejoined him, his powerful hands tearing into the soil. When they had dug so deep that they could barely see above the surface of the hole, they lowered Diana's body carefully into the grave. Pierre placed the last bit of earth onto the grave and they both spread needles over it. Finally, Antoine stood and stared at their work. In the dark, at least, the forest floor looked undisturbed.

Antoine turned to Pierre. "What shall we say?"

Pierre shrugged, then leaned down and drew an equal-armed cross in the earth, surrounded by a circle. He stood and brushed the dirt off his hands.

"Who are these Cathars, anyway?" Antoine asked. "I do not know any Christian blessings or words for the dead. Do you know any for Cathars?"

"I knew a Cathar once," Pierre murmured. "He told me that everything you see around you is really made of light, but that a king of all evil imprisoned the light into the world, so everything here is evil." He rubbed his belly and grimaced. "As if the Guardian's own earth could be evil! He was a good man, but I never understood him."

The package inside Antoine's mantle was warm. He was reluctant to part with it, but if his tent were searched it would be found. "Pierre," he said, pulling out the package and the necklace. "I am going to bury her necklace with her, and this," he unwrapped the silk, "I will bury nearby." It was an old stone cup. The outer surface was bumpy with letters or carving and there seemed to be something inside it. He touched the inner rim. A stone lay inside, but it did not move when he touched it. It must be wedged tight. When he touched the cup's surface, his belly warmed and a curious sense of peace flowed out to his heart, to his arms. He wrapped the silk around it again and buried it across from the grave.

Pierre looked at the sky. "Whatever you do, we must be going now, if we are to return before we are missed."

Antoine placed the necklace under the needles that marked Diana's grave. "You were a brave lady," he said. "We will do our best to keep your cup safe." He rubbed fallen oak leaves over his hands and face to take away the traces of blood and dirt. Then he and Pierre started their journey back.

HUGHES DES ARCIS reclined in his sturdy chair and examined the plan for the surrender of Montsegur. While he turned the vellum pages, he glanced up at his second-in-command, Henri de Bauçais.

Henri had busied himself with his incessant carving and was now deeply engrossed, making notches in what looked like the tail of a mermaid. He never went anywhere without his knives and small blocks of wood. Hughes had to admit his carvings were actually quite beautiful. When the Pope had put Hughes in charge of the siege of Montsegur,

Hughes had asked for Henri. He had known Bauçais since Henri was a wild, sweet and guileless boy. Hughes had watched him grow, had congratulated Henri's father on his three fine sons — Gilles, Henri and Guy — had even taken Henri as squire for a time.

Henri was humming while he carved. What tune was that? Something religious? Of course. Hughes knew Henri had been sent to the abbey to take training as a monk. How could Henri's father have allowed that? There were rumors, of course. Something about a girl. Ysabel? Some disgrace. And wasn't his mother mad? Hughes had heard she still wore a hair shirt. She would have her beautiful son chaste forever in an abbey, but Henri's older brother died. And his father, too.

Hughes folded the surrender agreement. A brilliant plan, really. It would put an end to this siege that had lasted nearly a year. Entirely too long, but the people of this region were clearly on the side of the heretics. Oh, they did nothing overt. But Hughes had the devil of a time keeping conscripts from deserting. And his supply lines were always disintegrating. Henri had changed that. His decision to use the Basque mercenaries had brought them the first real break they had in this campaign. And now this surrender agreement.

Hughes cleared his throat; Henri stopped carving and slipped the half-formed block of wood into a pocket on his mantle. A strong face, Hughes thought, a beautiful face. But the younger man's eyes were cold.

"This is a very good plan," Hughes stated. "How many do you think will recant? How high should our pyres be built?"

"What are you saying? Most of them will recant," Henri said, waving his hand.

"You think so?" Hughes raised his eyebrows but did not comment further.

"Anyone faced with burning to death will certainly see that it is much better to live than to die so horribly. I have a meeting with the guide I told you about," Henri said, "Jean Bernart. The one who can get us up to the eastern tower."

Hughes nodded. "How long do you think it will take to get us up there?"

Henri frowned. "It will take careful planning. I must climb the route myself first so I can see how long it takes, and how many of our men can get up there before the heretics know what we are doing." He reached inside his mantle. The knife he had used in his carving caught the light as his fingers played over the hilt. "I will not ask my men to do what I have not done myself." He turned to walk out the door.

Hughes smiled. Henri had never lacked courage. The soldiers of the king were certainly devoted to him. But the local inhabitants often shied away from Henri and made a curious sign with the pointing and smallest fingers of their hands when he strode past them. Hughes had meant to ask what this sign meant. Ah, well, he thought, we may never know.

"There is another thing," Hughes said as Henri reached the door. Henri turned to face him.

Hughes leaned back in his chair and selected his words with care. "There was an incident around Christmas," he said. "Someone from Montsegur tried to climb down and fell."

Henri nodded. "There was blood all over the snow."

"But no body was ever found," Hughes remarked mildly.

"Two of the Basques from my aunt's town had been on watch that night. Both claimed they had fallen asleep. I could not find fault with either story; except of course, there was the fact that they had fallen asleep on duty. Since everyone was doing double-shifts at that time, I was not surprised." Something flared within Henri's eyes. "I moved both of the guards who were on duty that night to the day watch just a few days after the incident." Henri's body was rigid now, and Hughes was favored with his icy stare, a gaze that many had warned Hughes would 'wither his bones.' Ridiculous, of course. Yet Hughes could not dampen the shiver that trembled his spine. The stare of a basilisk. Useful. But it could not wither one who had known him when he was a boy.

"Good," Hughes said. "I want you to keep an eye on them. The two Basques."

Henri raised his brows. The knife disappeared into his mantle.

"My sources have told me that something of value may have come down from Montsegur that night." Hughes paused, watching Henri's face thaw, watching the spark flare again in his eyes. "Something of great value."

"I will have them watched." Henri inclined his head, then swept out of the room.

A BLACK moon. There had been chanting earlier from the fortress above, but all was silent now. Henri had watched the black hulk of Montsegur for so long his neck ached. Jean Bernart, the guide they had bribed, stood sweating nearby. Henri knew that if they could secure the eastern tower, then they would control the entire eastern face and the siege would be nearly over, but he hated dealing with this traitor. He could smell him, an acid scent of both excitement and fear. The smell of the abbey.

His thoughts veered away, as always, from any memory of his time in the Fornault Abbey. His fingers found his carving knife and he nicked the skin of his ring finger. The sting brought him back to the task before him. He turned to Jean. "Lead me up there," he said.

ANTOINE lifted another iron bar and set it into place. It was nearly over

for him and Pierre. The fortress had fallen soon after Bauçais took the
east tower. Antoine had gone to the paymaster again as soon as the
trumpet was sounded, signaling surrender. But the blasted wretch had
simply smiled. "We have a task for such a strong man," the paymaster
had said.

So he was here now with Pierre again. Building a cage.

"Why do they want a cage?" Pierre had asked. "Will they put the
prisoners inside here? Why not in the dungeon of the fortress?"

"Maybe there is no dungeon." But Antoine felt uneasy. They were
building this cage so fast that it could not hold any number of folk for
long. The bars would collapse if too much pressure were placed on them
over time. True, they only had a few days now until the people inside
would deliver themselves to the pope's men. But how long would the
soldiers hold them? He shook his head. This cage was simply not strong
enough. He hoped they would not blame him when the bars collapsed.

Antoine paused and glanced up as Henri de Bauçais strode past
him, searing him with that icy stare. The man looked demented. But
Henri had won. He had given the people inside Montsegur fourteen days
to prepare themselves for the surrender. They would have time to decide
whether they would put aside their Cathar beliefs and live, or refuse to
recant, and die.

Antoine stared at Henri's retreating back. Henri paced all of the
time, now. But Antoine could feel the restless heat behind his cold eyes.
There was a passionate heart within that man. Antoine turned back to the
cage and saw men dragging bales of straw onto the platform he had
helped to build. What was the straw for?

Henri stopped at the edge of Hughes' tent. His stomach burned all
of the time now. The silence after the constant crashing of the siege
engine made the ears ring, and a curious tension had rippled through the
men surrounding the fortress since the heretics announced their
surrender. Henri could see that his men were jumpy. Quarrels broke out
everywhere, several of his men were coughing without reason, some had
developed tics as muscles in their jaws or around their eyes twitched
uncontrollably. He was at a loss. How could he deal with this?

A voice sounded from within. "Ah, young Henri." Hughes emerged.
"I hear you have some trouble with the men. Perhaps we could provide
some women or other entertainment for them?"

Henri forced his muscles to relax. "There are minstrels in the
village." He looked out over the camp. "I can have them come out to play
for the men."

Hughes merely nodded. "What of you, Henri?" His eyes did not
shift when Henri flinched. "Will you never be still? Why not find a
woman to warm your bed?"

Henri forced a smile. "You would recommend this? You, a man of the Church?"

Hughes shrugged. "As you wish, Bauçais, but get some minstrels for the men."

Henri ducked his head to acknowledge his dismissal and moved off toward the village, lengthening his stride. He averted his eyes from the cage, from the Basque Antoine who was stolidly raising bars and pounding them into place.

Tomorrow. The sixteenth of March. It would be over tomorrow.

THE SUN rose and slid behind a pall of heavy clouds. Antoine stood at one corner of the cage he had helped build and watched soldiers heap sticks of wood, straw, and pitch, all in several piles inside. At each of the four corners, extra straw was piled. Pierre came up behind him. "Is everything ready?" he asked, barely moving his lips.

Antoine felt the bulge inside his mantle. The cup the Cathar had given him rested in a sling next to his heart. He had avoided the guard, gone down to the burial site and dug it up just last night. "Are you sure you want to leave without the gold they promised?" he asked.

"I would like to leave right now," Pierre said, "but we cannot slip away until there are more people around. The soldiers watch us."

He lowered his voice even further. "Wait for the signal. As soon as you see me pull my ear, you must run for the forest."

Antoine looked back at the cage. "Maybe this is just to hold them."

Pierre grimaced. "If you believe that, you are a bigger fool than Bauçais." He moved away from Antoine with deliberate steps, looking for all the world as if he and Antoine had merely discussed the possibility of rain.

HENRI WAITED outside the gates of Montsegur. It was time. He sat there next to Hughes in the Pope's own wagon and watched row upon row of people walking out of the fortress. A procession of men and women dressed in dark blue robes marched down toward them, their voices rising and falling in the still air.

"What are they singing?" He leaned forward.

Hughes shook his head. "A Cathar hymn, I suppose."

Several other inhabitants of the fortress marched to the left: knights, merchants, some women and children. The Bishop's priests were everywhere, praying and approaching the people of Montsegur for their recantation of the Cathar heresy. Soon the area was filled with people. Soldiers pushed the blue robed folk toward the cage, but no priests followed them. The people from the fortress were milling around, mixing with the pope's soldiers, the priests. Henri stood up in his seat on the wagon. He could see women from the village now, and camp followers. They were still on the edges of the crowd, but would soon be among the prisoners.

He sank back into his seat and looked around in dismay. It was total chaos. There was no order to it, no way to tell who would recant and who would not. Swearing under his breath, he leaped out of the ornate wagon he occupied with Hughes and marched straight into the crowd. Someone had to bring some semblance of order and organization to the surrender. He would start with the blue robed people near the cage. "Form a line!" he barked out his order and watched in satisfaction as the group jostled around until a rough line was formed. He folded his arms across his chest. "Now," he said, "who will be first?"

THIS WAS going nowhere. Henri shook his head and moved to the next person in line, an elderly man with cloudy blue eyes. "Do you accept the teachings of Christ?" he asked this man, as he had asked all who stood silently in the line. So far, no one had responded to any of his questions. "Do you revere His Holiness, the Pope?" The man's eyes were mild. He met Henri's stare, but did not speak. None of them had. But this one was thin, so thin that a stiff wind might blow him away. Henri stepped back and allowed his gaze to travel over the man. Hughes had told him that the priests of the Cathars were often very thin. "Are you a parfait?" he asked.

The man's expression did not change. He still regarded Henri with patient endurance. All of them had looked back into Henri's eyes with the same maddening serenity. But this one spoke. "Yes," he said. "I am a parfait."

"Well!" Henri raised his arms. "Finally someone will speak to me." He leaned forward. "I wrote the surrender agreement," he said, pitching his voice so the others in line could hear. "And you must know what this is for." He pointed at the cage and saw the tremor that shivered through the man's frame. A quiver rippled through the people in line.

But the man's eyes remained calm. "Yes," he said. "We know." All motion stopped. The people now stood there as they had since they had come down from the fortress, hands clasped before them, faces serene and eyes bearing the same mild look as the man in front of Henri.

Henri leaned toward him again. "Then how can you let your people go into there? You are their priest." He allowed his voice to drop. "It is your duty to protect them." He glanced over at the cage, then back to the man. "We both of us believe in the Christ. Why let these people die for a small matter of doctrine?" The man's eyes grew alert, boring into Henri's. "Come now," Henri continued. "They follow you." He stepped back. "Tell them to recant and we can all of us go home in peace."

The man reached forward, his eyes still searching Henri's face. Henri felt his hands taken and held. The man's hands were dry and cool to the touch. One corner of the man's mouth lifted and he said, "For you, this is just beginning."

Henri felt the blood drain from his face. "What?" He backed away and looked down at his hands. The man no longer held them, but Henri could still feel his grasp. A touch on his arm brought his head around.

"My lord." One of the bishop's soldier's stood there; his red tunic and white cross made a garish splash among the deep blue robes of the Cathars. "It has already been decided." His words were courteous, but firm. "These people are to burn."

Henri jerked his arm away. "Nonsense!" he growled. "I wrote the surrender agreement. They are to be given the chance to recant." He turned back to the blue robed line. "I have barely begun my questioning." He opened his mouth to continue his interrogation, but a flash of red and white on either side stopped his words. Three other soldiers surrounded him. Two grabbed his arms, one removed his sword. Henri sputtered. "What is this?"

"Hughes des Arcis has ordered us to take you," the first soldier said. "We do not like this any more than you, my lord, but we must do des Arcis' bidding."

They dragged Henri back away from the line and held him fifteen paces from the cage. Henri glanced at their faces. Struggling would be no use. He knew these men. They would travel to hell and back again if their commander bid it. He could not countermand an order given by Hughes.

"Then take me to Hughes," Henri said, watching their eyes. They would not look at him.

"We cannot." The first spoke again. "We are to keep you here until it is over." His jaw set in a rigid line.

The gates to the cage were opened by the two Basques from his aunt's territory. Henri tried to break free, but he was held fast. He saw the people he had been questioning march inside. The old man glanced back at him before he entered. His mouth moved, but Henri could not hear what he said. The sound of voices raised in anguish tore at him. Women, now. They were dragging women to the cage. Some were walking toward it, but soldiers carried others. One woman's hair had come down from her cap, streaming in a black and silver blanket around her hips. She held her arms stiffly at her side and her eyes were so wide Henri feared they would bulge out of her head. His own arms strained against the men holding him. The soldiers herded children toward the cage. Children!

"This was not part of the surrender!" Henri shouted. "We do not kill children!" To the devil with des Arcis! This must end.

He relaxed in a compliant sag, then when he felt the answering slack in the soldiers' hold, jammed his arms forward and dropped to the ground in a roll, breaking free of their grasp. Shouts echoed in his ears, but he leaped to his feet and ran toward the cage. One child. If he could save just one.

Six more soldiers caught and held him before he could reach the cage. "What are you doing?" Henri saw other soldiers carrying the wounded from the fortress into the cage. "You are killing the wounded, too?" The pulse pounded in his temple. "This is madness!"

He sought the Basques from his aunt's town and saw the white face of one; it was Antoine, he thought. "Antoine!" he shouted. "Open the gate. For God's sake, man! Let the children out, at least." His voice failed. Now he could see tiny hands gripping the bars, tear-streaked faces pressing against the iron.

He froze when he saw the four men at each of the corners of the pyre, then screamed "No!" when they dropped their torches into the straw.

The men who had built the pyre had done their work well. No more Cathar hymns. Flames spread instantly and soon engulfed the entire cage; women screamed. The children ran to the blue robed priests, who stood in the center of the cage. The old man he had questioned put his arms around a boy. The boy could not have been more than ten.

Suddenly, Henri's arms were free. The men who had held him ran from the heat that blasted at him like a furnace. He remained where they had left him, arms hanging limply at his sides, eyes and ears filled with the sight and sound of over two hundred people. Burning.

He watched the flames, the bodies jumping, the hands clutching the edges of the cage, then fingers snatched away as the bars heated. And the children, my God! Smoke overcame them first and they lay huddled in pitiful little mounds. He tried to close his eyes, but his lids would not obey him. A powerful arm thrust hard against the bars, almost a blacksmith's arm it was, and still free of the fire, but the fingers curled and uncurled as the flesh started to crisp. A woman's silver hair floated up above her blackened face before it, too, burst into flames. A man crawled, his skin streaked with red and black, bleeding, desperately creeping away from the flames that threatened to engulf him. Fire ran over another man's body, burning his clothing off and bubbling the fat in his skin with an obscene sizzling. Henri turned, looked for the parfait again. Where was the old man? He could not see him at first. But the old man was there in the center, his arms still wrapped around the boy. Flames climbed his robes now. The boy was limp in his arms. The old man fell to his knees; fire leaped from his robes into a living torch.

Henri threw his head back and howled; a long, desperate cry of grief. He shouted his despair until he could barely make a sound. He did not stop when the bishop's men braved the heat to rescue him. He did not stop when they tried to pull him away, but sought instead to break free of their grip.

A bright flash of pain exploded behind his ears. And darkness fell.

HENRI'S EYES blinked open. He raised his head and saw the walls of his tent. "What?" His lungs clutched. Surely he had been somewhere with Hughes, hadn't he? But it was dark, night must have fallen. The last thing he remembered was sitting in the wagon with Hughes. His legs trembled. He sat, holding his head, forcing air in and out of his rebelling lungs. "What is that stench?" He swallowed. What were they cooking tonight? Staggering to his feet, he stumbled out of the tent.

It was not nighttime, as he had thought. The edges of the sky were still light gray with the low-hanging clouds of that morning. The darkness came from a pillar of thick black smoke rising from a huge fire. Even from where he stood at the lower camp he could see flames peeking through smoke and red-hot embers glowing angrily at the heart. Bodies. That was what burned there. Henri sank to his knees and threw back his head, but no sound would come out of his open mouth. He covered his face with his hands, but no tears would flow. In the end he simply sat there on the ground in the doorway of his tent, his eyes focused upon nothing.

THE SOLDIER'S voice sounded hoarse from the smoke and his eyes darted around the encampment. "He just sits there, my lord, and does not move."

Hughes des Arcis frowned. "How long has he been this way?" He had been occupied with administering the other conditions of the surrender and had not thought about his young friend for some time now.

"Since yesterday, about an hour after they knocked him out."

"Knocked him out?" Hughes asked in surprise. "What happened?"

"He wouldn't leave the fire, my lord. Just wouldn't go. We were afraid he would die there, the heat was so bad." The soldier wiped the sweat off his face with hands that trembled. "So we went back to get him, had to drag him back, but he fought us, and, you see, the air from the fire — it was burning our lungs." He coughed. "So we had to hit him over the head. But we carried him back."

"Thank you, commander," Hughes said, rising. "I would like you to take me to him now, please."

HUGHES HELD a pomander in front of his nose as he walked the short distance to the bishop's quarters. Although the burning had taken place three days before, there was still an ungodly stench hanging in the air. They all prayed for rain, but, although the clouds still hung heavily over the area, no rain had fallen.

For the past three days his second-in-command, Henri de Bauçais, had sat in his tent where they had placed him, neither eating, drinking, nor sleeping in all that time. Hughes drew in a deep breath in spite of the stench and knocked politely on the door of the bishop's chambers.

When he entered the room, he approached the desk and kissed the ring on the bony hand the bishop extended to him. "Your Eminence," he stated, then seated himself after the bishop motioned for him to sit. Bishop Durand was a large, angular man with deeply hooded eyes.

"Ghastly smell," Hughes remarked. "Seems to get into everything."

"It will pass," Durand said mildly. "Have you any word of the two Basques?"

Hughes hesitated. Antoine Jakintza and Pierre Brounnan had disappeared during the burning of the heretics. They had been commandeered by the bishop's men to help build the cage and take the Cathars into the pyre. When everyone had returned to his post from this grisly duty, the soldiers in charge found that the two men were missing. "No, your Eminence, they have not been found. However, I have a plan to find them that will serve a double purpose."

Durand leaned back and signaled for Hughes to continue.

"You remember Henri de Bauçais?"

A spark flared in Durand's eyes. "You mean the man who brought the Basques from Navarre, who took the eastern tower?" He bowed his head. "François de Bauçais's son, now Baron de Bauçais?"

"The very same. His older brother died nearly five years ago and his father died about — oh, three years ago," Hughes said, waving the pomander in front of his nose. Thank God for oranges and cloves, he thought, then said: "It was Henri who brought the two Basques from Reuilles-la-ville, on de Reuilles land."

Another spark flared in Durand's eyes. "We are familiar with de Reuilles," he said, then continued smoothly, "I had heard that there was some difficulty with the execution. That someone tried to pull heretics away from the pyre."

"That is not entirely true. Henri did try to get the heretics to recant, that is so, but he did not pull anyone out of the pyre." Hughes paused. "Henri believed that most of the heretics would recant. He is a brilliant man, really, but he lacks our experience in these matters."

"Unseasoned." Durand nodded. "This often happens with the first burning. Very well, go on."

"He stayed near the fire even after the others had gone to a safe distance. My men had to go back to get him, and even then he would not leave, so they had to strike him in order to remove him from danger."

"Indeed. Where is he now?"

"He is in his tent." Now Hughes leaned forward. "He has neither eaten nor slept for the past three days. I placed a guard on him. I was not sure what he would do."

Durand drummed his fingers on the table. "What do you propose?"

"Those men you are looking for come from the de Reuilles territory. I propose sending Henri there to track them down." If Henri ever came to his senses. "His aunt is Johanna de Reuilles, so he will have the confidence of the baron." He pulled a document he had written, ordering Henri to find the two Basques, out of his mantle and placed it on the table before Durand.

"Baron Louis-Philippe de Reuilles," Durand murmured, examining the document, "Yes," then: "Do you think he will be able to travel?"

"I cannot say. But I think it is worth a try and it may help him, give him a purpose, bring him out of himself."

"Let it be done, then." Durand signed the document in front of him. As he handed it back to Hughes, he added, "Now that we have succeeded here, we can turn our attention to other heresies." He leaned back in his red cushioned chair and regarded Hughes.

"Other heresies?" Hughes rolled the parchment into a tube and slipped it in the pouch upon his belt.

Bishop Durand waved his hand. "Oh, you need not be gone from your loved ones for long." His lids dropped and his eyes gleamed out from beneath. "I am not sending you to Jerusalem. Heresy is everywhere. We will have much for you to do here at home. Much to do."

HUGHES APPROACHED the tent where Henri sat unmoving and unresponsive. Holding the pomander by his nose, Hughes nodded to the guard he had posted by the door of the tent and pushed past the man to go inside. It was dark in the tent. He could see the shadow of Henri sitting on the cot, his haunted eyes staring out of his thinning face, the traces of a beard lacing his cheeks and chin. Hughes averted his eyes. It hurt to look at Henri, especially when he remembered the sunny, cheerful boy Henri had been. Hughes sat on a chair by the cot and produced the document the bishop had just signed.

"Good news, Bauçais," he said in a brusque tone. "Bishop Durand has another mission for you. You remember the two Basques who were on duty when the Cathar had an accident on the mountain?" He saw a brief flicker come and go in Henri's eyes.

"Well, they have both disappeared," Hughes continued. Really, it was unnerving to see Bauçais sitting there, so inanimate. He remembered Henri's incessant carving. Henri never could be still before. Now he was a statue. "Durand wants you to go to Reuilles-le-château to trace them."

"Henri," he whispered, then cleared his throat and his voice strengthened. "I had no liking for this campaign. Recapturing the holy land is one thing, but turning our soldiers against our own... well, I did not like it. But I am a soldier of Christ and I will always do as the Church commands." He looked at Henri. No change. "You should do the same. This was your first burning," he said. "There will be others."

Hughes waited, counting his heartbeats, then stood up to go. He heard a whispering rustle behind him, then Henri grabbed his wrist in an iron grip, and he cried out. The guard rushed in and Hughes motioned for him to return to his post.

Henri's eyes blazed at him. No more ice in that stare now. Henri released Hughes' wrist and took the paper he held. Hughes watched him as Henri read it though. Then Henri looked up at him, mouth set in a grim line.

"When do I leave?"

Chapter 12

ROSE AND gray colors of the fading night gave way to translucent blue. Everyone around her exclaimed their wonder at the spectacle of the dawn, but Maríana struggled to stifle a yawn as she sat on the back of her stolid, gentle mare in the meadow south of the château. Her eyelids blinked sleepily of their own accord, then flew open when she felt the stab of talons on her arm as her sparrow hawk, Isolde, moved restlessly, her bells jingling with a silvery whisper in the quiet of early morning.

Hawking was a weekly ritual at the château and Maríana had joined the throng with little Isolde.

She rubbed her eyes and surveyed the field before them where hounds were beginning to flush out game birds. The company milled around her—young squires, visiting knights, her father, Johanna, and Bernart. It was a small crowd, unlike the hawking parties that would visit the château later in the spring. Now it was the beginning of April, only two weeks into the cycle of the Ram. Though the slopes of Irati retained a thick coverlet of blinding white snow, in the valley below, tender shoots of plants and grasses strained up through the soil. All that was green and growing now had a chance to struggle and breed and die in the space between spring and autumn.

Up ahead, a cloud of pheasants and quail disturbed by the hounds ascended. In response, the fine falcons of the knights and squires surrounding her were released at once, ominously silent and purposeful, except for the jangle of bells tied to their powerful legs.

She watched them climb into the sky, Isolde still clinging to her arm, turning hooded head toward the burst of cheers from the crowd when their falcons captured prey. Isolde pinched her arm.

"How do you think you can compete with these aristocratic falcons? You're only a rather small sparrow hawk, you know! But don't fret. I'll take you where you can hunt safely."

She reined her mare away from the others, ducking several covetous, sidelong glances from the young, smooth-faced squires, and quite a few direct, appreciative stares from the older knights. Head still lowered, she lifted Isolde to block her view of their faces. Richard would soon marry Beatrice. He had left before her father's wedding and she had heard nothing from him since then. Anyway, her father would be choosing a husband for her, wouldn't he? She prodded her mare into a canter and left the hawking party behind.

At the forest's edge lay a small cleared area, bordered on two sides by a grove of birch, oak and pine. Sitting still for a moment, Maríana basked in the warm morning sun that sent tendrils of mist floating, streaming and curling around her. It had a fresh, green smell, and she drew in her breath, savoring her solitude. She inhaled again and smelled the tangy, sharp fragrance of fertile earth strong with the birth of growing things.

She tugged away the hood covering Isolde's alert eyes. "I have no hounds to flush out the game, but I think I can arrange something for you," she told the bird.

Closing her eyes, she quieted the chattering of her mind and drank in the fluttering movement of tiny lives all around her. She raised her hands, weaving a bright pattern in the air. "Come, now." The pattern bulged and strained, a wiggling dance of light and shadow. "Who will it be?" Ibrahim had taught her how to draw the pattern, but it was Iranzu who had shown her what it could do.

A small quail trembled in the grasses across the meadow. She felt its heart flutter. It was past breeding age and drawn to the piercing stare of her hawk even though it would mean death. It was the way of things. "So be it," she breathed. "Fly, then!" The quail lifted its wings.

At the flutter in the grasses, Isolde took flight with the speed and accuracy of an arrow, and pinioned the small quail in her talons. Maríana swung the red lure around her head, then held out her wrist as the bird gracefully floated down, landing with the dead quail still caught in her claws. Slipping the hood back on Isolde, Maríana removed the quail from the hawk's grasp, tying a bit of string around it and hooking the other end of the string to a notch on her saddle. She was so engrossed in her task that when a voice spoke by her ear, she jumped.

"Maríana. So your little bird caught something." One of the younger knights had come alongside her and was leaning close.

"Yes." He must have arrived that morning. She did not recall his face among the others last night. But he was familiar. Where she had seen him? Something about the tumble of hair across his forehead made her back stiffen, but perhaps that was because he was leaning too close. She hated that.

"Your father sent me here to accompany you back to the château. There have been rumors of bandits who have used these dark glades to ambush our kind." He smirked and turned his horse toward the château.

Ambushed. In an instant, she knew who he was. Arnaut, the same bully who had knocked her down so many years ago, grown up now and still a bully, although of another sort. The beard he had grown had changed his face enough so she did not recognize him at first, and his voice had deepened. Her father and grandmother must have forgiven him, otherwise why would he be here? Well, she did not forgive him. Arnaut reached down, grabbing the reins of her horse to lead her back.

But he brought his own mount up short with a surprised exclamation as Maríana's mare tore the reins out of his hands.

Maríana urged her mare to a full gallop, using special words Ibrahim had taught her to put fire into her mare's pace. When she reached the gate into the château, Arnaut was two hundred paces behind her. She dismounted and flung her reins at the nearest stable boy, who appeared to be trying very hard not to laugh at the expression on Arnaut's face as he came riding up behind her.

THE HALL was bathed in the gold and red glow from the central hearth, and still fragrant with the early morning meal. Maríana made her way across the floor to the stairway. She must return Isolde to her perch, feed her, and change into a fresh gown to help Ysabel entertain the guests who had slept late. She mounted the first step, then stopped.

In the dim alcove to the right of the stairs, a man stood staring at the de Reuilles mermaid tapestry that hung there. His inspection of the tapestry was so intent he must not have noticed her entry into the hall. Who had let him in? Had no one greeted him? There were others about in the palais. Arnaut would be blundering through the door at any moment. But for now, there was no one of any rank there to welcome this newly arrived guest to Reuilles-le-château. He must have been expected, for otherwise he would not have been admitted to the hall. It was definitely poor form to have no one of rank there to greet him.

She was annoyed at her father and at Ysabel for this minor breach of etiquette and at herself for a memory that tugged at her awareness but would not surface. Sighing, she stepped back off the staircase and approached the stranger.

Isolde was still perched on her arm, blood on the talons. Her gown was crumpled from her wild ride and her rich auburn hair had escaped from the braids she had plaited that morning, but she contrived to carry herself with as much dignity as she could muster as she said to the stranger, "It is very fine work, is it not?" He half turned toward her. "Actually, it is Flemish." She smiled as he slowly turned.

"I am sorry that no one was here to greet you properly. We were all out on the hawking fields," she said.

Maríana lowered her eyes and curtsied as she had been taught, so she did not see his face. All she could see were strong, capable, square hands and travel-stained clothes as she murmured a traditional welcome, inviting him to follow her to where he could bathe, change, and rest. One of the hands suddenly tightened its hold on the sword fastened to his belt.

Finished with the proper welcoming, she looked up, and all thought and words abruptly ceased.

Flinty, blue eyes looked directly into hers from a tired and stern face. Heat rose until she was sure her cheeks were flaming, but she held herself straight and stared back at him. He was of medium height, his body powerfully built. Golden brown hair barely brushed his shoulders. His cheekbones were high and broad; he must have ancestors from the cold island in the north. His mouth was both thin and wide, with a slight hint of something that might be cruelty-or pain-at the edges. His nose was firm and straight.

All taken, a very handsome man, dressed in russet and forest green. But it was the shadowed torment in his blue eyes that caught and pinned her so she could not move.

She would not look away, even though his stare raked her from head to foot. Her hands curled into fists and Isolde dug talons into her arm in response. Well! The boor did not even speak. He just stood staring at her.

She sealed her lips and stared back. Let him be the one to break this silence. She could wait. Although her legs trembled from standing so still and her arm threatened to droop and deposit Isolde on the floor, she would wait until he spoke. The man glanced at Isolde. The bird was restless, head bobbing, talons now penetrating the leather sleeve. She gritted her teeth against the slice of Isolde's claws.

At that moment the door swung open and Arnaut ran in shouting, "Maríana!" He was brought up short when he saw the two of them standing there and his eyes widened.

"My lord." Arnaut bowed. "Please forgive my interruption." The young knight backed away and walked quickly to the door.

She still faced the visitor, ignoring the dampness spreading under Isolde's talons.

"I am forgetting my manners," the man said, his voice a deep growl, but modulated and smooth, the texture of lamp oil. "I am Henri de Bauçais, nephew to your grandmother."

"Welcome, cousin." She dipped into a perfunctory curtsey. "Please follow me and I will show you where you can take refreshment and rest." Henri? Johanna had never mentioned an Henri.

He silently followed her up the stairs. She wanted to look back at him, but kept walking, cursing her disheveled gown and hair and the blood seeping under the hawk perched on her arm. Still, she knew her duty and led him to the large room that was reserved for guests of rank at the château. She stepped back and allowed herself a furtive glance at him.

He was looking at the row of wooden baths that were curtained and supplied with shelves so that guests, if so inclined, could eat while they bathed. "De Reuilles has quite a sense for beauty and comfort."

"What?"

He took a knife and carved wooden figure out of loose pockets sewn onto his mantle, placed both on the small table at the side of his bed. He turned to her again. "Your father placed the baths along the south wall opposite the windows, so only soft, even light will fall upon them." Flecks of gold shimmered in his blue eyes. Such eyes should be dancing with life, not shuttered.

She backed away and motioned to a servant who was cleaning the armor of a visiting knight. "You can stop that for now." She forced a crisp edge to her voice. "Prepare the heated water for my cousin's bath." The servant bowed his head and turned on his heel, running toward the kitchens for heated water.

Henri dropped his pack on his bed and unfastened his sword. His tunic and breeches would soon follow. She curtsied and nearly ran out the door, not stopping until she reached her own chamber on the other side of the palais.

ONCE MARÍANA had seen to it that Isolde was secured to her perch and fed, she tore her hair out of the restraining braids and made ready for her own bath, which Alys had just poured. It was still steaming. In the northern baronies the châtelaine often bathed honored guests. Did Henri expect her to bathe him? If her father chose a northern baron for her would she be expected to bathe visiting knights?

"You'll want to get downstairs soon to help Johanna." Alys stood at the door. "She is in a state this morning. Ysabel has taken to her bed again."

"Wonderful," Maríana hissed as she lowered her naked body into the hot water filling the carved wooden bath. She opened a linen pouch and sprinkled crumbled mint and lavender into the water. Then she grabbed the soap and lathered her hair and body vigorously.

What would Henri think of her? Her face burned with shame as she remembered the picture she must have presented to him, her hair all in tangles, her gown soiled, Isolde stupidly perched on her arm. If she were châtelaine she would be bathing Henri now, not herself, her hands would be rubbing his strong arms... .

Ah, well. He was her cousin, after all. Family. And ill-mannered at that. She took the pitcher and poured water over her head, rinsing the soap out of her hair, her eyes. What was Henri de Bauçais to her, anyway? What could he be to her?

But she dressed carefully in a dark green gown that gave her skin the hue of pearls, made her eyes take on the color of emeralds, and she brushed her auburn hair so it flowed freely down her back. Johanna entered the chamber while Maríana was still smoothing her hair back over her shoulders.

"A relation from the north, the Baron of Bauçais, has just arrived. I believe you met him downstairs. The dinner this evening will be in his honor." Johanna lifted a brush and motioned for Maríana to come closer.

"Ysabel is ill again and has taken to her bed. I need you to help with the preparations tonight."

"Are you all right, Grandmother?" Maríana asked, taking Johanna's hands and looking into her face. Johanna was pale and her hands felt clammy. "Don't worry, I can manage the feast. Why don't you go and rest?"

Johanna smiled and patted Maríana on the cheek. "I believe I will. But I will be at the feast. He is my nephew, after all."

YSABEL WAS in her chamber stretched out beneath the sheets of her bed, clutching the mannikin. The old woman had been right, the damn thing whispered to her, telling her horrible things — that she wanted to mate with her brothers, that she would never have the love of Louis-Philippe, that she would be dragged from the palais! She found it so difficult to ignore the insidious whispers that she spent most of her time alone in her chamber so she could argue with it where no one could see or hear.

Even worse than the whispering and the malaise that had struck her when she created the mannikin was the awful wiggling sensation against her abdomen. The wretched thing actually moved! She often had to take it out and spank it to make it keep still. Once she had hit it a few times it would cease to move, but it would not be silent. She had just slapped it when she heard a tapping at her door. Slipping the mannikin back into its pouch, she let her voice tremble. "Come in." If she sounded ill enough, whoever it was would leave her in peace. It was difficult to speak to anyone with the mannikin cackling in her ear.

Johanna entered the chamber and frowned. Striding over to the window, she pulled aside the heavy tapestry that covered it, allowing a flood of soft gray light to fill the room. Ysabel covered her eyes and cringed away from the light. Johanna walked over to the bed and felt Ysabel's forehead, her cheeks.

"Ysabel," she sighed. "I wish you would allow Jacques to come and have a look at you."

Ysabel nearly jumped as she heard the mannikin laughing. "No Madame," she said. "It is just my bleeding time. I have always been this way."

Johanna nodded, then drew her finger across the table next to the bed and frowned again at the dirt on her finger. "Well, I hate to see you miss the feast tonight."

Ysabel glanced up at her. "A feast? Who is it for?" Someone important?

Johanna smiled and sat on the bed beside Ysabel. "My nephew Henri de Bauçais has arrived."

Ysabel leaned forward and choked. Mary and all the saints! Henri!

Johanna's eyes widened. "My dear, what is wrong?" She reached for Ysabel's hand.

Ysabel waved her away. "It is nothing, really." She managed a weak smile. "I will be fine." Now she paused, calculating what she needed to do. "I think I can make it down to breakfast tomorrow."

Johanna patted Ysabel's arm and said, "Yes, do see if you can come down tomorrow. Henri will be here for quite a while."

AFTER JOHANNA had left and closed the door, Ysabel tore the mannikin out of the pouch and threw it against the wall. "I don't care what the old woman said!" she yelled at it. "I will not have you next to me any longer." Surely seven months was long enough! "I will have you baptized tonight." She got out of her bed and riffled through her gowns for a dark color that would help disguise her during her trip to the priest over in Reuilles-la-ville.

As she bound her hair into a kerchief, she thought of her first love, Henri de Bauçais. She had been a girl then, barely out of the nursery, and he had been even younger. Her mother and his were good friends, and they often visited each other, bringing their children. Henri was a beautiful, happy, charming boy — all the girls loved him. He had composed a song for her that she still treasured.

She stopped binding her hair as she thought of him. His body was glorious, all smooth brown skin and firm muscle. Her first experience of love had been on the ramparts of her father's castle, with Henri. They had been playing a tag-and-chase game, and he had caught her, then kissed her desperately until she had felt as if she were on fire. She had allowed him to push aside her skirts and take her right there on the stairs. Luckily, no one came by.

Of course, later, his mother had caught them; she was always following him around, that old cow! Henri had been sent off to an abbey and Ysabel, well, her mother had seen to it that she was watched. She shrugged. It had not taken long for her to find a way around her mother's vigilant eye. Henri's passion had awakened a need in her that could not be denied.

Ysabel snorted when she heard the mannikin speaking to her, telling her that there had been no man in her bed for the past seven months. "Tell me something that I do not know!" she taunted it. Her disguise complete, she went to the mannikin and pushed it into the pouch once more.

"It is too soon!" it shrieked, but she mashed it down inside.

"No one will keep me from my Henri," she told it. "Not even you." She slipped out the door and descended the steep kitchen stairs to the back door.

MARÍANA was in the kitchen again, watching Geneviéve move from hearth to cooling table, to oven and back again. Her aunt poked at the roasting pheasant and ladled butter over partridge and grouse, while Maríana stirred lake eels in saffron sauce. Lionel set bowls of almond cream on the long oak table, next to plates of custard lombarde and a marrow and plum tart. At the table's end, a large platter held the figure of a young man, sculpted from a thick wine jelly. Lionel caught Maríana's eye and beckoned to her, pointing at the wine jelly figure.

"This one is spring, eh?" he laughed, placing tiny buds of early lilac where the hair should be. "Shall we make him the green man?" He winked when Maríana glanced around and then held her finger to her lips. "Shall we give him a lover's prominence?"

"Quiet, now!" she scolded. "That is a heathen practice." Her words were stern, but she let her eyes twinkle.

"Ah, you will give me no pleasure in my work!" he sighed. "But what shall I do with him, then?" He frowned at the platter. "He needs something more."

Maríana looked down at the figure. "No lilacs," she finally said, "dark hair. And a harp shaped like a dragon." Why not? That way she could show everyone Richard was only a friend, nothing more. He would be married soon. Geneviéve told Maríana she had heard he was in Bourdeilles even now. Her hand hovered over the figure's face.

Lionel drew in his breath sharply, but all he said was, "De la Guerche." He frowned at the figure, then shrugged and started molding the jelly. Maríana stood watching until Lionel had made the hair from dark shavings of willow bark and was carving the straight nose, the wide and gentle mouth. She averted her eyes and moved away, to where Geneviéve stood with a ladle and a knife.

"Maríana," Geneviéve said. "Go up to the hall and tell them we will have games tonight."

"Which games?"

Geneviéve turned from the steaming kettle of leeks in ale and wiped her forehead with the back of her hand. "Ragman's roll, dice, and maybe hot cockles, maybe not." She reset the lid on the kettle. "My brother cannot make up his mind about that game." Another lid was lifted and set aside. Clouds of steam rose from serat, garlic boiled in buttermilk. "Oh, and watch the hearth up there. We are roasting two boars." She leaned forward to taste the serat. "Make sure they do not burn them."

"Very well." Maríana shook her head as she climbed the narrow staircase to the hall. Hot cockles was a game where men and women were blindfolded, then struck lightly by participants. The blindfolded players were asked to tell who had struck them by the touch. It was a silly game, really. Why would her father dislike it? At the top of the stairs, she held her breath. Henri might be there now. As she moved across smooth stone and meadow rushes to the hearth, she looked across the hall.

Her heart skipped. He was there.

HENRI SAT next to Johanna on the seat of honor, a raised dais that was cushioned and canopied. He wore a wine-colored tunic, trimmed with dark green, and red-brown breeches. Maríana let her breath out in a long sigh. Henri was beautiful, with his high, broad cheekbones, dark brows and golden brown hair. She was not the only one who thought so. Even she could see the quick glances and even bold stares women in the hall aimed toward Henri. The golden light from torches and hearth warmed his skin, but the warmth did not touch the ice blue of his eyes as he regarded Johanna, who leaned toward him in earnest discussion.

Louis-Philippe sat on his other side, rubbing his chin and regarding Henri. Her father made a brief gesture. Henri's mouth tightened and his eyes flared. Then the moment passed and Henri leaned forward toward Louis-Philippe. Her father laughed and turned to Johanna. But Henri sat back in his seat, his gaze searching the hall.

Maríana came to stand by the hearth after she had delivered Geneviéve's message about the evening's games to Guillaume. She watched Henri as he looked at people in the hall, occasionally subjecting one or two to a silent appraisal. Soon he would see her.

She lowered her eyes and watched him through her lashes. Surely his gaze would move on and continue around the hall, only brushing her lightly. Even the thought of the briefest of glances from those cold blue eyes started her heart pounding uncomfortably. But he did not look away. Should she acknowledge him? She could feel her face grow hot and quickly glanced up. Blast the man! His eyes were still upon her. She would not be stared at. She boldly met his gaze.

His eyes glowed, not shuttered, not cold. Was it the firelight? His stare was no longer coolly appraising, masking his inner thoughts. A deep hunger lived there in his face, but for what? She thought she saw shadows, despair. She struggled to turn away. Then Henri seemed to regain control and veiled his expression.

A touch on her arm summoned her.

Geneviéve stood beside her, beaming. "Why don't you retire to your chamber and change before the feast begins." She leaned forward and wiped a smudge off Maríana's cheek. As Geneviéve rubbed the smudge, she whispered, "He is no blood relation, you know." She looked up over Maríana's shoulder, nodded and gave a broad smile. "You can turn, now, my dear," she said. "He is talking to Johanna again."

"But he is my cousin." Maríana looked back to see Henri leaning toward her grandmother. He was showing Johanna something small, a carved figure, in his hands. A warm ache spiraled from her belly down her thighs. His hands. What would they feel like against her skin? She drew in her breath. What was she thinking?

"He is your grandmother's nephew through marriage only." Geneviéve dimpled and took Maríana by the shoulders, leading her to the staircase. "Though you would need special permission from the bishop." A shadow crossed her plump features, then her face cleared and she shrugged. "Why not wear your gray sendal silk," she whispered.

THE FANFARE for the first dishes greeted Maríana as she took her place at the family table. Johanna and Louis-Philippe were already seated opposite her, with an empty space between them. Geneviéve was at her right, Guillaume on her left. Maríana glanced at the head of the table. "Henri is not here?" she murmured to Geneviéve, but her aunt nodded at the central staircase, where Henri now descended to the great hall. Not as tall as Richard, but well-made... .

She wrenched her eyes away from Henri and stared at her trencher. So he was no blood relation. What of it? She kept her head bent. He must have arrived to take his seat. She glanced up. The head of the table was still empty. Where was he? She turned her head and looked into his face, the finely chiseled bones, the wary eyes. He had seated himself directly opposite her, waving his hand at Johanna when she indicated the seat of honor. But his eyes were upon Maríana.

Blast the man! How could she eat with him seated only an arm's length away? Why didn't he sit at the head of the table? She focused on her lap. Her fingers toyed with her trencher. They were serving the partridge, the pheasant. Guillaume offered her a slice from the pheasant's breast. She murmured her thanks, but kept her eyes downcast. Henri's hands rested on the table across from her. She could barely breathe. The sweet, moist flesh of the pheasant sat like ashes on her tongue.

Henri dipped crisp slices of roast game birds and chunks of hearty boar into bowls of crushed rosemary and fennel. The surrounding company joined the pipes in snatches of song. Laughter rang around her, but she sat quietly with downcast eyes. Her breath caught in her throat whenever she happened to see Henri's strong hands upon the table. How would she survive this dinner?

Henri never addressed her throughout the meal, never said a word to her. But her ears ached with the melodious, low rumble of his voice. He made short, polite comments to Johanna. He remarked on the beauty of the silver table fount spouting two kinds of wine, the one light and delicate, and the other deeply colored and sweetly heavy. He joked with Louis-Philippe. She listened, heart hammering in her chest. Would this meal never be over?

Then Jeanne was tapping her on the shoulder, handing her a fine bowl filled with warm, fragrant water sprinkled with dried rose-petals and crumbled lavender. "But I already have mine here," Maríana said, her fingers touching the small bowl on her left.

"No," Jeanne whispered. "This is for the Baron of Bauçais."

"Grandmother is châtelaine when Ysabel is not well." Maríana pushed the bowl away. "You have the wrong person. She should perform the washing ceremony." Tradition. At the end of a feast the honored guest would be presented with the finest bowl of rosewater to thoroughly wash his hands in full ceremony.

Johanna nodded to her. "Would you, my dear?" Her eyes were rheumy and the hand she held out to Maríana shook. "I am afraid I would drop it."

Maríana took the bowl. She could do this. If she did not look into Henri's eyes, she could do this. A murmur rippled out from the family table, spreading across the hall as she made her way slowly to where Henri sat. People grew silent; the music stopped.

What was happening to her? She had loved Richard for so many years, had never been afraid to look into Richard's eyes. Think of Richard, that is what she must do. Conjure him. See Richard's lips curving into a smile, the scar at the corner of his mouth making a silvery dimple. Feel Richard's eyes, the color of burnished leaves of autumn, reaching into her.

Finally there. She could see Henri's feet. He must have stood. Her eyes traveled up his form, the red-brown breeches, the claret and forest tunic. She could do this.

She offered Henri the vessel with a flowing motion that evoked a murmur of appreciation and even applause. Good. She had not failed. She could feel people staring. Were they sighing over the image of a chaste young lady, her maiden's tresses flowing smoothly down her back, eyes properly downcast, offering the gently steaming vessel to the square, powerful hands of the knight standing before her?

She wondered what the guests who sighed so sentimentally at the tranquil, innocent picture before them would think if they knew of the wild racing of her pulse, the trembling of her knees and the fluttering in her loins as she knelt before Henri, vessel in her upraised hands, head bowed. Henri's hand chanced to brush her arm as she lowered the vessel after he finished. Startled, she raised her head and looked squarely into his clear blue eyes, eyes that widened as they met hers. The gold flecks swimming in blue glowed and the pulse at his throat quickened as he took her arm, helping her to stand.

At that moment, the crowd was diverted by the commencement of the games. Dicing groups formed as tables were cleared of food, and wagers flew thick in the air.

The moment had passed, but she was strengthened by it. Henri reached for the cloth proffered to him by a waiting squire. His eyes did not leave her, remaining upon her as she returned the vessel to Jeanne, who offered it to other guests at their table. Servants cleared the plates away for ragman's roll and a minstrel scattered the curled slips of parchment across the table. Soon lots would be drawn for selection of the first verses.

"What is this game?" He was still beside her. His voice sounded in a low growl by her ear.

"The seneschal and minstrels write verses on these strips." She pointed at the fluttering bits of parchment. "Whoever draws one must act it out."

"They all can read?" A line formed between his brows. She fought to keep from reaching up to smooth it away.

"At this table, we all do." She raised her hand and gestured toward the seven other tables that filled the hall. "At the other tables, as you can see, games of chance are played."

She walked back to her seat. Henri was sitting across from her again, his fingers toying with one of the parchment slips.

"Will you play?"

A shadow passed across his face. He had decided something, she was sure of it. But all he said was, "No." He looked away. "I will watch."

The first verses were dull, she barely paid attention. Henri sat with his arms folded, listening, staring at the table where the verses rested. Now that he was not watching her, she could look at him, at the curve of his cheek, the glint of blue eyes beneath his thick brown lashes. Her throat tightened. Was this the man from her St. Agnes dream?

Someone shook her, jostling her shoulder. "What?"

"Your turn, Maríana." Geneviéve reached out to stir the remaining slips. "You must choose, now."

Maríana reached out to grab the first slip she could reach, but Henri's foot touched hers at the same moment and her hand jumped, flicking the parchment away.

"Ah, well," Geneviéve said. "You can choose another."

Henri leaned down, reaching under the table. "No," he said. "Here it is." The parchment was tightly curled. She extended her hand and jumped again when their fingers touched. This could not continue. She drew in her breath and pulled the slip open.

For a moment she frowned, the letters that sprawled across the parchment made no sense. "Lady Maríana," it said, "Would you meet me at the door of the chapel after the eleventh hour. Your devoted cousin, Henri." She choked.

"My dear!" Geneviéve pounded her back till her teeth clattered.

She pushed her aunt's hand away, cleared her throat and recited, "For indeed there is no more subtle passion under heaven than that of a squire for his first beard." It was an adulteration of a love song, but what could she do? She folded the slip Henri had handed to her and tucked it into the open seam of her surcoat. Johanna clapped her hands and sent Jeanne to borrow an ermine tippet from Lady Béarn so she could act out her verse.

She hooked the fur over her ears, lifted a clean plate that had been left behind when the table was cleared, and made a show of masculine preening. People howled until the next verse was drawn.

She returned the ermine to Lady Béarn and sat with the rest of them, smiling and laughing at the appropriate moments, but her thoughts were on the small slip of paper. It was less a request than it was a command.

He had replaced the slip she had dropped with his own message. Why the secrecy? She turned the thought over and over in her mind, wondering if she should indeed go to meet him, when she chanced to meet his eyes across the table. He had been sitting there regarding her silently, and, as she looked up at him, his gold and blue eyes captured and held hers. And he smiled.

She was lost. The smile transformed his face, softened the tired lines and the iron control of his jaw. The gold in his icy blue eyes glowed.

There was no doubt. Henri de Bauçais was the man in her St. Agnes's eve dream. There was also no doubt that she would make her way through the sleeping palais to the door of the great hall. She would evade the night watch, travel to the chapel to meet him. What else could she do?

THE ELEVENTH hour. She gathered her mantle around her head and looked out into the inner bailey. The heavens had opened that evening in the soaking downpour known as the siri miri. Good. The night watch would be inside the gate house, out of the rain. She moved from shadow to shadow, past the gate house, and through the inner gates to the chapel. Shaking the rain from her mantle, she shifted from foot to foot in the recessed doorway of the church. Where was he? From out of the pouring rain, she saw him stride across the cobbled ground to the church doorway. He had not hurried. He was drenched.

She handed him her outer mantle. He smiled wryly and ran it over his face and hair, then folded it with care. She waited in silence. He stood there before her, silent also. The moment lengthened. He had asked her to meet him here. It was for him to speak. Rain made a steady whisper on the cobbles. Dampness rose from the soaked mantle across her arm.

He broke the silence. "My lady, I apologize for the unconventional meeting. I needed to speak with you about your family, but I felt it would be impolite to do so in front of your father and grandmother, so I arranged our meeting here."

She watched his face. "My father and grandmother are my family. What do you have to say that cannot be said in front of them?"

"It is your other family I am speaking of, Jakintza," he said, his voice stumbling on the Basque name.

She froze. "Go on." Had he noticed her stillness?

"I have been sent to find a cousin of yours who lives in Reuilles-la-ville, an Antoine Jakintza."

Her breath caught in the back of her throat and she feared he had noticed. Stick with the truth. "I do not know him." Antoine had never been at the house when she went to see Iranzu and Leila. She lowered her eyes and controlled her expression as the image of her raven-haired sister leaped into her mind. "I doubt that I could help you."

He stood in silence for a while, regarding her. "Perhaps not." He offered his arm. "I will escort you back." He smiled. The gold in his eyes caught and held her again. "I promise to run this time."

She took his arm and they ran back to the palais, Henri barking out an answer to the watchman who challenged them. When they reached the door, however, they were both soaked and laughing. Henri walked her to her chamber door and, bowing deeply and gracefully, he took his leave. She shut the door and leaned up against it, her knees shaking. Why Antoine? What did Henri de Bauçais want?

Chapter 13

HENRI CURSED himself as he made his way back to his chamber. What could he have been thinking of, jeopardizing his mission by asking Maríana about Antoine right from the start? He should have gathered information before he approached her. Now she was alerted to his purpose here at the château. He pushed away the memory of her standing there gracefully like the goddess Diana with her braided auburn hair, green eyes fringed with black lashes and translucent skin glowing. Ridiculous! He was no longer a boy. He was immune to such things.

Someone laid a hand on his arm.

He fell back, reached for his sword, his fingers grasping air. No sword. Why should he wear it in the château of his aunt? Who was this?

Then the figure moved back and dropped the cloak covering its face. "Ysabel? Is it you?" It could not be. Surely she was in Gréves, or Blois. Wasn't there a rich merchant in Paris who had courted her? What was she doing here in Navarre?

"Yes, Henri. I heard you were here. But let me look at you." She pulled him closer to the torch placed in the wall sconce. "Every bit the handsome knight now." Her fingers toyed with a bag she held close to her body. "You have met my husband, Louis-Philippe?"

He stared at her. Except for a few lines at the corners of her eyes, and dark smudges beneath them, she had not changed a bit since they had been lovers ten years before. They had both been children then; he had just returned from his time as squire to des Arcis, and Ysabel was always seeking freedom from the restraints of the lady's bower. At the time he had been only too happy to aid her escape... and to accept his reward.

Of course, the result was his banishment to the abbey. His mouth tightened as he remembered the punishments the Abbot had inflicted upon him and he stepped back.

"So," he said. "You are Baroness de Reuilles now."

"I am." She turned away. "Welcome to Reuilles-le-château."

He watched her move down the hall. "Welcome indeed."

IRANZU LOOKED up when the door to the tiny stone house opened. Leila jumped, her latest drawings of Cecile's children dropping from her lap. Then a grin spread across her mobile features and she launched herself at the tall figure in the doorway. Iranzu stood and regarded Antoine as the younger man slowly entered his own home.

Antoine caught Leila and ruffled her hair, saying, "My beautiful cousin!" But his voice was muted and there were lines on Antoine's face that were not there before he went away. He had lost weight. His clothing hung around his frame.

"Cecile and I... and the little ones. We need to go to the mountain right away." He paused, rubbing hollow, reddened eyes. "I do not remember the way."

Iranzu held out his arms. Antoine stood back, shaking his head. Then tears streamed down his face. He hung his head and sobbed aloud. Iranzu nodded to Leila, and she guided Antoine to the table where he sat facing them, his chest heaving with even more tears that needed to be shed.

"I went for the money. Cecile and I, we found it hard to live, to feed our children in this place. But me, I am not from the mountain Jakintzas, you see; I am from here. My family is here. I wanted to stay, so when Bauçais' knights came and asked for soldiers I joined them." He gulped and blew his nose on the cloth Leila had brought him. "The money would have paid for the bakery I wanted to start. We would have been fine then." He murmured his gratitude and drained the cup of wine Leila had given him, then put his head in his hands and shuddered.

"They burned all of them," he finally whispered through his hands. "And me, I helped to put them there." He pulled his hands away from his face. "I must take Cecile and my family to the mountain," he repeated dully.

Iranzu reached over and gently patted Antoine's hand. "We will get someone to take you there." Had Antoine heard him? The younger man's eyes were empty.

"We must leave now." Antoine's voice was a soft whisper, barely leaving his lips.

"Where is Pierre?" Iranzu asked. A muscle below Antoine's left eye started twitching.

"Pierre was here in Reuilles-la-ville. He came back with me, but he did not want to wait for Cecile and the little ones. We came the long way back because the French — they were following us. Pierre said he already knows the way to the mountain so he kept going." Antoine looked down at his hands. "I cannot stay here." His face grew rigid.

"We will find someone to take you there," Iranzu repeated, his calm and serenity filling the space surrounding Antoine. The knotted muscles around Antoine's mouth started to relax and he slumped over the table, head in hands. Iranzu turned to Leila. "Get Cecile and the children and gather enough provisions to get them to the mountain." What terrible thing had happened to Antoine?

Leila looked from one to the other, clearly wanting to stay and hear what Antoine had to say. Iranzu pointed at the door. Sighing, she rose and trudged out.

"Antoine." Iranzu took the younger man's hands from his face and held them firmly in his own. "What happened?"

Antoine raised his face. "At Montsegur. They surrendered, the Cathars. Bauçais and des Arcis, the Bishop — they sent more than two hundred people to the flames." His teeth started to chatter. "I had to put them in the cage they made to burn them. I helped make this cage, you see. When they started the fire, Pierre and I, we ran. We left everything we had in our tents behind." He dropped his face, his haunted eyes staring at the table. "What else could I do?"

Iranzu sighed, patting the younger man's shoulder. "Do not worry. I know someone who will take you and your family to the mountain. There you will heal. It is a terrible thing, what you have seen." The younger man still would not look up.

"It is a terrible thing that I have done."

"What choice did you have?" Iranzu settled back into his chair.

"There is always a choice," Antoine finally said, then he pulled a silk package out of his mantle. "This is why I am here." He unwound the silk to reveal a stone cup.

There seemed to be a stone set inside it. Not a drinking cup, surely. How could anyone drink from it with the stone wedged inside? Now Antoine held the cup between his hands and closed his eyes, drawing a deep, shuddering breath. His brow cleared; his jaw set firmly. He opened his eyes and regarded Iranzu with clarity and peace. Then he offered the cup to Iranzu.

Iranzu gave a long, low whistle. His hands burned with the throbbing force radiating from the cup. He turned it around and around, trying to shake out the stone set inside, but it did not move. Then he set it aside and blew on his fingers. "Do you know what this is?"

Anguish twisted the young man's face. "No," he replied. "A Cathar gave it to me for our people. I thought I would just give it to you when I got here. You are the elder of our family, so you should have it, eh? But... I need it." Tears welled up in his eyes again. "It helps me forget the screams, the smell." He bowed his head. "It helps me remember a brave lady."

Iranzu regarded Antoine for a moment, then wound the silk back around the cup. "Here, my friend," he said, holding it out to Antoine. "I want you to take this back to the mountain with you." Antoine looked up in surprise. "You must use it whenever the pain is too great for you to bear. I want you to keep it for my granddaughter. Would you do that for me?"

Antoine took the package and carefully nestled it in the sling he had fashioned for it inside his mantle. "You want me to keep it for Leila?"

No, not for Leila. Iranzu took Antoine's arms with his hands and looked directly into his eyes, deep down into his soul. "You are not a bad man, Antoine. You are right that there is always a choice, but many times we cannot see the larger purpose." He paused, then smiled. "I want you to keep it for the Lady of the Cave, the Keeper of the Stone. She will be coming to the mountain someday. When she does, you will no longer need this." He squeezed Antoine's arms and turned to Leila, who was followed by a frightened Cecile and two drowsy children.

Iranzu smiled at all of them. He patted Cecile's round belly. "This little one will be born on the mountain," he said. "Gilbert will take all of you home." He rose, pulling on his mantle. "Come, we will get him now."

JOHANNA'S chamber had the largest window. The heavy tapestry covering the window frame and the oiled paper that sealed it in winter were gone, now that spring had arrived. Streams of sunlight cascaded through the open window and framed her bed. Maríana hovered in the doorway. Johanna had not come down to the hall to break her fast that morning. Jeanne had said Johanna seemed better, but Maríana climbed the stairs to Johanna's chamber to see for herself. Her grandmother was still pale, though the bruised circles under her eyes from last night had disappeared. Maríana turned to go, but Johanna raised her arms and gestured. "Come in, child."

"Grandmother." She smoothed the blankets, placed the back of her hand against Johanna's cheek. "You are better?"

Johanna shrugged, pulling Maríana's hands down to her lap. "As well as anyone my age," she said. "Did Ysabel come down this morning?"

"Yes." Maríana dropped her eyes, her fingers twisting the blankets. When she had descended to the great hall that morning she saw that Ysabel had taken the seat next to Henri. The entire meal, her stepmother had bantered with Henri. Louis-Philippe sat on Henri's other side, stolidly chewing his bread, drinking his ale, murmuring to his seneschal, Guillaume. Her father did not seem to notice when Ysabel leaned over to whisper in Henri's ear, did not seem to mind that Ysabel's hand was upon Henri's arm throughout the meal. "Who is this Henri de Bauçais? He says he is your nephew." Maybe Johanna would know why Henri was looking for Antoine.

Johanna stopped Maríana's twisting fingers by taking hold of her hands. "Why do you wish to know about him?"

"He is flirting with Ysabel."

Johanna leaned back. "So." She smiled. "And this disturbed you?"

"What do you mean?" Was she that transparent?

Johanna shook her head. "I was concerned," she started, "after de la Guerche left, well," she paused when Maríana turned away. "But you were asking me about Henri."

Maríana kept her face turned away. It was bad enough that Genevíéve had noticed her interest in Henri. Yet she needed to know why the Baron of Bauçais had come to Reuilles-le-château, why he was looking for Antoine. She glanced back. Johanna sat with arms crossed, eyes distant. Somewhere a door shut with a muted bang and the rise and fall of voices from the bailey below drifted through the window.

"We are related through his mother, my youngest stepsister. She was just a baby when I gave birth to Genevíéve," Johanna said. "A very pious girl, really. Wanted to enter a convent." She shook her head. "Her eldest died and Henri's father also died recently, I think..." The clatter of hooves on the stones of the inner bailey drowned the rest of her words. Maríana leaned toward her. "Henri is now Baron of Bauçais. He was a bit of a rascal when he was young, but seemed to straighten out after a few years at Fornault Abbey," Johanna finished.

Maríana swallowed. Henri in an abbey? Why did that frighten her? "Well. Thank you, Grandmother." Abbeys were for praying. And for books and learning. "Where is Jacques?" She could ask Ibrahim what to do.

"Louis-Philippe sent him to Roncesvalles last week. He should be back soon. But where are you going?" Johanna's hands fell away from Maríana's arm when she backed away.

"It is Moon day," Maríana replied. "Time for me to go to Reuilles-la-ville." And to warn Iranzu.

Johanna frowned, but waved her hand. "Very well, go find Guillaume. He will take you." When Maríana reached the door, her grandmother added, "And back before dark!"

Maríana turned so Johanna would not see her eyes. The past year she had gone alone to the healing circle. The people of Reuilles-la-ville would do nothing to hurt her, but it would grieve Johanna to know that she went alone to the town. She looked back over her shoulder and smiled at her grandmother so Johanna would not worry, then slipped out of the room.

HENRI EMERGED from the palais with a blinding headache. He had spent the two hours since the morning meal trying to escape Ysabel. Each time he gave her a gentle hint that he had other tasks to accomplish, she reminded him of their time together when they were young and an image of her naked body heaving below him flashed before his eyes, paralyzing him. Then she hauled him off to yet another section of the palais to show him what Louis-Philippe had added to his home. De Reuilles didn't help matters. He disappeared soon after the meal, bowing and saying that Henri was "in capable hands" with his wife.

Henri found that even though he disliked the type of woman Ysabel had become, his body still reacted to her. She knew it, too, which made matters worse. The gown she wore clung to her slender body and the rose scent she had always favored both aroused him and set his teeth on edge.

He was no longer a boy to be lured by such tricks. What was wrong with him? Finally, at the top of the central staircase, he gave a curt bow and told Ysabel that he must take his leave. He hurried down the stairs and strode out into the bailey, her cries for him to return ringing in his ears.

When he reached the stables, he looked back at the palais. Ysabel had not followed him out yet. He entered the stables and asked some boys who were rubbing down an Arabian gray to find his squire.

Had his squire been able to find Antoine Jakintza? Henri often used his squire Robert to obtain information. The boy had a sweet, open face and a fine memory. People liked to talk to Robert. Henri stretched his arms and rubbed the back of his neck. The fresh air muffled the pain constricting his head. When Robert approached him, Henri was almost smiling.

DAMN! HENRI pounded the stone wall that enclosed the narrow, twisting alleyway, then leaned up against it and put his chin in his hand. How was he going to find his way out of this bloody town, let alone find Antoine Jakintza? "Town!" he scoffed. "If this is a town then Paris is a province!"

There did not seem to be any coherent plan to Reuilles-la-ville. Two-room dwellings stood between great stone houses that rose the height of several men. Roads spiraled around and ended in blank walls. The cathedral stood out at the edge of the town, not in the center. Not that he could find the center. He had spent the entire morning asking the citizens in the market, in the alleys, in the church: where could the Rue des Anciennes be found, how could he get there, where could he find Antoine Jakintza? All he got for his trouble was a load of gibberish in a language he had never heard before and to top it off, he had just lost himself again for the ninth time in the twisting maze of cobbled streets that ambled across the town. Worse still, his headache had returned.

At least he had found a merchant who was selling bread and meat. It had cost him the small amount of gold he had brought for bribes, but the aroma of roasted meat set his stomach into a noticeable gurgle. Perhaps the food would sustain him through another twelve streets and alleys. Surely he should soon come upon some place where he could sit and eat.

He stomped out of the alley and rounded yet another corner, then stopped in surprise. An open courtyard, fashioned in the Moorish style with a number of houses opening onto it and colorful banners hanging from each doorway, lay before him. Against the wall by one of the doors, people of all shapes and sizes were gathered, from rotund merchants' wives dressed in rich colors to dirty street urchins.

Maríana sat in their midst, engrossed in bandaging the leg of a painfully thin woman whose body was barely covered by threadbare rags. Maríana smiled, giving the woman a small pouch she had pulled out of a dark gray sack.

"You will need to simmer these for at least an hour in just a little water so that it boils down into a paste." She pointed to the woman's bandaged leg. "Let the paste cool and then smear it all over the sore." Patting the woman's arm, she said, "It should be gone in a few days."

The woman shyly took the pouch and kissed Maríana's hands. Maríana laughed and said something to the woman in the incomprehensible language the people kept jabbering in the street. Then another took the woman's place.

What was this? It looked like some of the people gathered there had come to watch, while others formed a loosely configured line to obtain help from the girl.

Could he use this? Maríana knew something, he was sure of this. She had paled when he mentioned Antoine. He counted how many were left in the line. Perhaps she did not know where Antoine could be found. He pulled his hood around his face and covered the white cross of the crusades that was emblazoned upon his red tunic. But she may know someone who would know. He took his place at the end of the line.

MARÍANA pushed a tendril of hair back from her forehead and concentrated on the young boy before her. His mother had patiently waited while others had been seen, but the boy's ailment was much more severe than that of the others who had lined up before him. Although Maríana told them all each time she came that she needed to see the people who were really sick first, they still formed a line according to social position, with the wealthier at the front and the poor at the back. This never happened when Leila was there. Her half sister always marched up and down the line, glaring at the wealthy merchants and their fat wives until they dropped back to the end of the line.

Maríana examined the boy's red and swollen hand, then reached deep into her pack for the molds and mosses she used to treat such infections. Leila and Iranzu had decided to stay in Antoine's house today. Her news of Henri de Bauçais's presence and questions had not surprised them. Iranzu had seemed to expect Henri. How could that be? She pulled bread mold out of her pack.

"You must put this in his favorite food," she told the woman, handing her the green mold Ibrahim favored for this type of ailment. "See that he eats all of it." She cleaned the boy's hand using water she had sprinkled with powdered manzanilla and burdock. Then she took two different kinds of mosses, one from oak, the other from stone, and bound them to his hand with a clean bandage. "You must also soak his hand in the hottest water he can stand with this." She handed the woman a packet of crushed burdock. The boy had been silent through the whole examination and treatment. She pulled a small honey cake out of the pack.

The boy's mother thanked her with tears in her eyes and kissed her hand. "Jainkosa," she said over and over, "Jainkosa."

Maríana shook her head and crossed her hands over her heart as Ibrahim had taught her. She ruffled the boy's hair and was rewarded with his wide grin as he left with his mother. Behind the woman and boy stood a man, hooded and cloaked. The last one. She beckoned and he came forward.

His face was hidden by the hood. "What is your ailment, my friend?" she asked, as she had asked all the others.

"I have a headache," the man said, his voice rough and hoarse.

"How long have you had it?" she asked. What had Ibrahim taught her about headaches? They could mean nothing at all or be very bad. If a headache persists and vomiting is present, well... .

The man's voice cut across her musing. "Since this morning." He coughed.

Good, it was not likely to be serious. "Where does the pain start?" she asked, her fingers rummaging the depths of her pack.

He pointed both fingers up to his temples, still hidden by the hood.

She pulled her hands out of her carrying pack. The last of her supply of ground black willow bark and marjoram was in a tiny packet. Not much, but enough for a headache that had only started that morning. "Take this powder mixed in water," she told him. "Your headache should be gone soon." He took the small package. "If it does not, please send for Iranzu or Leila. They would know where to find me or could send word to Jacques."

He took her hand and kissed it. His touch started a trembling that traveled up her arm. Who was he? He raised his head and the hood fell back. Henri's icy stare caught her. She snatched her hand away. "Games, monsieur?"

He threw back his cloak, exposing the white cross on his tunic. The people who had not yet left the courtyard immediately scurried away. "See," he said. "I have frightened them away." A smile softened the tight lines on his face. "I should have stayed hidden."

"They are right to fear French lords dressed in the garment of the crusade against Cathars." Maríana sealed her pack and stood. "Toulouse is not so far away." He flinched, then visibly caught himself. Curious. Why had what she said startled him?

He looked down. "I would like to pay you."

"But no one..." Well, why not? He was a baron. She could give whatever he paid to Iranzu and Leila. "Very well."

"I have no gold with me now, but it is a fine day. Would you do me the honor," he swept his arm in a regal bow, "of joining me for a meal in the meadow by the lake?" He took her hand, brushed aside a tendril of her hair that had wandered onto her cheek. "I got the food from a merchant around the corner." He leaned closer. "I am sure it is quite good."

She averted her eyes and stepped back. "What do you have for this meal?"

He stood regarding her silently, then said: "Fresh bread, sliced roast pig, dried fruit."

She did not speak.

"At least you could instruct me on how much of this to take." He gently shook the packet of marjoram and willow bark.

She looked up. Perhaps she could discern his purpose if she spent time with him. He was her cousin. What could happen? "Well then, let us go."

Chapter 14

YSABEL FUMED. She had taken the mannikin off and had it baptized by a drunken, defrocked priest in a filthy hovel in Reuilles-la-ville. She'd soaked for hours in the tub last night, to rid herself of the vermin she had picked up just from being near the slavering idiot. Now that she did not need to hold the mannikin close to her body and was free to dally if she wanted, she had hoped to spend the entire day with her Henri and what did he do? He ran off to that accursed town! She savagely stabbed the mannikin again and again, delighted to hear its screams of pain. Finally, she tired of the game and wrapped it up, burying it in the depths of her cabinet.

As she dressed for dinner she thought idly of returning to the town and asking the old woman for a love charm. Then she stared at herself in the polished silver mirror. Why do that? If she could make a powerful charm like the mannikin, how hard could it be to make a love charm? She sat in a daze for a moment, then rose from her seat and tore around her chamber, feverishly gathering the materials she thought she would need for a love charm. She would make Henri want her again. After measuring and cutting a piece of red silk from an old gown, she went over to the early-blooming roses she had her servants pick for her every day.

Red, the color of blood. She picked the petals off a deep red rose. These would do. She chose the finest three petals and placed them on the little square of silk. It needed blood, too. She stuck her finger with her sewing needle, wincing a little as she squeezed some of her own blood out onto the rose petals.

It needed some of his blood, too. Blood that binds, blood that binds. And something else. She needed something Henri had given her, something from him. She pulled everything out of her chest, then picked up and discarded several things, an old shoe, a bracelet, a ring.

"Of course!" she exclaimed. "The ring he gave me when we were children — I still have it!" She tore into her jewelry until, with a cry of triumph, she held up the small ring of gold Henri had given her so long ago.

Sitting on the floor with the contents of her room strewn about her, she placed the ring in the center of the square of silk and gloated over her love charm. But it was incomplete. Blood. She needed Henri's blood, too. The old woman said that blood was the most powerful. She looked at her charm again. That old hag had better be right!

HENRI BLINKED his eyes, then turned his head to see the squat stone walls of his cell at Fornault Abbey. How did he get there? The short, cadaverous figure of the Abbot was bending over him, eyes gleaming. Henri tried to rise, struggling against restraints that bound him to his bed. "It is for your own good, Henri." The Abbot tested the strength of the leather straps that held him, and ran his fingers lovingly over the other restraint that had been anchored to Henri's body when he had first arrived. "You must learn to control your passions." The Abbot turned to leave, then stopped at the door. "It is the only way." He left the room.

Henri's jaw ached from clenching his teeth. It wasn't so bad during the day, when his thoughts were his own. When the sun reigned he found it easy to control his reactions, his emotions. When the Abbot sent beautiful young nuns from the convent in to tend to him, he concentrated on numbers, filling his head with figures so that his body did not have a chance to respond. When the Abbot sent in boys to look at the leather restraint attached to his body and he saw their pitying eyes, he nurtured his scorn until he could flay them with a few well-chosen words. He took a curious pleasure in these small victories.

It wasn't that bad during the day, but the nights! He simply could not govern his dreams. Night after night he fought to stay awake. He drove slivers of wood under his nails, he paced the floor, he made himself stand up straight so that he could not sleep. Night after night, he failed. His dreams were filled with women. Women he had known, the young nuns the abbot had sent in, Ysabel... .

He ground his teeth again. Ysabel was the reason he had been sent to Fornault Abbey, although it was not her fault. His mother had flown into a rage when she had found Ysabel and Henri together in his chamber. His father had accepted his mother's decision to send Henri to Fornault Abbey and he had been taken there the very next day.

The minute Henri arrived, the Abbot had him bound and placed the "belt" on him, a leather restraint with small metal spikes facing inside that fitted over his male parts, allowing him to urinate, but stabbing him if he became aroused. Henri removed it the first week — it was difficult, but he managed — and all that got him was an even more painful version of the belt, tighter and more difficult to remove.

Since then, he learned to avoid the pain by concentrating on his studies, on Latin, on numbers — numbers were best to quell his arousal. But he could not control his dreams and now the Abbot had taken away his ability to stay awake by tying him to his bed. Henri tried to bite off the leather straps, but only succeeded in tearing the skin on his wrist. He was defeated. He wouldn't cry, though. No, he wouldn't give them that.

He had heard other young boys who had been taken to the Abbot's rooms, heard them cry out in pain. After they came back to their chambers, they huddled on their beds, weeping in misery, but none ever spoke of what the Abbot had done to them.

"This is a man of God," Henri told himself. "It is for my own good." But when the dreams came and he woke screaming in pain, Henri cursed. He cursed them all — the Abbot, the brothers, the Church, God Himself. He hated and hated, and his rage took on a color, a form all its own.

He imagined horrible things — dismembering the Abbot slowly, bit by bit, so that he remained alive, but crippled. Yet the best, most satisfying image, the picture that would not stop the pain when he awoke from one of his dreams of women and felt the restraint's iron grip, but would make the pain bearable, was of him holding the Abbot's severed penis in his hands, forcing it down the Abbot's throat, choking him.

HENRI CRIED out, jumping up from his bed, his body soaked in sour sweat. He was panting, staring at the billowing curtains that divided his bed from the others in the long room. As he watched, the curtains fluttered again, then settled and hung straight from the rod that held them. Running his hands through his sweat-dampened hair, he made himself sit on the edge of his bed, breathing deeply to still his pounding heart.

A candle still burned on his table. He should move it before the curtains billowed out again with the breeze that had set them moving. The flame would set them alight. He stood and reached for the candle, then stopped. He had not left it burning when he went to sleep.

He placed the heel of his hand against his forehead and pressed between his eyes. A headache. The abbey dream. Just a dream. He stood and poured water from a jug into his basin, soaking a cloth to drape over his aching eyes. The water in the basin trembled. A single drop of red pattered on the surface, then sent pink fingers streaming.

"What?" He lifted his arms and saw a small cut on his wrist that was bleeding. "How the devil did I do that?" he wondered aloud, wrapping a dry cloth around it.

YSABEL FLEW down the passage toward her chamber. She opened the door and slipped inside, sighing in relief.

That was too close. Henri had almost caught her. Muffled, cackling laughter of the mannikin rose from the depths of her cabinet. "Shut up," she said, her voice muted. She had entered Henri's curtained area in the knights' room simply to obtain some of his blood — just a little. All the knights were sleeping. And Henri had not moved. He had remained still when she lit the candle and drew the blanket off his body. He had not moved when she cut him. She held the small vial under the lamp she had left burning in her room. Yes, that should be enough for the charm.

But she had been denied the kind of love she wanted for such a long time that she had not been able to resist running her hands gently over Henri's body, feeling the firmness of his muscles, the expanse of his belly and on down to his loins. He had not moved when she cut him, but the gentle touch of her hands along his glorious body had started a shaking in his limbs. A shaking that her own body answered. Damn! Her hands still shook. She moved with grim purpose to the love charm and poured Henri's blood over the ring and the rose petals. He would be hers tonight.

HIS HEAD was splitting apart, pounding with the blinding pain he had been prone to suffer since leaving the abbey. Perhaps that was why he dreamt of the abbey again. He groaned aloud as the pain intensified, then fumbled in his pouch for the packet of herbs Maríana had given him. A few grains of powder trickled into his hand.

    Not enough. He sat on the edge of his bed, holding his head. Maríana, he must wake her. He could not wait for morning; he needed relief from this now. He threw a robe over his naked body and stumbled out of the curtains surrounding his bed. His body shuddered as he staggered down the passageway to Maríana's chamber.

A THUMPING on the door, followed by soft groans, tore her from her sleep. Maríana pulled a robe over her gown and cautiously opened the door. She saw Henri leaning weakly against the wall, one hand holding his forehead and the other clutched around his middle. A cloth wrapped tightly around his wrist was stained with blood. "Henri!" she cried, then pulled him into the room.

    Wrapping a rag around her hand, she grabbed a flaming ember from her hearth and used it to light her Saracen lamp. Then she led Henri over to the divan against the window and seated him there. He rocked back and forth, retching. Retrieving the night basin at the side of her bed, she got it to him just in time for him to empty his stomach into it. He hung over it, gasping.

    Maríana rubbed the back of his neck firmly and said in the measured, soothing voice she had developed to speak with the people she tried to heal, people who were all in pain of one sort or another, "I want you to stay here on the divan while I get my pack. The basin is still here if you need it. Will you be all right if I leave you?"

    He nodded weakly, so she stood and, wrapping her robe more firmly around her, moved across the room to her store of healing herbs. "Black horehound, meadowsweet, manzanilla," she whispered, drawing out the packets. "Right." She looked over to where Henri huddled miserably on the divan.

    With a snort and grunt, Alys woke and sat up in her small bed, then yelped when she saw Henri, now reclining on the divan. Maríana frowned at Alys and held her finger at her lips. "This knight is very ill. He has come to me for healing. If you wish to help, you can come over and soak some cloths in the water by the bed. If you don't want to help, then stay out of my way." Alys sputtered, but subsided when Maríana glared at her.

"Where is the pain?" Maríana asked him.

"In my head again."

"And it is so bad that it made you sick in your belly as well?" When he nodded, she sat looking at the packets she had selected. Maybe she should send for Ibrahim. It could be something very serious. But she sat gazing at him, at the dark lashes covering his gold and blue eyes, the fine, proud forehead, the high planes of his cheekbones. His body rocked slightly against the pain.

Yes, it could be serious. But she could heal him. What could Ibrahim do that she could not? As she rubbed Henri's neck, she remembered their time at the edge of the lake; his eyes had warmed whenever he looked at her, but were always darting around, scanning the shore. His hand never strayed far from his sword.

"A soldier's reflex," Henri had told her when she asked why his eyes assessed the crowd, why his hand forever hovered over his sword. "It never leaves you." His lips had spread in a smile that did not reach his eyes.

But her father did not cling to his sword when he was in Reuilles-la-ville, and he was a soldier, too. She had asked Henri of his most recent campaign. He had told her, "I served Hughes des Arcis." Then his eyes became opaque. Even she could not penetrate the blanket that covered his thoughts. And he kept his distance from her.

She could do it. Ibrahim did not have to know. She raised her hands, then paused, staring at Henri. It would do no harm, would it? Ibrahim had said she could, if there were no other way. She had already given him the marjoram and willow bark. Drawing a deep breath and putting her hands on either side of Henri's temples, she closed her eyes and did exactly what she had promised Ibrahim she would never do. Henri's pain had dropped his guard. He could not keep her out. She felt her way into Henri's body and climbed into his mind.

And saw the bald head and black robes of a priest bending over Henri. A very young Henri. This priest had yellow teeth that showed when he grimaced. He was stroking Henri's groin, something was attached there. Something that was hurting Henri. What was it? Now young women dressed in the robes of the convent were coming into the room where Henri lay. The priest stepped back as they moved around the boy that Henri had been. Then the priest nodded and the women started to stroke Henri's body. Henri was holding himself rigid, but his eyes were frantic. The priest stood back from them but watched avidly, his eyes gleaming. And Henri screamed... .

She wrenched her hands away. Henri was still in the grip of his pain and did not notice her trembling. She sat still a moment, choking on the image she had received of a young man barely out of boyhood being tortured for his body's own natural responses. Drawing in another deep breath, she looked into him again. There were no yellow-gray flares, no muddied orange that would indicate disease. His body was still sound and healthy. This illness had its origin in his emotions and spirit, but had not damaged his body yet, though if left unchecked, it might.

She clutched the packets of meadowsweet, marjoram, and manzanilla. A mixture would help him, of course, but it would take time and would not stop future headaches from torturing him. He opened pain-glazed eyes. She could take away his pain, but he must free himself of the guilt and rage that shaped it. The healing was there, within his reach, if he were willing to face it. She tore open the packets and mixed the herbs in a cup of boiling water Alys had brought over. He would believe this was what healed him. She stirred the liquid with her little crescent blade, wiping the bitter mixture off when she was done. She had already disobeyed Ibrahim to help this knight. What harm could her touch do? He would think the herbs had stopped his pain. And if her touch guided him to the root of his torment, he would not know it was she who took him there.

"Henri, here," she spoke softly to him. "I need to lift you so that you can drink this." She pointed to the cup. He grimaced.

"At least try a little. You remember the willow bark and marjoram you had this afternoon? That helped you, didn't it?" He nodded weakly. "Well, at least try a little of this. You must help me get you up so you don't choke."

He slowly raised his upper body so she could hold the cup for him, and stoically drained the entire cup of bitter liquid.

She set the cup on the floor and gathered her energy as Ibrahim had taught her, using her breathing and her ability to form pictures and images in her mind to unlock to powers that were always there waiting. Placing her fingers lightly on Henri's temples again, she massaged them gently, so that Alys would not wonder what she was doing. Then she spoke the words of healing under her breath and felt her hands burning, as the energy was accepted into his body. Good. He wanted to be healed.

While she put away her carrying pack, she saw him sinking into a deep, natural sleep. Pulling some large pillows Ibrahim had given her over to the side of the divan, she made a cozy nest for herself close beside him. Alys' eyes grew wide and she started to cluck, but Maríana silenced her with a direct stare.

"He is not well enough to be moved," she said firmly. "I am staying beside him in case he needs something during the night." She smiled at the older woman. "Unless, of course, you would like to sleep here." She pointed to the pillows on the floor. Alys huffed and grumbled, totally scandalized. "Well, at least keep an eye on him while I clean out the basin." Maríana lifted the metal pan soiled by Henri's illness and marched out the door.

A COLD, PALE light pulled Henri up out of sleep. A dream again. Not the abbey dream. He fought to retrieve it, but it had fled. Where was the agony that had sliced through his temples? His headaches always lasted for days, once they had taken hold. He had only hoped for a brief reprieve when he went to the girl. Yet the pain was gone. Even more amazing, he felt wonderful! But where was he? He saw stone walls covered with tapestries, not the curtains that surrounded his bed in the knights' room. Gray light of a mist-filled morning touched his face from a window behind him, and someone was snoring.

Henri looked around the chamber. Alys lay on her pallet, her arms flung wide and mouth hanging open. Well, that explained the snoring. He sat up and froze. Maríana de Reuilles was sound asleep on some patterned cushions on the floor beside him. Seeing her there, her long black lashes fanned out on her creamy, ivory skin, triggered a memory of the dream he just had. In the dream he had been holding her — just simply, innocently holding her. He remembered the delight of exquisite sensations that washed over him in waves as he held her soft body in his arms and lifted the heavy weight of her fragrant hair.

Christ! How long had it been since he had a dream like that? What was he still doing here in her chamber?

He allowed himself another look at Maríana while she slept. Violet shadows smudged the fragile skin underneath her eyes. How late had it been when he came here last night, anyway?

He shook his head, then laughed out loud in delight. How long had it been since he had felt this way? For years, a dull ache behind his eyes had plagued him. He had not minded, as long as the gripping agony of his fierce headaches had not blossomed. What had brought the headaches back?

The abbey dream. Every six months he would dream of Fornault Abbey. Five years of his life had been spent there. Five years with his loins encased in leather and metal spikes.

But it had not all been bad, his time there. After the first two years, he had become accustomed to the restraint, and although he sometimes awoke in pain, he was able to bear it. It was at the abbey that he discovered he had a thirst for knowledge and devoured all the learning that the monks could give him. Eventually, he even made peace with the abbot. Perhaps the abbot was just doing whatever he had to do for Henri's spiritual development, however cruel it had seemed. But once they were on better terms, Henri had often noticed the abbot watching him, and the abbot had started touching Henri more often, brushing up against him, putting his arm across Henri's shoulders.

Then one evening, as he slept, Henri had felt soft fingers upon his chest that moved down his body, stopping at the restraint and circling his waist. He immediately awoke, rubbing his eyes to clear his vision. At first he thought it was a dream, but the feather touch continued down his back, enticing, familiar.

He had shouted and leaped up out of the bed, taking the intruder by the arm and swinging his own arm back to deliver a blow. His arm dropped to his side when he found himself looking into the glittering eyes of the abbot.

"Why?" Henri had breathed into the silence that hung in the room. "Why?"

The abbot had shrugged, spreading his hands and smiling. "To test you, Henri. Simply to test you." He had slipped easily out of Henri's bed and made his way to the door, but not before Henri saw the signs of the abbot's arousal through the fabric of his robe.

After that, Henri had quietly spoken to each and every boy who had been taken to the abbot's chambers and had come back whimpering and distressed. He found that all of them were orphans. They had no one to speak for them, no one to defend them. At first none would admit what had happened in the Abbot's chambers, but as time went on, Henri wore down their resistance with kindness, and they confirmed what he had suspected.

The rage he had felt during his first two years at the abbey threatened to overwhelm him again, but this time he was older, and hoarded his anger in icy depths that his boyhood self could not have imagined. Henri knew how to play their game. He sent a letter directly to the pope describing what the Abbot had done, bypassing the bishop who had given the abbot his post. This bishop was either in league with the abbot or somehow indebted to him. Bishop Durand. The same bishop who had later laid siege to the last stronghold of the Cathars. Montsegur!

Henri shivered and held his breath when Maríana stirred on the pillows next to the couch where he lay. He watched as her brow wrinkled, then smoothed. But his thoughts still ticked through the events that had haunted him for so many years. Before Henri wrote to the pope, he gathered evidence, enough evidence so that when the papal legate arrived to inquire into the matter, the only question the legate had to resolve was what they would do with the abbot. They swept it all aside, of course. It remained purely a church matter. No one thought to recompense the boys for what they had suffered. Why should they concern themselves with orphans? But the abbot was removed from the abbey and the belt of torture was removed from Henri.

Henri had no illusions about why they had allowed him to leave the abbey. His older brother had died, making him the next in line to inherit the Barony of Bauçais. The bishop was careful to make a conciliatory gesture to the future Baron of Bauçais, so Henri would not dig too deeply into Durand's relationship with the abbot. Henri had let it pass. What purpose could his persecution of the abbot serve? The Church protected its own and Henri was no longer a monk, no longer one of them.

Henri had left the abbey after that and spent the next year whoring and drinking his way throughout the Languedoc. He finally came to his senses in a rat-hole of an inn in Toulouse after a week he somehow could never seem to remember. For an entire month he stared at bugs crawling up the wall and felt the emptiness inside of him. Before his time in the abbey, Henri's universe had been orderly. God was in heaven, the kings ruled the earth, and people who lived good, or even just useful lives, were promised reward in heaven, as long as they were good Christians. As he watched the scurrying bugs, he came to the conclusion that everything was simply a senseless game. There was no God; there was only power.

Since then, he found the most satisfaction playing political games with the barons, so he traveled to Paris and offered his services to the French king. While he was there, he received word that his father had died. He was now the Baron of Bauçais. All of this meant little to him. He returned to his home only once, to help his mother retire to the convent at Fontevrault. He refused to speak with her or even see her, sending his men to escort her to the convent. "She is well cared for," he told himself. He left Bauçais in the capable hands of his younger brother Guy, who was only too glad to take over.

"I don't want to be restricted," he told his brother. "Run it any way you choose. I leave it to you." When his brother asked him what he planned to do, he laughed. "I will go wherever the wind blows."

At this time all of the pleasure went out of his life. Several times, he tried to make love, but he found that he could not. He wanted, wanted desperately, yet he could not complete the act. After two humiliating episodes, he gave up even trying. He took scant pleasure in eating and drink had little lure for him anymore. His universe narrowed to developing strategies and schemes to keep whomever he decided to serve in power. And that led him to... .

Henri veered away from thoughts of Montsegur. "Not yet," he told himself. "Not yet." He looked over the edge of the divan again and saw that Maríana was still asleep. Sitting up quietly, he pulled his robe more tightly around his body and got up from the divan, then straightened his back in a glorious stretch, hearing and feeling at least twenty bones pop. Alys snorted and blinked. Henri put his fingers to his lips, pointing at Maríana. When Alys nodded, he gave a sweeping bow and padded silently out of the room.

Chapter 15

A GRAY shadow stopped him as Henri crossed the smooth wooden floor of the palais toward the long knights' room. He had not meant to spend the night in Maríana's chamber. The girl had aided him, but it would not do to be found lying next to her, even with Alys there. He drew back in surprise as the figure flew toward him, its feet barely touching the floor. "Ysabel?" He peered into the pale oval of her face.

She caught his arm and pleaded. "Henri, come with me now. I must speak to you!"

"What?" He stared at her again, noting the tremor that shook her. "Very well," he said.

She pulled him into her room and leaned against him, shaking.

"Ysabel, I should not be in here." What if de Reuilles came in? Henri pulled his robe tightly around his middle. First he spent the night next to Louis-Philippe's daughter, now he allowed the baron's wife to drag him into her chamber. What would Hughes des Arcis say? No, he must leave.

Then he saw tears glimmering on Ysabel's lashes. Tears. The sight of tears was always his undoing.

"We cannot talk plainly anywhere else." Ysabel slipped beneath his arm and rested her ear against her heart.

"What is it?" He grasped her chin and raised her head, so she had to look into his face.

"Henri. I need you." Her dark eyes were swimming with unshed tears. He led her over to a chair and sat her down.

"Now," he said. "What is the matter?"

She began weeping in earnest. "It is Louis-Philippe. He never comes to my bed," she cried. "I must have a child to secure my position. If I do not, he could set me aside! How am I to have a child if he never comes to my bed?"

Henri sat on a low stool in front of her, chin in his hand. Ysabel had curled her legs under her and held her arms crossed around her ribs. Tears streamed down her cheeks and dripped into her lap. She was dressed in a simple gown, yet the fabric clung to her form, showing her trim waist. Shifting her weight, she moved her legs so that her shapely ankles and tiny feet peeked out from beneath her skirt.

Well. This was the Ysabel he remembered. Why had Louis-Philippe not honored his marriage vows? What was wrong here? Why was it that Ysabel did not share a room with Louis-Philippe? Henri had heard of such things in Paris, but lesser nobles like de Reuilles usually shared a chamber with their wives. "I am not sure what to say, Ysabel," he said. "I hardly know de Reuilles and I am certainly not in any position to lecture him on his duties as a husband." He paused. "Have you tried going to the château priest, or better still, to Johanna? Johanna must have an interest in an heir for the château."

Ysabel shook her head. "No. I have not gone to them. Perhaps I will talk to her. Only," Ysabel's lower lip quivered and tears started in her eyes again, "would you please hold me for a little while?"

He drew back. "This is not right..." But Ysabel looked so like a child sitting there, tears spilling from her eyes. A sad child. She held out her trembling arms to him. He moved over to her chair and gathered her into his embrace.

He could not seem to stop stroking her hair. It had been so long since he allowed himself to feel desire for a woman that he was not sure what he was feeling until Ysabel took his hand, placing it against her breast and the aching heat in his groin sent waves of urgent need through his body. He moved around in discomfort, seeking to break free of their embrace, but Ysabel held him close and began running her thumb along the inside of his arm, humming.

She looked up into his face and caressed his cheek. "It has been so long, so very long," she said, her voice catching, "and I need love, Henri. Everyone does."

Now he could not move. The years after the abbey, years when he had wanted and needed — and failed — all disappeared. There was only the hot ache in his loins and Ysabel in his arms. Her scent and the closeness of her body were awakening fires that he thought he had put out long ago.

"Yes," he answered. "Everyone." The air fled his lungs when her nails ran down the length of his chest to his groin. Then he lifted her in one sweeping motion, and covered the distance to her bed in two large steps.

He tried to leave. After his seed had been spent the first time, he rolled out of the bed in a daze and grabbed for his robe. He did not particularly care for de Reuilles, but had never thought to dishonor the baron in his own house. As he poked his arms through the sleeves of his robe, Ysabel wound her legs around his waist, pressing her breasts up against his back. Shivers cascaded from his head to the base of his spine when she ran her fingers slowly down his naked chest, finally circling around and around his navel, never quite touching the organ that was rejoicing in her efforts. It was driving him mad. He pushed her down on the bed and took her again.

He lost count of the number of times they joined. Ysabel was voracious. Her hands, her mouth, her whole body caressed him everywhere. He should be glad he could feel again, could desire and take a woman. Yet he felt drained and curiously, not satisfied. His body responded to her touch, but he found himself recoiling after he had taken her. When he heard footsteps pattering outside in the corridor, he leaped out of her bed and ran to the door, but Ysabel followed, wrapping her arms around his neck and winding her legs around his middle again. "No!" Henri pulled at her hands, but she evaded his grasp, running her fingers over his chest, her nails scraping his nipples. Heat flashed through his loins. He leaned his head back and groaned, then grabbed the low chair next to her bed and dragged it across the floor, propping it against the latch. Ysabel still clung to his back, but now she slid down, her tongue making a line of fire along his back, his waist, coming to rest between his legs. He buried his hands in her hair and shuddered.

It seemed that hours had passed when he finally stumbled out of the bed, grabbing his robe and shoving the chair away from the door. He did not care if he ran into anybody out in the passage — even de Reuilles, for God's sake! He had to get out of there.

The corridor was empty. He strode toward the knights' chamber and paused in surprise when he reached the entry. The room was dark. It was still early, although he could hear the other knights in the long room starting to stir. How long had he been with Ysabel? His vision blurred and he shook his head to clear it. It had felt like forever, but the sun was barely up even now and it had been just before dawn when he left Maríana's chamber. Parting the curtains surrounding his bed, he fell onto the mattress, sinking at once into a deep, dreamless sleep.

When he awakened again, it was early in the afternoon. His squire must have left him to sleep-the boy was nowhere in sight. He stretched his body languorously on the woolen blankets, feeling his strong muscles move against the powdery texture of the fabric. Wool usually scratched. De Reuilles must have had his people beat these blankets to make them so smooth.

Soft, silky cloth. He lifted a corner and rubbed it against his cheek. As he touched the blanket, he remembered the weight of Maríana's hair between his fingers as they sat in the meadow near the lake. His body responded quickly to his idle thoughts, a swell of wanting that he suppressed. Shaking his head, he scolded himself and rose up out of his bed, pulling on his breeches and shirt. As he opened the curtains that surrounded his bed, he stopped and frowned. What was he going to do about Ysabel? He could not believe that de Reuilles had not honored his marriage vows. It would be like Ysabel to create such a ruse to serve her purpose.

No matter. Ysabel would say nothing. How could she? She was Baroness de Reuilles now; she would not jeopardize her position here. He splashed water from the basin on his face and whistled through his teeth. If Ysabel continued to pursue him, he would keep his distance. But now he must return to Reuilles-la-ville to complete his mission. He strapped his sword to his side and unfurled the map Robert had drawn for him yesterday, then traced the twisting spiral of the route from the wharf to Antoine's house. He would make the crossing again by himself and find this fellow. Today, nothing would stop him.

HENRI STALKED the cobbled streets of Reuilles-la-ville, studying Robert's crudely drawn map and the buildings surrounding him. Left here, then this curve to the right. Rue des Anciennes. Such a name! Street of the ancient ones.

Henri counted the houses from the corner and approached a small stone house with a large wooden door. Two low windows, their shutters open to the cool spring air, were set on either side of the door. The scent of baking bread wafted out into the street. His stomach started a conversation with him, gurgling in a hollow roar. He had skipped the afternoon meal to avoid Ysabel and was regretting this now. He had been asleep earlier, so he missed the morning meal too. He should have eaten. Taking a deep breath, he knocked firmly on the wooden door.

The door opened. A young woman with hair the color of a raven's wing, the kind of black that harbors a deep, burnished shade of red in bright sunlight, stood before him. Black lashes framed eyes the color of the angry sea, a dark gray-green. His breath caught in his throat. Except for the sallow complexion and the dark shade of her hair, he almost thought he was seeing Maríana. "Yes? What do you want?" the woman asked in perfect French, wiping her hands upon her apron.

He smiled. "I have come seeking a soldier who served in the bishop's army recently."

She stood very still in the doorway.

"He left some of his things behind when he disappeared and I want to return them to him," Henri continued, pulling Antoine's shirts and a stone attached to a leather thong out of his pack. Hughes de Arcis had given Henri clothing and trinkets that Antoine and Pierre had left behind when they fled Montsegur. It was a ruse, of course. Henri had no interest in returning the items. He only wanted to find Antoine.

The woman glanced at the shirts, her face still and her eyes hooded. Then she yelled over her shoulder, "Grandfather! Do you know of anyone who served in the bishop's army?"

A large man with a long silver beard loomed out of the shadows behind her. "What did you say?" he asked querulously. "Whose army?"

The woman turned to him and spoke a few words in another language. The man simply shrugged and answered her back in the same tongue, then disappeared into the house.

She smiled, but her eyes were cold. "We only just arrived here,

Monsieur," she said. "I wish we could help you, but..." Her voice trailed away.

Henri had been expecting resistance. He pulled a small leather bag of coins out of his pack and shook a few into his hand, then looked up at the woman. The sight of gold often loosened tongues. But she only shrugged and started to pull the door closed. Placing his foot between the door and the frame, Henri said, "Please. Just a moment. I must make note of your statements for Bishop Durand." He watched her closely when he said the bishop's name, but he could see no reaction. If anything, the woman looked even more indifferent. But she could not close the door without shutting it on his foot and Henri did not think she would do that. He pocketed the bag of coins and shifted his sword. When she saw his blade, the corner of her left eye twitched. It may mean nothing, but he was encouraged. She knew where Antoine had gone. He was sure of this.

While she watched, he pulled a sheaf of parchment, a pot of ink, and his quill out of the pack he had slung across his shoulder. "What did you say your name was?" He carefully made notations on the parchment. This was a ploy he had often used. It did not work with clerics or nobles, but writing was magic to most. When people saw him writing they usually became nervous and would end up telling him whatever he wanted to know.

Henri was certain that Antoine had been here. He also was certain the woman was hiding something. Glancing up at her, he held his quill poised.

She looked down at his parchment and said, "I did not say. My name is Leila."

"What?" he asked. He was not used to people simply answering.

"My name is Leila," she said. "L-e-i-l-a." She spelled it out for him, watching him writing it. "Are you hungry?"

Henri jumped. "Hungry?" His stomach suddenly rumbled loudly.

"You are hungry, aren't you?" Her teeth gleamed in a broad smile. "Come inside, we will feed you before you go back." Leila's eyes became pools of blackness and he felt a thrumming in his head when he looked at her. Her fingers closed upon his arm. She was strong, this woman. Her grip on him was firm. His feet moved across the doorstep and the house swallowed him.

HENRI LEFT the house of Leila and Iranzu Jakintza, his stomach full of roast pork and fresh-baked bread and rich wine. He stood for a moment, breathing deeply, waiting for his eyes to adjust to the light. It had not been dark inside the house, but the pale early evening sky nearly blinded him. He blinked and stared back at the small stone house behind him. "Now, what was I there for?" He scratched his head. "Of course, Antoine Jakintza," he laughed, smiling at his memory of the old man trying to explain the Jakintza family tree to him.

"There are so many Jakintzas and we are all related," Iranzu had told him proudly. Unfortunately, to his apparent consternation, the old man could not find Antoine Jakintza on his list of the family. But Iranzu had shrugged and smiled engagingly, saying, "He must be there somewhere. More wine?"

The woman Leila and the old man told Henri that the previous occupant had left quite suddenly and that they had taken the house soon after. They seemed worried that he might come back to claim his house again, this Antoine who must be related to them, but whom they did not know. Henri found himself reassuring the two Jakintzas that he would make sure that they could stay in the house. He would speak to Louis-Philippe himself! Henri wanted to do whatever he could for them, although just before he left, a cold, measuring stare from Leila's gray-green eyes took the air right out of his lungs. He had gasped, but a moment later, she smiled at him warmly, her eyes grew large and black again, and everything was fine, just perfect.

HENRI SMILED at people scurrying to their homes. The final rays of sunlight caressed the blue and gray stones of the walls. He could smell meat roasting and caught the scent of ale through the rough-hewn door of a tavern. A perfect evening. Stars were just beginning to show.

He breathed in the damp smell of the earth near the lake, then stopped and shook his head. How did he get this far? Surely he had just left Antoine's house. But the house did not belong to Antoine, did it? It belonged to a man with a silver beard and a woman with gray-green eyes. He must write to Durand and tell him Antoine could not be found. They must stop looking. He shook his head again. Something was not right, his thoughts would not fit together. When he felt a hand take hold of his arm, he turned to see who was trying to catch his attention and found himself looking into another pair of green eyes.

"Maríana!" Henri threw his arms wide and embraced her. "So you are here in Reuilles-la-ville too?" Smiling, he waved his hands at the still waters beyond the wharf. "Look at the starlight on the lake! Isn't it a perfect night?" He looked down and saw his squire Robert hovering next to her. "Robert! What are you doing here? I told you to stay at Reuilles-le-château." Why were Robert's eyes so wide? Henri swayed on his feet and Robert moved to his side.

"It was my idea, Henri." Now Maríana was at his other side, taking his arm and draping it over her shoulder. "When you could not be found, I went to Robert." Henri felt himself propelled by the two of them to a raft at the end of the wharf. The same boatman who had taken him over that afternoon stood there, his pole held ready. "Come," Maríana continued. "We will take you back."

Henri wanted to tell her that he could take himself back, but now his tongue would not work. Then the pattern of ripples spreading out from the raft caught his eye and the next thing he knew, Maríana and Robert were guiding him off the raft and walking him up to the walls of Reuilles-le-château. His legs trembled. It took all of his concentration to make them move. He heard Robert whisper, "He has never been like this. What is wrong?" and saw Maríana shake her head at the boy.

"There is nothing wrong," Henri assured them, pulling his arms away from their hands. "I had the most wonderful meal with an old man and his granddaughter." His hand swiped at the bag at his side. "I wrote their names down." But the bag was empty. "Where are my parchment and quill?" It hurt to think and the walls of Reuilles-le-château looked so far away. He forced his right foot to move, then his left. The walls did not seem any closer. "Perhaps I do need your help." He held his arms out and felt their grasp again.

When they entered the château grounds, two young girls were herding huge pigs through the arched entrance to the inner bailey. Henri collapsed with laughter. He could not stop laughing, but Maríana and Robert pulled him up off the ground and hurried him past the gates, around the back way into the palais.

When they reached the knights' room, Robert shoved Henri onto his bed while Henri chuckled and grabbed at Maríana's gown. Henri tried to pull her onto the mattress with him, but he was unable to hang on to anything for very long. His hands did not seem to have any strength in them. He lay back and watched Maríana's face as she helped Robert remove his sword and boots, then she sent the boy away and pulled the blanket up around his shoulders.

"Maríana." He reached out to touch her cheek. There was something he wanted to tell her, but her eyes held him and he could not speak.

"You need to sleep," she said, then placed her palm on his forehead. Her hand felt warm and grew even warmer. He wanted to tell her to take her hand away; it was burning his forehead, but as soon as the thought formed, he felt his eyelids drop over his eyes and sleep wrapped its dark blanket around him.

MARÍANA sat on the edge of Henri's bed, hearing his breathing lengthen, then grow steady. As she watched the rise and fall of his chest, she rubbed her burning palm against her skirt. This was the second time she had used her gift to help this knight. Ibrahim would be furious. But she could not leave him to suffer from the effects of whatever herb or root Leila and Iranzu had given him. She was sure they gave Henri a plant to take away his will and the force of their words to convince him that Antoine could not be found.

So like a boy... his face relaxed in sleep, dark lashes swept across his cheeks. She sat and watched him until he turned away, wrapping his arms around his middle. She would not help Henri find Antoine, but she also would not allow her family to harm this knight. Reaching forward, she traced the curve of his cheek with her fingers, then stood and pulled the curtains around his bed.

Chapter 16

YSABEL ROSE up out of a terrifying dream. In it, the mannikin had grown into a huge creature made of some kind of straw or twigs, covered in vines and flowers. It had a gigantic, dark grinning mouth that was opening to swallow her. She struggled, then felt her own mouth working as she gagged and choked. Her eyes opened and she saw the black sky and cold light of a full moon streaming around the edge of the tapestry she had hastily pulled across her window earlier that night. Her pillow was soaked with sweat. She groaned and swallowed again, trying to still the spasms in her belly.

Why was she shivering? Her chamber was warm enough. It was early June. The approaching summer heat already made the air heavy and laden with fragrance. Perhaps the scented air had caused her stomach to rebel. Or the lavender-strewn bowl of water she had to present to guests at the château every evening. She had asked them to use rose petals, but they kept sprinkling lavender in the bowl.

Ah, well. At least the washing ritual gave her a chance to touch Henri. He had managed to avoid being alone with her for the past two months, but she was sure she could eventually break his resistance. He had not gone away and she could continue to watch the play of hearth light across his face. She had watched Henri for the past two months, seen him coming and going from Reuilles-la-ville, saw his eyes as he looked upon the servants and family at Reuilles-le-château. He was always assessing, judging, her Henri was, always searching for something. His eyes usually looked distant and cold. It made her shiver with desire, wanting to bring fire into those eyes.

But when he was in the palais, Henri's eyes followed her stepdaughter.

Ysabel swallowed again, then stroked her belly. Whenever Maríana was near, Henri stared at her. As far as Ysabel knew, he did not talk to her stepdaughter, but wherever Maríana went, Henri watched her and his eyes burned with longing. Ysabel gritted her teeth. Henri had never looked at her the way he gazed at Maríana. Every time Ysabel saw Henri watching Maríana the raw desire on his face made Ysabel's loins turn to butter. Even Johanna had noticed his interest in her granddaughter.

Ysabel had set several traps for Henri after their first liaison. She had him called to the garden, where she awaited wearing her thinnest gown and nothing underneath, followed him to Reuilles-la-ville, waylaid him in the corridor. But Henri had outwitted her. He had his squire

Robert with him all the time and would not send the boy away, even when Ysabel asked to be alone with him. Could she season Robert's food with a sleeping draught? Yes, and send a message to Henri that Mariana awaited him. A shiver started at her neck and ran down her legs. Henri would answer such a message. Why not do it now? She sat up and swung her legs over the edge of her bed, then clutched her middle.

Ysabel waited for the waves of nausea to pass. Was it the leeks at dinner? But she had always been able to eat anything. She pulled her wet hair off the back of her neck, then scowled at her cabinet where the mannikin howled with laughter.

"What do you have to be happy about?" she asked in irritation. As if in answer, it started humming a tune. She waved her hand. The thing was mad. Someday she would have to... she sat up straight as she recognized the tune it was humming. Then she ran to her pile of moon-stones. Her mother had given her the stones when she had her first bleeding time. She counted the tiny black stones, then started her count again. The black stones marked days that she did not bleed. Ysabel faithfully placed a moon-stone in the line on her shelf every morning after she visited the privy or used the chamber pot, black for no blood, stones with a red circle for her bleeding time. Her fingers shook. There were too many black stones, twenty, thirty, forty, forty-five, forty-eight, fifty-three. Surely there should be no more than thirty. She counted again, then leaned back against the bed, her mouth hanging open in astonishment. The mannikin was still humming the cradle song.

"SHUT UP," she told it. "A child."

Ysabel rubbed her belly, still as taut as ever, yet even now she could feel a slight hardness inside where her womb was starting to grow. "Henri's child." Would its eyes be blue and gold?

The mannikin started shrieking with laughter again. "Henri's child!" it roared.

She gasped and counted again. "Not even two months gone yet," she said. "Not very much. Babies come early sometimes."

"Not that early!" the mannikin shrieked. "With your husband never in your bed at all!"

Ysabel threw her pillow at the cabinet. Then she sat back to ponder. Could she get Louis-Philippe so drunk that he was senseless and fool him, tell him that they had made love? No, that would not do. He might not believe her, and anyway, she wanted to seduce him, have him, steal him back from Ibrahim.

The mannikin howled again. "Try cutting your tits off!" it screamed.

Ysabel started to throw her moon-stones at the cabinet, then stopped, her mouth dropping open again. "Of course!" she laughed. "I can dress like a man!" She held her sides and chortled. "I used to dress like a boy when my brothers would go riding so I could go with them where maidens were not allowed. Why didn't I think of this before?" The mannikin was incoherent with rage. "I'll bet you never thought you would help me, did you?" she taunted it, and was rewarded by blessed silence.

Ysabel tore into the chest filled with gowns she had brought from Touraine. At the bottom were the plain shirt and breeches her brother had given to her. Humming the cradle song, she pulled on the breeches and laced them up tight. She wiggled into the shirt, swept her hair back and tied it with a leather thong, then stuffed it into a jaunty cap she found tucked away in the bottom of the chest. Viewing the results in her polished silver mirror, she grinned at her reflection. Finally, she retrieved the needle from underneath her mattress and held it triumphantly in her hand, tossing it into the air and catching it easily.

"Here I come, Baron!" Ysabel waved at her image, then strode purposefully out the door.

LOUIS-PHILIPPE was sound asleep and snoring. Ysabel breathed a prayer of thanks that the baron did not have his manservant sleep in his chamber. All the de Reuilles loved their solitude. When she had first arrived at Reuilles-le-château, Ysabel had been shocked to find that her husband-to-be would keep his own chamber and that she would have a separate chamber. Such a thing was unheard of in Gréves, although Ysabel had heard rumors of this practice in Paris. She was glad they did not keep the traditional ladies' bower, though. To sit all day in a room full of jabbering women made her head spin.

She crept around the edge of the large mattress and looked upon his face as he slept. An ache of longing brought tears to her eyes as she gazed at his smooth brow, the straight line of his nose, his lovely full mouth. Henri may be beautiful, but Louis-Philippe was glorious.

And he was hers — would be hers, totally hers. She would steal him from Ibrahim. Her breath caught in her throat when she hid the needle underneath the far edge of Louis-Philippe's pillow. Then she drew her hand across her eyes, dashing her tears away, and reached out to shake him awake.

His arms shot out and he grabbed her, as he exclaimed, "What? Who are you?" He sat up and rubbed his eyes with one hand, the other holding her fast in his grip.

Ysabel smiled at him. "It is only me, your wife, my lord."

Louis-Philippe frowned, then his eyes widened. "Ysabel?" He waved his hands at her costume. "What is all this?" He did not sound displeased.

"A game, my husband." Ysabel ran her hands down his chest. "Just a game. Please indulge me." She got up from the bed, remembering to move with free, broad strides as a man would, and came around to the other side. "It is just you and I, after all," she continued, pleased to see the effect her words had on him as his eyes upon her warmed with desire. "What we do in our marriage bed is our own business," she finished, lowering the timbre of her voice.

"Indeed!" Louis-Philippe pulled her toward him in a deep embrace, then he tore off her breeches and pinned her to the bed, stretching her arms wide and lacing her fingers in his own.

Ysabel shuddered as she felt the length of his body against her, felt the proof of his wanting parting her thighs. She whispered words in his ear, words her brothers had told her, words she could never say aloud if another lady were present. He shivered and held her even closer, then covered her mouth with his. She gripped him with all the strength she could muster as he entered her body. He moved against her three times, then she heard his gasp and felt the pulse of his release.

Ysabel had barely remembered to wince at the proper time and now reached under the pillow for the needle, stabbing her thumb and smearing the blood underneath her on the bed as she moved out from under him. Indeed! That was over quickly. She glanced at him through her lashes. Perhaps he would improve with time. She started to slip out of the bed to return to her chamber when Louis-Philippe caught her again and gathered her into his arms.

"Madame." He grinned at her surprise. "You know and I know that we are not through yet." Louis-Philippe pulled her onto her side and breathed gently upon her chest. "So tiny," he said as he nuzzled her breasts.

Ysabel mouthed another prayer of thanks, this time for her child-like chest, while Louis-Philippe's fingers played over her skin, finding centers of pleasure that she had no idea she possessed. Now he whispered to her, lovely words, words that flowed out of his mouth and curled around her. What language was he speaking? His hands caressed her until she shook and cried out for him to take her. This time, he moved slowly and she exploded several times before he was spent.

Her own pleasure was so intense that she did not care that his eyes were tightly shut. Had he truly whispered "Ibrahim" when he quivered with the force of his release? She did not care — she was here in his bed, not the Moor. Louis-Philippe sighed, wrapped his arms around her and was asleep the very next moment.

Ysabel smiled and curled up, her back against his belly. "Louis-Philippe's child," she whispered to herself as she drifted off to sleep.

Chapter 17

MARÍANA took her place at the family table, keeping her eyes lowered. Henri was already seated and sat watching her again. Usually, Ysabel frowned at Maríana when Henri kept his eyes on her, so Maríana was careful to avoid his stare. Maríana had found that annoying Ysabel could be costly. Ysabel even stopped Maríana from visiting Ibrahim. Her stepmother had convinced Johanna that Ibrahim was the reason Maríana refused the suitors who still came to Reuilles-le-château. Maríana had not seen Ibrahim for the past two months.

Ysabel had also prevented Maríana from going into Reuilles-la-ville. "Too dangerous," she had said and Johanna concurred. But recently, Ysabel had paid no attention to her stepdaughter. Maríana saw her stepmother wander about the palais with a half-smile hovering at the corners of her mouth, rather than her usual pout. If Ysabel was distracted, perhaps Johanna would allow visits to Ibrahim again. Geneviéve had told Maríana that Ibrahim was unwell. He might need her. She must try to see him.

Maríana looked up and froze. Henri had moved to the seat across from her. He merely nodded to her, but the naked wanting in his face drew an answering cry from her own body. She held her hands clutched tightly in her lap. What was she to do? He was her cousin. Geneviéve was wrong about special permission from the bishop. A dispensation to wed would be nearly impossible. Johanna had looked into this. Yet Henri had remained at Reuilles-le-château, long after his mission was completed. Maríana had seen the messenger from the bishop arrive and depart with Henri's report. Antoine and Pierre were nowhere to be found. Why was Henri still here?

Now it was near sunset at the end of July, and all the vassals from the surrounding area had been invited to the château for a special feast. There were visitors from Béarn, from Navarre, from as far away as Carcasonne. Maríana saw her father descending the central staircase, his eyes bright with suppressed excitement. He took his place at the end of the table and glanced around the hall, then motioned for the musicians to sound a fanfare. The blare of the shawms brought everyone to a halt, even the servants running from table to table with large goblets of fresh, sweet mead. Maríana watched her father as he stood holding his goblet aloft. She could still feel the warmth of Henri's gaze, but Ysabel stood beside Louis-Philippe. If Maríana looked at Henri now, her stepmother would see.

"A toast!" Louis-Philippe's voice rang out across the hall. "A toast for a new member of the de Reuilles!" He turned to Ysabel, who smiled and blushed. "A child to be born next March!" He bowed to Ysabel as the company filled the hall with shouts and laughter and good wishes.

Maríana heard a stifled exclamation from across the table. Henri stared at Ysabel, his eyes hooded and brooding, his mouth a tight line. Following his stare, she saw her father beaming at Ysabel and a hollow ache started in her belly, a pain she had not felt in years. She wished that her birth had been accompanied by such fanfare and good will, but she was pleased that her father had finally seemed to find some measure of happiness. He had tried to hide his longing for Ibrahim, but Maríana knew he had suffered when Ibrahim refused to continue their alliance.

Another child. A hand on her arm pulled her out of her thoughts. She turned to see Jeanne standing at her side, holding a scrap of vellum. "What is it?" Jeanne placed the paper in her hands, curtseyed, and fled.

Maríana opened the crumbling scrap, then slid it into her sleeve. She looked around the table. Henri was still frowning at Ysabel, Johanna was fussing with Louis-Philippe's trencher, and everyone else was digging into the food. Pushing her chair away from the table, Maríana rose and made her way to Geneviéve.

"Is this not wonderful?" Geneviéve was beaming. "A baby!"

"Aunt," Maríana said, "I must check on the rosemary wine sauce." She did not wait for Geneviéve's nod, but pushed through the crowd to the doors, then slipped out of the hall and into the bright summer evening. She nodded to the guard and skipped over the stones to the entry of the garden. No one would wonder why she was there. If anyone did ask, she could say that she needed to harvest more herbs for the feast. It was near dusk. Maríana was still the only one who would enter the garden after dark. Except for Ibrahim.

When Maríana was sure she was the only person in the garden, she paced the pathways again, this time stopping at the farthest end of each of the four directions and sending images into the air — images that would cloak where she had passed. Ibrahim had been very clear in his message that she should not be followed. She made her way to the back of the garden and dipped under the rose wall that guarded the secret gate. The metal groaned when she pushed the lever that opened it, but she did not pause. She left the château walls and climbed up to the palace.

IBRAHIM SAT on a pillow in the middle of a circle of candles, with stones: lapis, sandstone, garnet, and gold, all guarding the four directions. He was pale and there were lines around his mouth that had not been there before. Moving closer to him, Maríana felt his forehead. It was clammy. She reached for the pulse in his neck. He stopped her, taking her hands.

"There is nothing you can do that I have not already done," he said. "Do not worry, it will pass." She stubbornly remained where she was until he ordered her to sit. Then she placed a pillow directly in front of him within the circle and sat facing him.

"Did anyone follow you?" he asked, gazing at her, his eyes smudged with fatigue.

"No. I made sure. I covered my path and scattered the images to the four directions as you have taught me. Anyone who even tried to follow me would go in circles until he found himself where he had started."

He nodded. "I have called you up here, even though it is dangerous, even though there are guests at the château, because I need to complete your training."

"But my training was complete two years ago," she said. "One year was what my father gave us for our work."

"Yes that is true, but we have continued just the same. Our meetings in the garden were all part of this training." His cheek dimpled in a smile when she made a wordless protest. "Yes, I know Johanna forbade you to see me." His eyes darkened. "And I know who was behind her decision." He reached out and rubbed the middle of her palms. "But it is better that we have not met these past months. With Bauçais at the château... well, we must be careful."

"Why so much fear of my cousin Henri?" she asked. "Surely, as family he can be trusted." But he had sought to find Antoine. She still did not know why.

Ibrahim regarded her a moment, his eyes opaque. Then he said, "Bauçais is just the first wave of the outside world that will come to the château. You might say that he is no more or less dangerous than anyone else coming here now, in these times." He shifted his position on the pillow. "A change is coming and I believe he is its messenger. Since we will not be able to meet anymore to discuss the healing herbs or plants, how to call someone to you, the motion of the stars, or any of the other things I would like to teach you, I must complete a link with you to pass on to you all that I know... and all that your mother knew."

She leaned forward, taking his hands. "How can this be done?"

"The process will be simple for you. We have already laid the foundations with the disciplines I imposed. But be warned, the linking is not without risk, to you or to me. There will be no secrets between us. Everything that I am or was, everything that you are, will be laid bare. Once we have started, there can be no going back."

"You must know I will not be frightened away by that. What have I to hide from you?" A shiver went through her as she remembered healing Henri.

He sat back, his hands still holding hers, and looked at her. "It is what you will learn from me that concerns me. But it must be done."

Ibrahim rose and walked over to the altar, bringing back a small bowl filled with frankincense and cedar from the east, pine and mugwort from the north. Placing the bowl between them, he drew his staff and closed the circle, as she had seen him do many times, saluting the guardians, creating the space between the worlds. As always, when the circle was closed, Maríana felt the humming in the air and in the earth. She looked at the boundary Ibrahim had drawn and felt the presence of the Door, the translucent membrane separating them from the world outside. When she looked back at Ibrahim, he was igniting the fragrant woods, sending smoke billowing around them. After sprinkling frankincense and mugwort on the glowing embers, he placed the bowl between them and told her to breathe.

She watched his face. He was still, but the pulse in his throat was visible. When had age etched its signs upon his brow? She remembered their first meeting, the kohl outlining his eyes, those absurd bracelets. But now he was raising his hands, palms facing forward, reaching toward her. Her hands sought his, almost against her will. Their palms touched.

They remained touching, breathing the sharp and woodsy smoke from the smoldering bowl. Maríana felt herself tumbling. She squeezed her eyes shut to stop the room from spinning. When her dizziness cleared, she blinked her eyes open and looked over at Ibrahim.

She found herself looking into her own face, her wide, dark green eyes, her mouth parted in surprise. A trembling started deep within her and spread to her limbs. But it was Ibrahim's hands that shook. Maríana clamped her will over her fear and moved Ibrahim's arms. She could feel his illness, a spreading blackness deep within his gut, but she also felt his strength as she flexed his strong muscles. His heart beat steadily. Then she allowed herself to look at her own body again. She saw Ibrahim looking at her through her own eyes, startled and pale, and she felt another stab of fear. But he said he had already done this, he knew what to expect! What was wrong?

WITH THAT thought, she abruptly found herself somewhere else, still inside Ibrahim's body, crawling through a close tunnel. Now she could not stop his body from what it was doing. She could only observe what was happening, peering out from his eyes. A faint light glimmered at the end of the cramped tunnel. Ibrahim's hands pushed through a barrier of mud and stone. She felt his body squeeze through the narrow opening.

Darkness, intense and enveloping. And a sour reek. Ibrahim's feet slipped on excrement carpeting a frozen stone floor. Slimy mold painted the walls — the faint shimmer of ooze dripped from the wall beside him. The chamber Ibrahim had entered was large. His footsteps echoed. A small glow shone in the distance. Maríana watched from behind Ibrahim's eyes as he crept toward the light, breathing shallowly, his heart speeding and slowing.

A woman huddled on filthy straw beside a squat candle. "Thérèse," Ibrahim whispered. The woman lifted her face. He choked. "Thérèse!"

Maríana looked out of Ibrahim's eyes into her mother's ravaged face. "Ah, God!" Maríana tried to speak, but Ibrahim's mouth would not move with her thoughts. The eyeless water creature from the pond so long ago — was that truly her mother trying to come back to find her? And Maríana had denied it, sent it away.

Thérèse's lids sagged over empty sockets. Several recent burns made shiny tracks across her face and neck, but she was calm, saying, "Hush, my love. They will hear you." Then, while Ibrahim gulped and trembled, she said, "It is too late, my Ibrahim. You cannot help me now, you will only make things worse for you and Louis-Philippe." Her lips twisted. "It is ironic, no? They took my eyes, but they gave me a candle." She moved her elbow close to the tiny flame. "I can feel the warmth from it."

Ibrahim moved closer. "I cannot give you your eyes back but I can save your life." He reached out. Thérèse stopped him with the palms of her hands. He wavered, then stifled a sob.

Someone had wrenched all of Thérèse's fingernails from her. Ibrahim looked at fingers that were swollen to twice the normal size. "I cannot go anywhere," Thérèse said, her voice halting. "You see, the first day they broke both of my legs." Ibrahim gently held his hands over Thérèse's legs, not quite touching them, and Maríana felt him force his eyes to look down. Her mother's limbs were purple and swollen, not only broken, but shattered.

"You need not worry," Thérèse was saying. "I have told them nothing." Ibrahim was crying openly now, his grief and rage battling with the need for silence. "Don't cry, my love." Thérèse's voice broke. "I have been able to stand the pain, but I really could not bear it if you cry."

Ibrahim held his breath; his whole body shook, yet his thoughts were cold. Maríana could feel him assessing his options, examining and discarding several routes of escape, finally settling on a course that set his gut trembling.

"You must not hate Louis-Philippe," Thérèse continued. "I brought this upon myself. I did not listen to him or to Johanna. They are suffering, too." Thérèse reached out to find and finally touch Ibrahim's face with her hand. "So please, do not blame them."

Ibrahim dug into the leather pouch on his belt and pulled out a packet. "I brought a packet in case..." His voice failed him.

Thérèse became very still, then shuddered. "What is in it?" she finally asked.

Ibrahim sprinkled a powder and what looked like shredded leaves into the palm of his hand. Maríana could feel the fine grains of some ground herb and the weight of a crumbled plant upon his skin. "I have balm and a plant from the land of al-Din Sinan — the assassins. The balm will make you sleepy and the plant of the assassins..."

"Will kill me," Thérèse finished for him and shuddered again. Then she drew a deep, ragged breath. "Thank you, my love. I have been able to bear what they have done to me, but the flames, the flames!" Her head dropped. "Especially when I cannot see them, cannot escape into my mind before they envelop me."

Ibrahim sat staring at the powder and plant matter in his hand, then squeezed his hand shut. "I cannot give it to you, for then I would be killing you, and I have taken the oath never to kill."

Thérèse felt for him and grasped his hands. "Is it in this hand?"

"No." He opened his palm again. "This one." He held his hand still and Thérèse touched it.

"Then I will take it from you of my own free will," Thérèse said. "So you are released from your vow."

Thérèse opened her mouth and Maríana felt her tongue lick all the powder and leaves off Ibrahim's hand. Ibrahim was shaking, but he did not stop her mother.

"You must wash it off soon," Thérèse said, her voice beginning to slur already. "I do not know this plant you have used, but it may be taken in through the skin."

Ibrahim unhooked a water skin he carried in a sling around his neck. "Don't worry about me. Here, have some water, it will make the poison move faster." He poured a stream into her mouth.

Thérèse gulped and choked, the water ran over her cracked and bleeding lips. Then she sagged against the wall. "The plant I took from you. Will it make me ill?"

Ibrahim moved behind Thérèse and put his arms around her shoulders. "No. You will feel nothing."

"I cannot feel my legs even now," Thérèse said, her voice dipping.

"I will stay with you."

"No!" Thérèse rallied, lifting her arms. "It will all be for nothing if you are found here."

"I cannot leave you."

"But you must," Thérèse said, touching his face. "I am counting on you to watch over Maríana."

"She has Louis-Philippe," he said, gently caressing her cheek.

"Does she?" Her voice was heavy. "Louis-Philippe never understood anything. If there is any danger, you must take Maríana to the mountain, to my father." Thérèse yawned, her jaw stretching. "Promise. Promise."

Tears coursed down Ibrahim's face. "I promise," he finally said. But Thérèse sagged in his arms. "Allah be with you," he whispered.

MARÍANA'S vision blurred with Ibrahim's tears, and she sobbed uncontrollably. "Mama!" was what she cried. "Mama!"

Then she fell through a vast distance. There was a rhythmic pounding everywhere. Stone giants were striking mountains with enormous, ancient trees. But the world steadied and she looked out of her own eyes again. She curled her body into a ball, her face wet with tears. Ibrahim's arms wound around her, his hands stroked her hair. He murmured silly things, children's songs, and words that had no meaning to her. Yet his voice touched a place deep within her heart. The knot of anguish in her throat loosened. She straightened her limbs and raised her eyes to his face. "Thérèse," she said.

"I know," Ibrahim said. "I know."

"Why?" Maríana stood and paced. "What use is it — all that we know, all that we can do, all of our powers?" Her voice cracked. "What use is it, if she could not even use this knowledge, this power, to save herself? Why couldn't she open the Door? Why couldn't she make a mist to confound them?"

Ibrahim just sighed. "I am sorry," he started to say, but Maríana moved toward him, put her fingers over his lips.

"Not a word," she said. "Not one word." She kissed his cheek. His face was damp, too. "Thank you," she said simply. "Thank you for what you did for my mother." Ibrahim drew her into his arms. Maríana sat held against his chest, listened to his heartbeat, slow and steady. Then he released her. Standing, he doused the candles and brought the still-smoking embers of the aromatic wood ashes outside to wash off into the fountain.

When he returned, she asked him, "How?"

"People came to her to be healed," he said. "She healed them."

"That is why you would not let me..."

"Yes." He touched her face. "Do you love him, then? This Bauçais?"

"I don't know, Ibrahim. I think so."

"When you healed him, you forged a bond, you know."

"I am sorry, Ibrahim. He needed to be healed, so I healed him." She looked down at her hands.

"Be careful," he said, holding her eyes with his. "Be very careful. With this linking you will be much more powerful than either myself or your mother. This ritual allowed me to transmit the knowledge to you without your awareness. It is a part of you, now." He paused, glancing down at his feet, then continued, "What we have done, the essence I have passed on to you, has been passed on to all the chosen of your mother's line for hundreds, perhaps even thousands, of years."

He took her face in his hands. "I do not know what the combination of our knowledge will create in you. When your mother linked with me before they took her away, my power increased tenfold. You will find that you know things you did not know before, that you can do things you could not do before. You may be tempted to use this knowledge, this power, openly, but you must not! With this power come both the gift and the curse."

"What is the gift?" she asked, looking into his deep brown eyes, at the flecks of gold swimming around his pupils.

"The power itself," he answered.

"And what is the curse?"

He smiled. "The power itself."

She shook her head. "Riddles again."

"Think on it, Maríana. And remember your mother." He hugged her tight against his chest, then let her go. She gathered her skirt in her hand and slipped out the door.

Chapter 18

THE GUARD at the eastern gate barely glanced at Maríana when she approached and asked for entry. They were used to her wandering. He opened the smaller door set beside the massive wood and iron gate and stepped aside to allow her entry. In the distance, she heard voices and the beat of drums. The celebration had moved outside. But she could not join them. Not yet. Her feet took her to the edge of the garden, where she paused by the hawthorn trees. She could stay there until she was ready to face the crowd in the palais, until she could soothe the raw ache inside her, still the rage that made her hands clutch the fabric of her gown, making wrinkled creases.

She paced beside fragrant beds of flowers and herbs: marjoram, to cure an aching head, valerian to calm the spirit, lavender to scent the soul and give gifts to the Hawthorn God, and roses. There had always been roses in her mother's garden, blossoms to provide balm for a crying heart. Now Ysabel had planted even more.

Another child. Maríana's hands balled into tight fists. How could Louis-Philippe invite those people to Reuilles-le-château to celebrate the coming birth of his child? How could he feed them, give them ale and wine? Any one of them may have exposed Thérèse, brought her to the priests, burned her. Maríana dropped to her knees by the sweet violets and ran her fingers across their silken petals. Louis-Philippe had not loved Thérèse. Even if he had, could either he or Johanna have saved her?

Maríana bowed her head. Ibrahim had loved Thérèse and he could not save her. The gift and the curse. So be it. But she would not help any who may have tortured and burned her mother. There would be no more healing circles in Reuilles-la-ville. Her gift she would use, but only for Johanna, only for Ibrahim or Geneviéve or Alys. "I will survive, Mama," she said, lifting her head to the stars that now dotted the heavens. "I will survive."

"WHAT DID you say?" The low, musical voice of Henri came from behind her.

Maríana drew in her breath and stopped herself from spinning around. How could he have come upon her? How could she have been unaware of his presence? She forced herself to look at him without flinching. He stood before her, his face solemn and grave, eyes steadily regarding her. Starlight softened the sharp planes of his face, darkened his blue-gold eyes. "You do not join the others?" he asked.

"Where is Robert?" His squire was always with him, but she could not see the boy.

He looked toward the shouts and laughter from the palais. "They are going down to the lake. I told him to join them."

"Will you join them, too?" She stood and brushed the skirt of her gown. No one else from the château would come to the garden this late. Didn't Henri know it was haunted? She looked down at the sword strapped to his side. Perhaps he thought he could battle spirits with its sharp metal edge.

"I thought I would accompany you there." Henri did not reach toward her, but she felt his touch just the same. "There will be bonfires." Now his teeth gleamed as his face relaxed into a smile. "And dancing."

"What?" She could not stop her hands from clenching again. "Fires?"

He did not answer, but his eyes held hers. "Who will survive, Maríana?" His voice dropped, made the speaking of her name a caress.

She tried to look away. His eyes were glowing now. Or was it the starlight? "Survive?"

He reached toward her and the white silken cross that covered the front of his tunic shone. She fell back, her throat closed. The image of her mother's ruined face rose before her.

"Why do you ask me who will survive, soldier of Christ?" The words slipped past her lips. "We set bonfires for celebrations here at Reuilles-le-château, not to burn people." Her voice shook, but she could not stop. "And that is what you warriors of Christ do best, is it not?"

His face paled.

"Well, will you burn me? Will you burn my home? Will you burn my violets, too?"

Henri grabbed her arms. "What are you saying? It was not my fault, do you hear me?" He shook her so hard that her head snapped back and forth. "Not my fault! Not my fault!" he repeated, then released her and covered his eyes.

"What am I doing?" He dropped his hands from his eyes and took hold of her arms again, but his touch was gentle now. "Are you all right? Did I hurt you?" He held her at arms' length, staring at the ground, fingers stroking. His chest labored, then quieted. He raised his head. "I am sorry," he started, then held very still as their eyes met. The pulse beat rapidly at his throat.

She looked away. "Take your hands off me." Her voice was faint. "Please." The heat of his skin burned through the fabric of her gown. The urgent hunger in his eyes was answered by a shivering ache below her heart that was spreading in slow waves out to her limbs. She must get away from him. But she could not move.

"Very well." His voice was strained, yet his fingers still stroked her. "Maríana." He pulled her forward and lifted her, holding her close to his chest. His lips sought and found hers, a soft pressure that increased, then demanded. His arms tightened around her until she felt the whole hard length of his body against hers, felt his desperate need.

Every part of her yielded — her mouth parted under his pressure, her knees bent, her arms rose up and wrapped around his neck. The longing that had been a part of her since she had first seen him blossomed. Her limbs trembled and ached. All else faded. There was only the strength of his arms and the singing in her blood. She feared that if he did not enter her, if she did not welcome him into her body, she would burst. He held her with one arm now. His other hand fumbled at his waist. His sword fell to the ground.

He sank to his knees in the bed of violets, dragging her with him. "God forgive me!" He groaned aloud as his lips traced a fiery line from her mouth to her neck. He touched the soft swell of her breasts. Her nipples rose in a peak when he ran his fingers across them, sending a wave of molten need from her loins to her heart. He shuddered while his hands worked inside her gown. She cried out and leaned into him, her face resting beneath his chin. But he pulled his hands away and pushed her from him. He knelt in front of her, shaking. "No." The word was wrenched from deep within, and he held her at arms' length again. She reached out, touched his face. He was struggling. She could see the sheen of moisture on his brow and his fingers gripped her arms.

"Look at me, Henri." Was that her voice? She knew she was speaking, but it seemed to come from somewhere else, from some other throat. "Am I so difficult to look at?" Deep and melodious, this voice was. She could not believe it was hers.

Her last question brought his head up and he stared into her face. Then he made a sound somewhere between anguish and joy and took her mouth again, buried his fingers in her hair. He shook. His arms enveloped her. Then he pushed her down into the bed of violets and covered her body. He pulled at her long skirt, fingers seeking and finding warm skin. She could not seem to catch her breath.

"Maríana." His voice had deepened and he was breathless too, his chest laboring. The weight of his body settled into her, his hands continued to move under her gown. She wound her arms around his neck and opened to him. No thought of stopping. Her legs moved by themselves. The heat of his skin now burned against her. He cried out once, a hoarse shout, then buried himself in her, thrusting past her maiden's barrier in a powerful rush. A ripping, then a sharp twinge, and now warmth and fullness as he moved. She pulled him closer. Every part of her ached for this, for his touch, for the weight of his body, the heat as he filled her. He was panting, moist breath warming the space between her neck and shoulder. Then he stiffened, and another hoarse cry slipped past his lips. The hot spill of his seed flooded her.

She lay very still beneath him, feeling his weight upon her, his slowing breath moving strands of her hair. The ache within her was still there. She did not want him to leave.

"God," was his first word. He started to roll off of her, but she caught him, arms wrapping around his back, her legs imprisoning his.

"Not yet," she whispered.

A strangled laugh was his answer. She felt the heat of his lips on her neck again, and a breeze cooled the skin where they touched. They were surrounded by violets, the sweet aroma curled around her. She could stay there forever.

But he spoke. "Maríana." There was laughter, and uncertainty, underneath his words. "I must move."

"Very well." She unwound her legs and released him. He rolled off her into the violets, his motion casting an explosion of fragrance into the air.

He let his breath out in a long sigh and worked his right arm underneath her shoulders, pulling her toward him and kissing her hair. "Robert told me that no one would come here after dark."

"Yes." She did not know what to say. He was now deep in thought, eyes remote, judging, assessing.

She reached down and pushed her skirt across her legs. "No one comes here except me, so no one will see." She would tell no one. How could she? Harlot. That is what Alys would call her. She looked at his face again, at his brooding profile.

"If you are worried..." she started, but his voice stopped her.

"Why did you think I would burn you?" He had turned toward her and his eyes searched her face. His mouth tightened. "Did someone tell you of Montsegur?" He looked away again.

"Montsegur? I heard somewhere..." Iranzu and Leila had told her of Antoine — the story of the burning. But they had not mentioned Henri. "I don't know who told me," she said. "Are you saying that you were there?"

He would not look at her. "I was there," he finally said, then he turned and kissed her hair again. "It is not important now. Our task is to decide what we will do."

She did not pretend to misunderstand him. "We should return to the palais separately." She stole a look at the lines of his finely sculpted face, his high brow.

"They are expecting us down at the lake." He smiled at her start of surprise. "I was sent to find you."

She sat up and started to brush violets and bits of earth from her gown. "Then we shall go to the lake together."

He remained where he lay, his eyes gleaming in the starlight. "Not yet." He grasped her arm and pulled her beside him again. She nestled her head on his shoulder. "Maríana, I have written to the bishop."

"Will you be leaving soon?" He had not found Antoine. Would they send him somewhere else?

A frown creased his brow. "No." He turned his head. "I wrote asking permission to wed."

She choked, raised her hands to her throat. He gave a soft exclamation. "Did I hurt you?"

He had asked permission to wed. She counted the stars she could see sparkling above her to stop the tears from gathering in her eyes. Richard had been taken from her, now Henri would walk away, go to his bride. After she had given herself to him.

When she could speak, she asked, "Who will you wed?" She tried to keep her voice from betraying her, but it caught on the last word.

His eyes widened and his lips parted in a slow smile. He took her hand and raised it to his lips. "My lady Maríana, would you do me the honor of consenting to stand at my side as the Baroness of Bauçais?"

Now her throat trembled and a shudder passed through her limbs. Could this be? Then she remembered what Johanna had told her. At last she could only whisper, "But you are my cousin. Grandmother said... And what about your family? Won't your family object?"

Henri laughed and rose to his feet, pulling her with him and helping her brush off the bits of dirt and flowers still clinging to her gown. "Why would they object? You would bring them the blood of the Capets!" He stopped laughing when she flinched. "Do you think we did not know Johanna's parentage?"

He held her, tenderly stroking her arms with his fingertips. "You and I share no blood relation. Johanna's mother was with child and Louis needed to find a worthy mate who would take her and ask no questions." He raised his hand and caressed her cheek. "Johanna's mother died and my grandfather married my grandmother later."

Henri looked younger now and a dimple creased his left cheek. "But I am telling you nothing you do not already know." He pulled her out of the bed of violets and onto the path. "Tiens, who is there to object? I am the baron, and if I agree to leave the reins of Bauçais in my brother Guy's hands for a while longer, he will say nothing." He wound his arms around her. "Bishop Durand counts the degrees of blood kinship, not kinship based only on marital alliance," he said, his voice smothered again by the weight of her hair as he buried his face in it. "Still, I needed to ask for special permission from him. But he owes me," he breathed, his lips brushing the skin of her neck.

He backed away. "We had better go to the lake now. If we stay out here much longer, I cannot say what I will do."

"But if we are to wed..." Worse than a harlot, that is what Alys would say. But María did not care. She wanted him near, wanted to feel his need, to ease the heavy ache of longing she held within her.

He reached out; his hand hovered in the air near her face, then dropped to his side again. "No." He smiled now, but his eyes were sad. "I cannot say that I am sorry about our joining," the dimple in his left cheek deepened, then his face grew solemn again, "but I have dishonored you." He looked down. "We should not meet alone again until we are wed."

María watched as Henri lifted his sword, bound it to his side. "Very well," she said. He paused in fastening the belt that held his sword and looked up at her, brows raised. She touched his lips. "Until we are wed."

Chapter 19

YSABEL STORMED around her room, throwing her clothing and goblets against the wall in her rage. Once she had broken nearly everything in sight, she collapsed upon the bed and stared at the wall. Louis-Philippe had grown more distant as her body began to take on a more womanly shape. It was October now and no matter what she did, she could not disguise the bulge of the child growing in her belly. She stroked her middle. "My child will inherit the château, not Maríana." Henri had somehow gotten permission to wed her stepdaughter. Louis-Philippe had announced their betrothal last month. Ysabel was outraged. Cousins marrying? She had never heard of such a thing. How did Henri convince Bishop Durand to allow this?

Ysabel had watched Maríana and Henri going everywhere arm-in-arm. It had choked her to see them, but it had been at least somewhat bearable while Louis-Philippe was in her bed every night. Now she found herself unable to sleep, pacing and always stopping outside of the long knights' room. But Henri had his squire sleep on a pallet next to him every night. She could not visit Henri there.

She had even sent a note to Henri from Maríana, asking him to meet her in the garden, and to come alone. Ysabel had waited, seated upon a stone shelf next to the pond. Henri never appeared; Robert came instead. She had watched as the boy searched the garden, then left shaking his head.

Ysabel pummeled her pillow and growled. She was sure the girl was breeding, too. Johanna had sent for the midwife from Reuilles-la-ville just last week. At first, Ysabel thought the woman had come to see her. After all, she carried the heir, didn't she? Yet the midwife had breezed past Ysabel and entered Maríana's chamber. Now Ysabel wrung her hands, making reddened blotches on her palms. A scarlet and black wave curled up from her belly when she thought of Maríana having Henri's child.

She hissed, "No one can take him from me! I will have him back. I will have him *and* Louis-Philippe!" But how?

A hushed murmuring issued from her cabinet. The mannikin was speaking again. Ysabel rolled over onto her back and waited. It had left her alone after she had used its taunts to get her into Louis-Philippe's bed, but now it whispered to her. She scowled and waved her hand. "If you cannot speak clearly, I will not listen." True, it had helped her trick Louis-Philippe into believing that the child she carried was his, yet it had not meant to help her. "What good are you, anyway?" she added. "Ibrahim is still alive. You have not done your job."

"So you want him dead now?" Its voice floated out from the cabinet.

Did she? "Yes," she said. Why not? With Ibrahim out of the way entirely she would surely tempt Louis-Philippe back into her bed, after the baby was born and she could fit into her brother's breeches. But she did not want to wait until then. She wanted Henri now.

"You took me out too soon," the mannikin said. "Now you must wait."

Ysabel sniffed and rubbed her belly. Why did she bother speaking to that thing? Still, there must be something she could do to capture Henri. Another mannikin? She considered it briefly, then shook her head. She would not go through even one month of that madness again. She ignored the deep chuckles emerging from her cabinet.

Her fingers traced the expanse of her belly. The baby followed her motion when she did this, jabbed her with his feet or elbows. Her baby. Louis-Philippe might recoil from the swell of her belly, but Ysabel had often seen Henri's eyes drawn to her middle.

Henri was no longer in Maríana's bed, of that she was sure. She knew frustrated lust when she saw it. Whenever he looked at her stepdaughter, his eyes burned with suppressed longing. For the past month, Ysabel had seen Henri stalking the corridors of Reuilles-le-château at all hours of the night, Robert stumbling along at his side. Blast the boy! If Robert were not always present, Ysabel was sure she could get Henri into her bed. His need was held in check, but there were ways to break the barriers he had set.

Henri still found Ysabel beautiful. She knew this. He avoided her. That told her a lot. She had asked Johanna to put Henri beside her at all meals. Since last month, Maríana had been taking all of her meals in her chamber, so Johanna agreed. At each meal, whenever Ysabel touched Henri — reaching for her goblet, pushing her sleeves up, leaning toward him to speak — he became very still. And she felt the heat emanating from his arms, his thighs. Henri had even taken to immersing himself in the lake every morning. Ysabel knew from her brother that priests recommended cold water as a cure for lust. Her brother had told her that it was painful, this cure, and did not entirely soothe the heat in his blood.

Just last week Ysabel had come upon Henri after his morning swim in the lake, had seen him rise up out of the frigid water, his golden brown hair darkened, sparkling drops flying when he shook his head. She should have looked away; it was unseemly to stare at his naked form, but she could not tear her eyes from the glory of his body. Jeanne had pulled at her gown, tried to bring her away. It was the silly woman's chattering that had drawn Henri's eyes to where Ysabel stood. He had turned aside and draped the cloth Robert handed him across his shoulders, hiding his body from her sight.

But Ysabel had felt the heat behind his eyes. His fire was banked, but what would it take to fan the flames? Her pathetic stepdaughter spent all her days and nights huddled in her chamber with Alys or puking in the privy. Stupid girl could not even keep a baby in her. Ysabel sat up so quickly that red and black spots floated before her eyes. That must be why Henri could not bed Maríana! The midwife must have told Johanna that Maríana would lose the baby, and Johanna would allow nothing to harm her precious granddaughter.

So, Henri was barred from Maríana's bed, was he? Well, Ysabel could use this. She would continue to follow Henri, wait for the opportunity to approach him. He could not hold himself in check forever.

But what if Maríana recovered? Ysabel ground her teeth. The thought of Maríana and Henri together made her stomach churn. Ysabel would not use a mannikin again, but there must be some way she could eliminate her rival. A scandal? Perhaps she could plant evidence of a prior lover, that de la Guerche knight. But no. Richard had been gone for too long. No one would believe it. Ysabel's thoughts drifted now, turning in slow circles. A scandal. No one ever talked about Maríana's mother. That was strange, wasn't it? What had happened to her? Thérèse had been young when she died, that was all Ysabel knew. She leaned forward and vigorously rubbed her forehead. An idea had started to form, but she needed information first.

Servants' gossip. That was what she needed. Servants were always ready to tell tales. Ysabel rose from the bed and looked around her. She needed someone to deal with her chamber, to sweep up the broken goblets, to repair the torn garments. Jeanne always cleaned Ysabel's room. She would find this Jeanne.

YSABEL DESCENDED the central stairs to the great hall. The palais was filling with guests for her stepdaughter's wedding. The ceremony was set for late November, but many were arriving early to avoid early snow storms and to enjoy Reuilles-le-château hospitality. Ysabel snorted. November was a stupid time for a wedding, but Henri and Maríana could not wait, could they? Most of these guests would be staying until the snows melted in the early spring.

She glanced at the young knight walking at her side and smiled. After Jeanne had told her to ask Richard about Maríana's mother, Ysabel had gone to the knights' room to find Richard and discovered that he was expected, but had not yet arrived from Bourdeilles. However, a friend from his days as a squire, Jean-Pierre Rhomboid, was there talking to Arnaut Vaillancourt. Jean-Pierre was now a stalwart knight from his fief near Paris, thoroughly French, and utterly disgusted with the free and easy life he saw at Reuilles-le-château. He had left the knights' room with Ysabel, explaining that he was quartered in the donjon because the palais was overflowing with guests for the wedding. Ysabel had gritted her teeth at the mention of Maríana's wedding, but had formed a smile and asked if he would have some mead with her in the great hall.

After they settled into cushioned chairs near the hearth, Jean-Pierre was only too happy to talk about Maríana. Ysabel sat and stared at him as he told her a tale of a green and gold light that Maríana had woven into the air, causing a great storm of wind to arise. Nonsense, all of it. The girl was just a pale shadow. Maríana could not possibly have the power Jean-Pierre was describing. But Ysabel could use this, yes she could. She gasped and smiled at all the right moments as the pompous dullard gave her everything she needed and more. He said he had not been able to get the image of the green-gold light out of his mind, so he had looked into the history of Maríana's mother.

"They are all witches," he whispered. "Priests from Carcasonne came here while Maríana was still a child, and they took her mother away." Here he nodded sagely and patted Ysabel's knee.

"What did they do to her mother?" Ysabel ignored the hand Jean-Pierre had placed upon her knee and widened her eyes.

Jean-Pierre looked around to see if anyone was listening, then made a sound like the crackling of flames. "They took her all the way to St. Jean Pied de Port to burn her," he said. "They would not have allowed her to be burnt around here. Too many of them here are also witches," he sniffed. "I only came to the wedding to honor Baron de Bauçais."

YSABEL THANKED him for his tale, then nearly spun up the stairs and down the corridor to her room. She went to her table and drew out quill, parchment and ink. Seating herself, she wet the quill carefully and began to write: "Your Eminence..."

She paused. Why not accuse Ibrahim, too? That would rid her of two enemies. Her hand flew across the parchment, only stopping to sprinkle sand across the ink to dry it. When she had finished, she knew that she had sealed Ibrahim's fate and Maríana would join him on the pyre.

She sealed the message with wax imprinted with her mark. Her fingers shook as she carried it down the central staircase and out into the bailey. Could she trust this with Guillaume? He usually saw that messages from the château were delivered. Eh bien. She had no other alternative. Smoothing her expression, she handed the sealed parchment to Guillaume and told him to see it sent to Carcasonne. Then she stood and watched as Louis-Philippe's seneschal placed her document in the leather pack strapped to his servant's horse and ordered the man to carry it to the bishop's residence in Carcasonne.

With any luck, the messenger should reach Carcasonne before the end of October. Ysabel clasped her hands across her belly and turned toward the palais to see Henri stride out of the doors to the great hall.

Chapter 20

HENRI WAS pacing again. All the days seemed to merge. He found himself striding through the corridors, through the great hall, the bailey, even the kitchens. Robert scurried to match his restless motion. The boy said nothing but Henri saw the shadows beneath his eyes. All night, every night they walked the upper hallways, the stables, the top of the donjon. Henri did not pace during the day. There was much to be accomplished at the château now that Johanna and Louis-Philippe were taken up with the preparations for the arrival of Ysabel's child and Henri and Maríana's wedding.

Henri gladly assumed many of the day-to-day details of the management of the barony. Every day he took Louis-Philippe's place in the great hall, hearing complaints and dispensing justice. Most of his afternoons were spent on the jousting fields watching the progress of the squires. But the nights were endless.

He stopped in front of Maríana's chamber and Robert nearly collided with him. Henri caught Robert easily and looked into the boy's pale face, at the green tinge around his mouth. "Robert." The boy lifted his head and stood ready but his hands trembled and he blinked away a trace of moisture in his eyes. Henri sighed. Robert's father would never forgive him if the boy sickened. Glancing up and down the empty corridor, Henri took Robert's arm and said, "Go to bed."

Robert's face sagged with relief. The boy gave a quick bow and stumbled back toward his pallet in the long knights' room. Robert would rest now. God willing, he would not grow ill.

Henri watched his squire's retreating form. He had used Robert as a barrier, first to keep Ysabel at bay, and later to protect the chastity of his betrothed. Now Henri leaned against Maríana's door and shuddered. What was wrong with him? He had gone without a woman for years. During his time in the abbey, desire brought pain; afterward when he found that he could no longer complete the act, he avoided women.

His breath stopped as he thought of Maríana asleep on the other side of the door. He had not needed a woman for years. Yet now he could barely go through a single day without the heavy ache of wanting driving him to pace the corridors all night. He caressed the slick wooden surface of the door, felt its cool smoothness.

He moved away from the door and looked up and down the corridor. Louis-Philippe had his palais arranged for comfort as well as beauty. He had artisans smooth and polish the floors, the doors and frames.

AT FIRST, Henri had dismissed the baron as a weak courtier, interested more in the symmetry of an arched window than in strength of arms. But after watching Louis-Philippe on the fields he revised his assessment. De Reuilles was an able opponent and a wily strategist. And he had readily agreed to the alliance between Bauçais and de Reuilles. When Henri brought the message from Bishop Durand approving the marriage of Henri de Bauçais and Maríana de Reuilles to Louis-Philippe, the baron's eyes had widened in surprise. But he had agreed to the match, even before Maríana knew that she carried Henri's child within her. His child.

Johanna was angry with him. Henri remembered the frost in her eyes when she told him that his betrothed was expecting his child. A flood of joy had warmed his heart when he heard her words, but the midwife had cautioned him. Maríana was bleeding. Johanna had ordered her granddaughter to stay in her chamber, nursed by Alys and the swarthy gardener who somehow seemed to have free access to everywhere in the château.

Once, Henri even thought he saw the raven-haired woman and silver-haired old man from his fevered dream of Reuilles-la-ville coming out of Maríana's chamber. But that could not be. After he recovered, Henri had gone back into Reuilles-la-ville, to the house of Antoine Jakintza, and found it deserted. He must have imagined what happened there. Maríana told him the illness that had confined him to his bed for days after his first visit to Antoine's house in Reuilles-la-ville may have caused the strange dream of a woman with angry gray-green eyes and a man with a silver beard. It must be true, because since that time, Henri had found no one who could tell him of these people. And he could not remember their names.

NOW, HENRI'S breath puffed out between his teeth and his hands clutched the door latch. All he had to do was open the door, order Alys to leave, crawl into bed beside his beloved, hold her... but he could not. The midwife said that he would endanger Maríana's life if he took her now.

"Forty days," the midwife told him. "If we can stop the bleeding for forty days, then we shall see."

Forty days. Henri counted the days, counted them as he paced. Thirty-nine, thirty-eight, now there were thirty days left. Guillaume had noticed Henri's heated pacing, had cautiously recommended one of the kitchen maids. The girl was eager. She joined with all the visiting knights. Henri even went to the kitchen, seeking the girl. But something stopped him. He could not say what it was. The girl was fair. Her face was pleasing. Yet he could not approach her. So he paced.

A groan issued from his throat and he pushed away from the door.

His foot trod on something soft. A single yelp of pain echoed behind him. "Robert? I thought..." Henri turned and looked into the wide brown eyes of Ysabel. "Baroness de Reuilles." He caught her as she stumbled against him and held her steady. "I did not hear you. Please forgive my clumsy feet."

"Henri." Ysabel searched his face. "It would seem that you and I suffer from a similar malady."

"What is that?" He could not seem to let her go.

"My husband cannot abide me in his bed now and your bride-to-be cannot have you in hers."

He forced his hands to drop from her arms. "What?"

She reached out and traced his mouth with her fingers. He shivered in response, then ground his teeth. She smelled of roses and warm skin.

"You know where my chamber is." Ysabel backed away. "I will wait there for you."

Henri watched her progress down the corridor, heard her door open and close. "Never." He ran his hand through his hair, felt the skin of his scalp tingle. Why did the touch of Ysabel's hand against his mouth set his blood on fire? He had felt no desire to bed the kitchen maid, yet his body now warred with his will, demanding he join with Ysabel. Never.

THE NEXT night Henri stopped outside Ysabel's door for the hundredth time, and placing his hand upon the latch, opened it. He had left Robert sleeping on the pallet next to his bed. The chamber was dark, but he could still see Ysabel. She was sitting in the bed, naked except for the blankets wound around her.

"Don't worry," she said. "Louis-Philippe never comes to my chamber, and none of the servants would dare enter without my permission. If you like, we can prop the chair against the door..."

Ysabel lifted her arms to him and the blankets dropped away. Henri stood in the doorway looking at her, then he closed the door and dragged the chair over, placing it so entry would be difficult. He stood a moment longer, his eyes taking in the curves of her body. Her breasts had ripened, the nipples a dark pink hue. Her arms had rounded and the curve of her belly drew his eyes to the space between her legs. She had folded her legs, sitting tailor-fashion. Henri swayed, his hand slipping from the chair that barred the door. He went into her embrace.

Chapter 21

YSABEL READ the message Guillaume had given her. "This cannot be right!" she cried. "They cannot be coming for my Louis-Philippe!" She had quivered when she saw the Bishop's seal on the parchment and carried it up to her chamber to open it. Her hands gripped the page and she read through it again. What had gone wrong? She had named only Ibrahim and Maríana. Her eyes scanned the message once more. Yes, Louis-Philippe as well as Ibrahim and Maríana appeared on the list. "What can I do?" Her feet took her to the opposite side of the room and back again.

As she paced, she started speaking to the mannikin. It was something she found herself doing more and more these days. "I will remove Ibrahim. Mother Utarilla can tell me how. Then they cannot know that he and my Louis-Philippe were..." Her throat closed on the word. She wound her mantle around her body, arranging the hood so it hid her face. It was early in the day. If she hurried, she would have enough time to go into Reuilles-la-ville and be back before anyone missed her.

UTARILLA looked the same. Her bright eyes stared at Ysabel when she walked through the door.

"I need to kill someone, old woman," Ysabel said, seating herself across from Utarilla and smoothing her gown.

Utarilla cackled, waving her hands toward Ysabel's belly. "Someone has been riding you, eh? Seems the charm worked."

Ysabel pressed her hands against her belly. "You could say that. But now I need something more and I will pay well."

Utarilla waited, her eyes half-closed.

"I need plants that will kill. Something I can put into drink or food, something that has no taste so he will not know."

Utarilla rubbed her forehead. "Not many things that can do that, no." She closed her eyes and murmured, "Not again. Once is enough, but if I help her again..."

Ysabel leaned forward. "What?" Once is enough? Had the old woman lost her senses?

Utarilla opened her eyes, but she did not seem to see Ysabel. Her eyes blinked twice, then cleared. "There is one thing. The bones could do it, yes. Yellow water." She rubbed her lips and chin. "But you must put it in something sweet and the herbs must be freshly ground, or else it can be detected."

"What must I do?"

"You must make it yourself." Utarilla leaned forward and caught the edge of Ysabel's mantle. "Gather belargusia at the black moon. Dry it in total darkness for three days, then grind it up into dust."

"It is November, old woman. The gardens are all cut back and the beds are all made ready for winter."

Utarilla's eyes grew larger, the dark part filling the sockets so that no white showed at all. A shiver ran through Ysabel, but she refused to let the old woman see her fear. She tossed her head. "There was ice on the lake this morning. I cannot wait till spring." Ysabel stood and walked toward the door.

"Wait." Utarilla spoke softly, yet her voice throbbed with a humming sound that compelled Ysabel to stop where she stood. "You will find that there is still belargusia in the garden. Ask one who knows the plants." She chuckled, a low hollow sound. "Some call it 'belladoña,' the beautiful woman. Just ask." Her eyes grew even blacker, even larger. "During the same black moon you must dig up a corpse — child's corpse is best — take the bones of that corpse and boil them with the powder. Once it is done, drain off the yellow water from the top, put it into a sweet drink and serve it. No matter how little he drinks — even if he just touches it to his lips-his fate will be sealed."

"How much do I pay?" Ysabel opened her bag and spilled the gold pieces out onto the bed.

Utarilla looked at the gold. "I must take enough," she murmured. "For my grandson and his wife. It must be enough for the smithy he wants to build. Then I can die in peace." She paused, fingering the edges of the coins. Then her ancient, ropy hands swept up the entire amount of gold Ysabel had poured out on the bed.

YSABEL KNEELED in the herb garden. She had waited three days until the new moon after having Yves show her what the Basques called belargusia. She was now digging up just enough to make the yellow water.

The old hag had been right. There were still some herbs and plants in the garden, though not many, and this belargusia was poison, all right. Yves had asked her some very pointed questions when she inquired where it grew, only falling silent when she threatened to have him thrown in the dungeon for his impertinence. Then he showed her where to find the tall plants only under continued threat. The dolt actually had the nerve to smile and bow to her after he had shown her to the belargusia!

Ysabel huffed as she dug three plants out by their roots. She had already obtained the bones of a baby that had died at birth. Dug it up herself, as the old woman had commanded. Really, it was just a bag of bones, anyhow, and a small, fragile skull. She ignored the single tear that slipped down her cheek and her mouth twisted in scorn as she stuffed the long, spindly plants into a bag she had sewn together for this purpose.

A slithering wet sigh came from the direction of the pond. Ysabel held her breath and listened. Snakes. It must be snakes. She shuddered, scanning the ground where she huddled. There was nothing near. No black forms crawled toward her. But she could still hear something moving. It sounded like it was in the pond. She kept hearing water dripping. Could Henri be swimming in the pond? Ysabel caught her breath and peered into the silver and gray shadows.

No, this was not Henri. Someone was singing a lullaby. Ysabel listened to the hollow voice and her blood chilled. She did not want to meet the singer of that song. The melody rose and fell. Some words were whispered, others crooned. Whatever it was, it was in the pond. She could see a dark form move across the waters.

Putting her hands out to steady her ungainly body, she heaved herself up off the ground and then scurried out of the garden, her heart beating like a bird imprisoned within her chest. Her baby squirmed and kicked. "Stop that!" she scolded it, tapping her belly. She breathed deeply in relief when she reached the palais and closed the door on the night. Clutching the bag, she made her way to her room to dry the plants for her potion.

IBRAHIM SAT wrapped in his white robes, his head nodding now and then as he went in and out of a light sleep. The black sickness that had started in his bowels months before had spread throughout his body now and he knew that the end would come soon. The illness had spread quickly after he helped heal Maríana. But he had to give of himself to help her, to try to save her baby.

He might have had a month or two more if he had not used his energy in that healing, but what was a month or two? He had seen people taken by this before. It was his own body eating itself. He gave a short laugh without mirth, but also without bitterness. Eating itself like the serpent devouring its tail. He thought of the story Thérèse had told him about the three serpents. "Only one will be left, my love," he whispered into the air.

Ibrahim felt that Thérèse was close these days, and wanted to join her, but he hoped to be able to stay alive long enough to see Maríana's baby. Yet he was not certain that they had been able to save it. Even Iranzu and Leila were not sure. The passage of time would reveal their success or failure. His eyes closed and he drifted for a while in a reverie, then raised his head when he heard feet crunching across the new snow that carpeted his courtyard and clogged his fountain.

He pulled his robe tighter and waited. Perhaps it was Geneviéve.

She had been visiting him every day since he found he could no longer walk without difficulty. He became weaker by the hour, it seemed. He liked her visits. She did not mind the fact that he was dying, and only sought to either bring him cheer, or bring him the herbs and plants that would take the edge off the crushing pain he experienced all the time now. If only she would stop asking him to tell Louis-Philippe about his illness.

Louis-Philippe would give himself away if he knew. Ibrahim was sure that the baron would not stay away. No, it was better that he not know. Louis-Philippe was married now, with a child on the way, finally safe from whispers and speculation. He no longer had to worry. They would not burn him. But if he saw Ibrahim dying, he might forget why they had sent for Ysabel. He might come to the palace, stay with Ibrahim while he died. The whispers would start again and he would be in danger. And for what?

Ibrahim was going to die anyway. Nothing Louis-Philippe could do would stop that.

Ibrahim knew that he could trust Geneviéve to keep the news of his decline from Maríana. He himself had placed barriers to prevent Maríana from sensing the seriousness of his illness. There would be no purpose in her suffering along with him. She could not help him and it would only grieve her to watch him die. He shivered. The dead were already stroking his skin with their cold fingers. He looked up as his door opened. But it was not Geneviéve.

Ysabel entered the room, carrying a large goblet. What did she want? "Baroness." He gestured for her to sit down.

Ysabel placed the goblet on the low table in front of Ibrahim and maneuvered her body into the chair he had indicated.

"What is this?" Ibrahim pointed to the goblet.

"Methegelin." Ysabel smiled. "Geneviéve said you were unwell, so I thought a little of the baron's favorite drink might help you."

Ibrahim brought the goblet to his lips. Taking a mouthful, he swallowed. Ysabel was leaning forward, delight now spreading across her face. Why was she suddenly so happy?

"Well, I will not keep you from your rest," she said with a brittle smile, her eyes glittering. She spent a few moments struggling to get out of the chair as Ibrahim looked on in amusement.

"God be with you," he said to her as she was on her way out, and was startled to see her flinch.

IBRAHIM EXHALED, then brought the goblet to his nose again. What was in this? Did she really think to heal him with it? It was not like anything he knew, except the faintest odor of gentian. Was she giving him a fever-reducing herb? He frowned. If she only knew. There was nothing she could do to help him. He considered various reasons for her visit, then drew his breath in a labored groan as pain broke through the barrier he had drawn with his own herbal mixture.

He lurched unsteadily to his feet to go to the kitchen where the mixture waited, promising blessed relief. On his way there, next to the windows, a curtain of black dropped down over his eyes and he dimly felt his body hit the ground. When he opened his eyes again he found that he could not move, but the pain was also gone. He was not sure how long he had lain there when a shadow fell across his body and he saw Ysabel bending over him, her face twisted in hatred.

"Still awake, eh? Don't worry, it won't be for long."

Curious. His eyes were open and he could still see and hear, but he could neither move nor speak, except to blink his eyes. He could hear her rummaging in his kitchen, finally returning to the larger chamber carrying a jug of the sweet white wine he loved. What did she want with it? Why had she come back?

He heard her sniff, then snort. "That old hag!" she exploded. "She told me no one would be able to smell it, but I certainly can!" Now footsteps padded to the door and he heard the sound of liquid hitting the snow-covered stones. More furtive sounds followed. Was she wiping something? Then the clank of an empty cup being set down. Next, the pop of the stone covering his jug of wine and a silvery cascade of liquid filling a cup.

"I don't have time to do more," she said, her face swimming into view as she leaned over him. "But no one will know what I have done. No one saw me come up here. When they see the two cups they will know you have been murdered, but no one will suspect me."

Ibrahim stared into her eyes. How could she think her gentian had killed him? She had not killed him. He still breathed, but he knew the end was near. It was the blackness eating inside of him that was his killer. He closed his eyes. Fatigue was wrapping its noxious cloud around him. Why would she want to kill him?

"You were taking too long to die," Ysabel stated, as if she could hear his thoughts. He opened his eyes. She was watching his face. "I had the mannikin baptized with your name. Then I stuck it with needles. When you became ill I thought that would be all I would have to do. But that didn't work, did it? I did not keep it next to me for long enough."

Suddenly she started to cry. Her tears pattered down on his face in a warm, salt rain. "I just received this." She held a scrap of parchment in front of his eyes. He saw a flowing signature, but the words did not make any sense. It looked like a list of names. "It says that the Inquisitor will be here soon. I cannot let you drag my Louis-Philippe down with you.

"You twisted my beautiful Louis-Philippe. You ruined him so that he could never want me as a man should want a woman. Once you are gone maybe he will love me." She paused, wiping her eyes with the back of her hand. Then her voice and face hardened. "Even if he never wants me again I will have more children." She laughed bitterly. "They will all look like Henri, but who cares?"

Ibrahim's eyes widened, and he started to choke. What was she saying?

"Oh, that got a reaction, did it?" Ysabel sneered. "Well, your precious Maríana won't have my Henri. I have enough evidence to burn her. I will have Jean-Pierre accuse her of trying to kill you! All I have to do is have others discover the evidence so that Henri does not know that I am the one who will destroy that puny brat!"

Maríana! Ibrahim struggled to send out his thoughts, his feelings to her. She was deeply asleep, that much he could sense. But he could not reach her. He had never been good at the Jakintza mind-talk. Why hadn't he practiced it more, as Thérèse had wanted? Ysabel kept talking to him, but he could not understand her words. His eyes fixed upon the piece of parchment she held. Could he take it with him, take it to Maríana? He knew his end was upon him and he had seen a dervish who could transport objects by leaving his body. But could he do this? Sweat beaded on his forehead as he focused. Something like an arm lifted from his body, sprouted fingers, closed upon the parchment that Ysabel held. There! He had it. But the chamber flooded with a light that was all colors and no color, a light that lived and breathed and sang. Ibrahim drew together all the energy he had left and leaped out into the living light he saw shining all around him.

YSABEL WATCHED him die. A quiver started in her belly as she watched his breathing fail, heard the rattle deep within his throat and chest, saw his eyes glaze. She drew back. It was not unlike what she felt when she held a man inside her, this quiver. Tiens! Ibrahim had stopped shaking and all animation left his body. But his eyes were still open. Well *she* would not close them for him! She pulled her bulk up off the floor where she squatted. She looked across the chamber, at the pillows, the rich tapestries, the wooden chests. Maybe she would turn this into her home. Maybe when Louis-Philippe saw her there he would make love to her, once she had regained her shape and could play at being a man again.

Where was the message from the bishop? Surely she had just held it in her hand. She paced the floor of the palace, skirting around Ibrahim's body. Perhaps it had fallen beneath him? She approached his inert form and stopped several paces away.

His sightless eyes seemed to glare at her. No, she could not move him to see if it was there. If someone found the message under his body, she could say she had sent it up to him. After all, it had his name on it.

Yes, she would say just that. They could think what they liked. She was Baroness de Reuilles.

Louis-Philippe was safe, now that Ibrahim was dead. That was why she had done this. She glanced around the chamber again. It was time to get back before she was missed. She had told the guard she was going to the lake to pray for the health of her baby — many of the people in this region shared this superstition. The guard had accepted this, but if she was out for too long, he might suspect she was doing something else.

She exited the chamber, leaving the door slightly ajar, and lifted her face. Snow was falling again. Her tracks would be hidden. Raising her head, she marched back down the path to Reuilles-le-château.

Chapter 22

IBRAHIM WAS in her chamber. Maríana blinked and sat up in her bed. Glow from the banked hearth fire gave a muted illumination to Alys asleep on her pallet, the dark mounds that formed the divan and her tapestry frame. But no Ibrahim.

She leaned back against her pillow. Why did her stomach tremble? The nausea that had plagued her for the past two months had fled. The midwife had even allowed her to go down to the great hall that evening. Henri's eyes had shone when he saw her descend the staircase. He had kept her at his side as he went around the family table, greeting guests who had come to Reuilles-le-château for the wedding. Their wedding.

She lifted her arms up over her head and stretched. Baroness Maríana de Bauçais. Henri had told her that Bauçais was north of Paris. His fief bordered the sea that separated the Kingdom of France from Britain. But he owed fealty to Louis of France. Would he take her to Paris to see the king? She would like that.

And the sea. Henri had told her that in Bauçais he awoke every morning to the sound of gulls, the salt and sea weed fragrance of the ocean. He would take her there after the wedding, as soon as she was well enough to travel. Perhaps after the baby was born. The midwife had not let her stay for the feast. Johanna had ordered her to return to her chamber before the first course was served. Still, she was growing stronger each day. It would not be long until she would be able to join her Henri. To wed him.

She looked at the far corner of her chamber where her wedding gown hung. She knew every stitch, had tried it on every morning since it had been made. Jeanne had done well with this gown. Pale embroidered violets trimmed the ivory silk. After she tried it on, Maríana had made Alys cover it with a blanket. She did not want Henri to see it until she stood before Father Gregory with him.

Henri came to her each day with tales of his fief, of Bauçais. Of green fields and thick forest that stretched from Gréves to the sea. His fief supported three large towns! Her father's fief only supported Reuilles-la-ville. Henri said that his château was smaller than Reuilles-le-château. As if this mattered! His eyes had warmed while he told her of Bauçais, of his brother Guy. But when she asked about his father, his eyes had dimmed, and when she mentioned his mother, a flash of something like rage had shone from his face. A puzzle. His mother still lived, she knew that.

Ah, well. She need not worry. His mother had retired to Fontevrault Abbey. And Henri assured her that his brother Guy would adore his bride, his Maríana. Still, she would be far from everything she had ever known. Far from Johanna, from Geneviéve. Far from Ibrahim.

She wriggled deeper into the bed. A whispering rustle drew her attention. Her hand rested on something slick and dry. Something that crinkled when she moved her fingers.

She picked it up. A note? Could Henri have left a message? Warmth spread through her and she absently patted the slight bulge that curved outward from her loins to her navel. "Your father left me a message," she whispered. Since the midwife told her the danger was past — she had stopped bleeding — Maríana found herself talking to the baby.

She swung her feet off the bed and groped for her slippers and robe. It had snowed earlier and her toes curled against the chill as she stumbled to the hearth and used an ember to light her night candle. Alys muttered. The blankets covering her heaved, then settled, as she turned toward the wall. Maríana held her breath. She wanted to read Henri's note by herself, not with Alys leaning over her shoulder, asking what he said.

How had Henri entered her chamber and left this note without waking Alys? He was not clumsy, but there were many objects in her chamber that would trip a fellow; pots of seedlings filled one corner of the room and Maríana had strewn the loose woven sacks she used to dry her medicinal plants across the floor. She shrugged. Henri would have to tell her later how he had gotten the note on her bed.

She scanned the message, dropping first to the bold signature and seal at the bottom. A finger of ice traced her spine. This was not Henri's writing. The signature curved in on itself, difficult to decipher. She looked at the top and read, By the order of His Eminence Bishop Durand, the Inquisitor Jean Becier will be sent to Reuilles-le-château to look into the matter you presented to us. Following this was a list of names.

The paper slipped from her nerveless fingers. Three names. Her name was at the top of the list. She shook her head and retrieved the paper from where it had fallen. This must a jest. The signature looked like H, then Arcis. No, it was des Arcis. Didn't Henri say that he served under des Arcis? She stared at the list of names and her throat closed. The second name was Ibrahim Al'Khaldun. No one but her family and Bernart knew him as Ibrahim.

She turned the paper over. Who had received this? She touched the name on the outer surface. Baroness Ysabel de Reuilles. Ysabel? But that could not be. Maríana turned it back to the list of names. The third name was Louis-Philippe. Ysabel was expecting Louis-Philippe's child. She would not bring the Inquisition to Reuilles-le-château! Maríana stood holding the parchment, staring at the message. It fluttered as her hand shook.

What should she do? Take it to Johanna? But that would alarm her grandmother. If it was just a joke, there was no need to frighten Johanna. Should she go to Ysabel? She had heard that her stepmother often wandered the corridors late at night. Just a few weeks ago, Maríana had been wakened by her stepmother's voice outside her door. And Ysabel seldom appeared in the great hall until the sun was well into the sky. Johanna often complained about this. What was the hour now? Maríana had not heard the watch since she awakened.

She creased the note. Ysabel. She must see her now. This would not wait until morning. She would go to Ysabel, ask her stepmother what this meant.

THERE WERE still people in the corridors; perhaps it was not that late. As Maríana left her chamber, she heard the watch proclaim the hour. Midnight. Well, if need be, she would awaken her stepmother. She passed Lady Béarn, inclining her head and dropping into a brief curtsey when the older woman smiled. At the end of the corridor, three knights huddled around a young girl from the palais kitchen. One knight raised his head as Maríana passed, but he did not speak. The corridor beyond was empty. To the left was the long knights' room, to the right and around a corner lay her stepmother's chamber. One more turn now.

Who could have placed the message on her bed? Perhaps Jeanne? Jeanne cleaned Ysabel's room; she could have seen the message and taken it to Maríana. But no. Jeanne could not read. Ysabel herself must have left it. It was an odd sort of jest, but Ysabel could be strange. Several times, Maríana had heard Ysabel conversing with someone, only there was no one near her stepmother.

Maríana did not hear Ysabel's door open until she was almost upon it. The door swung out and she backed away, retreating around the corner that led to Ysabel's corridor. She did not want to speak of this matter in front of someone else; she would wait until Ysabel was alone. But a man's voice, raised in anger, stopped her feet.

"I told you it is over. I will not visit you again." The last words dipped. Maríana peeked around the corner. The door hid his body but there was no mistaking the voice.

The door swung wider. Maríana's hands curled into fists until her nails bit into her palms. Henri stood there, arms folded and face stern. He glared at her stepmother. Ysabel did not flinch. She laughed and moved forward, then spoke to him, her voice low and breathy. A lover's voice. She reached toward Henri, brushed her fingers against his waist, then moved her hand slowly across his loins.

Maríana swallowed the sour acid that spilled into her mouth, that burned her tongue. Henri did not withdraw from Ysabel's caress. As she watched, Ysabel moved closer to Henri, wound her arms around his

neck, pulled his mouth down to hers. Henri's back stiffened and he
pulled away, but Ysabel grabbed his hand and shoved it into her gown,
plastered his fingers against her breast. He threw his head back, then
groaned as he bent toward Ysabel and folded into her embrace. Ysabel
pulled him with her as she backed into her room. Neither glanced over to
where Maríana stood, rooted to the floor.

Maríana forced herself to move. She reached the door as it shut. She
lifted her hand to rap its surface, then stopped. Think. She must think.

But no thoughts would form. Only the image of Ysabel in Henri's
arms, his lips upon her stepmother's mouth. Her betrothed. How long had
they been meeting, Ysabel and Henri? Why had he asked Maríana to be
his wife? The air was so thick, she could not seem to fill her lungs, and
her hands wrung themselves together so her fingernails pulled at her
flesh.

This could not be! Henri had said he was taking her to Bauçais.
Ysabel would be here in Reuilles-le-château. But Ysabel was from
Gréves, wasn't she? Gréves was next to Bauçais. Maríana looked down.
There. Her hands were still now, rolled into fists again. She could think.

Would Henri harm her? Would he have her burned so he could be
with Ysabel? No, impossible! He could not be a part of the message that
now crinkled in her leather pouch as her fists pressed against her belt.
But he had served under Hughes des Arcis. So. The message.

Pieces that did not fit before now flew into place in front of her.
Perhaps Henri was not part of the message, perhaps he was. This did not
matter now. If Maríana and Louis-Philippe were burned, Ysabel would
have Reuilles-le-château. And she would have Henri. He was Baron de
Bauçais, a Soldier of Christ. When the Inquisitor came, would Henri turn
away from his betrothed? Must Maríana watch his eyes turn to ice when
he discovered that his bride-to-be worked magic with Ibrahim
Al'Khaldun?

Ibrahim! He was in danger, too.

She could not stay; she must consider her own safety, and
Ibrahim's. He must leave with her. They could not be there when the
Inquisitor arrived. Red spots floated past her eyes. How long had she
been standing there staring? She blinked the spots away, then a low ache
spread around the base of her spine, gripped her womb in a vise. Sinking
to the floor, she wrapped her arms around her middle as undulating
agony flowed from her back through her belly, then settled in her spine
again. Someone was whimpering. Was it she?

The pain faded. She drew in her breath and leaned her head against
the door, felt the cool wood against her sweat-dampened face.

And heard the grunting moans. Heard Ysabel's wordless shout of
triumph. Heard Henri's panting cry of need.

Enough! Gritting her teeth and ignoring the pain that lanced her again, she leaped away from Ysabel's door and flew down the corridor to her chamber. Her night candle still burned. Alys had not moved.

Sliding to the floor, Maríana rested her cheek against the inner surface of her door, waited for the pain to dwindle. She must leave Reuilles-le-château. Even if she trusted Henri, could he save her? Henri and Ysabel were not even careful. Anyone could have come along in the corridor and seen them together, as she did. Who else knew that Henri and Ysabel were lovers? Did her father know? He was on the list, too.

No, she must leave. She could not stay to help her father. Could she at least warn him? Did she have time? The message. She would slip it under Johanna's door. Louis-Philippe had not saved Thérèse, but he could save himself. Johanna could call upon the King of France to save her son's life, couldn't she?

Still clutching her belly, Maríana stood and moved in silence to the shelf where her night candle burned. She found the pot of blackberry ink and her sharpened quill, and scrawled Johanna's name across the outer surface of the paper.

Thérèse had not been of their kind; she had been easy prey. Maríana was her daughter. The quill slipped from her hand as she bent around the receding pain and caressed her belly. No time for grief. No time to feel the empty hollow ache left by Henri's betrayal. She must save herself.

Maríana would not stay to stand beside her father, would not risk the life of her child. She pressed her fingers gently into the curve of her belly. The pain had gone away. Now she must see what damage had been wrought. She leaned against the table, then sucked in her breath and raised her gown. After she counted to three, she lowered her head and looked between her legs, sighing in relief when she saw no red stain, no black clots.

Where could she go? She would not draw Alys into danger. If she opened her chest to retrieve her mantle, Alys would waken.   Ibrahim. She must go to Ibrahim. He would know what to do. Her mother had made him promise to take Maríana to Iranzu. But Iranzu and Leila were still in Reuilles-la-ville. She must contact them, let them know of the danger she faced. And slip the message under Johanna's door. It was the best she could do.

Alys was still asleep. Maríana tiptoed across the floor, eased the door open and slipped out before Alys could see her. At best, she would have until dawn, when Alys would awake and see that she was not in the room. Food. She would need food. And warm clothing. But where? She could not get her gown or mantle from her room without waking Alys.

Maríana leaned against the wall and glanced up and down the empty corridor. The donjon. Alys had left her old gowns in their chamber in the donjon. It was now used for storage. If she were lucky, the chest with Alys's old gowns would still be there. Maríana moved down the corridor toward Johanna's chamber. First the note, then food.

And then, the donjon.

LIONEL WAS kneading dough for the morning bread when young Maríana entered the kitchen. "Ah," he said, beaming at her, "wandering again?"

He pulled her to the fire in the hearth, sitting her down on a stool and fetching a small loaf of freshly-baked bread for her. Her face was drawn. Poor thing. Her life had not been easy, they all knew that. Too bad about young de la Guerche, of course. But the Baron of Bauçais seemed a good match for her. She smiled and accepted the bread with thanks. A delight she was, always polite, unlike her stepmother.

He sighed. That was the way of things. Maríana would go away to Bauçais and Ysabel would remain at Reuilles-le-château to make his life a misery. He went back to his kneading.

"Lionel?" she asked.

"Yes, little one?"

"I really am so very hungry. I could not keep my dinner down, and now..." She broke off.

"I will fix up something nice, eh?" Lionel set about gathering the tastier remains of the evening's dinner, pushing chunks of roast meat, bread, and a skin of wine into an empty grain sack. He flung it over his shoulder and started toward the stairs.

"No!" she cried, going pale. He stopped and looked at her, puzzled. "That is," she continued, "I thought to take it to Grandmama's room, and..."

He nodded. Johanna and he had never gotten along, that was well known. "But can you carry it?" he asked. She looked so frail.

"Of course I can, see?" Maríana hefted the bag over her shoulder easily and blew a kiss to Lionel. "Thank you, dear friend! Farewell." She walked purposefully toward the stairs that led to the upper corridors.

Lionel watched her ascend the stairs. Then he shook himself and went back to his baking. Something was not quite right there, but he just couldn't place it. Why did she say "farewell?" He would be seeing her in the morning. Ah, well. The dough was ready now. He reached for his special knife to cut it into pieces for baking. But the knife was not there. Now that was strange. It was there just a moment ago. He searched the tables for it, then asked the boy who was working the bellows, "Have you seen my knife?" The boy shook his head.

Lionel stood with his hands on the table, fingers splayed out. Well, he must get another knife, then. He trotted to the end of the kitchen where all the pots, kettles and cutlery were stored. Who would want his knife? His shoulders lifted in a shrug as he selected another. It would show up later. He returned to the bread dough and began dividing it into loaves.

AT THE TOP of the stairs, Maríana turned and made her way to the back door leading to the pit where slops were thrown. The staircase that descended to the slops pit was deserted, as she had hoped it would be. The smell kept people from lingering nearby. Now she must go outside, walk to the donjon. Would it be locked? When there were many guests, it was often unlocked until quite late. She grasped the thin cloth of her gown and robe and looked at her flimsy slippers in dismay. It had snowed earlier and might still be snowing. If anyone saw her, she would surely be stopped. If she tried to retrieve her mantle, Alys would awaken. Alys could not lie. Her face would betray her. They would catch Maríana. She would burn and Alys would burn, too, for trying to help her. That left Maríana with no choice.

Her breath puffed out in white clouds and her feet grew numb as she walked through drifting snow to the tower. She could not run. She would trip on the cobbles. No one challenged her. The watch must have gone inside to keep warm. She caught glimpses of people in the distance, but their heads were lowered, watching their feet. It still snowed. Her footprints would soon be completely covered in a layer of feather-soft white snow.

Maríana crept up the stairs in the donjon, shivering. Her toes were frozen; she kept hitting them against the stairs. But she blessed these stairs — the door had been open. No one had stopped her. She pushed on the door to her old chamber and slipped inside, then stopped in surprise. It was warm. A hearth fire sent out a gentle glow. Why did they have a hearth fire burning in a storage room?

She felt her way down the three stairs and over to the chest where Alys had kept her clothing and candles. She must have more light. She found the candles and took one to the hearth, lighting it from a smoldering ember. The chamber's windows were so narrow and high up in the walls that no one would see it. She could sit now for a moment, allow her hands to warm.

Maríana wrapped her arms around her ribs and closed her eyes. No more pain in her belly now. Oh, a twinge or two, but still no blood. The baby was not moving, but it was often still for long periods of time. The midwife had told her just yesterday that this was normal, not to worry. She would be with Ibrahim soon. He would know what herbs to take with them to save her baby. But now she must try to reach Iranzu.

She had used the mind-touch Leila had taught her, but never over so great a distance, and never over water. Iranzu and Leila were in Gilbert's home in Reuilles-la-ville. She could not go there, but she must try to contact them. They might be in danger, too. Warmth now spread across her body; she felt the tug of something that she could not name capture her spine, wind around her.

Then she saw a room with two, no, four people laying on straw mattresses upon the floor. Another two huddled together upon a real bed. All sleeping.

Chapter 23

MARÍANA slumped forward. Had she reached them? She flexed her hands and trembled, felt a quiver run up her arms. Usually when she used the mind-touch, she felt colder and her arms tingled. If they had received her message, they would know to flee, to join her at Ibrahim's palace. If she had reached them. The candle she lit had barely burned down. Clothing. She must have warm clothing.

She pried open the latch that fastened her old chest and lifted the lid. The smell of damp and musty wool, of garlic and sprigs of lavender rose from its depths. She pulled out a large woolen gown and tugged it over her nightdress and robe. It flowed out in a loose bulge around her waist, but her belt would cinch it in. She removed the belt and refastened it over the woolen gown, slipping Lionel's kitchen knife in between, so its hilt rested against her side.

A thick mantle lay at the bottom of the chest. Maríana wrapped it around her and fastened it at the neck, hiding her face in the shadow cast by the hood. If anyone saw her now they would not recognize her. The chest closed with a thump. Now shoes. She kicked off her slippers, then put them in the bag Lionel had given her. There must be no sign that she had been in this room. She crossed the floor to where Alys kept her shoes. Stale rushes and dust puffed into the air as her feet shuffled over the stones. She sneezed. Her hand covered her mouth, but the sound rang in her ears. She pinched at her nose to stop another sneeze, then dropped to her knees to retrieve the shoes.

A sharp rustling came from the direction of the bed. Rats?

That side of the chamber was in shadow. She could barely make out the sagging form of her old bed, but something moved there. Her hand slipped into her belt and she stood, fingers playing over the hilt of Lionel's knife.

"Jean-Pierre?" A man's voice, thick and hoarse with sleep, sounded from the bed. "Back already? She must have been disappointing!" The voice broke off as he raised himself on one arm. He saw her. She pulled the knife out of her belt and held it ready. The man grabbed a sword Maríana could now see standing against the wall next to the bed. What was a knight doing here? She raised the knife to throw it, to put it in his throat before he could reach her with his sword. But something stayed her hand.

The man took up his sword and leaped to his feet, advancing on Maríana. "Who are you?" His angry voice rang off the stone walls. He was tall, this man. Tall and well made. And completely naked.

He was closer now. The light of her candle fell upon him, illuminating the black hair framing his face, the tilted, deep brown eyes that widened in recognition.

"Maríana!" he exclaimed, his sword clattering to the floor as he retreated to the far side of the bed. He grabbed a shirt and breeches that lay there, speedily pulling them on. "What are you doing here? You live in the palais now! What are you doing in those clothes?"

Her fingers closed convulsively and she felt the warm flow of blood from where the knife sliced her hand. Raising her hand to her face, she dropped the knife to the floor. She would have buried it in his throat.

He moved forward and took her hand, wrapped his sleeve around the cut. "I don't think it is serious," he said, wiping away the blood that now seeped from the shallow cut on her palm. "There, see? It stops."

She could feel the warmth of his breath upon her hand, see the dark lashes hiding his eyes as he examined her wound. "Richard." How could she sound so calm? "What are you doing here?"

He dropped her hand and backed away, then shifted from foot to foot. "The floor is cold," he said, and moved back over to the bed, dragging heavy boots from beneath it. As he sat on the bed and pulled them on, he explained, "Johanna put Jean-Pierre and me here until they can find more suitable accommodations. The palais is so full with the other guests that there was no room for us there. It wouldn't do to put us in with the squires, now would it?"

"No. It would not." Of course. People who had come for her father's wedding had been put in the donjon, too. She had forgotten. "I did not see you at the feast." No one had told her Richard would be at her wedding, but Johanna knew how she felt about him. How could her grandmother have said nothing about his presence?

"I was at the back of the hall." He looked down at his feet, then shook himself and lifted his eyes to her face. "I saw you." There was a bright challenge in his eyes. Yet he fell silent, now.

The knife still lay upon the floor. She bent down and retrieved it, wiped dust and blood off the blade. They would question Richard, she was sure. Even torture him if he refused to speak. "Richard." Her feet moved by themselves, carried her to where Alys' old shoes rested on the floor. "I am leaving the château."

"Leaving?" A spark flared in his eyes, but was quickly doused. "Oh, you mean you and the Baron of Bauçais are leaving." His hands gripped the side of the bed.

"No." Maríana pushed her feet into the shoes. These were too large, also. She searched the chamber for rags she could stuff in the toes. "I am leaving. Just me."

He frowned. "But you were to marry the Baron of Bauçais." So the gauntlet was thrown. His words rang in her ears.

"And you were to marry Beatrice." There! It was his betrothal to Beatrice that had ended her hopes. When Henri had asked her to marry him, she had been free to say yes. Henri... . She knelt and shoved pieces of an old gown into the shoes, blinking away the moisture that fogged her eyes. She looked at Richard.

"I know." His mouth twitched. "She would not have me." Was that a shadowy grin she saw?

"What?" Maríana flexed her feet, returned to the chest and straightened the clothing left there, smoothing over the signs that she had removed things from it. She turned back to look at him. What had he said? She could not have heard right. Why did he smile?

Richard lifted his mantle from a metal hook on the wall. "She would not have me," he repeated. "And I will not have her." He was no longer smiling.

She froze. "Did she have two heads, this Beatrice?" Richard was free? A trembling seized her limbs, then drained away, leaving her limp. She could not be with Richard. Not now. The Inquisition was seeking her. He would be in danger.

He fumbled with the hood of his mantle. "No." He would not look at her now. "Why do you ask?"

"I was hoping you could go to Bourdeilles," she said. No. This was not true, but she must make him understand. She put her hand on his arm. His muscles stiffened under her fingers. "You cannot stay here, either, Richard." He started to speak, but stopped when gestured. "Hear me," she said. "The Inquisitor will be here next week."

He went very still. "He is coming for Jacques, isn't he?" His skin drained of color. "And for you, too?"

"Yes." So even Richard had heard of her healing circles and the work she did with Ibrahim. Well, her healing was no secret, was it? But how did Ysabel know of the work she did with Ibrahim? Father Gregory always looked the other way when Maríana went into Reuilles-la-ville. He knew that Maríana had spent a year with Ibrahim, yet he had not objected. When he said the mass, his words were always of love, not hatred. Ibrahim had told her of the danger, but she had not listened. "They are coming for my father, too."

"It cannot be." His mouth made a stubborn line.

She touched his hand. "My dear friend." Her voice broke. "I am sorry that you are here. I would rather have you safe with Beatrice, or in Brittany with your family. But if you stay here and they find that I had been here..." She raised her fingers to touch his lips and stop the argument she saw forming there. "They will torture you to find out where I had gone." His lips were warm and soft. She quickly drew her fingers away.

"I will go with you." He moved to the far side of the chamber, lifted a leather and metal helmet. Light glinted off his chain mail as he hefted it to his shoulder.

"You could go to Brittany — leave a message that you had been called back home. You would be safe. I don't think they would follow you to Brittany."

"That is not why I am going with you, to avoid their questions," Richard said, setting his jaw. He was sorting through his shirts and stuffing them into a bag. "I am no coward."

"You don't understand," she said, then broke off as he glared at her. "If you were to come with me you could not take any of your things other than the clothes you wear. They would start looking for both of us right away if all your things are gone. It must look as if you had just stepped out for some air, or..."

"Or gone to visit one of the kitchen maids," he finished for her. "Of course, that will give us more time. I will write a note to Jean-Pierre." Dropping his helmet and chain mail upon the bed, he reached in his bag and pulled out parchment, quill and a pot of ink. She watched him. He wrote with ease, now. She remembered his struggle, the hours he had spent copying letters Johanna had written for him. "We should leave soon." He leaned down and grabbed a handful of rushes and dust from the floor, then sprinkled it on the page and shook it off. "I do not know when Jean-Pierre will return."

Tears blurred her eyes. "You may never be able to go home, you know." If he went with her, they would be after him, too. How could she do this to him?

He turned toward her, took her hands in his. "I know." His face was still again, but his eyes reached into her. Then he grabbed the hilt of his blade. "Surely I can take my sword. It would look strange if I did not. I take it everywhere I go, and we may need it." He leaned closer to her, his lips barely grazing the top of her head as she looked down.

"Then you must take it," she said. "Are you ready?" It was his decision to go. She should argue, tell him she did not want him, send him away. But she could not stop the warmth that filled her, the glow that formed around her heart.

He lifted the bag that held the food and her slippers. "We should take candles." She pushed several into the bag he held and extinguished the candle she had lit.

"I will check the stairs for the guard." Richard climbed the three stairs to the door, but before he opened it, he took her hands in his and looked directly into her eyes.

"You really do not need to leave, you know," he said. "I am sure that the Baron of Bauçais would protect you. We could just go to warn Jacques." She shook her head and Richard continued, "But I have heard that you are carrying his child... Bauçais' child." His voice stumbled over the name of her betrothed.

She looked into his clear brown-amber eyes. Did Richard really think she should stay with Henri? Didn't he want her? Was his concern only that of a friend? "It won't make any difference," she said. For the first time she wondered whose child Ysabel carried. No, she could not risk it. For the sake of her own child, she must flee, trusting that Johanna would save Louis-Philippe.

"VERY WELL, then. We will go." Richard eased the door open, peered out, then turned back to her. "The watch on the tower is not due to change for a while, I think," he whispered. They crept down the stairs. When they reached the door, he reached for the latch. She took his hands and pulled him toward the back of the hall where more stairs led to the dungeons.

He followed her into the cold darkness. As she neared the bottom, the steps grew slippery with moss and stone-sweat. The pungent odor of fungus and dried blood, of cold stone, and earth and fear surrounded her. It was pitch black.

No one had inhabited the dungeons for some time. The guard's chambers had been empty for years. It was through the guard's rooms that she led him, feeling her way along the greasy stone of the wall. She stopped at the back of the last room, her fingers searching for the lever Ibrahim had shown her. "Wait while I open the passage," she whispered.

"I am sure we can risk lighting a candle," he said. His hand on her shoulder shook.

"Not yet." She knelt, her fingers following the space where wall met floor, seeking the glyph Ibrahim had carved into the stone that would open into his tunnel.

"Where did you go?" Richard was shuffling his feet along the floor. She felt a breeze from the motion of his arms as he tried to find her.

"Be still." A loud grating and whisper of air told her the space was open. "Here." He jumped when she took his hand and pulled him to the floor beside her. "You must duck down." He bent over and squeezed through the narrow opening, his sword scraping against the sides. On the other side the air was dead, but it was drier than the dungeon. She searched along the wall and found the latch to shut the small section of wall she had opened.

"Now we can light a candle," she said. Richard pulled his flint box out of a pouch on his belt and lit the candle she gave to him. His hands still shook. The candle light danced on the walls.

He looked around, eyes wide with surprise. He stared at the stone corridor, stretching into darkness beyond their candlelight. "What is this place?"

She rose to her feet and rubbed her hands against her skirt. "Ibrahim's people built this tunnel." She lit another candle from Richard's, holding it away from her gown as the wax dripped. "My father wanted another way from Reuilles-le-château to the Irati caves." She started down the tunnel, then stopped when she saw him standing behind her, his fingers tracing the stones that formed the walls.

"These are fitted so closely together that I cannot even fit my fingernail in the joints!" He looked back at her, then hoisted the bag to his shoulder. "Who knows of this tunnel?" He was beside her now, his loping stride shortened to keep pace with her. "Where do the caves lead?"

"Father had the donjon cleared while they built it." The candles threw their shadowy silhouettes into relief on the walls, elongated black shapes dancing alongside them. "He wanted a secret way out, so only he and Guillaume know the trick to open it. Ibrahim's people all went back to Egypt after they built it. The Irati caves lead to my father's Saracen palace."

"The house with the fountain?" Richard was smiling; she could see his lips curve. "And the arched windows?"

"Have all the squires been up there?" That would be the first place they would look after they discovered she was not anywhere on the château grounds. She increased her pace, ignoring the low ache that grabbed the base of her spine.

He winced. The flame of his candle dipped, then flared. "Well, I know we were not allowed to, but anything forbidden..." His steps slowed.

"It does not matter, now." She tugged on his mantle, pulling him along. "We don't have much time." Anxiety put an edge on her voice. He lengthened his stride, following her down the corridor into the shadows.

Chapter 24

HENRI awakened slowly. For a moment, he thought that he was back at Montsegur. His lungs ached again with fumes of burning corpses. When he opened his eyes, he saw that some candles had been left to burn and had burned all the way down. Cursing, he leaped out of the bed and then looked around in confusion.

What was he doing in Ysabel's room? His clothes were strewn in untidy piles across the floor. He looked back at the bed. Ysabel lay sound asleep, her arms curled around her middle.

As he gathered up his clothing and started to dress, he tried to remember why he had come to her room. He was sure he had intended to tell Ysabel that he would no longer visit her. The midwife had told him just that evening that she felt it was safe for Maríana and him to wed. Maríana had stopped bleeding and the danger was past. He would not visit Ysabel any longer. Yes, that was why he had come to her. He had stood there and told her this. But Ysabel had laughed and pulled him into her room, and he had gone willingly, had moved into her embrace, taken her.

Afterward, Ysabel had started talking. He had been exhausted, drained, and could barely keep his eyes open, but he had heard her voice. She had not seemed to be speaking to him and her words had not made any sense. Her voice had risen and fallen in a rhythm, then had grown sharp with anger. Something about a list, about an agreement. She had mentioned Durand several times, and a name. It had sounded like Raheem.

Henri frowned and ran his hands through his hair. This was not his concern. There would be no more visits to Ysabel. If need be, he would use Robert as a barrier again. He left her room, walked along the empty corridors to Maríana's chamber, where he stopped in surprise. Her door stood ajar. He waited for a moment at the door, listening. Hearing nothing within, he pushed the door open and slipped inside. "Maríana," he whispered.

It was totally dark. No fire burned in the hearth, but room still held the smell of hot ashes. Henri stumbled across the floor, his feet catching on mounds of cloth that lay strewn across his path, then sank down upon the bed. He fruitlessly searched the surface for his bride-to-be.

"Damn!" Stalking over to the candle shelf, he groped across its surface, grabbed the first he could find and struck the flint to light it. A blue flash, followed by a flickering glow, showed the empty, rumpled bed. Alys was stirring on her pallet. He put his hand on the bed again. Ice settled over his heart. He turned his head as Alys sputtered and complained.

"Hush, woman." Her eyes grew wide, but her grumbling subsided. "Where is your mistress?"

Alys heaved her body off the pallet and peered over at the bed. "Perhaps she went to Johanna's chamber?"

"Go and see if she is there." He waited as Alys drew her robe over her gown and stuffed her feet into slippers, then ran his hand across the cold bed again when she went out the door. Where could Maríana have gone? She was not well enough to go far. He searched through the gowns hanging in her cabinet, then lifted the lid of her chest. Her mantle was still there. He pulled it to his face and inhaled. It smelled of her, a blend of earth and sun-kissed skin. He raised his head and dropped the garment when Alys entered the room. Her eyes were wider now, white showing around the rim.

"She is gone!" she choked. "I cannot find her anywhere."

BLUE LIGHT beckoned Richard and echoes of dripping water surrounded him. Ice formed in white strands around the mouth of the cave that joined with the tunnel Maríana had just dragged him through. The journey had seemed to take hours. Twice, Maríana had taken a false turn and they had retraced their steps. But now they stood at the mouth of the final cave.

Maríana had doused the candle, yet he could see the terrain outside clearly. It had stopped snowing. Light from the heavy, threatening clouds bathed the snow covering the rock and earth and trees in an uncanny glow. Richard stared at the slope that fell away from his feet into a shallow ravine.

Maríana took his hand. "We must go down into this," she said. "It is easier if you sit down and let yourself slide." She went first, crouching sideways and descending in a graceful skid. He shuddered, but tried to imitate her and managed to get down with most of his skin intact. At the bottom she stood holding her side and pointed upward. He swallowed.

Gleaming white walls and exquisite arched windows; poetry in stone and tile. The Saracen palace glimmered in the heavy atmosphere, seemed to float on top of the cliff before him. He had only gone there once, when he was still a squire. The elegant rise of pillars that supported the walls, the glistening white of the stone, the dancing pattern of the tiles, all of these had moved him. He had been just a boy when he first saw it and had made a vow to travel to Byzantium.

He stared at a path cut into the bare rock of Irati, winding up to the crest of the cliff on which the palace stood. Maríana started up the path, one arm still wrapped across her waist. Had she hurt herself? He moved to her side, asked if she was hurt, but she kept walking, would not look at his face. "Jacques is up there," was all she said.

HENRI STOOD in front of the central hearth, one foot placed upon a stool beside the huge oak table that stretched the length of three men across the floor of the kitchen. The head cook leaned away from him, his head lowered, mouth forming a surly streak. "You say Maríana told you she was going to her grandmother's room?" Henri repeated. This one was stubborn. What was his name? Ah, yes. Lionel. "To Johanna's room?"

"Yes, that is what she said," Lionel stated, then added, "She often went to see her grandmother."

"In the middle of the night?" Henri looked at the kitchen servants. All who had been there that night were gathered around the long oak table. Their faces appeared pale and worried. "I have just come back from Johanna's chamber. Maríana is not there and Johanna does not remember her being there at all tonight."

"You woke the dra... er, the mistress?" Lionel's eyes bulged.

Henri could see that he wouldn't get much more out of this one. When Alys told him that she could not find Maríana, his mouth had gone dry. He had gone to the knights' room, wakened Robert, gathered his men together, sent all of them out to search the buildings of Reuilles-le-château. She could not have gone far. They would find her.

Henri himself had searched the palais, questioning anyone who was still awake. Three knights had told him they had seen Maríana in the corridor after midnight. They thought she had gone toward Ysabel's room. When he heard this, ice had gripped his heart again. But Maríana could not have gone to Ysabel's room. Who knew that better than he?

Now Henri looked at Lionel again. So Maríana had come down for food. That was not so unusual, was it? And it was a good sign that she was hungry. He dismissed the cluster of servants who stood around him, thanking them for their help. It was time to search all the rooms, even if it meant waking the guests.

RICHARD followed Maríana around the palace's outside wall. When they reached the courtyard and could see the door, she stopped so abruptly that he collided with her and both fell to the ground. He lifted her in his arms, dusted the snow off her gown, again asked if she was hurt. But she still did not answer him. She stared at the door to the palace. It stood open to the courtyard. No one would leave a door open in this weather; there would soon be ice on the floors and walls. Her heart pounded so hard, he could feel it through her thick woolen gown. He must go to the door, see if it was safe. But she pushed away from his grasp before he could order her to stay. She hurried to the open door, her feet stumbling and sliding.

"Maríana! No!" He followed in her wake and nearly knocked her down again when he moved through the door behind her.

Lamps burning, three of them. And rugs upon the wall. He had never seen walls that held rugs, never seen fabric woven in such rich colors. Indigo and scarlet and gold danced in curling patterns across their surfaces. He glanced at the floor. Something lay there, just inside the door. He could not see it clearly; Maríana had stopped in front of him and stood there, trembling.

He must protect her. At his touch, she sank to the floor. He caught her as she fell, caught her before her head hit the tiles.

"Maríana!" An old man came from the arched doorway to the back. Richard reached for his sword, but the man knelt beside him, gently touched where Maríana's neck met her jaw, then peeled back her left eyelid.

Richard pushed his hand away. "What are you doing? Leave her be."

The man drew back and smiled. "She has only fainted. Do not worry." He rose and turned toward a young woman who had entered.

"Who are you?" Richard asked, then bent toward Maríana as she stirred. Her face was waxen.

"Grandfather," she whispered. She touched Richard's cheek. "It is my grandfather. You need not worry."

Maríana's grandfather leaned forward, raised her chin so her eyes fell upon his face. "Maríana," he took her right hand and chafing it, "there is nothing we can do for Ibrahim. It is too late."

She stiffened, then pulled away from his arms and climbed in an unsteady lurch to her feet. The old man backed away, nodded to the woman who prowled the chamber.

"Have you found it?" he asked.

Richard drew in a breath when the woman turned and glared at Maríana. "Not yet," she said. She turned to look at Richard. "Who are you?" Her voice was hollow.

Richard opened his mouth to speak, but Maríana answered the woman. "He is with me." She dropped to the floor beside the bundle Richard had seen when they entered. A man lay there! Richard's heart thudded in his ears. What had happened here?

"HIS BODY is cold." Maríana ran her fingers across Ibrahim's high cheekbones, across his lips.

She no longer shook, but Richard could see the rapid rise and fall of her chest.

"We think he has been dead since moonrise." The woman stared at the man on the floor, but Richard could not read her expression. He moved to Maríana's side, saw the black and silver hair that flowed away from the face of the man laying in front of her.

"That is Jacques!" Who killed him? Was the Inquisition already there? His eyes darted around the room, came to rest upon the dark-haired woman.

"Is he always this slow?" The words were hostile, but the woman's voice sounded mild. Who was she? Her raven hair hung free, streaming down her back. Her skin was fine, golden, browned by the sun even though it was winter. She had returned to her search of the chamber, now pulling cushions and mats aside, peering underneath them.

"You knew him as Jacques. But his name is Ibrahim." Maríana closed Ibrahim's eyes, pulled the lids down over his fixed stare. Then she raised her head and pinned the woman with her stare. "Leila." Maríana's voice sliced the air. The woman's eyes flashed hot, yet she halted. "What you seek is in the chest near the kitchen."

Leila dropped the blanket she held and strode to the back of the chamber. "You will need his key," Maríana said. She fumbled with a chain around the dead Ibrahim's neck, her hands shaking and catching in Ibrahim's hair.

Richard leaned across her. "I will get it." This he could do for her. The old man nodded at him, then gripped Maríana's arms and lifted her away. Richard raised Ibrahim's head, worked the chain up over his face and off. The woman Leila grabbed the chain from his grasp. "You are welcome," he said as she marched away with the chain and key. She snorted but did not halt, bending to the chest and opening it.

"Got it." Richard saw her lift a book up out of the chest. Then she dropped to her knees and sputtered, "Blessed Mother!" She pulled lengths of emerald green silk, golden sashes, and purple robes out of its depths, then held up golden earrings, bracelets.

Maríana gave a small cry and moved to Leila's side. "Ibrahim's secret woman disguise," she said. "He never burned it."

Secret woman? What was this? Richard looked at Ibrahim's face again. He had heard many strange things about this man, that he was from Egypt, that he dabbled in sorcery. Yet he liked him, this Jacques, or Ibrahim, rather. Ibrahim had treated his wounds when he was learning to fight, had set his arm when he broke it.

And Ibrahim had seemed to care for Maríana. Several times Richard had seen Ibrahim gazing at her when she was still a girl, his dark eyes following her while she walked through the garden. Warmth had lived in those eyes, a father's proud regard. Richard had thought it odd at the time, but his heart had been glad. Maríana's father had not spoken to her when she was little, but this man had loved her.

"We should burn these now." Leila dropped the fabric and pushed the book she had taken into a loose woven bag, then hefted it to her shoulder and strode to the door.

"No," Maríana said. "We will take all of it with us." She beckoned to Richard. Ah, finally something she wanted him to do. He grabbed the bag he had carried for her and held it open as she stuffed the gowns and jewelry inside. Three more books lay at the bottom of the chest. "Ibrahim's medical texts," Maríana said, pushing these into the bag on top of the gowns, "and my mother's herbal."

"What!" Leila stalked across the chamber and peered down at the book in Maríana's hands.

"Why don't you carry it?" Maríana offered it to Leila, who stood staring at her.

Leila reached for it, then her hand fell to her side. "No," she said. "You keep it." Her voice was the same hollow rasp as before, but her eyes had softened.

"Why are we taking these things?" Richard whispered to Maríana as he placed the last book inside and drew the bag closed. She turned to him. It was difficult to look at her. The ball of grief she held tightly inside radiated from her eyes.

"There are things in these books that would endanger the people we leave behind." She turned to her grandfather. "Especially my father." The last words were nearly inaudible. Richard looked at the bag he held. What was so dangerous about these books? But a shudder rippled through Maríana; she shut her eyes and curled forward. Her hair fell over her shoulders, surrounded her face.

"Are you ill?" Richard bent toward her. Lines of pain stretched across her forehead, around her mouth. She waved him away, drew her body straight and shook her hair back.

"Grandfather Iranzu." She took Richard's hand. Her fingers twined around his. "This is Richard de la Guerche. He comes with us."

Iranzu nodded and said softly, "Lady's greetings, Richard de la Guerche."

"You know my family?" Richard still held Maríana's hand. Her fingers felt like ice, but her grip was firm.

Iranzu shook his head. "I know of your mother, Marguerite, but we have not met." He turned to where Ibrahim lay upon the floor.

"We must bury him," Maríana said.

"No time." Iranzu said. When Maríana cried out in protest, he added, "Louis-Philippe will see that he is properly buried."

Maríana dropped Richard's hand and walked over to Ibrahim. "I could not even say good-bye." Her eyes shone with unshed tears.

Richard sighed. He wished he could help her, but her grandfather was right. The ground outside was solid ice. In order to bury the man, someone must light bonfires to thaw the earth. This they could not do, for fire they lit would be seen.

"No time for good-byes, either, sister." Leila placed her arm around

Maríana's shoulders and pulled her toward the door. Richard remained frozen where he stood. This woman was Maríana's sister? He felt a touch on his arm and looked up to see Iranzu beckoning. Richard still clutched the bag. He threw it across his shoulder and followed Iranzu out, dragging the door shut behind him.

"Are we ready?" Iranzu asked. Leila nodded and lifted two stout packs that sat by the fountain. Iranzu lifted another and strapped it to his back. Richard slung the bag he had carried from the donjon over his right shoulder and extended his hand to Maríana.

"I can carry something." Her voice was faint, her face still and ashen. But her eyes glittered.

Leila glared at her. "No you won't," she said, her voice firm. "You have a baby inside you and you are carrying that baby too low already." She tossed her hair back and said to the three of them, "Come on!"

It was snowing again, little flurries of perfect crystals settling into the footprints they left in the courtyard. Iranzu and Leila led, followed by Maríana and then Richard in the rear. Thick stands of trees hugged the edges of the path. Anyone could be hiding there. Richard continually watched the bushes and trees that crowded both sides of the trail and stopped every few steps to look behind him. His hand remained on the hilt of his sword. He felt naked, exposed. Iranzu carried a thick staff, but only Richard was armed. It was he who would protect Maríana.

He wished he had his mail shirt. The links would not stop a sword, but might protect his back from an arrow. Skin at the nape of his neck tingled. But he heard nothing over the crunch of their own steps.

One hundred paces down the path, Iranzu and Leila entered the forest. Richard, following Maríana, backed off the path into the trees, his eyes searching for movement. The air was still-no scuffling rodents, no beating of wings. Snow fell in a soft white blanket. Their steps would be covered. His breath puffed out in relief, made filmy clouds on the air in front of him.

Turning, he saw the others up above him. They were climbing now, feet sinking into thick drifts of pine needles, feathery snow. They followed no path, just the precipitous slope of Irati.

Swiveling back toward the path, he scanned the open space that led back to Reuilles-le-château, to his life before this flight. He stared at the path, yet did not see it. He saw his sister crying, his mother white with grief, his father burning with anger. Soon they would hear the news from Bourdeilles, that he had broken his betrothal. After that, the news of his disappearance.

He knew he could never return. They would all know he was with Maríana. He had only bought her a small amount of time by not taking his harp and his chain mail. Richard hoped Baron de Reuilles would have his things sent to la Guerche. His sister would like his harp. Not that she could play it. He had tried to teach her, but she could not seem to get the fingering right.

He rubbed away the moisture seeping down his cheeks. What had gotten into his eyes? No matter. He pulled his sleeve across his eyelids and blinked. Then he turned and trudged into the blue stillness of deep forest.

Chapter 25

LOUIS-PHILIPPE answered Henri's knock and bid him enter. Henri moved into the chamber. Several lamps burned. The walls were overlaid with tapestries and a long oak table covered with rolled parchment stretched the length of one wall. Louis-Philippe sat upon the bed, pulling on his boots. Maríana was not in the room.

"My mother came to get me after you spoke with her," Louis-Philippe said, retrieving his mantle from where it lay upon his bed. "Have you found Maríana yet?"

"No." Henri waited until Louis-Philippe looked up at him. "We have searched every building in the château."

"The donjon?"

"Every building, and the inner and outer bailey, the garden, the watchtowers." Henri took his carving knife from his belt, ran his fingers over the hilt, the blade. "We are still questioning servants and guests."

He had been sure they would find her, so sure that he avoided picturing what might have happened to her. But images now filled his head; of Maríana at the base of a cliff, of blood on the snow.

"Is anyone else missing?"

"Do you think someone..." Henri broke off when Louis-Philippe shook his head. "One of the guests is away from his chamber. We are still trying to find him." He slid the knife back into his belt.

"Who is that?" Louis-Philippe strode to the table, riffled through the parchment rolls.

"The Breton."

"What?" Louis-Philippe raised his head, his blue-green eyes alert and sharp. "De la Guerche's son?"

"The same." Henri watched as Louis-Philippe's eyes widened and he leaned against the table. "Do you think he has taken her?" Young de la Guerche. Henri could not remember his face, although he had met all the knights who had come for the wedding.

"Taken her?" Louis-Philippe's forehead creased. "No. He was my squire. But they were childhood friends."

"Childhood friends." Why did the image of Ysabel leap into his thoughts? Henri shook himself and added, "We have covered all of the places inside the château." If this Breton was with Maríana, he would take him apart. Slowly. Then he would kill him.

"There is another place she could be. Nearby, but beyond the château grounds." Louis-Philippe moved toward the door. "You will need your mantle and boots."

Henri followed him out the door. "Where do you think she might have gone?"

"I have a house outside the walls, on the lower slopes of Irati."

Henri retrieved his mantle, pulled heavy boots over his shoes. A house outside the château walls? Why would Louis-Philippe have built a house that was outside his defenses? De Reuilles was an odd one. But if Maríana were in this house, Henri would thank him.

Louis-Philippe waited until Henri finished, then wheeled about and marched toward the great hall.

"Why do you think she might be there?" Henri asked, lengthening his stride to keep pace with Louis-Philippe. Really, the man's legs were uncommonly long.

"Jacques the gardener is there."

Oh, well. That explained everything! The gardener, indeed. Henri shook his head as he descended the staircase into the bustling space below. All were awake now and pages darted from table to table carrying bread and ale. A smothered hum of voices rose and fell in uneven cadence. "How could she have gone there in the snow without her mantle?"

"There is a way, but why she would take it is more important than how." Louis-Philippe covered the distance between the base of the stairs and the door of the great hall in a lope, then threw open the door.

FRIGID AIR pinched Henri's face, laid icy fingers across his neck. Maríana had left the warmth and safety of the palais to travel in this? He followed Louis-Philippe out, watched as a page pulled the door inward, sealing in the radiance of golden hearth flame, the fellowship of murmuring voices. No, she could not have gone willingly. Someone must have taken her. She would never have put her life or the life of their baby in jeopardy.

Henri sprinted after Louis-Philippe, sliding in the snow and then catching his balance. "Where are you going?"

"The east gate," Louis-Philippe plunged ahead.

Henri increased his pace. He had no breath left to talk. He followed de Reuilles out into the falling snow, along the frozen ground. Women had strange fancies when they were expecting. Could Maríana have gotten an urge to see this house outside the walls? But that was not like her.

As he hastened to keep up with de Reuilles, his thoughts whirled in his head. And kept returning to the notion he had avoided until now. His years as a soldier told him that people do not leave the safety of home unless they are abducted. Or fleeing.

The path they followed climbed in a rising slope up the side of the mountain. Fallen branches made the going treacherous. Henri stumbled several times, but Louis-Philippe seemed to avoid all the pits and buried sticks that caught Henri. One would think de Reuilles could see underneath the snow. Or that he had traveled this path so often that even his feet knew the way. But now Louis-Philippe halted, his hand lifted to stop Henri.

THE SKY WAS brightening, yet clouds still made a thick blanket across the heavens. Henri halted and stared. White walls, tile, arches. A Moorish palace? Someone had told him that de Reuilles had been to Jerusalem. But why build this here?

Louis-Philippe pulled a key out of his shirt and forced it into the door. After a sharp push, it swung inward and he preceded Henri through the arch calling, "Jacques!" Henri followed him into the main chamber, looking intently from side to side. Rich fabrics, golden lamps, silk-covered cushions surrounded him. Lamps were burning, but two sputtered. Henri placed his hand against the side of one. It was merely warm, when it should be hot. Had they burned all night?

A ragged inhalation alerted him. Louis-Philippe stood in rigid silence near the door. A body lay at his feet.

"What!" Henri strode over to the olive-skinned moor who lay upon the floor. This the same man he had seen coming out of Maríana's room back when the midwife had confined her to her bed. Dropping to his knees, he felt underneath the nose for breath, then touched the back of his hand against the smooth cheek. "Dead." Standing, he rubbed his hands together. "For some time, I think." He looked back at Louis-Philippe, who still stood there frozen, eyes unfocused. What was this? "De Reuilles?"

Louis-Philippe seemed to collect himself. He turned his face to Henri. "What?" His voice was faint, almost a whisper.

"This man has been dead for several hours, I think." Henri found it hard to meet Louis-Philippe's eyes. They were fixed and staring, but Henri did not think Louis-Philippe was seeing anything.

"I will search the house," he added when Louis-Philippe did not answer. The main chamber where the body lay was filled with cushions and tables, a low chest at the back. Henri strode to the back. Only a kitchen which held a simple hearth, bowls and knives. No one was there and there was no place anyone could hide. The only other chamber held one straw pallet. Henri stalked through all the rooms one more time. Empty. Maríana was not there. Why had de Reuilles been so sure she would be there? Is that why he had stood like a statue? Because she was still missing? Henri returned to the main chamber, chafing his hands again. It was colder in the palace than it was outside. He stopped when he saw de Reuilles.

Louis-Philippe stood by a chest, its open lid in his hands.

"Is anything missing?" Henri asked. Was de Reuilles ill? His face was bleached of all color.

Louis-Philippe dropped the lid. "I do not believe so." His movements were stiff and awkward. "Maríana is not here." He turned to the man who lay on the floor. "And Jacques is gone." His last words rang with sorrow.

Henri sighed. He knew what it was like to lose a cherished family servant. His falcon master had died when he was a boy and he had grieved for weeks. The gardener had been with the de Reuilles for some time. But they must continue the search for Maríana. "I am sorry," he said.

Louis-Philippe raised his head. Henri spread his hands. "Will it be hard to replace this fellow?"

Louis-Philippe turned his head away. "There are no marks on him that I can see, and there are two cups on the table there."

"Someone was here with him." Henri picked up one of the two goblets standing on the table. "Curious. One is full and..." He held the goblet away from his face and turned it over. Nothing fell out, not a drop. "Wiped clean," he said.

He went to the body and touched the mouth, raised the hands and examined the nails. Finally, he sat back on his heels. "I do not know what killed him. Perhaps some kind of poison? You may want to get your physician in to confirm."

Louis-Philippe had gone even paler. "He was my physician," he said softly and continued to stare at the man on the floor.

"We will need to get back to continue the search for Maríana." Henri strode to the door. "You can send someone up here to remove the body."

"No!"

Henri stopped at the door. Louis-Philippe had dropped to his knees by the body, was gathering it into his arms.

"He is not heavy," he said, standing. "I will carry him."

"As you wish."

THERE WAS something strange here, but it would have to wait. Henri held the door open and followed in Louis-Philippe's steps. They returned to the château on a different path, circling the Moorish palace to the back.

Henri let his hand trail along the side. He must ask de Reuilles how he had built this. The work was quite fine. He would ask, after they found Maríana.

Something in his gut twisted. She had been gone for several hours now. He looked up to the sky, where clouds held the promise of more snow. Was she out in this?

Louis-Philippe waited for him, holding the gardener. Henri walked forward, then stopped dead. He stood on the edge of a cliff that fell into a ravine. "How?" He looked across the ravine to another arm of the mountain that reared into the clouds.

"There is a path we will follow." De Reuilles edged off the cliff onto a road that seemed to be cut into the mountain. Well. It was tricky, but he should be able to navigate it. Still, Henri could not see the château from there.

"This leads to the château?"

"What?" Louis-Philippe turned; the body's head lolled against his arm.

"This will not work." Henri walked up to him, reached for Louis-Philippe's burden.

Louis-Philippe backed away, stopping when he hit the side of the cliff. Henri dropped his arms and said, "I was going to help you place him over your shoulder." No response. "He will be easier to carry."

Louis-Philippe lowered his head. His eyes closed. Then he nodded and allowed Henri to reposition the body. As they made their way down the track, Henri ticked off the names of his men, the areas of Reuilles-la-ville he would assign to each. "We will search Reuilles-la-ville next."

"What?" A whisper.

"Reuilles-la-ville," Henri remarked, adding, "It is the most likely place for her to have gone." He stared at the lowering sky. "As soon as we get back..." He paused. They had reached the bottom of the ravine. "Does that look like a landslide to you?" There was a dark slash that flowed down from a ledge high above. "There is just a dusting of snow there, but it covers everything else."

"It has been snowing all night," Louis-Philippe said. "Until just a little while ago."

Henri moved to the place where the snow sat lightly upon dark soil. "Damn!" He peered at the raw gash in the earth. "Someone slid down this tonight!" He pointed to the side. "See? A hand print here. And here." Well. They were getting somewhere now. He started the climb the slope. "We will need several men to conduct the search, and dogs, as well."

Henri stopped to look back at Louis-Philippe climbing up behind him. The man's eyes were closed again! How could he hope to see where he was going? "De Reuilles. I will need your help with this." Henri stood waiting.

A shudder moved through Louis-Philippe's body. His eyes opened and he looked at Henri. "Yes," he said. "I am going to show you another way into the château. I trust you will keep this secret."

"You have my word."

Louis-Philippe continued to stare at him in silence. With anyone else, or were it any other time, Henri might be insulted. Such a stare! But the man's thoughts were clearly far away. Henri watched as animation slowly returned to Louis-Philippe's face.

"There is another door into Reuilles-le-château." Louis-Philippe's arms tightened around the body slung across his shoulder. A spasm shook his limbs. But he continued, as if he had not paused at all. "A back door," he said. Then, "We will find Maríana."

Louis-Philippe straightened his back and climbed ahead. Henri watched him for a moment. But de Reuilles seemed to have returned to himself. His step was sure now. Henri followed him up the slope.

Chapter 26

LEILA AND Iranzu were always ahead. From time to time Iranzu would stop and wait, but he did not allow Richard or Maríana to pause. They had been traveling for hours, and it was snowing again. Richard bent and grabbed a handful of snow, stuffing it in his mouth and feeling his tongue go numb as it melted. It did not satisfy, but it took the edge off his thirst.

Iranzu halted and looked up at the sky. "Good," he said. "It looks like a heavy snow will be falling soon. The snow will cover our tracks."

"They will have dogs," Maríana's voice was faint. "Dogs to find us." She had been dropping behind and was sweating, but when Richard touched her forehead it felt cold. She trembled. He glanced over at Iranzu and saw the old man's concern for Maríana. Good. Perhaps Iranzu would let them rest. That was what she needed.

Iranzu held her hand for several breaths, then sighed. "Then we cannot stop," he said. Maríana nodded and moved forward, plodding through the snow that piled up around them. Damn! Richard plowed behind her.

"Dogs." Iranzu whispered to Richard, "If we could reach the first shelter before the snow gets too bad, perhaps then..." The rest of the old man's words were lost as he increased his pace. He caught Maríana's elbow, propelling her forward.

They continued to climb.

WHEN HE came to the ledge, Richard's foot hung in the air and he lurched forward. The weighty pack strapped to his back slipped to the side and nearly carried him back down the mountain slope they had been climbing. But somehow Leila was there, pulling the pack from his body, helping him over the top to the space that stretched out before him. He stood there, just breathing, surprised by what he saw. The ledge was two hundred paces wide, at least, and another hundred paces deep.

He looked back down the slope they had climbed. Reuilles-le-château was no longer visible. He could not even see the Saracen palace.

He turned again, back to where Irati had continued to climb in a gentler slope to where clouds sat upon the trees. Pine and scrub straggled across the ledge, but at the back where the slope continued, a massive oak tree stood, its trunk the width of seven men. Leila and Iranzu were already there, stretching a blanket across one of the lower branches, making a shelter.

Finally. They would stop there for a time. Richard looked behind him for Maríana. She struggled through the drifts, seeking his footsteps. She had fallen behind again, but was almost there. He waited at the edge and grabbed her arm when she reached the top.

Pulling her to the ledge, he brushed snow and pine needles off her gown, then knelt and dug packed snow from inside the tops of her boots. She held her skirt aside, shivering. "You should take these off when we reach your grandfather and sister," he said. "We can try to dry them before we go on."

His words caught in his throat. Something warm and red dripped on him. He pulled away and held out his hands, saw the ruby stain, looked down at Maríana's feet.

"No!" He heard her cry as she, too saw the crimson pool widening around her.

HENRI PACED the length of the great hall. A page carrying a tray of ale scurried out of his way. Earlier, Henri had thrown two of them aside when they blocked his path. Now he stopped in front of the roaring hearth fire. He felt chilled straight through. The search was not going well.

He strode across the hall toward the door, his eyes on his feet, hands clasped behind his back. The château had fifty men out searching for Maríana. Four of these were his own men from Bauçais and Burgundy, from Paris and Gréves. He halted at the door. Ysabel had not come down to the great hall for any of the meals today. Would she have any idea of where her stepdaughter might be? Henri leaned back on his heels. No. Ysabel was only concerned with her own pleasure, whatever that might be. She would not know where Maríana had gone. Henri released his breath in a sigh, then shook his head as three more servants scrambled away from him, their hands trembling and eyes rimmed with white. Good. If they feared him they would work all the harder. He wheeled around and marched back to the hearth.

When he had arrived at Reuilles-le-château with Louis-Philippe, the Baron had taken the body he carried up to Johanna's chamber, where he remained even now. Henri snorted. De Reuilles was useless. Henri had been forced to organize the search. Fortunately, de Reuilles' men did not balk at orders from Henri. They were worried about Maríana, he could see that.

But Louis-Philippe! A dead gardener was more important to him than his own daughter. Henri had been aware that Maríana's place at the château was secondary to her stepmother, to the child Ysabel carried. But that was as it should be. Maríana was a daughter, not a son.

Still, her father should have some concern for his daughter's whereabouts when she was missing. Henri felt a tug on his arm and raised his eyes in an even glare. Robert shrank from him, stammering.

Henri tempered his stare, reached out and patted Robert's shoulder, "I am not angry with you, boy," he said, then, "What news?"

"Guillaume just got back." The boy's voice trembled. "He is in the stables."

Henri had sent most of the men over to Reuilles-la-ville with Guillaume. They were searching the town house-to-house. The rest of the men were outside the walls, covering the forested area down to the lake and marsh. Henri knew the most likely place to search now was Reuilles-la-ville. Where else could she be? But this took time. it was getting late. He looked up as the door opened and Guillaume walked in, snow dropping from his mantle.

"Well?" Henri barked out. The hollow space inside his chest lurched when he saw Guillaume shake his head. Where now? Henri folded his arms across his waist and stared at the floor. The only place they had not searched was the mountain. So be it.

"Collect all the men." Henri moved toward the stairs. "We will be camping up at the Saracen palace tonight."

They would climb the mountain at dawn. Henri trudged up the stairs. Louis-Philippe must join him in this. De Reuilles knew the territory. He must provide experienced climbers for their search. And dogs. Henri strode along the upper corridor and knocked on Johanna's door.

MARÍANA lay on her back under the shelter of the blanket Iranzu and Leila had stretched across the oak branch. Richard held her head in his lap. He wiped her forehead with a damp cloth as she gritted her teeth, her body stiffening with each wave that rippled through her belly. From time to time she whimpered, "It is too soon, too soon," and then her body would become rigid and she would turn her face against his belly to muffle her screams. Every whimper, every groan she uttered stabbed him, from his stomach out to his limbs. And yet he was glad.

This gladness tore him into pieces. How he could be happy when she was in such pain? When new life would not be born? But he was glad she would not have Henri de Bauçais's child, glad this baby would die. The cloth he used to bathe her forehead and face was growing hot. He dipped it in the snow, then caressed her fevered skin.

Leila knelt at Maríana's feet. She had lifted her sister's skirts and was examining her. Richard watched as Leila's hands ran over the expanse of Maríana's belly, then moved between her legs and even up inside to check the expulsion of her baby. He could not bear to watch and averted his eyes. He had assisted foals into the world and knew what Leila did, but seeing it brought a giddy shiver. This was Maríana he cradled in his arms, not a horse. He focused on her face to still the grinding contraction of his belly. Her eyes were shut tight and tears squeezed out the corners in a continued leak.

The rustle of cloth brought his head up. Leila stood now, gazing down upon her sister, her eyes soft. He cleared his throat and she looked at him, then shook her head slowly as she wiped her hands. Dropping to her knees again, Leila crawled under the shelter of the blanket, coming to rest next to where Richard held Mariana's head. "It will not be long now. You are not very far along in carrying this little one, so it will be coming out soon." She paused as Mariana opened her eyes and stared up at her sister in a silent plea.

"I will not lie to you." Leila's voice was firm, yet her face sorrowed. "It is too late, but you have done nothing to cause this. It was placed too low in your womb." She stopped again as Mariana closed her eyes and more tears leaked out, wetting Richard's hands. "I have seen this before, sister. I have delivered many babies, many. Some living, some not. It is the way of things." Her voice trailed off. Richard could feel the shift in Mariana's body, saw the set of her jaw as she gathered herself together. "Do you want to see it when it comes?" Leila asked softly. Mariana shuddered, then nodded. "I am glad," Leila gave Mariana's shoulder a gentle squeeze. "It is better to say good-bye."

Mariana opened her mouth to speak, but a wave surged through her belly and she arched her back against it, then a keening wail poured out of her, its echo crying back to them from the sides of the mountain.

"Silence her!" Leila returned to her position at her sister's feet while Richard grabbed Mariana's head and held her mouth against his stomach.

"Grandfather," Leila said shortly, placing her hands between Mariana's legs, "I will need the water and cloths now."

Iranzu came to her with melted snow he had heated over the fire they had taken the risk of making, and several torn pieces of a surcoat he had arranged in the sort of breechcloth women use during their bleeding moons. "And the mosses and yarrow from my pack," she added as Mariana convulsed, her legs whipping out and back curling.

Richard continued to hold Mariana in his arms. He leaned toward her and whispered, "You are doing well, it will be over soon."

Mariana drew her legs up and held her breath. Then a tremor rippled through her and she started to cry in gulping sobs. Leila swiftly drew her hands out from Mariana's skirts and gently cleaned what they held with one of the cloths Iranzu had brought her. Leila was holding something in the palm of her hand, something small. She blinked her eyes furiously. "A girl." Then she turned to Mariana, who was sobbing into Richard's belly. "Mariana," she said. "Sister, are you ready to see?"

Mariana drew in her breath and shuddered again, then nodded and turned her face to Leila. Richard closed his eyes. He could not look.

"She is blue," Mariana said. Her voice had deepened and was

hoarse from screaming. Blood was everywhere. But all he wanted to do was draw her into his embrace, take care of her.

"She had already died within your womb, Sister," Leila told her. "Perhaps as long ago as two or three days."

Silence. Richard opened his eyes cautiously. Leila still knelt at his side, but she had covered the tiny form she held in her hands. She looked at Maríana. He almost thought they were talking, but he could only hear the hushed whisper of snowfall outside their shelter.

Leila nodded. "I will bury her so that no animal will dig her up," she said. "But first I need to stop your bleeding." She went around to Maríana's feet again, handing the tiny form to Iranzu, who wound a cloth around it.

"Am I bleeding a lot?" Maríana asked. She shifted, drew her arms up, pushed against him.

"No. But it is best that we pack you right away so we can continue." Leila bore down hard on Maríana's womb and held her hand between her sister's legs again for a moment. Maríana's breath rattled in her throat, then something else slithered into Leila's hands. "There. That should do it." Leila turned away, handing a glistening red lump to Iranzu. "Bury this with the baby."

Maríana drew her legs up further and leaned forward, pulling away from his arms. He released her and watched as she rose to her knees under the sheltering blanket. There she swayed for a moment, her arms held out for balance, then she reached down and tugged her gown free of her knees, pulling it up and over her head.

"What are you doing?" Leila fell back as Maríana pushed out at her, flinging her gown into the snow, staggering to her feet outside the shelter. Now Maríana pulled at her nightgown, shredding the gossamer silk in her haste to remove it. Her feet were bare — they had set her boots next to the fire-and she sank into the snow up to her ankles, stumbling away from Leila's reaching hands.

He jumped to his feet, grazing his forehead against the underside of the oak branch that held their blanket. Leila stood in his way, staring at her sister, her mouth hanging open. Maríana was shrugging the torn nightgown over her head, down along her arms, casting it into the snow on top of her woolen gown. He picked Leila up by her arms and set her aside, ignoring her sputtered protest. But he stopped when Maríana turned.

She stood naked, an ivory statue in the midst of snowflakes and darkening sky. Her gaze passed over Leila, Iranzu, the oak tree, the shelter, coming to rest upon Richard. When her stare fell upon him, he shuddered. Her eyes were icy, remote. And yet he felt the sharp pressure of her glance as keenly as the edge of a sword against his skin. Leila moved toward her sister. She held the cloak Maríana had rested upon in her hands and was shaking the snow from it with a practiced snap of her wrists. The hot metal smell of blood rose from its folds.

Maríana remained where she stood, pinning Richard beneath her haunted gaze while Leila approached her, spreading the mantle with her hands. "Put this on until we can get fresh clothes for you from our packs." Leila's voice was quiet, but it cut through the stillness of falling snow.

Maríana still did not move. Her eyes darted to her sister. Leila wavered, then stopped in her tracks. "You said I was not bleeding very much," Maríana said.

Leila drew the mantle against her chest and stepped back. "Yes, but..."

Maríana looked away from her and Leila stumbled. As if she had been released. "Well, I have a use for it, this blood," Maríana said, then extended her hand to Iranzu. "My knife."

Iranzu said nothing. He bent over the jumble of Maríana's clothes and drew a kitchen knife from under the old woolen gown Maríana had taken from the tower. Holding it aloft, he brought it to Leila. "Leila must consecrate it," Maríana said, inclining her head toward her sister.

Leila stared at Maríana, her face ashen. "Are you mad? You will freeze!" She stuck out her jaw and glared at her sister. "I need to pack yarrow against your womb or you will bleed away your strength."

Iranzu placed a hand upon Leila's shoulder, murmuring in her ear. The mantle dropped from her hands and she took the knife from him, her face frozen in a snarl.

"Very well." She stalked over to the fire.

Richard wanted to retrieve the woolen cloak, drag it from the ground and throw it over Maríana's body. But his limbs would not obey him. This was not his Maríana, this alabaster image that held him in its thrall, the face bleak, the eyes frost.

Leila was chanting. He caught the frenetic motion of her arms at the periphery of his vision and tore his eyes from Maríana's stare. But his arms dangled at his side. He still could not move.

"Air! Cure it!" Leila shouted, rotating the knife to cut a circle in the air. She fell to her knees and thrust the blade into the fading blaze of their dying fire. "Fire! Seal it!" Now she dug through the snow to bare ground, her other hand slammed the knife into the soil up to its hilt. "Earth! Bind it!" Both hands wrenched the blade from the earth, held it now in the water still steaming in the pot on the fire. "Water! Bring it home!"

Leila raised the knife again, holding it away from her body, striding toward Maríana. When she reached her sister, she turned the knife and handed the hilt to Maríana.

Maríana made a slow turn where she stood, one hand with the knife held over her head, the other pointing at the ground. Her eyes closed, but

Richard could see them moving behind the lids. When she stopped turning, she bent down and drew patterns in the snow, the knife dancing in an undulating wave as she walked, moving in a spiral outward from where she stood. Blood trickled down her legs, tracing its own red-brown pattern upon the snow.

She was humming. No words, just tones that rose and fell, then floated upon the air. Richard's arms still hung useless at his side, inert and heavy. His knees were locked. He looked up at Leila and Iranzu. Leila's face was fixed somewhere between horror and pity. Iranzu gazed down at his feet. Richard looked back to Maríana. He remembered the green-gold light she had held between her hands, how he had broken her spell, how she had sent the light away. But whatever power held him in its grip would not release him.

She had already covered the space of a small chamber with her spiral. The tones emitting from her throat were deeper. He could feel them in his feet.

The air was stretching. Something unwound, coiled around him in a lazy, exultant shimmer. He could feel its pressure against his skin; its breath hissed in his ears. A guttural cry sounded across from him and he looked up to see Leila holding her ears. Her mouth was moving, but he could not hear her words above the throbbing murmur that emanated from the ground, climbed into the air.

Words spilled around him, yet he could not grasp their meaning. They seemed to come from the air itself, but it was Maríana's voice he heard. She was standing now at the edge of the spiral she had drawn, the knife in her left hand, arm raised to the sky. The earth beneath him shrugged in a pulsing ripple.

Then silence. The air around him held only snowflakes, tracing moist, icy kisses across his face.

Whatever held him relinquished its grasp. He bent and grabbed the mantle, strode over to where Maríana shivered, her legs wobbling, arms wrapped across her chest.

As he drew the woolen cloak around her shoulders, she whispered, "The dogs will not find us."

But her voice was sad.

Chapter 27

THE BLASTED snow had covered everything; obliterated all tracks. Henri waded across the wide ledge to where his men had gathered near a huge oak tree, its branches heavy with the snow that was everywhere. One of de Reuilles' men led the two hounds they had brought. The dogs whined and strained on their leashes. It was early afternoon, but they had already traveled for hours. Henri approached Guillaume, leader of the team of expert climbers. "Well?" he asked in irritation. "What have you got?"

"It's the dogs, my lord," the man with the hounds answered. "When we got up here they went crazy."

"Indeed?" Henri said. "But what have you found?"

The man spoke again. "It looks like someone was here by the tree," he said. "Not long ago, either."

Henri gave him a sharp glance. "Where? Show me."

The man handed the leashes of the hounds to Guillaume and led Henri to where the gnarled roots of the tree parted to reveal bare ground covered with only a dusting of snow.

"A footprint," the man said. "We would have missed it, but the dogs came over here right away and started digging in the snow." He knelt and traced the footprint with his finger. "We removed the rest of the snow and found this."

Henri looked at the footprint. "Small," he said. "Perhaps a woman's foot?"

"Maybe," Guillaume said, shifting from side to side.

Henri could see that the men were afraid, their eyes kept darting around, and Guillaume's hold on the dogs' leashes was so tight his knuckles were dead white. "All right," Henri said, clasping Guillaume's shoulder. "Out with it. What is bothering you?"

Guillaume's tongue darted out, moistening his lips. He was sweating, his forehead beaded with it. "I don't much like this place, my lord, can't say exactly why."

Henri turned to the other man, brows raised in question.

"It... it's like a vibration," the other man said, and both nodded. "Or a sound you can feel but not hear." He knelt down and placed his hand flat on the ground, then jerked his hand away and stood up, shaking. "Like drums beating inside the earth," he finished.

Henri sighed, but he also kneeled down and placed his hand against the ground. "I see." He could feel something of what they were describing, a sort of rumbling shudder. "Probably water running underground." He shook the dirt off his hand and stood up to see the two men grinning, their faces shining with relief.

"Yes, my lord, that must be it," they both said in unison.

"Is that all?"

"No, there is a place over there." Guillaume pointed to a clear area several paces from the oak. "The dogs keep wanting to go there, but whenever we get closer to it they veer away."

"Show me," Henri said.

Guillaume brought the hounds to the clear space in the center of the ledge, Henri following close behind him. They were nervous, these hounds. One dropped its head and growled, pulling on its leash.

"Let him go," Henri ordered.

Guillaume hesitated briefly, then released the hound. Once freed, the dog went to one area and sniffed along the ground, following some scent around and around in the snow as the other dog hid behind Guillaume and shivered. It was uncanny, the way the dog circled around in a spiral. Its back legs were shaking so hard its rump kept hitting the ground. Suddenly the dog stopped dead in its tracks, lifted its muzzle to the sky and gave a long, mournful howl. Henri shivered. The dog turned and showed its fangs. Then it bolted over the edge and down the mountain in a streak of brown fur.

"Get him!" Guillaume shouted. But the dog had disappeared.

Henri turned to Guillaume. "Try this one," he said. "But keep the leash on him." Guillaume nodded and brought his hound over to the spot. The dog whined piteously at first, then started sniffing around the same circular pattern the first dog had taken. Guillaume had wound the leash around his wrist and he could barely keep up. This dog's legs did not shake. But it gagged and vomited upon the ground. "Let up on his leash," Henri ordered. There was no need to choke the poor animal. Guillaume loosened his hold and the dog lifted its nose, gave an eerie, barking howl, a howl that was answered in the distance. Then it turned on Guillaume, fangs bared, low rumbling growls emitting from its throat. Guillaume backed away and was shaking so hard that when the dog fled, the leash whipped over his wrist and slid right out of his hands. As he reached out to grab it, he fell onto the ground.

"Well!" exploded Henri. "There go our dogs." Wonderful! What else could go wrong? He marched over to the edge just as de Reuilles was swinging his ungodly long legs over the top.

"What is going on up here?" Louis-Philippe asked as he rose to his feet. "We saw both the dogs run past us as if the devil himself were after them." He looked back over his shoulder. "The first dog fell most of the way down."

"They have never done this before," Guillaume said as he picked himself up off the ground and dusted snow off his cloak. "But what is this?" He pointed at the ground where he had fallen.

Henri got down on one knee, brushing aside more of the snow. There were red-brown lines on the ice underneath. "What the devil?" he muttered, then looked up in surprise as several men approached Louis-Philippe, jabbering away in that ghastly southern tongue, waving their hands wildly. Louis-Philippe merely nodded and gestured toward the slope they had just climbed.

"Come here, de Reuilles." Henri stood and motioned to him. "What do you think of this?" He watched as Louis-Philippe knelt down and frowned, then brushed at the snow with his gloves, uncovering a swirl of rusty lines, peppered with dark red splotches.

Louis-Philippe raised his glove up to his nose, then jerked his hands away from his face and out of his gloves, dropping the gloves in the snow. "Blood!" he exclaimed, looking at Henri, then, "Are you all right?"

Henri stumbled back and fell to his knees. Blood on the snow. His heart raced; he willed it to slow. It could be animal blood. A wolf's kill. Wolves often drag their prey away. But wolves also killed people. Maríana was such a little thing. She could never fend off a wolf.

The sharp trill of a hawk brought his head up. He watched as the dark wings beat, then held rigid, riding the winds. Hawks often flew near wolf kills. Most people thought that hawks were noble creatures. But after wolves had eaten their fill, hawks and vultures both would feast on the remains.

Henri lunged toward the blood, his arm flailing across the snow in a desperate sweep. What could they do if there were bits of cloth, clumps of auburn hair among the blood? He set his jaw against the acid that spilled into his mouth. All he could see was Maríana, her body torn and bleeding, her eyes closed forever.

"Henri."

Someone called him, but he could not seem to stop the motion of his arm. A hand touched his shoulder now, took hold of his arm.

"What?" He turned to see Louis-Philippe staring at him.

"Bauçais." Louis-Philippe's blue green eyes reached into him. "This is no wolf kill."

Henri looked down at his hands, rolled them into fists to stop his shaking. Louis-Philippe squeezed his shoulder. "Stand and look."

Henri rose and looked down upon the area he had uncovered. Louis-Philippe still had his hand on Henri's shoulder. The firm grip steadied him. "And not much blood, see?" Henri followed the motion of Louis-Philippe's finger as he pointed to the pattern on the snow. There were marks scored into the snow, and the blood curled around in a spiral.

"I do not know what this is," Louis-Philippe said. "But we must continue our search."

Henri shuddered. De Reuilles was right. His eyes swept the ledge. There were only a handful of men left there. He counted seven. "Where did the others go?"

"The others are afraid of this part of Irati. We are too close to Canigou." Louis-Philippe bent and retrieved his gloves. "They will go no farther."

"Canigou?"

"Another mountain farther on." Louis-Philippe nodded toward the slope that swelled behind the massive oak. "They call it the Lady's mountain, but Canigou is not a lady you would like to meet."

"Well." Henri looked at the cluster of men. Guillaume was still there and several of the squires. Henri caught the eye of his own squire and gestured for him to come forward. He was aware of the eyes of all the men upon him. A deep breath steadied his shaking hands. He raised his voice. "We will continue on up the mountain," he said, then turned to Louis-Philippe. "Who is your best climber?"

Louis-Philippe regarded him for a moment, his eyes cool and assessing. Then he nodded shortly and waved his hand at Guillaume. "Guillaume shall still lead." He extended his hand to Henri. "Come," he said. "We will climb."

RICHARD awakened with a jolt. His ears rang and his mouth tasted of rancid butter. He could hear the others breathing, but his own breath caught in his throat. The air was bad. He leaned toward the reed they had worked through the laced slit that sealed them in the tent. Looking through the tube, he saw nothing. Snow must have covered them. Iranzu had said this might happen. Richard drew in as deep a breath as he could manage and blew with all his might into the reed, then inhaled in relief as fresh air flowed through.

He blinked at a circle of light that shone on his hand beneath the reed. Peering through it again, his eyes were dazzled. How long had they slept? Richard looked at his three companions. Iranzu was wedged next to him, and Leila was on the far side of the cramped space. Sheltered between Iranzu and Leila lay Maríana. They were still asleep. Why not let them rest a while longer?

He closed his eyes and drifted. Everything that had happened whirled around in his head, all of it jumbled into a dance of images. Maríana shivering in the cloak he had wrapped around her. Leila ordering him to dig a grave between the roots of the oak. She had brewed a pungent drink over the embers of their fire, had made everyone down the bitter brew.

Leila had taken pity on him. She had pushed a steaming cup of the vile stuff into his hand after he had dug down a full measure, had ordered him to drink it and to help Iranzu take down the shelter, while she buried the baby. The drink had revived him somehow. It was the most amazing thing, this drink that tasted of tree bark and rotting weeds. Richard had been certain that Maríana could not take another step. Yet she had climbed steadily beside him through the remainder of the night, over ground that glimmered in the half-light of clouds reflected off icy slopes.

As the sky grew lighter, they had pitched Iranzu's goat skin tent beneath a twisted pine. Iranzu had put Leila and Maríana in first, then had climbed in after them, leaving Richard to follow, showing him how to lace the opening together and position the reed through the slit so they would not smother.

Iranzu had told him that he hoped snow would cover the tent, that the Jakintzas often traveled in winter and used the small tents, pitching them where snow would insulate them and disguise them. Their tents were small and the goat skin was tough and black. When covered with snow, the tents looked like rocks.

It was good to sleep in such tents, even though everyone must curl into a sphere in order to fit. Richard moved his elbow now and held his breath as the elbow joint made an audible crack, then his heart skipped in his chest when he heard something outside. A bear? Leila had told him there were bears up there. He held his breath and listened. No. It was footsteps he heard. Footsteps crunching in a regular gait through snow drifts. And voices.

"Not here, my lord," he heard, then very close, Baron de Reuilles' voice.

"Check over there, will you? I will search this area."

Maríana's father. Surely they could go to him, couldn't they? But no, Maríana had told him Louis-Philippe's name was on the Inquisition's list. Richard pulled his lip between his teeth when he heard more footsteps and another familiar voice.

"Find anything?" It was Bauçais. Richard knew this voice, the northern inflection rendered in a low rumble. His blood chilled. Bauçais wore the red and white of the soldiers of Christ. Richard had heard stories of the swath they had cut all across the south, of mutilations and burnings. As he had traveled through Provence on his way to Bourdeilles, he passed more than one manor house that was no more than a blackened skeleton against the golden hills.

He reached for his sword where it lay at his side.

"No, we are just about done with this area," Louis-Philippe was saying. "Maríana must have traveled all night."

"She is not alone." Henri's voice sounded strained. "My squire found tracks, underneath the pines back there, that the snow had not covered."

Richard heard a heavy scraping, then the walls of the tent quivered.

He clutched the hilt of his sword, drawing it up to his cheek and feeling the chilled metal against his skin. Bauçais must have leaned against the tree that stood beside their tent.

"We think there may be two or three others who are with her," Henri was saying.

"Perhaps we will catch up with them," Louis-Philippe said. "But we must be cautious. If she has been taken for ransom, she will not be harmed. If we alarm whoever has her, they may panic. I would rather pay the ransom."

"Do you still doubt that she was taken?" Henri's voice was louder the louder of the two, with a rasping edge.

"There was no ransom note."

"They still may send one."

"I have left instructions with Johanna on what to do if she receives one."

"But you believe Maríana was not taken." Henri's voice was barely a whisper now.

"Not out from under our noses, no." The tent shifted again. Richard was holding his sword so tightly his fingers were going numb. He forced his grip to relax. Louis-Philippe was speaking. "If she were taken when she was outside the walls, yes. But everything we have found so far tells me that she left of her own will." Silence now. Richard kept his ear by the reed. He heard the steady drip of melting snow. The sun must be high, the day warm.

"Why would she leave?" Richard could not tell who was speaking. The voice was ragged and hollow.

"I cannot say for sure." This was Louis-Philippe. "When her mother died, I gave Maríana to Johanna and my sister to raise. From all they have told me about my daughter, she is very like her mother. Stubborn, but strong."

There was a long pause. Voices floated on the air. Richard tried to distinguish them, to count the searchers, but Louis-Philippe's voice cut across the others. "They never saw her cry, not once." Another stretch of silence followed, then, "I believe that if she fled, she had good reason."

There was silence for a few heartbeats, and Richard heard Henri again. The iron was back in his voice. "But we will continue to search."

"Yes." Footsteps now. "We are finished here, but there is a place over there that..." The voices faded into the distance.

Richard let out the breath he had held. If the searchers came for them he could cut through the laces, roll out of the tent and come up swinging and take several men down before he fell, but could Maríana and the others escape? How many knights were there? Of the four of them, Richard was the only one who was armed. He listened. There was shouting in the distance, Bauçais was yelling out orders, and closer, the tapping of water against crisp snow. Richard took several deep breaths to slow the speeding of his heart. Then he shook Iranzu's shoulder. "Wake up!" he whispered. "It is daylight and some people were here."

"Who?" Iranzu whispered back.

"The Baron and Bauçais. And maybe some other men," Richard said quietly. "They may come back. We need to get away."

Iranzu reached over and touched his two granddaughters. "Maríana," he said. "Can you travel?"

"Yes."

The tent shifted as Leila felt Maríana's forehead, her wrists. "She is fine. When do we move?"

"Soon now. But we must take down the tent and gather all our things in perfect silence," Iranzu warned. "Even if we are out of their sight, sound travels far in winter stillness." He touched Richard's knee. "We will travel northeast to Canigou. You must follow us and keep watch behind. But do not speak. Speed and silence are our only hope now."

A moment later the four flowed out of the tent. Richard saw tracks everywhere. He could not tell if the tracks were made by many men, or by a few walking over their own footsteps. There was no time to assess the marks they had made, but he could not see anyone nearby when he peered around the dense pines. From time to time voices drifted to where he stood, setting his heart racing. Yet each time he heard them, the voices seemed to be receding.

Richard watched as Iranzu and Leila took the tent apart, their hands working together in an elegant dance. He moved toward them, then stumbled. "What?" He reached down and uncovered the chunk of metal that had tripped him. It was a knife, a hunter's knife. The hilt was black, but silver was worked into the side. His fingers traced the pattern. The de Reuilles crest.

Had Baron de Reuilles lost it? He could come back for it! Richard froze in alarm. But all was still. Nothing moved. He held the knife in his hands, felt its weight. Did the Baron leave it behind? Richard looked over to where Leila and Iranzu stood. They had finished taking the tent down.

Leila caught his eye, motioned toward the thickest part of the forest and pushed Maríana ahead of her into the space between the trees. Richard tucked the knife into his belt. Louis-Philippe might have left it as a sign. Her father must now know why Maríana had fled. Yet Richard could not be sure he would understand their flight. After all, they were abandoning Louis-Philippe. The Inquisition was seeking him, too. Richard stared at the trees behind him, seeing only snow-burdened branches. No, they could not count on Baron de Reuilles to lead the searchers away from Canigou. Richard must be more vigilant. He followed Leila into the woods.

AH, IBRAHIM. Louis-Philippe tramped through the snow in slow, deliberate steps. He had taken Henri and the men to the southwest slopes of Irati. Pines grew in thick clusters here. It would take them hours to search this area. He scanned the forest around him every few paces, but his thoughts turned again and again to Ibrahim.

When he had seen Ibrahim laying upon the floor, his had heart seized. He could not believe it; he wanted to go over to Ibrahim, shake his arm, see Ibrahim's eyes flash up at him, see the corner of Ibrahim's mouth lift in a wry smile. But Louis-Philippe had found that his feet were frozen to the floor. Even when Bauçais had told him that Ibrahim was dead, *dead*, he could not move. While Henri had stalked the rooms of the Saracen palace, Louis-Philippe had stood over Ibrahim, looking down at his face, seeing the curve of his lips, the sweep of his brow. He was not sure later what had drawn him to the chest in the back, the chest that held the silken gowns, the bangles. Ibrahim's penance. The chest had been empty. More than anything else, that had told Louis-Philippe that Ibrahim would never breathe again. The books were gone.

Who would have taken the books, the gowns? And why? There were no marks on Ibrahim. Not that he would fight. That was not Ibrahim's way. If bandits had come, Ibrahim would talk to them, make them laugh, tell them a tale of the southern winds. He never had any sense, his Ibrahim. No sense at all. Now he was gone. *Ibrahim.*

The first time Louis-Philippe saw him, Ibrahim had been so angry his eyes threw sparks. But Louis-Philippe was captured by the fire in those eyes, by the dramatic gestures, by Ibrahim's tender heart, his unflagging kindness.

Johanna had held Louis-Philippe after he had brought Ibrahim's body to her chamber, had held him as she used to when he was a baby. She had cradled his head underneath her chin while he shook and his breath whistled in and out through his teeth. Then she had smoothed the hair back from his forehead and pushed him away.

"Now," she had said. "We must think of Maríana."

Johanna had told him that she knew Maríana had fled. She did not tell him how she knew, but had made him promise to join the searchers. He was to do whatever he could to make sure that Maríana was not found. But if she was found, he was to take her directly to Johanna.

Louis-Philippe watched Henri prowl. Henri's head turned first one way, then the other, his cold eyes moving in a methodical sweep. Johanna was right. No time for grief. When he had seen the snow-covered hump under the pine, the black reed pointing into the sky, Louis-Philippe remembered Thérèse telling him how her family buried themselves in the snow when they traveled. It could be anyone there under the snow, of course, but he had used his body to hide the reed from

Henri's eyes. Bauçais may not know how the Jakintzas traveled in winter, but he was not stupid. If he had seen the faint mist rising from the end of the reed, he would know that more than a snow-covered rock rested beneath the contorted pine.

Louis-Philippe had taken Henri away, but before he had herded the searchers down the slope, he had dropped his hunting knife. If Maríana were there underneath the snow, he hoped she would find the knife. He must trust that his message would be clear, that she would know he was on her side.

HERE THEY were on the southwest slopes of Irati, heading north. Henri had swept the area all day, but they were getting closer to Canigou. Louis-Philippe looked up at tattered clouds filling the sky, their edges and centers darkening. In a few moments, night would claim the mountain. But that cloud there, it looked like a wing. Yes, that sharp edge had feathers. He really must tell Ibrahim. *Ibrahim.*

Louis-Philippe stood, head bent back, and waited for the anguish to wash in a frigid stream from his heart down through his legs. His giraffe legs. He let the grief pass from his feet into the earth. This was not the first time he had given his woe to the ground today. He was leaving pieces of his mourning all over the mountainside. But it was fitting. And wherever he was now, Ibrahim would be amused.

Louis-Philippe drew in a breath and looked at Henri again. Bauçais had stopped. His squire leaned toward him, whispering. Then a voice yelled from the knoll that rose ahead of them.

"Over here!" It was Guillaume. "Tracks!"

Allah! Louis-Philippe ran with the others to where Guillaume knelt. Why hadn't he taken Guillaume aside, told him to kick over any tracks he found? Guillaume would not question this; he never disobeyed orders. Now, it was too late. Henri was kneeling and inspecting the footprints. Louis-Philippe looked at the sky. Soon darkness would slow the search, but it would also curb the pace of Maríana and whoever traveled with her. Merde!

Bauçais was staring at the tracks. Then he lifted his face to the fading light. His eyes glimmered under his strong brow, but he did not speak. The men stood around him in a clump, their arms dangling at their sides, waiting.

"What moon is there tonight?" Henri finally spoke, but his eyes were still fixed upon the darkening sky.

"Black," Guillaume answered.

Henri's face dropped and a muscle in his cheek jumped. Then he stood and approached Louis-Philippe. "It is for you to decide, de Reuilles," he said. "These are mostly your men and you know the area." Henri's eyes were direct. Where was the frost that usually blanketed his gaze? "Do we continue with torches, or wait until dawn?" He stopped an arm's length away.

"The day was warm," Louis-Philippe replied, watching Henri's eyes. "The snow may shatter." Something was unsettling Bauçais. His face was naked, stripped of the reserve that usually thrust people away. Henri was not a fool. He must know these tracks were fresh, that their best chance of finding Mariana was to pursue. So what was the desperate plea that shone from his eyes now? "We would risk avalanche if we continue in the dark." Louis-Philippe hoped that whoever was with Mariana would consider this also. He did not want to come upon Mariana's twisted body at the bottom of a ravine. Ibrahim would never forgive him.

Henri inspected the tracks again. Some struggle within him was traced clearly upon his face-a struggle, and sorrow. "Would we endanger the men if we continue?"

"We would."

Now Henri drew in his breath, his face lifted again. "I will not endanger you or your men," he said. "We will camp here."

He gestured to his squire and the boy brought him a length of ash, cloth wound around its end, the smell of animal fat rising from it. "I will follow the tracks as far as I can." No one moved or spoke as Henri struck his flint and blew the spark into a steady blaze. "No, Robert," he said as his squire made to follow him. "You will see to my squire, de Reuilles?" His eyes sought Louis-Philippe. How curious. He had not noticed Henri's eyes before. Beautiful eyes, those. In a fine-boned face. He could begin to see what Mariana had found in this man. Louis-Philippe nodded. "You can follow me at first light," Henri said, then turned to go.

The men used their staffs to clear a space for their camp. He was aware of the swirl of motion around him, the sharp tang of burning pine branch as they made their fires, the ripple of voices. But his eyes followed the golden flicker of Henri's torch until he could no longer see it.

Chapter 28

A SHEER WALL of stone halted Henri. The air held the luminous sheen of dawn. Another warm day. Beams of sunlight settled upon icy slopes, cleaving snow that had melted, then frozen again under the stars. The crack and groan of fracturing ice drifted to where he stood.

Last night he had been stopped in his tracks by the mounting roar of snow and rock tumbling and sliding somewhere on the mountain. He had waited, torch clutched in one hand and sword held ready in the other, while the thunder of collapsing snow faded to a rumbling lament. When the night was silent again, he had looked in surprise at the sword in his hand. When had he drawn it?

He had followed the footprints through the night, searching the ground for signs of human passage. Several times he lost the trail, was forced to retrace his steps and follow an orderly search, fanning out from the last tracks he had found until more traces of his prey appeared. At first, he had noticed nothing around him except the faint marks upon the ground, signs that would lead him to his Maríana. But the torrent of rolling rock and snow had unnerved him. De Reuilles had been right. It was dangerous to travel in the dark over this terrain.

Now, he surveyed the granite and slate cliff barring his way. Last night, he had hunted for a route around this barrier which towered into the clouds above his head. But the cliff continued far into the distance. And the trail ended here.

Henri looked down at the scraps of beef and crumbs of bread scattered upon the ground. They had stopped here, he was sure of it. A hurried meal, but then where did they go?

The gathering light revealed more of the cliff that reared above him, scored and pitted, with twisted fissures. Henri was no climber. His fief was on the northern coast. The sea did not daunt him, but this mountain defeated him. He had spent the night seeking the fissures in the rock, handholds that he might use to ascend the sheer wall. At one time, he had mounted the height of three men before he could go no farther and he was forced to come down again.

This mountain would not suffer his touch. It repelled him at every turn. He had hung suspended, the promise of broken bones and twisted limbs awaiting him below, until his toes found a resting place. He could not scale this wall of stone, but de Reuilles had experienced climbers. They would find a way.

The steady crunch of feet upon snow heralded the arrival of de

Reuilles and the men. Henri watched the group, noting the men's pallor, the way they averted their eyes from the cliff. Was this the mountain Canigou? These men seemed to fear it.

Louis-Philippe came forward, stopping next to Henri. He grunted a greeting, then peered up at the granite barrier, bending his head back and shading his eyes.

"They were here," Henri said. He released some of the crumbs he had. Louis-Philippe's eyes darkened when he saw the bits of bread flutter to the ground.

"Guillaume." Louis-Philippe snapped his fingers, then gestured toward the cliff when Guillaume approached. "Can this be climbed, or can we go around?"

Guillaume considered, glancing up and down, then across the length of the granite wall. "It will take time."

"How much time?" Louis-Philippe drew his gloves over his knuckles.

"Hard to say," Guillaume answered. "One week, perhaps two?" He shrugged. "Maybe more."

Louis-Philippe turned to Henri, reached out his hand. "Come, Bauçais," he said. "Guillaume will stay with two men and try to find a way up or around." He waved his other hand at the men. "We have done all that we can here."

The air was still, hushed. No more cracking ice now. And De Reuilles was right again. They would do better back at the château where Henri could question the servants and visiting knights a second time. His earlier interrogation had been cursory. He had been so anxious to find Maríana that he had not followed the system Hughes des Arcis had taught him during his time as a Soldier of Christ. Henri was still a warrior of the Pope. They had not reassigned him yet. He could use this. Tongues tended to loosen when people were confronted with the garb of the Inquisition. Even de Reuilles' men watched him, became very still when he came near. They were watching him now, though they did not know he caught their sliding glances. He brushed the rest of the crumbs from his breeches, looked at the group of men surrounding Guillaume.

He would don his silken tunic with the white cross as soon as he got back to Reuilles-le-château. Once they reached the château, he would find the knight who had shared a chamber with the Breton.

The Breton. Why did he not remember this man's face? He could picture all the other knights, even the squires. But not this man. Guillaume was pacing the base of the cliff, shading his eyes, peering upward. Henri was sure Guillaume would find a way up. He must.

The chill of damp stone radiated from the granite wall before him. Henri turned his back to the cliff.

A STACCATO howl shivered and echoed around her. Maríana clung to the wall on her right. The stone felt gritty under her fingers. Iranzu and Leila were in front of her on the ledge. Maríana knew they were there from the taut pull of the rope that Iranzu had used to connect them all, just as she knew Richard was behind her from the tug and slack of the rope that tied him to her. But when she held her hand up a finger's width from her eyes, she could not see it. How could Iranzu see? He was leading.

Leading inside Canigou.

They had stopped at the doorstep of the Lady's mountain last night and shared their remaining food. Maríana had eaten. She was sure of this. Leila would not have allowed her to refuse. She had been aware of the weight of bread on her tongue, the bulk as it slid down her throat, but it had no taste. Plaintive voices kept speaking to her. They had started their chatter in her ears after she had drawn the spiral in the snow. She could still hear their faint whispers, though these were now fading. Once or twice she had answered them, but stopped when she saw the keen glance Richard gave her, the worried furrow between his black brows.

When Leila had pulled her to her feet and pointed to the cliff that soared above them, Maríana had blanched. How could she climb this glassy surface?

But they all had. Iranzu had tied them, one to the other, and led, finding handholds on the sheer wall. He had sent images of where he placed his hands and feet, marking the spots somehow so when Leila and Maríana followed they could see a faint glow upon the rock's surface.

It was Maríana who talked Richard through the climb, who told him where the fissures and chinks in the stone lay. This had slowed them, but talking to Richard helped her. It stopped the giddy flutter in her belly whenever she had to look down and saw the ground fading into the distance. She could focus on the next place to put her hands, how to tell Richard where to reach for the indentations in the rock so that he could follow. Richard looked up at her the whole climb. She caught the gleam of his eyes in the starlight. It was a miracle, the way Iranzu guided them, showed them all the places where the ice had not settled, where they could drive their fingers and feet into the side of the mountain.

They had climbed the height of thirty men before Iranzu pulled her up onto the ledge. She shook with the effort of the climb, her muscles taut and hands burning. Yet Iranzu had not allowed them to rest there. He had waited only until Richard reached the ledge, then he had turned and disappeared into the cliff wall, pulling Leila, and then Maríana and Richard behind him into blackness. He had placed Maríana's hand against a flinty, icy surface, telling her to keep to the wall. They could not risk a light. It would be seen. When they had gone far enough into the mountain, then Iranzu would light his torch. She must have inched along this wall for hours now. They would be in this mountain forever, she was sure.

Her face now leaned into the wall as the chirping cry bounced off the walls around them again. Richard touched her shoulder, his hand a firm, warm pressure. "Bats," he whispered. "It is only bats. We must keep going."

Maríana nodded and shuffled forward, her hands following the wall, slackening the rope that held her to Leila and Iranzu. Richard gave her shoulder a gentle squeeze. His touch captured her breath. He could never return to Brittany. Not now. Not ever. He had left everything behind, even his harp. Everything except his sword.

It was her fault. If she had not gone to the tower, had not wakened him, he might be safe now. Or he might be out with her father, searching. Her fault.

But she was glad that he came with them. She could feel him behind her, feel the warm push of his breath on her neck when he drew close. The deep timbre, the rich wine-dark resonance of his voice traced a path from her ears to her toes. He had held her when she lost the baby. She swallowed the clot of sorrow that filled her throat and her foot wandered to the left, hung in the air.

Nothing there! She drew in her breath and pulled her foot back, listened to the clatter of pebbles falling into the blackness.

The rushing gurgle of water somewhere below and the scrape of feet upon stone reached her ears. Their breath had its own music; the deep rhythm of her grandfather, the quiet inhalation of Leila, the steady whispering murmur of Richard. The fresh dampness of mist and the warmth of their bodies mingled. But over it all, a sharp vinegar bit her nose, drifted toward them from somewhere up ahead. The rope pulled her to the right around a sharp corner, then it slackened. They were stopping. A slick tearing rasp, then the distinct brilliance of flint striking was followed by the warm glow of torch light, revealing Iranzu's profile as he lit fabric he had tied around the end of his staff.

The passage they had come through yawned behind her in a blackness so deep it swallowed the meager light thrown off by their torch. Maríana let her head fall back, raised her eyes and saw a pitch-black sky filled with tiny stars. Were they out of the mountain now? But these stars were restlessly moving, and a trilling wail pulsed in the air.

"They are just bats. Out there it is daytime, so they come in here to sleep." Leila was watching her, but her face was kind. For now, there was no censure in her sister's eyes. "They piss in a great pool under where they hang — that is the stink — but they will not harm us. Ignore them."

The immense cavern echoed with every step. Iranzu led in a circular path around the deep pool of excrement underneath thousands of bats dangling from the ceiling. Maríana kept a wary eye on the waves of movement up above, jumping now and then as one or two of the bats disengaged from one spot and fluttered over to rest on another part of the dome of the cave. Iranzu turned back to her. "It is not far now. This way." His words echoed throughout the cavern. He pointed to his right where a narrow passage branched off from the main cave.

Here rocky walls gave way to smoothly finished blocks of stone, the floor spread out in a level stretch. Maríana knelt and touched the bits of polished stones that made up the floor. Pink granite and smooth gray river stone ran in diamond patterns toward the walls. She looked up and saw Richard standing in the middle of the passage, his eyes wide, entranced.

"There are people in these walls." He pointed down the tunnel to where Iranzu and Leila were walking.

Leila looked back over her shoulder, then shrugged. "They have always been here."

Maríana moved to where Richard stood. The walls were carved into the life-size likenesses of men and women in a continuous row that marched into the depths of the tunnel ahead. She reached out and let her fingers trace the features of a woman molded into the rock of the wall. The eyes of the figure were sloped, tilted upward at the outer corner, like Richard's eyes. The nose was straight and fine, the lips curved in a gentle swell, the cheekbones were high and well-defined. The forehead rose to a patterned head covering that bound the hair. As her hands caressed the figure, the stone grew warm. An image of the woman's face captured the likeness upon the stone, the skin turned golden, the brows black, the eyes trembled and started to open.

Maríana snatched her hand away and fell back against Richard, felt his hands steady her. "What did you see?" His voice was hushed.

"Nothing." She looked up ahead where Leila was beckoning.

"We cannot stop here," Leila said. "Farther down this path is a room where we can rest for a while." She turned and started down the tunnel again.

A room inside the mountain? Maríana looked at the figures on the wall, then up at the ceiling. Lines curled and twisted there in a meandering serpentine coil. As she moved her eyes along it, the coil started to unwind. "What?" But Richard was taking her hand, pulling her down the tunnel.

"Don't look at it," he said.

Maríana sped down the tunnel next to Richard, following the glow of Iranzu's torch ahead. She slowed when the floor warmed underneath her feet. The air was growing moist. Glancing to the side, she saw that the line of carvings had ended, but the walls were sweating. A green-blue mold clung to the sides of the tunnel and the floor became slippery. Yet she felt a radiance emanating from the corridor, pulling her forward.

What was this? It captured her heart, flowed out along her limbs in a golden shimmer.

She started to run. Richard cried for her to slow, but she could not. All she saw was the corridor stretching before her, faint light from Iranzu's bobbing torch. Then the walls abruptly angled outward, formed a six-sided room. She could not see the ceiling, but the echoes told her they were still in the mountain. Iranzu was at the center, where a block of stone rose into a central hearth. He was lighting sticks and what looked like bits of dung.

"We can stop here and rest," Iranzu said. "I packed snow into our wineskins. Leila has dried apples and twice-baked bread." As Mariana entered the chamber, she felt the walls embrace her, cradle her. Kindling in the hearth caught and sent its own fiery welcome. Richard stood close by her side again, but his eyes were wary. Didn't he feel the room greeting him?

"The next passage is longer, but it leads straight to our village." Iranzu's lips lifted in a smile. "We will be safe there."

Leila placed her hand on Mariana's arm. "We will soon be home."

Home.

HENRI FOCUSED his most potent glare on the young knight in front of him. Jean-Pierre Rhomboid perched, sweating, on a stool below the raised platform where Henri sat in the great hall. Henri had secured the chair de Reuilles used when he meted out justice. It was a solid, massive black oak edged with gold and cushioned with burgundy silk. The raised platform forced people he questioned to look up at him.

His eyes still fixed upon the quaking knight, Henri moved his shoulders so the white cross that spread over his tunic rippled with the tensing of his chest muscles. It was good to remind people exactly what he represented.

When he looked upon the cross on Henri's tunic, Jean-Pierre distinctly quailed, but his voice was steady. "We all squired for Baron de Reuilles," he said. "De la Guerche and I often spoke with the Lady Mariana." A film of moisture coated his upper lip. "I am not sure where Richard has gone. Perhaps he had to return to la Guerche."

Henri stroked his chin. There was something this one was not saying. Jean-Pierre had changed his story three times. First, he said that Richard had been visiting one of the kitchen maids. No surprise here, this fit the message de la Guerche had left in the chamber. But none of the maids remembered seeing the black-haired knight. They might be lying, of course, but Henri doubted this. Three of the maids admitted to him that they would have welcomed a visit from Richard de la Guerche. When Henri told Jean-Pierre what the maids had said, he changed his story, asserting that de la Guerche had gone to Reuilles-la-ville. Now he was saying that the Breton knight had returned home.

"You say you are such good friends." Henri softened his expression. "Why would he not tell you the truth of where he had gone?"

Jean-Pierre's shoulders twitched up in a rigid shrug. "Richard always kept his own counsel."

Henri nodded. Jean-Pierre visibly deflated in relief, then tensed again as Henri let the silence broaden. He watched Jean-Pierre squirm.

"Perhaps there was some other reason. If Lady Maríana knew that Jacques was dead, maybe she went away on some quest with Richard." Jean-Pierre's voice was pitched low, and fractured on his friend's name.

Henri looked down his nose at the young knight. "Are you saying that Maríana's disappearance was a childish jest with de la Guerche? Some girlish whim?"

Jean-Pierre paled and shook his head. "No! I meant that she would want to find the killer! The Lady Maríana never acted like other girls." His voice rang out into the room.

"Explain."

"She never said anything when we teased her, when we played jokes on her. Always quiet — you never knew what she was thinking." He was warming to this, his face shining with earnest zeal. "And she never cried. She would never give in, even when all she had to do was say something to get us to stop." His eyes grew opaque. He seemed lost in some memory. "All she had to do was say it."

"Say what?" Henri leaned forward.

But Jean-Pierre continued speaking as if he did not hear. "It was unnatural, her silence. We all talked about it. Arnaut thought he could make her cry. He asked me to come with him. But I did not knock her down, it was Arnaut!" Jean-Pierre's voice was surly with an old grievance. "She made a light with her hands. A light that brought the wind. She was never like other people. There were things that she could do..." Jean-Pierre broke off and looked up at Henri, then drew back, stammering, "That is, she, uh." The color faded from his face. Droplets of sweat made bright beads across his forehead. "I mean, she..."

"What light? What wind?" This was nonsense. But there might be something here that might reveal why she had left. Henri veiled his eyes, dampened the wrath that gripped him. He had no use for bullies, but this one might have information that would lead him to Maríana. "Did de la Guerche hurt her, too?" He would run him through.

Jean-Pierre moistened his lips. "The light... she conjured a light to punish us for knocking her down." He leaned forward, his words tumbled out. "Everyone remembers the wind from that night. It blew the fowl pen apart. Ask Guillaume! Or anyone else."

"Did de la Guerche knock her down?" Henri repeated. Could the Breton have taken Maríana away as some sort of revenge?

"No. Richard would never hurt her." Jean-Pierre's eyes were distant, abstracted, then the whine returned to his voice. "She made Baron de Reuilles send Arnaut and me away in disgrace."

"You said that de la Guerche would never hurt her."

"No." Jean-Pierre looked directly into his eyes now. There was no deceit in his face. "He loved her," he said. "He always has."

Henri bounded out of his seat, the oak chair toppling with a resounding crash. He struggled to control the tensing of his muscles, the swelling of his throat. He reached for his sword; his fingers closed on the air. Of course. His sword was in the long knights' room with Robert. Counting his breaths until the red haze before his eyes faded, he looked down at the trembling knight. Bullies. But this young idiot would not be worth endangering his fief. Lashing out at Jean-Pierre would bring Louis of France down on Bauçais. No, he would let this one live.

Henri turned toward the stairs, then spoke over his shoulder to Jean-Pierre. "Leave the palais." His voice was pitched low, but it filled the hall. "And stay out of my sight for as long as you remain at the château." He paused. "If you do not, I will call you out." Henri strode to the stairs. He heard scrambling footsteps patter across the floor, heard the door creak open. A puff of frigid air touched Henri's back as it closed.

It was good that he could not picture de la Guerche. If he could, the image of the Breton knight with Maríana would haunt him, interfere with what he must do to find her. There was more to Jean-Pierre's tale. Henri would start with Johanna. She should know of any dalliance between de la Guerche and Maríana. He would have his answers.

Chapter 29

A BREEZE kissed Maríana's face, carrying the tang of amber sap, the clean, unsullied aroma of black pine. The exit from the mountain formed a tall rectangle. Light from outside fell softly through it and spread across the paved floor, caressing her. She stepped from the passage's door into a grove of trees. Oak and ash, hawthorn and beech-not pine-surrounded her. But the gentle slope of the mountain that curved away from the tunnel, all the way down to the silver gleam of a river far below, was carpeted by a sea of dense, glistening pines. She looked up at the gray and violet sky that pressed down on the earth and embraced the valley below. Home.

Richard stood beside her, his face shining, his chest rising in a long inhalation. "It is good to breathe without the stink of bat."

A breeze washed over them again and the air filled with the chime and clang of bells. Wind lifted Maríana's hair, brought the sharp trill of silver, the musical clatter of brass, and underneath, a humming drone of plainchant, of monks singing wordless tones of joy. "What is this?" she stepped forward.

Richard grabbed her arm and shoved her behind him, drawing his sword in the same motion.

Leila gave a shout of laughter. "Put your sword away, Frenchman." She pointed at the trees around them. Countless rows of bells dangled from the tree branches. Wind sent their melody into the air. She pulled Maríana out from behind Richard. "You will not need your sword here."

"I am Breton, not French," Richard whispered as the voices sounded again, then he added, "But who is singing?"

Leila drew Richard and Maríana to where a massive oak stood, its branches strung with gut and woven strands of vine. "This one is dead, so we hollowed out the center. My cousin Marc strung the branches." She released their hands and stood grinning at them.

"It is a harp." Richard reached for the lowest gut string, plucking it gently. "Maríana." He turned to her, his face alight. "See? The air has a voice."

Maríana stood on her toes and peered inside the oak, then leaned back and looked up into the branches. She counted thirty strands fastened to the larger, more stable limbs. Deep tones resonated throughout the empty space within, flowed out toward her, hung in the air. Some strands were barely thicker than the string of an oud. Others were almost as thick as a rope. Richard plucked the strings, his fingers tentative, searching.

Leila drew her away from Richard. "In the winter, after the first snowfall, all of us come up here at sunset to tend to the bells." She tapped three brass bells hanging from the branch of a hawthorn. Pure notes fell into the air, joined the hymn the wind played over gut strings. "Each bell is for one of us who has crossed the river into death. During the year, some fall off or become tangled. Sometimes birds nest in them."

"Why tend them in winter?" Maríana stepped away and scanned the branches. Hundreds of bells.

"The barrier between life and death is thinnest in winter, so that is our time to tie them back onto their branches, to polish those that have tarnished, or to hang a new bell if one of us has gone ahead that year." Leila shook the branch. The bells answered her motion with a frenzied pealing.

"How many are there?" Maríana asked. "How long have you been hanging them?" A continual melody reached out, touched, rejoiced.

"You would have to ask Grandfather." Leila wandered over to where Richard was still plucking the strings, his eyes closed, listening. His fingers were more sure now. Maríana could almost recognize the song he played. But Leila extended her hands and ran them in playful tugs across the other strings. A discordant trickle of notes cut across Richard's melody. His eyes flew open, then he gave Leila a wry smile and joined in her random song, grasping and plucking strings that she could not reach.

Maríana stood back. Leila must have decided that Richard was worthy of her attention now. This was better than her caustic digs at him throughout their flight. Still, her heart ached at the sight of her sister and Richard together. But how could that be? She had been just a child when she loved him. Love did not have the same meaning then.

She had set aside any fantasies when Johanna told her of his betrothal. Oh, she had waited. And, in the night, had nestled next to him in her dreams. Until he sent her away, telling her he could not come back to her. But those were dreams, weren't they? She looked up, saw the curve of his grin, the honeyed lights in his eyes. He had come back for her wedding, hadn't he?

She turned away from Richard and Leila and faced the entrance, where Iranzu stood, then stumbled in surprise. "Blessed Mother!" Two immense statues stood on either side of the tunnel, each reaching the height of ten men. How had she walked right past them, unaware?

"Who are they?" Richard asked. Color flooded his cheeks and he averted his eyes from the statue to the right of the tunnel. It was a figure of a woman, bare-breasted, but clothed in a pleated kirtle that fell from her waist to her ankles. The hands were clutched into fists at the figure's side and one foot stepped forward. Sloped eyes stared sightlessly out onto the valley below, and the same proud forehead and gentle curved mouth as the figures on the walls inside the mountain shaped the face.

"The woman is the Guardian." Leila was watching Richard. Her lips twisted when he looked away from the statue. "And the other is the Beacon."

The statues had the same face, yet there was no mistaking the virile essence that imbued the Beacon with robust power, nor the softer edges and yielding that suffused the figure of the Guardian. "How long have they been here?" Maríana grasped Richard's hand. His fingers felt cold as his hand closed over hers.

Leila shrugged. "Forever, I guess." Then she waved to Iranzu. "Grandfather! I want to get to the house before dark."

"Let us go, then." He gestured toward the slope that descended into the valley below, the pine-covered cliffs on the other side that plunged to its floor. "Welcome to our home," he said and spread his arms.

IT WAS TOO warm in the chamber. Henri stood before Johanna de Reuilles, watching her eyes and feeling sweat trickle in rivulets from his neck down the middle of his chest before collecting in a damp patch on his belly. She was wily, this old woman. Her hearth was filled with blazing logs. The blast of heat alone would cause most to cut short any visit to Johanna. Her withered body seemed unaffected by the scorching atmosphere. It was often so with the old. Well. He could use this device himself sometime. But for now he could bear the heat in her chamber. Johanna would not be rid of him.

"So de la Guerche and Maríana were childhood friends?" He ran his sleeve across his forehead.

"I taught him to read." Johanna shrugged. "He took his lessons along with Maríana. I suppose you could say they were friends."

Henri pulled a stool from the corner and set it in front of Johanna, noting the twitch of surprise flutter across her face when he sat. "Rhomboid told me that de la Guerche loved Maríana." He leaned toward her. "But he did not ask for her hand?"

"He was betrothed." She was clearly deciding how much to say. "I believe his family chose someone from Bourdeilles."

"Then he did love Maríana? Could he have taken her away to compromise her?" It would not work. No matter what happened, Henri would have her back. But if he had touched her, this Breton knight, Henri would have his head on a pike. He looked at his trembling hands, forced the muscles to relax, then raised his face again to Johanna.

"Who can say if he loved her? He never said anything to me." She was good at masking her feelings, this Johanna. But Henri was skilled at reading faces and could see the struggle she tried to hide. He used his sleeve to wipe the sting of salt from his eyes. When he looked at her again, Johanna had decided something. Her face relaxed. She settled back into her chair.

"If he did go with her," she said, her gaze sharp and direct, "it was to protect her. I am sure of this."

Henri leaned toward her. "Protect her from what? If she were in danger, shouldn't her father protect her? Why didn't she come to him?" His fingers dug into his knees. "Or to me?"

"Her father cannot protect her." Johanna's eyes blazed now. "Nor can you."

"What!" This was really too much. "State your meaning."

She did not flinch. "It seems that her stepmother," Johanna began, pausing when he drew back from her, "has made some accusations."

Ysabel. What accusations could she have made? She was jealous of Maríana, this he knew. He had thought her jealousy silly. Ysabel was Baroness, after all. If her child was a boy, she was carrying the future heir of Reuilles-le-château.

Henri planned to take Maríana to Bauçais after the wedding. Women were strange. The last time he had seen her, Ysabel had clung to him, had said that she would never let him go. Surely she would not have told Maríana of her assignations with him! Maríana would have told her father and De Reuilles would have put Ysabel aside, if he knew.

No. Henri was sure that Louis-Philippe did not know. De Reuilles had not called him out, had he? Ysabel had said nothing, of this he was sure. Yet if she wanted to rid herself of Maríana, what would she do? He focused upon Johanna's face. She had remained silent. Light from the blazing fire painted crimson patterns across her features.

Light. Patterns. Wind... .

"Damn!" He pounded his knee. "Ysabel has called in Durand!" Jean-Pierre had handed him the answer with his story of eerie lights and great storms. Childhood fancies, of course. No one could command the elements. But he had seen less evidence result in a protracted interrogation up north in Gréves. A shudder gripped his bowels. He bit down, tried to stifle it before it could shake his limbs. Torture had sealed the fate of the woman in Gréves. There were few who could withstand crushed limbs and hot iron.

He turned away from Johanna, fought to suppress the shaking that moved through his arms. Fire. The blast of heat from Johanna's fire conjured an image, of tiny fingers grasping iron bars, the acrid breath of burning straw, of cloth. It always came back to Montsegur, didn't it? Burning Cathars. Burning witches. No wonder Maríana fled. He would have run, too.

"His minion will be here soon." Johanna was watching him closely. How much did she know? "So you see..."

"What do you know about this light she made with her hands?" He cut into her speech, saw her eyes fade into puzzlement. "I am told there was a great wind, a storm that blew apart the fowl pen."

She was hesitant. "I remember the wind, but I know of no light." She took his hand. Her fingers were strong. "Jeanne told me of a woman in Reuilles-la-ville, a woman who may be helpful in sorting this out. I was going to see her myself, but it would be better if you went." Johanna's eyes darted to the white cross on his tunic, now pressed wetly against his skin.

"Jeanne?" He was with the church, after all. And he was Maríana's betrothed. Who better to see how far this foolishness had gone?

"Jeanne is a servant. But she has kin in Reuilles-la-ville and she can take you to this woman, this Utarilla." The pressure of her fingers increased. "Will you go?"

He stood, towered over her frail body. Yes, he would start the investigation before Durand's lackey arrived. That would be his best hope of controlling it. Who would Durand send? Hughes des Arcis would be a good choice. He was reasonable. This nonsense about magic would not impress him. Des Arcis followed the rules. Heresy interested him, not spells and potions.

He nodded. Johanna shifted in her chair, hands tightly clasped, her face still, waiting. "Where is this Jeanne?" he asked.

MARÍANA followed a narrow path that wound down the slope to the valley's floor, where it widened to allow the passage of carts. On either side, cozy granite and slate houses sat surrounded by huge bushes and trees. Each chimney sent a fragrant plume of white smoke into the cold winter air. Candlelight twinkled through the slats on the wood-shuttered windows. Occasionally, shutters opened and people peered out at her. At the path's end, a larger stone house with a steeply sloping roof rested below the rearing slope of the mountain. A tall woman dressed in a russet gown waited in the doorway. Her two thick raven braids shot with silver that hung below her waist. She was wiping her hands on a midnight blue cloth hanging from her belt and her warm hazel eyes beamed. "Lady's greetings, Father!" she called out.

Leila ran on ahead and Iranzu slowly approached the house, but Maríana stopped, felt the blood drain from her face. "Mama?" she whispered.

"What is it?" Richard tried to turn her toward him, but she would not take her eyes off the woman in the doorway.

Maríana shook herself. "It is nothing," she reassured him. Not her mother. Just her mother as she would have looked had she lived. Richard still held her arm, looking uncertain. "Let us join them," she said.

Arm-in-arm with Richard, she walked the final steps of her journey to the house of the Jakintzas.

"I am Adelie," the woman said. Warmth and the smell of bread and meat wafted toward Maríana. "Lady's greetings, child of my sister" Adelie spread her arms wide.

Maríana walked to Adelie, fell into her arms. "You must tell me everything," Adelie whispered. "But now," she raised her voice to the rest, switched to the langue d'oc, "hot food for all of you! Bucket is over there for washing-water is warm." Still holding Maríana, she nodded toward the right side of the large room. "And make sure you use it! We wash before meals, here."

Maríana looked around the room in amazement. The stone house consisted of one large room. A small hut, outside in the back, was visible through the slats covering a window. Along the far wall three curtained box beds stood. The rich burgundy curtains and coverlets were embroidered and appliquéd with symbols in bright colors: circles with triangles inside, Arabic letters, the four-petaled flower of her mother's necklace, and others that she could not decipher. The woolen rug was made in the style of the East, with patterns of curling designs in reds and golds.

The oak table stretched nearly the width of the room, facing a deep, wide hearth where a fire roared and crackled. The table was set for eight, with red-brown crockery dishes, thick goblets, wooden spoons and metal knives. A large pot, filled with something rich and savory, emitted wisps of steam.

Richard vigorously bathed his hands and face. A youth with a triangular fine-boned face and deep-set green eyes stood beside Richard, waiting his turn. Behind the young man were two small boys, their bright eyes regarding Maríana.

"That is my Marc," Adelie said, "and Tomás and Paxti."

"WE HAVE ample livestock, so each winter we must slay at least a dozen cattle to keep the balance." Leila helped herself to great slices of bread on which she slathered fresh butter and then dipped the buttered slices into the steaming pot. "This is good oxtail stew, Aunt Adelie." Her mouth was full and the words blurred.

"What is in this?" Richard lifted his spoon, sniffed at the top of his dish.

"Carrots and leeks and onions, all from our gardens. The herbs are thyme and rosemary. Fennel and rosemary are also in the bread," Adelie said.

The stew was rich and delicious. Nearly three days on low provisions had made Maríana ravenous, but unable to eat much at one sitting. She soon pushed back from the table and watched, as Marc and Leila dished up the remainder of the stew and wrapped the bread for storage in the cold house outside.

Leila opened the door, carried the remains of their meal to the cold house. The light was fading now and a gray-blue mist settling on the land. Sounds were muted. Leila's steps crunching over the snow were nearly inaudible, even though she was barely ten paces away.

"We have made a place for Mariana in Leila's bed over there." Adelie pointed to the box bed in the back corner of the room.

She turned to Richard and smiled. "This young knight," she said in langue d'oc, "he shall have his own house." She motioned for Marc. "My son will show you the way."

Dismay spread across Richard's face. Marc was already at the door, gesturing for Richard to precede him. Richard looked at Mariana. "If you need anything..." he said, but he did not look at her.

"She will be well," Adelie answered. "You must not worry." Some silent message passed between them. Adelie nodded. Richard straightened and then bowed gracefully before he followed Marc out into the night.

"Richard does not speak Basque," Mariana said. He had stayed at her side throughout the meal, had listened to their rapid speech, to her replies. A shiver worked its way out from her heart. With Richard gone, the house chilled. Adelie bustled around the chamber, but Mariana did not know this woman who was her aunt.

Adelie stopped, looked into Mariana's eyes, and smiled. "Your young knight will manage, I am sure. Now," she motioned for Mariana to come with her, "into bed with you." Adelie helped Mariana into the box bed, pulled the covers up around her. "Leila told me some of your story," she whispered, "that you lost your baby."

A tiny blue body cupped in Leila's hand... "We had to flee." Mariana choked.

Adelie placed her fingers against Mariana's lips. "You need not speak now. There will be time for speaking, and healing, too."

Kind words. Caring eyes. But a jumble of images danced before Mariana's eyes. Henri in the corridor with Ysabel. The parchment with the list of names. Ibrahim lying still upon the floor. The tiny form of her baby entering the frozen ground. She rolled up into a ball and shook, but no tears would come.

Warm arms enveloped her. "The world has come down upon you, as we say here," Adelie murmured. "You must wash it away with your tears."

"I do not cry." Mariana could not stop shaking. She curled her hands into fists, but her arms would not be still. "But I did cry! I did. When the baby died." She could not remember ever crying before, yet she must have. Children cried, didn't they? "I did not cry when Ibrahim..." She could not force her words past the lump that continued to grow, reaching from the middle of her chest into her throat.

Adelie rocked Mariana and stroked her hair. "I remember Ibrahim.

Thérèse brought him here after you were born."

"He is dead." Maríana's words were strangled, but the clot that blocked her throat was easing.

"Ahhhh," Adelie sighed. "I see." She stroked Maríana's hair in silence for a moment. "He was a great one, your Ibrahim. We will mourn his passing. But he was just one of your guides. There will be others. And you will see him again."

She stated all this as a matter of fact, as if Ibrahim had just stepped out the door and would be returning soon.

The knot in Maríana's chest loosened, but now there was a noise, a gasping, wrenching howl, a desolate, furious sobbing. Who could be making such a sound? Maríana buried her face into Adelie's shoulder. The sound was smothered now, yet it would not stop. She tried to speak, tried to tell Adelie to make it stop. But she could not find her voice.

"That is better." Adelie pulled her even closer. "It is good to cry."

Maríana de Reuilles does not cry. She struggled to draw in her breath, to tell Adelie that this ravaged weeping could not be from her. Yet no words would come, only the dreadful wailing that flowed out of her, that poured in a flood past her lips. Adelie's shoulder was wet. Maríana really should stop this. Her tears were making a sodden mess of Adelie's gown. What would Adelie think of her?

But the arms circling her did not leave. Finally, the tears slowed. Soft blankets were wrapped around her and a pillow fragrant with pine needles and lavender cushioned her head. The room faded, echoes of her weeping dwindled until there was no more sound.

Chapter 30

THERE WERE few about in the inner bailey and the area beyond the gates when the pope's representative arrived. Twelve soldiers dressed in the papal livery surrounded him, their dazzling white crosses shining. He kicked his horse's ribs and rode slightly ahead, assessing the fortification, the thickness of the walls. Frowning at the open gate. Was de Reuilles so arrogant that he left his gate open for anyone to ride in? Blood of Jesus! He could see that conditions here were lax. Three pages were just standing in the entry to the stables. They should be out in the bailey, helping his men to dismount.

Now he let crisp air flood his lungs, chill his throat. He stared at the graceful arches of the palais. Reuilles-le-château was quiet. The pale winter sunlight provided light, but no real warmth. Well, it was nearing Christmas, time for preparing home and livestock for the shortest day and for the winter storms still to come. He had seen this himself on the ride from Carcasonne. For the past few days the sun had warmed, loosening some of the icy grip of winter. But today the air had suddenly become heavy, promising another hard frost. Delicate crystal webs were already forming across standing water that had thawed. Perhaps the servants of Reuilles-le-château were busy in preparation for winter.

Or they were preparing for the Inquisition. He felt a fluttering in his belly. There were three names on the list des Arcis had given him. He was sure to find more.

Now he urged his horse in front of the palais and frowned. "Do they not challenge armed men here?" he asked a boy who had finally hurried forward to help him dismount.

The boy looked startled. "Why should we?" he asked simply, then offered his hands to help the man down. "Our watchers on the tower have already seen you coming across the lake. They saw your livery."

He smiled at the boy and allowed his fingers to caress the silky hair on the boy's head. "I see that I have been among the heretics of the south for too long," he sighed. "Such trust, such piety!" He glanced around the inner bailey. Not a large holding, certainly. His gaze took in the grounds surrounding the palais, the tower, the outbuildings. No, not large. He had seen much larger, and grander, too. But Reuilles-le-château was solid, comfortable. He dismounted, still caressing the boy's head. Then, gesturing for the twelve men to follow him, he marched up to the door and entered.

Pulling his gloves off, he turned to the servant who approached him. "Tell the Baroness Ysabel de Reuilles that Jean Becier is here."

HENRI SET Mother Utarilla on a chair inside the entry of the tower. He would ask Johanna to find the old woman a bed. When he and Jeanne had arrived at Mother Utarilla's stone house, the old woman had shouted out a greeting. She had cackled like a hen. Her ancient eyes peered out from folds of papery skin at Henri, raking his form, rudely assessing his height, his face. He had nearly blushed, but Utarilla turned to Jeanne, babbled at her in that gibberish the town people spoke. Jeanne had answered her in the same tongue, then Utarilla said, "What can I do for you, young knight?" in perfect French.

Henri had pushed his mantle aside. He could question her himself without a translator. But when Utarilla saw the white cross stretched over his chest, her mouth had trembled. She fell silent.

She had not spoken since.

Henri decided to bring her back to Reuilles-le-château when he saw her hands tighten on her bony knees at the mention of sorcery. He felt sure that she had information, but it would take time to convince her to speak. He needed to befriend her first, gain her confidence. Whatever little potions or drinks she brewed to heal would not place her in jeopardy, not with him. He could tell her this in all honesty.

There was no such thing as magic. Oh, he had never said anything to des Arcis or anyone else in the Pope's army about his own belief. Or rather, lack of belief. But he knew that if there was no God, there was also no Devil. Once Utarilla realized that he did not seek to bring her before Durand or the Inquisitor for dabbling with herbal remedies, she would open up, tell him what she knew of Maríana's disappearance. He was sure of this. Wasn't Maríana a healing woman? These women all knew each other.

Now he patted the old woman's hand and told Jeanne to stay with her while he went to Johanna. Not that he needed anyone to guard her. Utarilla could not walk. Her withered legs would not hold her. Henri had carried her all the way from Reuilles-la-ville. She was not going anywhere.

When he left the tower, he had to push his way through a herd of horses, milling on the stones of the inner bailey just outside the palais. Where were the squires? He pushed two of the horses out of his way and barked out an order to three pages who stood in open-mouthed astonishment at the fine stallions stamping and huffing on the stones. While the pages each led a horse into the stables, Henri fingered the red silken blankets that lay under the saddle of the horse standing near him. Livery of the pope. Well. Des Arcis must have arrived. These horses must be seen to immediately.

He roused four squires to help with stabling the thirteen horses. Really! What was wrong with de Reuilles? After they buried the dead gardener, Louis-Philippe had closeted himself in his chamber with jugs of wine, not even emerging for meals. Ysabel had kept to her room, also. And Guillaume was still on the mountain, trying to find a way up Canigou. Everything had been left to Johanna and to Henri. Indeed. He waited until the last of the horses was in the stables and the squires he had collared were unsaddling and brushing them down before he made his way to the great hall.

HE SPOTTED Father Gregory first. Of course, the château priest should be there to greet the representatives of the pope. De Reuilles should be there too. But it was Ysabel who stood beside the priest. Henri's eyes caught the bulge of her belly before he saw her face. She seemed to be pleading with someone who stood behind Father Gregory. All three of them were at the end of the hall by the roaring fire in the hearth.

Henri stopped in surprise. White robes. A Dominican? This was not des Arcis. Henri caught a glimpse of ivory skin stretched over the man's skull. Had he shaved his head completely? How strange. They usually left a ring of hair. Of course, he could be very old, but this man did not hold himself as an old man would. Yet Henri felt that he was not young, either.

Now the bald man turned to face Ysabel, moved out from behind Father Gregory. His profile stood out against the red of the fire. Lush, scarlet lips curved as he smiled indulgently at something Ysabel was saying. Dieu!

Henri backed into the shadows by the outer door, heart thundering in his chest. He could never forget that face, the pale skull, the swollen lips, the hooded, glittering eyes. A taut constriction seized his loins. He fought to still the fury that threatened to overwhelm him. Jean Becier. He had never thought to see that hated face again.

A wave of ice flowed through his veins and stiffened his back. He was no longer a helpless boy. He was the Baron of Bauçais, knight of King Louis of France, as well as Soldier of Christ. And he had brought down Jean Becier once, hadn't he? Shedding his mantle, Henri pulled his body up to full height and strode forward toward Ysabel.

Ysabel was still pleading. "I tell you it must be wrong!" she said tearfully. "My Louis-Philippe would never..."

Jean took her hands and patted them. "Calm yourself, Baroness, calm yourself. I am here now to assess the truth of these matters. No need to worry!" He ran his tongue across his lips, his eyelids blinking rapidly. "You must be patient. These things take time."

"Of course these things take time, Ysabel," Henri said, throwing his leg over a chair standing near them and plucking a cold apple off the tray beside it, as he slid down into the chair with ease. "They expect you to feed and house them for as long as it takes." Henri waved his hand toward the twelve men seated at the long tables, feasting on bread and wine.

He was pleased to see Jean jump at the sound of his voice. *I'll bet you can never forget me, either.* "Hello, Jean," Henri said.

Jean Becier turned slowly toward Henri, his lips stretched in a broad grimace that some might take for a smile. "God's greetings, Henri de Bauçais." His voice held the texture of heavy oil, smooth and liquid, just waiting for a spark to set it alight.

"Baron de Bauçais," Henri said, his mouth full of apple, satisfied to see the flash of hatred come and go in Jean's eyes.

Ysabel looked back and forth between the two men as Father Gregory tried to fade into the background. Henri casually sprawled in the chair eating his apple. His other hand rested upon his sword. Jean stood beside Ysabel, his back straight and his hands clasped in front of him, bowing his head. Becier always did play this game. The perfect cleric.

"D-do you know each other?" Ysabel wrung her hands.

Henri spit the core out and tossed it to some stable dogs laying by the hearth, who fell upon it, growling. De Reuilles had never let these dogs in the great hall before. Henri must tell Johanna to have them removed. He stood up from the chair, placing his right hand upon his sword, watching Jean's eyes flicker over to his soldiers, Jean's tongue dart nervously along his lips. "Yes," Henri said, giving Jean his best icy stare. When had he started enjoying this? "What was the name of that abbey?" He made the pretense of searching his memory, scratching his head.

"Fornault," Jean practically hissed through his teeth.

"Exactly!" Henri turned to Ysabel. "May I introduce to you the former Abbot of Fornault." He made a sweeping bow to Jean.

Father Gregory cleared his throat. "But Fornault Abbey was disbanded." His voice faded into his throat when Jean turned reptilian eyes upon him.

"You are correct, Father," Henri said. "Several years ago."

Jean's face went very still. "Yes," he finally said. "We left the abbey at the same time, I believe."

Henri smiled. "I went to France to serve the King," he said. "Where did you go?"

Jean recovered. "I went to serve the King of all men. We have routed out the Cathars, but there are other heretics we must pursue now. His Holiness asked me to assist Jacques Fouret in the Inquisition against witches." He bent his head toward Ysabel. His voice once again held the smooth, heavy essence of cold oil.

"Actually, I am glad I found you here," Henri said and was pleased to see Jean jump yet again. "I brought an old woman from Reuilles-la-ville to the tower. She may have something to tell us." The devil she would. One glimpse of Jean Becier and Utarilla would seal her lips for good. Or go back to speaking that gibberish. Henri looked at the soldiers sprawled around the long table, tankards at their fingertips. Drink up, you bloody bastards. With any luck, Jean would be tied up with the old woman for days while his men drank the ale and ate the bread and meat of Reuilles-le-château. And Henri would be free to continue his search for Maríana.

When he found her, he must take her away immediately. Out of Jean's reach.

"The woman's name is Utarilla." Henri caught an abortive movement out of the corner of his eye. Ysabel was clutching her belly. Was she ill? "Ysabel?"

But Jean Becier moved closer. "Indeed," he said. "You will question this woman?" His eyes gleamed.

"Yes. If you would care to accompany me over to the tower we could both question her."

"Of course." He gave that grimace again and turned to Ysabel. "Baroness, I must take my leave now." He kissed her hand.

Her face and her hand trembled. "Ysabel, are you ill?" Henri asked.

"N-no." Ysabel surreptitiously wiped her hand on her gown, then placed it upon her belly. "Just tired." Her eyes flashed something that looked like fear.

What did she have to fear? What had she been saying about Louis-Philippe? Ah, well. He would ask her later. Henri watched Ysabel as she turned and clambered up the stairs.

Jean also watched her. Henri caught his frown. But Jean turned to Father Gregory. "Father?"

"I have never made an interrogation," the priest stammered. "I would be in the way, I'm sure."

Henri shrugged. Ysabel seemed to be able to make it up the stairs. Johanna could see to her. "Eh bien. Are you coming, Jean?" He swung about and looked back over his shoulder. Jean followed close behind him.

WHEN THEY reached the tower, Henri started climbing the stairs to the door, but stopped when he felt Jean's hand on his sleeve. The skin on his arm tensed. It took all his will to stop himself from striking the man, to stand and simply look back at Jean. "Yes?"

Jean dropped his hand, his eyelids flickering rapidly in that lizard blink Henri remembered so well. "Hen... Baron de Bauçais?" Jean swallowed. "This old woman is in the dungeon?"

"They have no guard for the dungeon. It has not been used in years, so there has been no need."

Jean was aghast. "You mean Baron de Reuilles has no one guarding his dungeon? What kind of place is this?" He rubbed his hands together, scowling. "I can provide the guard and we can place her there."

"Enough time for that. You will see she cannot escape. I had to carry her here." Henri turned to continue up the stairs but the pale hand on his arm stopped him again. He looked back, focused his eyes on the palais. Ice was starting to form at the peaks of the arches. "What now?"

"Another thing." Jean's lips drew back from his teeth. "About Fornault."

Henri remained silent, crossing his arms.

"I am willing to let the past rest if you are," Jean said.

Henri considered, then said, "How is it that you were not defrocked?" Answer that, bastard!

Jean blinked at him again. "I went through the mortification. I did all my penances. And I was assigned to the Dominicans." He drew himself up, threw his shoulders back. "I helped to eradicate the Cathar heresy."

Henri shook his head. "Now that is strange. I did not see you at Montsegur."

Jean swallowed again. "Y-you were at Montsegur?"

"Under Hughes des Arcis."

Jean's tongue darted out, wet his lips. "If you served there you know how important this work is."

Henri again remained silent.

"So you will say nothing more about Fornault." Jean waited.

"Fornault?" Henri laughed, then shrugged and raised one brow. "What is there to say?" He turned and marched purposefully up the stairs. *If he lays a hand on me again I will kill him right now.*

Jean followed some distance behind.

Henri threw open the door. "Utarilla?" Jean climbed the last steps and barged past him, shouting, "I am the Inquisitor, the representative of His Holiness, the Pope." He approached the old woman huddled in the chair, holding his crucifix out toward her.

"Who are you?" Mother Utarilla whispered. Henri started. She would speak to Jean?

Jean put his hands together and scowled. "I am the Inquisitor, that is all you need to know, old woman."

She watched him as he looked around the entrance to the tower. "My men will be coming to take you to the dungeon tonight," he stated. "After I have questioned you."

Her lids lowered, eyes stared out through the slits. Jean had struck a pose, his chest puffed out and head raised, staring down his nose at her. Yet she spoke. The blasted woman spoke. She said, "What is it you want to know?"

Chapter 31

YSABEL SAT in the middle of her bed, rubbing her belly. She had come up to her room to take the mannikin out of her cabinet and burn it, but a terrible lethargy overcame her and she found herself collapsing on the mattress.

The mannikin crooned. Then her loins grew hot and she thought she saw Henri coming through her door, but her visitor had cold blue skin and looked exactly like Ibrahim.

"So handsome!" She sighed as she felt him run his hands over her body and rub her between the legs. "Ah, God! You are such a good lover! I am sorry I killed you." Her breath left her body in a long sigh again. "You should have loved me, not Louis-Philippe!" She opened her arms to him and felt his weight upon her as he entered her.

A knock sounded upon her door. Ibrahim disappeared. "No!" she cried. "Come back!"

She levered her body up off the bed and searched for him, pushing blankets aside, peering behind the tapestries. "Ibrahim!" she whispered. "Where did you go?" The knock came again and she went to answer the door.

Jean Becier stood there. Henri was behind him. But why... the mannikin! She cringed, coughed to disguise the spasm in her throat. "What is it you want?" Her voice sounded weak. Good. No man would trouble a sick woman. A woman who was with child. She thrust out her belly. "I was sleeping." And she was, or was she? Hadn't Ibrahim come to her? She jumped when the mannikin started a whining plea. Let me out. "Oh, shut up!"

"What?" Jean had moved into the room and was regarding her with those blinking eyes. She stepped back, but stopped when the back of her knees hit the bed. "Baroness de Reuilles?"

She forced her eyes to remain steady, to resist the pull from her cabinet. Henri was looking at her so intently. What was he trying to tell her? Had Utarilla told them anything? "Yes?" she asked, clasping her hands in front of her.

Jean bowed his head, then told her that the old woman had made accusations against someone she described as a "brown-haired woman in rich clothing who was with child." He spread his hands and shrugged. "We are here to dispel the notion that the woman she described is you."

Ysabel bent her head, covered her mouth with her hand. So Utarilla did not name her? Well, how could she? Ysabel had never given her name to the old woman. So she was safe. She raised her head. "Of course." But now Henri was shaking his head, pinning her with his razor stare. What was he trying to tell her?

Henri cleared his throat. "Jean," he said. "I believe we should have Baron de Reuilles here, yes?"

Jean frowned. "Why?"

Henri leaned back and studied his toes. "This could be rather... ah, delicate, don't you think? After all, she is Baroness de Reuilles. We must make sure proper procedures are followed."

Procedures? What did this mean? Ysabel gripped her hands together, kept her eyes on Henri, away from the cabinet, where the mannikin was chortling. Didn't they hear it?

Jean looked at her, his brow furrowed. "You are correct." The words came out slowly, with great reluctance. "Very well," Jean added, his voice sharp with irritation. "Send for him."

HENRI SPED down the corridor to Johanna's chamber, paused at the entry. Taking a deep breath, he knotted his hands into fists, then forced them to relax, to fall at his side. He must tread carefully now. This matter was slipping out of his control. When Utarilla had told Jean of the woman who had come to her asking for poison, Henri was puzzled. Why would Utarilla implicate herself? But when she refused to identify the woman, it became clear. Utarilla wanted to trade her own life for the life of another. She refused to give any further information until Jean assured her of her own safety.

Jean did that. He had promised Utarilla that she would be given only penances if she recanted. Utarilla had made him swear it in front of Henri and Jeanne. Then she had whispered of a brown-haired woman, dressed in rich clothing. A woman who had come to her twice. A woman who had asked for her help in destroying an enemy.

Was this why Maríana had fled? Did Ysabel plan to poison her?

No, that was absurd. But the situation was becoming dangerous. Jean believed in this nonsense, and if Ysabel had been foolish enough to dabble in potions, she was in grave trouble. Henri had heard of cases where the Dominicans had circumvented the Capitulum Episcopi of St. Boniface and Charlemagne, the doctrine that placed these matters in the jurisdiction of common law. If Jean could do this, everyone was in jeopardy.

So. For the sake of their childhood friendship, and for the child she carried that might be his, Henri would try to help Ysabel. Even though her actions had caused his Maríana to flee, she did not deserve the punishments Jean would devise. Henri rapped on Johanna's door and entered without waiting for her invitation.

"No time, dear aunt," Henri cut off her exclamation. "The Inquisitor Jean Becier is in Ysabel's room looking for evidence of witchcraft."

Her eyes narrowed, then her lips curved in a smile. "Her room."

What was this? She did not seem at all surprised.

"You must go and rouse the baron. I have requested that he be there for the search." Henri started from the room, but stopped to say over his shoulder, "Make sure that he is sober." Harsh words, yet there was no time for careful phrasing.

If Louis-Philippe showed up drunk, that would tell Jean he could do whatever he pleased, and what pleased Jean was inflicting pain. Henri did not want to see Ysabel's foot crushed in the iron boot. She was foolish, yes. Annoying, too. But no one deserved torture.

When he entered the room, Jean was already rummaging through a trunk filled with Ysabel's clothing, while she stood by, twisting her hands. Henri frowned, but Jean was not deterred. "We must start," he said. "De Reuilles can join us when he will."

Jean pulled boy's tunics and breeches out of the bottom of the chest and examined them, looking over at Ysabel.

"My brothers' clothing," she said and bit her lips.

Jean shrugged and threw them down. "Bauçais." His voice rasped. "Help me here, please."

Henri sighed and moved over to a cabinet by Ysabel's bed. When he touched it, a shiver started within his belly and spread outward to his arms and fingers. Curious. Rubbing his hands, he looked over at Ysabel and saw the color fade from her face. What could be in there? He started to draw back from the cabinet, but Jean was watching him now, so he opened it and stuck his hand among the gowns hanging on hooks along the back.

When he pulled out his hand, he held a bit of red silk, bundled into a packet and stitched in a circle. When he closed his hand around it, something hard and small rolled in his grasp. Puzzled, he picked at the thread and the whole thing fell open, revealing some dried rose petals that appeared to have been soaked in some kind of dark liquid. A ring fell out, wrapped in another piece of silk with more of the rust-colored liquid, and letters written across it. He was trying to read them when Ysabel spoke.

"My pomander!" Ysabel exclaimed, reaching for the bundle. "You have found my rose petal pomander!" He handed it to her. "Thank you!" She crushed it together and held it to her face.

Jean had leaped up when Henri pulled out the red silk package, but after seeing Ysabel with the rose petals, he waved his hand and went back to his own search. While Henri continued to rummage around in the cabinet, Louis-Philippe entered the room, nodding at Henri and bowing to Jean, who mumbled a cursory greeting. Henri uttered a prayer of thanks. He did not know how Johanna had rendered him sober — from the green undertone of the baron's face, he figured she must have taken drastic measures — but Louis-Philippe was awake and aware.

Henri had started to close the door when Jean said, "Wait a moment!" He strode to Henri, looked back at Ysabel, then bent his head, peering at the bottom of the cabinet.

Jean leaned down, drew out a cloth doll, the face no more than a blank piece of wool, the stomach sewn in a circle. He held it up and shook it. "What is this?" His eyes flared. "A mannikin?" With his bony fingers, he deftly removed the thread that closed the stomach, pulling out a thin woolen packet.

Ysabel sank onto the bed, fist crushed into her mouth.

Jean continued to suck breath through his teeth as he swiftly opened the packet, revealing a lock of long black hair that he held up in triumph. "The hair! Let us see if the nails are there." He placed the hair on the bed and retrieved a smaller packet from inside, shaking several white slivers out into his palm.

"The fingernails!" he crowed, then spread the wrapping out on the bed. "Bloodstains." He pointed to several blotches the color of dark rust. "And a name." He peered at the cloth, reading aloud, "I-B-R-A-H-I-M?"

He turned to Henri in puzzlement. "The man who was accused of sorcery?"

Ysabel had backed away from the contents of the doll, her face dead white. "What is that thing?" she asked angrily. "Who put that thing into my cabinet?"

Louis-Philippe had made a single utterance when Jean read the name. Not a shout, nor a sound of grief, but something in between, something that still shivered the air. Henri now watched the baron pick up the lock of hair and hold it to his nose, smelling it, his eyes tightly shut. Becier was staring at Ysabel and did not see de Reuilles fingering the hair.

"The gardener," Louis-Philippe said. "The man who was accused."

Jean now swung his head toward the Baron, but Louis-Philippe had already returned the lock of hair to the bed, his fingers caressing it a moment before he let it go.

Henri groaned inwardly. Even more intrigue. Just when he thought that he could keep this under control.

Jean Becier approached Ysabel, who now stood with her arms wrapped around her, her eyes blazing. "That is not mine!" she shouted. "Anyone could have put it there in my cabinet."

Jean studied the mannikin, his lower lip pulled between his teeth. "She is right," he said after a long pause. In the silence, Henri could feel his own heart beating in every part of his body — all the way to his fingertips. Whatever happened next would seal her fate. He was sure of this.

"Anyone with access to fine silk thread and..." Jean examined the material with blood on it. "This looks like it was torn off a gown. May I see the pomander you hold, Baroness?"

Ysabel started. "This? Why?"

"Just an idea." Jean was reaching for it. "Please indulge me," he said softly, his red lips curving in a seductive grimace.

Ysabel snatched it back. "Must I?" She narrowed her eyes.

Jean withdrew his hand. "No, you need not. There is another test we can perform to determine who made the mannikin." He grabbed the packet of nails and the lock of hair and stuffed them back into the doll along with the blood-stained cloth, pulling the threads to close it up again. Then he took the doll over to the blazing hearth and made a motion to throw it in.

"What are you doing?" Ysabel screamed, rushing over to him. "You cannot do that to my baby!" She tore the mannikin out of his hands and sank to the floor, cradling it in her arms and crooning. "No one will hurt you. You are safe now. Hush, hush."

Jean stood looking down at her, his face blank. Then as she crouched at his feet, busy with the mannikin, he plucked the rose-colored silk packet from out of her grasp and opened it up, reading the message written there. "A love charm," he said shortly, his eyes flickering briefly over to Henri. He stuffed it into a pouch on his belt. Stepping over Ysabel, he moved quietly to where Henri stood and whispered, "I am going down to get some of my men to take her to the dungeon. Please remain here and do not let her leave."

Henri collected himself. What the devil was going on here? "You need your men to help you take a pregnant woman to the dungeon?"

"Watch her!" Jean warned, his eyes flashing. "Watch carefully what happens when we return. You will learn something." He went out the door.

Henri turned back to Ysabel. She was sitting on the floor, cradling the mannikin in her arms. As he watched, she pulled the top of her gown apart and tried to give her nipple to the mannikin. He looked away, felt a flush start across his face. His eyes fell upon de Reuilles, who still stood by the bed. The Baron's face was motionless, but his hands were clutched into fists and his eyes flamed. "De Reuilles!" Henri cried out his warning as Louis-Philippe moved toward Ysabel.

The Baron stopped and turned to Henri. He must have read something in Henri's expression; he nodded and straightened his shoulders, then dropped to his knees beside Ysabel, touched one of her hands. "Ysabel," he said, "Ysabel, why?"

She looked at him blankly.

"Why would you do this?" He gestured at the mannikin. "Why would you want to kill Ibrahim?"

A sweet smile trembled upon her lips. "Shhh!" She looked down at the mannikin. "My baby is sleeping."

"Why, Ysabel?" Louis-Philippe repeated.

"Why?" Her face twisted. "He bent you, my beautiful husband. He took you from my bed." Tears started in her eyes. "But everything is well now." Her face cleared and her voice brightened. "He came to me, you know, Ibrahim did. And he is the best lover! Better than both of you!" Her eyes darted to Henri, then she nuzzled the mannikin and started hummed a lullaby.

Damn the woman! She must be mad. Henri saw a wave shudder through Louis-Philippe's body. De Reuilles slowly got to his feet, moving like an old man.

"Can this be true?" Louis-Philippe whispered. "Can she have killed my Ibrahim with this... thing?"

Jesu. What was he saying? No, this could not be, could it? Henri found himself moving away from Louis-Philippe, then stopped and focused upon Ysabel until he trusted that his eyes would not betray him. Was de Reuilles a sodomite? He was Maríana's father, this man.

Henri glanced up. De Reuilles awaited his answer. Henri shook his head. "I do not believe she killed him."

"You knew her before she came here. What could have led her to do this?" Louis-Philippe gestured toward the mannikin.

Had he ever really known Ysabel? "We were just children," he said. "She was fond of getting her way, but then most girls are, aren't they? I don't know why she would want to kill the gardener," he sighed. But she had just given them the reason. Hadn't de Reuilles heard? She had also spoken of her dalliance with Henri. Had he missed that, too? He watched as the Baron looked away from Ysabel, stared directly into Henri's eyes.

"She had reason to hate him." Louis-Philippe shivered, but his voice remained steady.

Amazing. De Reuilles? No, he could not mean this. Ibrahim was a trusted servant. Ysabel must have been jealous of the time they spent together, her husband and this gardener. Yet Henri could not stop his face from reflecting the distaste he felt broiling inside. All those boys Jean had hurt. And, after Fornault, well, any hint that a man was sexually interested in him drove him to his sword. He had killed three men in Toulouse who had made the mistake of caressing his loins while he was drunk. He was not even sure that their intentions had been sensual. Perhaps they had been seeking the gold in his belt. But this was Louis-Philippe, Maríana's father. He must have heard wrong. De Reuilles was watching him, his face still.

"Well, Bauçais," Louis-Philippe said. "What will you do now?"

Henri lowered his head. No one could possibly believe Ysabel. The woman was clearly mad. Whatever else he might be, Louis-Philippe was Maríana's father.

"Remember, baron." Henri spoke softly, watching Ysabel. "She has lost her wits and does not know what she is saying." He looked directly into Louis-Philippe's eyes. "Who is to say exactly why she hated Ibrahim?"

There. And if Louis-Philippe was... well, Henri did not want to know.

Louis-Philippe regarded Henri for a long moment, then asked, "Whose baby, do you think?"

Henri did not pretend to misunderstand. "I cannot say. We should know in a month or two." He backed away. "Do you wish to call me out?" If he had to fight, he would. But he did not want to fight this man.

"No, no." Louis-Philippe shook his head, drew in a deep breath. "I will not fight you." He stared at Ysabel. Grief and regret made twin dents at the sides of his mouth. "Will they allow her to live that long? To have her baby?"

Henri set his jaw. "Oh, they will." He watched Ysabel rock the doll. "They will." Ysabel would have her baby, but what happened after that, he could not say. He caught Louis-Philippe's gaze. "I am not your enemy." Nor his friend, either. Still, he respected this man. This surprised him. When Ysabel had made her outrageous statements, Louis-Philippe had not flinched.

Louis-Philippe nodded. "We will see what they will do." His eyes held a question. "But I do not think that Maríana should be found."

So. It was said. "I was going to take her away to Bauçais when I found her."

"Do you think that is wise?" Louis-Philippe nodded toward Ysabel. "I do not believe they will stop with Ysabel."

"Perhaps not." Henri drew in his breath. "Very well. We will stop looking for Maríana." Footsteps pounded down the corridor. "For now."

The door flew open.

Jean burst into the room flanked by four of his burly guards. "Hold her!" he ordered them. Two of them moved forward and grabbed Ysabel by the arms. The other two took hold of her legs.

"Is this necessary?" Henri demanded angrily, but subsided when Jean tore the mannikin from Ysabel's hands. Petite, delicate Ysabel flung one of the men into the wall and nearly upended the other in her frenzy to get the mannikin back. But the two holding her legs still had her in a firm grip and the first two returned to wrestle her into their grasp.

"What are you doing? Let me go!" she screamed, spitting and hissing at them. Then a foul stream of obscenities flowed out of her. The men seemed to know their job and ignored her, lifting her and carrying her bodily out of the room.

"Take her to the dungeon. Here, this way!" Jean ordered. He

walked on ahead of them holding the mannikin, leading them down the back stairs to the kitchen.

Henri followed close behind Jean. Louis-Philippe strode at Henri's side, his face stunned. Jean, Henri thought, must have expecting Ysabel's reaction. The corridors were empty — no servants, no squires or knights. Six more of Jean's men joined them outside, forming a barrier around Ysabel, shielding her from the curious and terrified eyes of the servants milling around the inner bailey. Jean marched ahead, his eyes moving from left to right, never still. Was he appraising the assets of the château? Well. The former Abbott of Fornault had finally found his calling.

Henri looked at the frightened servants and knights. Some were glancing away, some avidly watching, their mouths hanging open, others were fearfully making the sign of the cross. A shadow chilled his side. Louis-Philippe had come over and stood beside him.

Avarice, greed, pity, terror, grief, and curiosity spread out before him. The scent of blood was gripping the crowd, the promise of torture. It was exciting them.

Louis-Philippe looked into Henri's eyes. His own were haunted. "And now," he said, his voice heavy with sorrow, "it begins."

Chapter 32

RICHARD threw down his woolen gloves in disgust. The bright blue wool lay against blinding white snow. Perhaps there was some poetry, some song there, if only he could see it. But his soul was cold. He raised his face to the mountain that soared around the valley where the Jakintzas lived.

Where he lived, now. His new home.

He retrieved the gloves and pulled them on. Adelie had given him these gloves just last month. Or he guessed it was last month. They did not count time in this valley as they did elsewhere. Richard had tried to work it out, starting with the days in flight. He thought that it was now close to Christmas. But he might have lost a day when they were inside the mountain. When he had asked Iranzu what day it was on the calendar, the old man had raised his brow and asked why Richard wanted to know. Did he plan to return to his life outside this valley? At the time, Richard had backed away, said "No, of course not." But now he was not sure.

He studied the mountainside again. The snow was brittle. Richard did not know what this meant. They had snow in Brittany, yes, and Reuilles-le-château seemed to be buried in it all winter. Even so, he had not known there were different types of snow. But Marc had told him that this fragile snow threatened them. All of them.

A line of peaks enclosed the valley. A dense blanket of pines climbed nearly all the way up the sides of the mountain, but snow covered these pines, clung to branch and earth in a deadly shroud. When the air suddenly warmed, and then froze again, snow could shatter, sending boulders and snow fields down upon them. Marc and his brother Alain were up there now with the other men from the village, checking the areas where snow lay deepest. From time to time, Richard heard the roar of avalanche bellow out from somewhere up above. He always cringed, glancing around for a moving wall of white to descend upon him. But Marc had told him not to worry. They would set the snow moving in the areas where it was most fragile. They could control the flow, somehow, so that it did not rain down upon their houses.

All the young men were up there, even Alain, who was recently wed and had to tear himself away from his bride. Marc was there, and he was just a boy. They were all up there. Except Richard.

He remained below with the old men and the women and children. Oh, he knew his inexperience with snow made his presence dangerous. They did not want him to blunder into a pocket of shattered snow and start a slide. Still, to be left behind soured him. Iranzu had said they would teach him how to tell fragile snow from solid. Next year.

Richard looked across the fence. Iranzu was there, waiting. He had not missed Richard's tossing of the gloves, then.

"Are you coming?"

Richard vaulted over the fence, landing beside the old man. Guillaume had made the squires jump fences several times a day when Richard was training to be a knight. Agility and strength, these were important.

Iranzu sighed. "Such energy." He turned and moved farther into the pens.

Richard filled his lungs, drew in the foul odor that hung in the air around the pens until his nose was so full of the stench that he did not smell it anymore. Then he followed Iranzu. Richard de la Guerche, who had fought at the side of Burgundy and Angoulême. Richard de la Guerche, only son of Geoffroy de la Guerche of Brittany. Tending pigs!

Iranzu had stopped again, was watching him. "If you are to stay, you must find a place among us." This was not the first time he had said this.

"Do I have any choice?" Richard muttered bitterly.

HE HAD HARDLY seen Maríana since they arrived. Only at meals, and then only across the table. Well, there was much work to do. He was glad of that, even though this work kept him away from Maríana. He did not mind tending the sheep and cattle, bending his back in labor to shore up rotten wood in fences, repairing roofs. All of these things he had done on his fief in Brittany. But pigs?

Ah, well. He had chosen to follow Maríana to this place. He had thought she would know that the sun rose and the moon set upon her in his eyes. After all, he had given up everything to come here with her, hadn't he? But she had fallen back into her distant regard. Oh, her eyes upon him were warm, to be sure. But he wanted more. His fingers itched to take her by the arms and shake her, and, well, do other things, too. But she just sat at her place by the table, face lowered. She seldom looked up from her bowl.

Marc had noticed that Richard's eyes were always on Maríana. From the time he sat down at the table till the time the meal was over, Richard watched her face. Even Leila had noticed this. Maríana's sister never passed up an opportunity to tease him when Maríana barely looked his way. But did Maríana take notice of this teasing? No! Richard ground his teeth.

At least Marc cared. He often visited Richard in the stone hut he now called his home, brought him news of Maríana, brought him what news they had of the world outside. Richard watched as Iranzu singled out three sows from the herd standing within the pen. News — hah! No one knew for sure what was happening out there. Richard's slow grasp of the Basque language hindered any conversation with Marc.

Iranzu had told him that the pope's men had come to Reuilles-le-château, but had known nothing more than this. It was too dangerous for people from the valley to venture forth into the outside world with the Inquisition so near.

They had even been forced to seal the cave where all the bats dwelled. Somehow Iranzu had known that Baron de Reuilles' men were on the verge of discovering the cliff entrance to the caves. How the old man knew this, Richard had no idea. But if Maríana could do what she had done — made a light with her hands that called the winds, drawn a spiral in blood upon the snow that had made the earth shudder — what could Iranzu do? Richard had believed the old man.

Iranzu had ordered men from the village to pile boulders around the place where the ledge they had followed opened into the larger cave. Richard had gone with them, helped stack the stones to bar entry. After they had finished, it looked like God Himself assembled that pile of stones. Richard had felt hope then. He had even touched one of the stone men who lived in the walls of the tunnel on his way back, had whispered a greeting. After they came out at the place where the giant statues stood, Adelie had met them in the bell forest with jugs of ale and they all drank and danced while Richard played the air harp and Marc played the bells.

BUT THAT WAS last week. Now, here he stood, feet mired in swine offal.

"This one is not ready," Iranzu remarked, pushing down on the largest, who promptly wiggled her gigantic form out from underneath his hands. He chose another, pushing down firmly on her back. She stood still, only bowing her legs slightly under his weight. Iranzu's face split into a huge grin. "Now, this one, she is ready."

Ready for what?

Iranzu removed his hands and wiped them, gesturing for Richard to open the inner gate. "What's the matter with you?" Iranzu laughed. "Didn't you ever watch animals rutting when you were a boy? How else do you learn what life is all about?"

Richard felt his cheeks grow warm. He opened the small gate that led to a narrow pen. "Of course I watched the animals. Everyone did. But pigs? I never thought to look at them." And he did not want to now.

"Come, let us get her into the lover's pen," the old man said. Richard helped Iranzu herd the reluctant sow into the pen set apart from the others. Iranzu put his fingers to his lips when they closed the gate upon her. "Privacy," he said, his eyes twinkling. "That is how we always have little piglets running around in the spring." He nodded and winked.

"Privacy?" Had Richard missed something?

Iranzu nodded. "Some others, they allow the lover into the pen with all the sows to do what he will, but me? I make sure he has the chance to woo her a little." He shrugged. "That is how we have such good fortune with our sows. They all become pregnant, and the lover is not worn out chasing those who are not yet ready."

Well now, this made sense. And Iranzu did seem to have the most pigs. Perhaps this would work with sheep and cattle. Horses, too. How would they do this, though? They would need to build special pens for the sheep and cattle, perhaps another paddock for the horses. Richard chewed this thought as he helped Iranzu climb out of the larger pen onto the path that ran alongside it.

ALARM SHOT through Richard's body, stopped his breathing. Adelie stood just outside the fence watching them, her face still and grave. Had something happened to Maríana? Adelie seldom left the house and small field where she cultivated her vegetables and roots.

Adelie and Iranzu stared at each other in that ghostly Jakintza silence. Then she nodded. "Healed enough, anyway," she said.

What? Had he missed something? Again?

Adelie turned away, toward the main house. "Richard, you must come with us," she said over her shoulder.

What could be wrong? Who is 'healed enough'? Ah, they would not answer him anyway. They seldom answered any questions he asked. And when they did it was often with another question that just set his head spinning. Well, at least he would get to see Maríana before mealtime. That was something. He trotted after them.

Maríana looked up as they all trooped into the stone house, and smiled broadly at Richard. He felt absurdly giddy and stupid at the same time. Here he was, so worried about her. There she sat, her face glowing. Well, he would take advantage of the empty space beside her. He sat next to Maríana, ignored Adelie's frown. The little ones, Tomàs and Patxi, were outside playing in the snow in front of the house. He turned to Iranzu. "Where is Leila?"

"Leila is out by the ice pond," Iranzu said. "It would be too cruel to include her in this discussion."

Why? Richard started to speak, but Adelie was already talking.

"Maríana," she said, "Your grandfather and I need to talk with you about your preparation to serve as Lady of the Cave. We are going..." Adelie stopped in mid-sentence as Richard leaped to his feet and moved toward the door. "You are needed here, too. Please stay." He felt the weight of her eyes upon him as he returned to his seat.

Why did they want him? What was this Lady of the Cave? In Brittany, the rituals were women's concern. His mother told him of her journeys into the long barrows, but she had always chased him from the room whenever she spoke of the charms and spells she created.

Of course, all of these were in supplication to Saint Cecile or to the Magdalen. But they were spells nonetheless. The men had nothing to do with this. Especially his father. Richard looked down at his hands, let Adelie's words wash over him. He had participated in the circle fires of spring. Except for the priest and Baron de la Guerche, all the men in his fief did. He had even gone to the stones of Cairn'hac one year, where bonfires were lit and the young people leaped over the flames. He would never speak of what they did afterward. No one would. But children were always born nine moons later.

And now Adelie was describing a circle fire much like the ritual blaze at Cairn'hac. He felt his skin flush, turned his face away. So Maríana was to be initiated at the circle fire of late spring. Was this initiation the same as what they did at Cairn'hac? Well, that was three moons away. Time enough to win her heart. If he could. He stole a look at Maríana while she sat listening to Adelie and Iranzu, a faint line forming between her brows.

"But I do not feel anywhere near ready," she said after Iranzu fell silent. "Why are we in such a hurry?" She leaned forward. "And why can't Leila do this?"

Iranzu reached over and took her hands. "Leila does not have the ability to do this, even if I taught her. And she did not link with Ibrahim." He touched Maríana's lips, stopping the words that trembled there. "Ibrahim told me of your linking."

His eyes pleaded. "We have need of your skills, Maríana. It has been thirty years since my mother died. The boundary she wove to protect this place is growing thinner and thinner."

His face looked drawn and ashen. How old was this Iranzu? Richard could not remember his own grandparents. Yet Iranzu's mother had died thirty years ago, and he must have already been a man then. Baron de Reuilles had seen at least forty summers and Maríana had seen twenty, so Iranzu was, at the very least, sixty. Yet this old man had guided them up the cliff, through Canigou.

"People are still looking for you, and they may find one of our paths to the valley. I cannot weave the boundary — the stone will not accept me — but I can show you how," Iranzu continued.

"What about my mother? Didn't she ascend to the cave?" Maríana's eyes grew darker, deep forest green instead of emerald.

"It was my fault," Iranzu said, releasing her hands and rubbing the side of his neck. "I thought we had so much time, you see. I thought she would have your father help our people down below in the town and the area surrounding the château, that she had time to come back to our valley and ascend to the cave."

His eyes were haunted with grief. "But I was wrong. She came here only once, with Ibrahim. Then she returned to your father and stayed at the château with you, and, well, you know the rest." He looked down at the table.

Adelie took one of Iranzu's rough, grizzled hands in hers. "We cannot always see the purpose behind what happens, Father," she said, softly, then turned to Richard. "Soon it will be the hawthorn moon. I will work with Mariana on the rituals we perform at that time, but she will take part as a participant, not as the Lady." Her fingers kept stroking Iranzu's hand.

"This we will also do for the stirring-time when day and night are equally divided." The dark part of her hazel eyes suddenly grew large, nearly filling her eye sockets. What kind of creature was she? Cold fingers played along Richard's back.

"But, at the circle fire," Adelie continued, "Mariana must serve as the Lady and must ascend to the cave soon after that. Which means bringing the Lady through by coupling within the circle with the representative of the Lord."

Richard looked down again. His face alternately burned and froze. He focused upon Adelie's hands.

"After stirring-time we will start making the guardians for the circle fire," she said, her hands moving expertly over Iranzu's fingers now, soothing, kneading. "All the women in the village help in the making of the maiden, the mother and the grandmother." She blew softly on Iranzu's swollen knuckles. "Mariana will assist in the making of the maiden because she has not yet borne a living child."

Richard jumped, glanced at Mariana.

Adelie seemed to ignore the flash of anguish that came and went in Mariana's eyes. "The men will make the lord." She took Mariana's hands now. "Well, sister-daughter. Will you join us?"

"What does it mean," Richard blurted, placing his hands upon the table next to Adelie's fingers, "going to this cave, communing with this stone?" Adelie flashed her black-hazel eyes at him, but he continued. "What is the cost?" They wanted this too much. There must be something more to it that they were not saying.

Iranzu answered. "It is dangerous," he said. "If she is not well-prepared, she could be lost in the stone."

"And this means?" Richard's voice made a jarring echo in the room. Mariana touched his hand, but he would not be deterred. "What if she gets lost in this stone?"

"She will die," Iranzu said, "as my mother did when she last drew the barrier."

"Then Mariana will not do this..."

Mariana's fingers dug into Richard's hand.

"This is why you brought me here, isn't it?" Her voice was soft, but something hard and knowing sounded behind the words.

"No." Iranzu turned to Adelie, who was sputtering. "Hush." He added, "But, as the daughter of Thérèse, we hoped that you would want to do this." Regret rang from his voice.

Maríana bowed her head. How could she even think to consider this? Well, Richard would not lose her, not after he had gone through so much to save her. He was about to say this when she spoke.

"And if I do not?"

Iranzu drew back and his shoulders sagged. "Then may all the gods help us. The world would be at our doorstep if you do not succeed in doing this."

Richard could not contain the bitter laughter that rushed past his lips. "Whatever for?" he asked. "You have nothing that they would want, no gold, no silver, no jewels." He waved his hand. "I do not believe that they would come all this way for your pigs."

"It is the stone they want," Adelie said. "People have sought this stone for thousands of years. First the desert people, then the Romans, then the northern tribes." Her eyes bored into his. "We use the stone to draw the barrier."

She turned to Maríana. "But there are other uses for it."

"It is merely a legend out there now," Iranzu said. "Yet there are still those who seek it."

Thousands of years? What else could this stone do? But no, this was a ruse, all this gibberish about other people wanting the stone. He would not allow Maríana to do anything that was dangerous. "No," he began, but Maríana turned her green-fire stare upon him. He felt the pressure of her gaze, his tongue grew thick and heavy. Damn! She was stealing his voice.

"You will be prepared," Iranzu was saying. "We will do everything we can to make it safe for you."

"And if I do this thing," Maríana said, "the valley will truly be my home?" She drew in her breath. "I will have a place here?"

This was it, then. There had never been a place for Maríana anywhere. She wanted this desperately, to please them, to ensure her place here. Richard could see it shining from her eyes. Merde! He tried to tear his gaze from hers, but she held him fast.

Adelie and Iranzu were nodding as one. Maríana turned from Richard, released him. Her green eyes were luminous, but filled with something that looked like sorrow. "I will do this," she said.

Blast it! Richard stood, fists leaning on the table, staring in fury at Maríana. "Do not ever," he said, "use your sorcery on me again." He strode to the door and passed out into the fading day.

Chapter 33

THE WEATHER had plagued him all week. Henri leaned forward into the gale that whipped snow and hail into his eyes, that stung his forehead, that painted ice upon the scarf he had placed across his nose. It was fortunate that the distance between the palais and the tower was short. If it were even a cubit longer, he would have refused to make such a journey. As it was, the door to the tower was a monster. It took all of his weight to pull it open against the wind that battered him. But Johanna had made her request. And he would honor it.

One of Jean's men was on the other side of the door. He was the leader of the soldiers Jean had brought to Reuilles-le-château. What was the man's name? Was it Pierre? Henri could not remember, so he made a noncommittal grunt as he removed his mantle, and shook snow and ice from the wool.

"Has she regained her senses?" he asked. This was Johanna's greatest fear. If Ysabel recovered her wits, Jean would begin his interrogation. Every day, Henri came over to the tower and asked the same question. And hoped that Ysabel still wandered in the dark dream that had claimed her when the mannikin was snatched from her hands. Once the real questioning began, she would break, tell them anything to stop the pain. He was sure of this.

"Not that I can tell." The man's eyes drifted to the white cross covering Henri's chest.

Henri wore it all the time now. Then he could come and go as he pleased, while Louis-Philippe could not. Henri used this freedom to watch Jean's progress, his procedures. Jean had already made mistakes. Henri had used what he knew of the Inquisition's own methods in a letter to Durand, objecting to Jean's seizure of the tower and his near-imprisonment of the de Reuilles family.

Not that it did any good. Oh, Durand supported Henri's objections. But he would not chastise Jean. Henri straightened his belt, nodded to Jean's man and crossed the stone floor to the entrance of the dungeon.

Becier was in the great hall every morning with his pots of ink, his quills, his parchment. Henri had passed him when he left the palais to come over to the tower. For the past two weeks, Henri had watched Becier in the great hall, a line of people snaked across the floor to his seat upon Louis-Philippe's raised platform. Jean spoke with people between morning mass and the afternoon meal, noting their words in minuscule scribbling upon his parchment.

At least Jean's plodding observance of Inquisition procedure had allowed Henri time to advise Louis-Philippe. De Reuilles was carrying out all of his duties as Baron of Reuilles-le-château as if the Inquisition were not there. Louis-Philippe had even recalled Guillaume and his men from the slopes of Canigou. He did not want to leave a trail for Jean, a path that might lead to Maríana. Let Jean think that she could never be found.

Henri descended the steps to the guard's room. When he reached the bottom, he stopped in surprise. Three of Jean's soldiers sat around the long table. A feast was spread in front of them, jugs of wine, chunks of pork, slabs of beef, fine-meal bread. Well. He knew exactly how much Johanna sent over to feed the Pope's men. She was generous, but this went far beyond what she would send. Where had they gotten the rest?

There were the ribs of roasted lamb that Johanna had sent over for Ysabel. And that other basket had a familiar weave. Since Utarilla had been imprisoned, her grandson came each day with a basket of food for her. The soldier nearest Henri reached into the basket, pulled out a crisp meat tart and bit into it. Henri watched as garlic and beef dropped out of the tart, made wet tracks down the man's tunic. This was the grandson's basket, Henri was sure of it. If the soldiers were eating food sent over for the prisoners, what were they feeding Ysabel and Utarilla?

"Did Jean order this?" he asked. "Did he say you could take the food we provided for these women as well as the provisions we have given you?" He fingered his carving knife, traced the length of its handle.

"Well, we were feeding them." One of the men scratched his belly. "But they are witches, yes? Why should they be fed?" He continued slicing roast pork while his companions nodded and kept eating. "We are just going to burn them."

They were starving the women? Obscene! Ysabel had not even been questioned yet and Jean had promised to release Utarilla. If this was true, Jean was killing them both already, and killing the innocent babe within Ysabel's womb. Without thought, Henri drew his sword, swept it across the table, scattering bread, wine and meat into a jumble upon the floor.

The soldiers stared up at him, their mouths open in shock. The harsh rasping of their breath echoed off the walls; the remainder of the meat tart crumbled in the soldier's fingers. Henri stood with his sword held in battle stance and allowed his eyes to sear them. Blast the consequences. He would have this out, now.

"Well?" he barked out his challenge.

The soldiers exchanged glances and slid toward the edges of the chamber. A whispering scrape alerted Henri to the sword being drawn behind him and he whirled around.

"In the back?" he shouted, deftly evading the blade and slamming the flat of his own sword along the side of the man's head. He did not wait to see the man fall, but turned to face the other two soldiers, who rushed him with blades flashing in the air. He retreated, placed the wall at his back, met the blow one man aimed at his side. Pain traveled in a bright flare down the length of his left arm; blood flew against the wall as he swung his blade. The second man had moved in, bringing his sword around for another slice at Henri's arm.

Henri ignored the hot flow of blood coursing over his elbow, kicked out at the man who had injured him, caught the man's groin with his heel. The man fell, bellowing. Henri swept his sword in a crescent strike, sliced through the leather breeches of the other man, opening a wide gash in his leg.

His lips set in a cold line against the throbbing in his arm, Henri spun toward the man who had wounded him. Blood streamed out of his arm as he lifted his sword to strike.

The soldier had already staggered to his feet and met Henri's blade with his own. Henri parried the blows raining upon him, risking a quick glance at the others in the room. One still lay unconscious upon the floor. The other cried out in agony, hands clutching his leg. So far, no one else had come in to join the fight. His limbs were growing cold. He must end this soon.

The soldier he fought was skilled, but the man's blows followed a pattern. Two to the right, one left jab, then a sweep across the middle. When the man shifted his weight to make his left strike, Henri drew in his breath, brought his sword around in a fierce arc that caught the soldier's blade, ripped it out of his hands. As the sword clattered to the floor, Henri drove the man into the wall with his foot, pinning him there and placing the point of his sword against the man's throat. Henri lowered his head, close enough to feel the man's breath stop when he saw the heat of Henri's gaze. "Was this Jean's idea, starving the women?"

The door to the guard's room crashed open. The leader of Jean's men stood there, sword in hand, eyes hostile. His mouth tightened as he took in the scene before him, then his eyes lighted again upon the white cross on Henri's chest. Dismay cut a path across his features.

He snapped out an order to someone on the other side of the door and lowered his sword.

"Bauçais," the leader turned back to Henri. "What happened here?"

"Did you know your soldiers were confiscating food we sent over for the prisoners?"

Jean's man frowned, then looked from Henri to the rubble upon the floor. "No. I did not know."

This man had honest eyes; his gaze did not slide away. So. He was not Jean's lackey. Still, it would not be good to press him too far. An ally might be needed, later on.

Jean's man blanched when he saw the blood steadily coursing from Henri's arm. It had slowed, but continued to stain his tunic and shirt. "I will help you walk back to the palais."

"My thanks," Henri grabbed the cloth that still covered the table and cleaned blood off his sword, watching the one soldier bind the other's leg wound. It would be a while before that one would walk again. "But I do not need your assistance." Sheathing his blade, he strode out the door. Jean would not get away with this.

He did not notice the wind or hail, only his feet as he placed each upon the uneven stones that paved the bailey. Twenty steps to the palais. He tucked his left arm against his side. Ten steps. His gait faltered. He sucked in his breath, pulled open the door and entered the great hall. The edges of his vision were darkening. He must be swift. Shouldering aside the people in the line that led to the Inquisitor, he came to stand next to Jean, hugging his left arm close to his body.

"Still like little boys, Abbot?" he whispered in Jean's ear. The pulse surged in his arm and there was a roaring in his head, but he held his body erect, stared into Jean's face.

Jean's hand tightened on his quill until his knuckles were white. "What do you want, Bauçais?" he hissed between his teeth, then shivered when his eyes fell upon the blood covering Henri's tunic.

"The prisoners will get decent meals, no more confiscating food, and Jean..." Henri paused as Jean regarded him. Becier's face was still and pale. But there was an avid spark burning in his eyes; his tongue darted out and moistened his lips. Henri leaned in toward him. "Remember I was at Montsegur, and I am a soldier of the King. If you cross me again..." His right shoulder lifted.

The shrug cost him. Black spots floated in front of his eyes. Henri forced himself walk up the stairs, one by one. When he reached his bed in the knights' room, he collapsed, tugged weakly at his shirt. It was stiff with his blood. "Robert..." he whispered, then stopped in surprise at the pale anguish on his squire's face. "Get Johanna," were the last words he could mutter before the roaring tunnel that sought him tugged his eyelids down and he knew no more.

THE BARONESS de Reuilles was singing again, her voice pure and clear, the voice of a child. It was an abomination, that such a creature should have the angelic tones of a beardless boy. But women were the source of all evil. God had given this truth to him, hadn't He? Daughters of Eve... .

Jean cocked his head and listened. What language did she use? He could almost make out the tune. It was something from the south, Castile, maybe. There was a rhythm to it. But the words ran together in a liquid stream, glided past his ears, rang against the stone and iron that formed the cells of the dungeon. It was not Latin.

He clasped his hands and descended the steps, stopping in front of her cell. Whenever he tried to question her, Ysabel just stared at him. Or grunted and howled. It set his teeth grinding. When she was first taken to the dungeon, he had placed a hot iron against the tender skin on the inside of her elbow. She had screamed in fury. Then, she had laughed. When his men heard her unholy laugh, they had backed away. After that, they all refused to touch her.

His teeth slid back and forth, clicking and gnashing. He did not like waiting. But he must wait until his men would hold her or tie her down so he could use what he had at hand to wrest answers from her. He could not touch her, not with his hands. A shudder moved through his arms. He never touched women.

Ysabel had fallen silent, rocking back and forth on her heels. There were so many questions he wanted to ask, so many mysteries here. Why had she written to Durand? Ibrahim the Moor was dead. No one could wring the truth out of him. Maríana de Reuilles had disappeared. As for Louis-Philippe, well, Durand had ordered Jean to wait. He could not take the baron. Not yet.

But Jean had sent some of his own men out to retrace the steps of de Reuilles and Bauçais, up to that mountain where they had stopped. Canigou. Ghastly name. Their pitiful search was a ruse, he was sure. Well, perhaps Henri had tried to find her, this Maríana. But Louis-Philippe? Why would he bring his daughter back to face the Inquisition? De Reuilles probably helped her escape. Ah, this did not matter now. His men would find Maríana de Reuilles.

Jean moved toward Ysabel, stopping before his robe touched the rust-covered bars. What was that sound she was making now? Was she whispering? A constant hissing sibilance was flowing out of her. There did not seem to be words.

Did this creature really think that her accusations against the Moor and her stepdaughter would mislead Jean Becier? That it would blind him to her own vile sorcery? He pulled his lower lip between his teeth. Well, it may have. For a time. He had not suspected Ysabel. It was only the vigilance of Henri that had uncovered the heresy of the Baroness de Reuilles.

Utarilla lay huddled upon a moldy blanket in her cell. Stupid old woman. Every day she begged for a priest to hear her confession so that she could receive her penances and be set free. A laugh sputtered through his lips.

He must be careful. Henri had heard him promise to free Utarilla, once she had made confession and recanted. Jean could not torture her. Not yet.

Ysabel. This demented creature had even made a love charm, a spell to entangle Henri de Bauçais. Jean had read the name she had painted upon red silk. He knew of these things, had seen the workings of such sorcery. He would tell his Henri of this love charm. When the time was right, he would tell.

His Henri. A shiver started somewhere near Jean's navel and traveled lower. When Baron de Bauçais had first sent his middle son to Fornault Abbey, Jean demanded a portion of the income from his fief to pay for the boy's upkeep. Jean did not like taking the spoiled sons of minor barons into his abbey. More to his liking were orphans, sweet young boys who had no mother, no father. He took them in and made them his own. His family.

But when the young Henri arrived with his mother, Jean's heart had leaped into his throat. He had been blinded by the boy's splendor. Henri's own mother had approved the use of the belt to quell her son's evil desires, and Jean happily complied. He had tried to turn the young Henri from the wicked snares of the daughters of Eve, tried to bring Henri into the one, true fellowship of men. Jean had treasured every cry of pain, every whimper that found its way past the boy's glorious lips.

Henri the man was even more beautiful, glowing with a cold and merciless radiance. Henri de Bauçais, brilliant, shining angel of God. Henri the beloved.

Henri the betrayer.

Oh, he had long ago forgiven Henri for his betrayal. It could have happened at any time. Anyone could have discovered Jean's secret indulgence.

But it was Henri who had broken him. The temptation was too great. Henri's eyes had drawn him, the fierce glare, the quick shielding of pain. Such pain lay behind Henri's frosty stare. Jean could see this pain Henri tried so hard to hide. It had finally drawn him into Henri's bed, led him to break his first rule. Jean had never before approached any of the children of knights or barons who had come to Fornault Abbey. It was too dangerous. Yet he had approached Henri. He had grown careless. This would never happen again. No.

Ysabel's hair hung in clumps around her face. She smelled like the slops pit. Henri could not have bedded such a creature. Not his Henri. Even when Henri had staggered into the great hall, blood staining his shirt and pattering on the floor, the glory of his beauty dazzled and burned. Henri's dangerous eyes, his magnificent stance commanded, compelled. Henri could barely stand, yet he had marched over to where Jean sat, had delivered his message, jaw set against the pain of his wound, against death itself.

Jean's teeth ground again, sent splintered shocks into his skull. Durand had censured him, had ordered him, Jean Becier, to feed these wicked creatures. Yet Jean did not blame Henri. No, it was not Henri's fault. Jean's own soldiers had caused this with their flagrant display of the food he had allowed them to confiscate. They should have hidden the food and shown respect to Henri. They should not have fought him.

It had been two weeks since Henri was wounded. Bauçais had not come down into the great hall since that time. The old hag Johanna said Henri had not yet recovered from his wound. Jean grasped the cold metal of the cross that rested next to his heart. He missed seeing Henri's face. But God was merciful. Bauçais would heal.

He caught a glint from under the mat of hair that surrounded Ysabel's face. She was staring at him, now. Would she speak? He leaned closer. Her lips parted.

"Bismillahi'r-Rahmani'r-Rahim." Her voice was quiet, with barely enough breath to move a feather.

Air puffed out between his lips. Gibberish again. More nonsense. Well, perhaps tomorrow. Jean turned and climbed up out of the dungeon.

HENRI STOOD before Johanna, scanning the document she had just given him. "You are only showing this to me now?" He impaled her with his stare. She returned it in full measure.

"I had to be sure where your sympathies lay," she said. "After you fought Becier's soldiers to ensure adequate food for the prisoners," her face softened, "I felt that we may trust you."

"Indeed." Three weeks had passed since he fought with Jean's soldiers. He traced the raw scar that ran the length of his arm. Johanna had given him wine and yarrow to build up his strength and to promote healing. Still, it had been an entire week before he could stand. Now he could walk, but it would be a while before he could fight again.

He looked at the parchment in his hands. It was a document des Arcis had sent Ysabel. As he read through it, a cold lump settled in his belly. This was not the method used in these cases. Charges of sorcery were referred to the local priest first, then to the seigneur. They always restricted their inquiries to the names that were given. Other names might arise during questioning, but not before. The names of Ibrahim and Mariana had come from Ysabel, he knew this now. But Louis-Philippe?

"Could Ysabel have sent them Louis-Philippe's name?"

Johanna silently handed him another page of parchment. It was Ysabel's letter to Durand. "How did you get this?" It must have cost a fortune. Durand guarded his correspondence closely.

She did not answer. He returned to Ysabel's letter and skimmed the contents. Mariana's name. Ibrahim, too. No other. He lifted the message from des Arcis, held it beside Ysabel's letter.

No, this was not the method used in cases of sorcery. But it was familiar. It was the procedure Henri had used when he first came to des

Arcis.

It was the way they found Cathars.

Three names-he remembered this. They liked to start with three names. And they always went after the rest of the family. Des Arcis liked to proclaim that heresy infected the entire family.   The   real   reason they questioned whole families was to use each family member as a lever, to branch out from those who were first named, to capture as many as they could. By pursuing family members from the beginning, they were often able to obtain the names of other heretics outside the family. A man may resist the questioning himself, but if you took his mother, his wife or child? He would break sooner.

Henri stared at Johanna. "We are all of us in danger," he said.

A knock sounded upon the door, three soft raps. Johanna took the documents from Henri's hands, tucked them underneath her and said, "Enter."

One of Jean's men sidled into the room, hands twisting the fine red silk tunic he wore. "M-My lord, lady, the midwife has disappeared."

Johanna frowned. "So?" She leaned back. "Is the baby coming, then?"

"Can't tell." The man was a wreck. Henri knew that this one had recently been given guard duty in the dungeon. Robert had told him that no one lasted long there anymore, even though the tenants of the dungeon were still only Utarilla and Ysabel. "She screams all the time now, but today her screams are more drawn out and more like an animal," the man whispered the last part.

"Have you looked elsewhere for a midwife?" Henri stared at the man. Sweat was pouring down this one's face.

"I went to the town," the man said, then swallowed. "No one would speak to me."

"And this surprised you?" Henri's eyes traveled over the pope's livery hanging from the man's body.

"What?"

He was oblivious, this man. Henri turned to Johanna. "Aunt," he said. "I will go over to the tower and see what I can do."

Johanna's eyes were hooded, but Henri detected a gleam as they darted from the man to him. "Ysabel is not due until the end of March."

Henri placed his hand upon the hilt of his sword. He was too weak to wield it, but Jean's men would not know this. "Who can say? Babes come early sometimes. I will see Ysabel and go over to Reuilles-la-ville for a midwife myself, if she needs one."

LIGHT FROM a single torch threw its glow across the floor between the cells. A wailing howl shivered along the walls, drove into his head, reached his teeth. Henri fought the urge to cover his ears, to step back.

No wonder Jean rotated the soldiers here. How did the old woman bear it? Ysabel and Utarilla had been kept together in the dungeon for over a month. He turned to the soldier.

"When were the cells last cleaned?" The stench of unwashed bodies and human waste reached him, along with the rasping grunts issuing from Ysabel's cell.

"We tried yesterday." Hands shaking, the man poked his key at the lock.

Johanna had insisted that the cells be scrubbed. Utarilla's cell was clean, that much Henri could see from the feeble glow of the torch. But no matter how much soap and water were applied to the walls and floors, the place still smelled of old blood. He suspected that no one would go near Ysabel's cell to clean it, just as no one would go close enough to gag her. Ah, well. He could not blame them. It was better for the de Reuilles family if the pope's men were afraid of her.

Utarilla huddled in her cell. Henri knew Becier had so far refused her requests for a priest to hear her confession, so she could recant and receive penance. It was an old trick. Jean must hope for more names.

Henri took the cell key from the man's trembling hands. Ysabel's howls were growing deeper. "How long has she been like this?" He unlocked the door and pushed it open, dropping to his knees next to where Ysabel crouched.

"For the past week. When she is not sleeping, she screams and wails." The man's voice came from behind him. Jean's brave soldier had retreated to the stairs. Henri leaned toward Ysabel. Matted hair hung around her crimson face. She did not seem to know he was there, yet her screams now dropped into a gurgling pant.

"Babe is almost here." A gruff voice floated out from the other cell. "Best get the midwife now."

"No one will come." Jean's man was at the top step now, his hands reaching for the door.

"Thought so." Utarilla nodded, then struggled to rise. "Very well. You must do as I say then, and we will bring the babe in."

Henri's stomach contracted. "What?" Had he heard right? "I will go over to Reuilles-la-ville."

Her eyes glinted at him. "No time." She leveled a fierce glare at Jean's man. "Go to the palais," she told him. "Find Jeanne and send her here." The man stared at Ysabel, then lumbered back up the stairs and out the door.

Henri stepped out of Ysabel's cell and unlocked Utarilla's door. "Well?"

She raised her arms. "Bring me to her."

He took her feather-light angular body in his arms, placed her directly opposite Ysabel. The old woman lifted Ysabel's skirt all the way up. "Too late for Jeanne," she murmured. "See?" Her gnarled finger pointed. "Babe's head is already there."

Henri forced his eyes to follow the old woman's finger, saw a dark lump emerge from between Ysabel's legs, then recede as Ysabel drew in another long breath. "Shouldn't we lay her down?"

"It is good that she squats. Have you a knife?"

He pulled out his carving knife. The familiar blade had a black sheen in the torch light.

Utarilla nodded. "Take it over to the torch and run it through the fire three times." Her hands traveled over Ysabel's belly, pushed at the laboring woman's legs.

"Why?" He stared at the knife. Anything to avoid the sight of the dark mass protruding from between Ysabel's legs.

Utarilla looked up at him, her eyes were crinkling with something that looked like amusement. "The Lady Thérèse taught me this." She waved at his knife. "We need to cut the cord when the babe comes out. Running your knife through the flames kills any evil that may be on the blade." When he stood glancing from his knife to the torch, she raised her voice. "Just do it, man." Amusement still curled around her words. "It will not harm your knife and it may be safer for her." She turned back to Ysabel, who was now straining. "Hurry."

Henri plunged his knife into the torch flames three times, placed it blade up in his belt and returned to Utarilla, who gestured for him to take her place in front of Ysabel. "When the shoulders come out, you must grab the baby and pull." She crawled over to the side.

"Why?" He focused on the top of Ysabel's head. Her hair seemed to quiver. Lice. "You have brought babes in before." He looked at the old woman. "I have not."

"I am too weak to do this, so you must pull." Ysabel was panting in heavy grunts. "Not hard, mind you, but steady." Utarilla's eyes glinted at him again. "Like pulling a sword out of a body."

"What!"

But Ysabel rocked back on her bottom, drew her thighs up. Even he could see the pale bump of a tiny shoulder squeeze out of her, the fragile curve of a tender ear. He hesitated, hand wavering between Ysabel's legs, then he reached for the little body and tugged. Now a rubbery arm came free; the warm and slippery body squirmed. Ysabel's head lolled back, then bent forward, chin pressing into her neck. Her face grew red, then purple as she strained. Henri still held the wiggling arm, one hand supported the damp head. He looked up to see a wave start at the top of Ysabel's belly and travel down to her navel. At the same time, the baby shot out toward him. He barely stopped it from hitting the floor.

Silence pressed in. Ysabel had either fainted or had fallen asleep; she lay flat on her back now. The birth cord was a pale snake from her to the baby Henri held in his arms. "A boy child." Utarilla's voice had grown hoarse. "Give him to me." She reached out.

He found himself reluctant to release the boy. The baby was not crying, just making mewling grunts. The boy's eyes opened, looked straight into Henri's. Deep blue, solemn eyes. A tiny hand took hold of his left thumb, gripped it hard. He wondered what his own child would be. When was Maríana due? He thought it was April or May. The baby he held shifted in his hands, the face crumpled. Still, he did not want to let the boy out of his grasp.

He looked down at Ysabel where she lay on the dirt of her cell. It hurt, having a baby. He knew this, yet he had not thought of the pain Maríana would suffer. Sometimes, women died giving birth. He pulled the baby in against his chest and the crumpling face relaxed. Louis-Philippe had told him he thought that wherever Maríana had gone, she was well. But how could her father know this? How could anyone know? Henri tried not to think about her. Even thinking of Maríana would fill his senses, dull his judgment. He could not let this happen, not now. The boy had latched on to his tunic, was grunting and seeking its silken fabric with his mouth.

"Give him to me," Utarilla said. "I will not harm him, and you must sever the cord." Her voice cut across his musing. He pulled the baby boy away from his tunic, offered him to Utarilla. It was odd. His hands felt so cold and empty now.

"First tear some of your shirt to tie off the cord." Utarilla was staring at the baby, then her eyes lifted to him, searched his face. What was she seeing? "Well," she said. "He looks like you."

Did he? "All babes look alike to me." Perhaps the boy was his, perhaps not. He could not claim him, could he? De Reuilles must raise him. He ripped the bottom of his shirt, sawing a narrow strip, then tied the pulsing cord.

Utarilla leaned forward. Her eyes traveled from the baby to Henri's face, lingered on his forehead, his nose. "I have helped many babes into the world. They are all different." She ran gentle fingers over the baby's jaw, along his brow. "See, his chin and the set of his eyes are like your face."

"Where do I cut?" He held his knife ready. The edge flashed as he turned it. Maríana would have his baby. When all this was over, he would find her, find the baby, take them both far away.

Utarilla settled back. "Very well, then." She turned to Ysabel, where another wave pulsed through the sleeping woman's belly. But this time a gray and red lump squeezed out, plopped on the floor. Ysabel did not even move. "You may cut here." Utarilla pointed with her gnarled finger. His knife slit through the cord easily. She looked up at Henri. "So this is the Baroness de Reuilles."

"Indeed." There did not seem to be much blood, and the baby was whole. "Are you a healing woman?" He had never asked her. But she seemed to know what she was doing.

She let out her breath in a long sigh. "Once I was." Her arms made a gentle rocking motion; the baby's eyes closed. "I hope she does not come to her senses," she continued. Ysabel was stirring. Her hands twitched and her head moved from side to side.

"Why?"

"Think I am stupid?" She shook her head when he bristled. Her finger stroked the baby's cheek.

He reached out, grazed the top of the baby's head. A curious pride and bleak resentment warred in his heart. The boy would never know him. He drew his hand back, stepped away, looked down at Ysabel. "Why did she go mad?"

"The mannikin," she breathed. "Some of her went into its making."

"Nonsense."

Utarilla's eyes glinted up at him. "Think so?"

But Ysabel was lifting her head, struggling to rise. He went over to her, pulled her up to where she could sit. Her eyes were unfocused brown smudges in her dirty face. Then they sharpened, darted to the bars of the cell, rested upon Utarilla. Shock and puzzlement swept across her face. She looked up at Henri.

"Henri?" Her hands raised to touch him, then stopped. She frowned at the filth encrusted on her palms. "What?" Now she looked around her again. "What am I doing here?"

Chapter 34

RICHARD climbed the slope from the river, his arms filled with his
share of the wool, bound and wrapped in leafy ferns. He had washed
away the smell of sheep in the river with the other shearers. His skin
tingled from the sand and leaves he used to scrub his arms and legs. It
was nearly May, trees were in full leaf, the sun bore down on him. He
had even taken off his shirt. His body ached and his muscles screamed
with fatigue. Yet he was glad. He would be able to sleep tonight. That
was very good.

He did not sleep well, here in Canigou. It was not because of the air,
air that at first had numbed his fingers and parched the back of his throat,
air that now pressed fragrant kisses against his face. The silence that
blanketed the mountain every night did not trouble him. No, none of
these things tore him from his sleep. He stopped and shifted his burden,
peered up ahead to where his one-room stone hut waited.

Marc had moved into Richard's hut. Oh, Marc had given Richard a
story of how he had fought with his mother and she had chased him from
the house, but that was not true. Adelie had ordered her son to stay with
Richard. They were worried about him, about his inability to sleep. Many
nights, when Richard's eyes blinked open, the first thing he saw was
Marc's lanky form sprawled across the bed in the corner of the hut. Not
that Marc awakened him. Richard dropped the fern-bound wool on his
doorstep and pushed the door open. It was dreams that wrested Richard
from his sleep. Dreams of Maríana. Again!

He had banished her from his dreams, so many years ago. Then he
had thrown away the bloodstone and invited her back, only to find that
the banishment was complete. She had not returned. At first, Adelie had
tried giving him plants that would make him sleep- valerian and
manzanilla, vervain and violets. In desperation, he took her sleeping
draught, drank it every night for the first month he spent in this valley.
But the plants erased his dreams and he treasured these dreams, even
when they hurled him into wakefulness.

Marc seemed to know this. Every time Richard awakened, writhing
from dreams of his beloved, Marc would also awake.

"What is it?" Marc would always say.

"Go back to sleep," Richard would always say.

Then Richard would take the flute he had carved from a bough of
the ash tree, throw his mantle across his shoulders and climb the path all
the way to the bell forest. Beneath the trees, amidst the chime of the

bells, the drone of the air harp, he would raise his flute and play the anguish that lived inside him. The flute had a fine resonance; his breath shaped sounds that lived, rich and ripe tones that lingered in the air. Slowly, the melody would allay the aching in his heart, easing his torment and enabling him to return to his hut and sleep the short while until sunrise.

For the past several nights, even his music had failed to give him solace. It was not Maríana's distance that troubled him. It was her presence.

She had appeared on his doorstep all last month. At first, she had questions; how could she divert water from the stream to feed Adelie's garden, how high should she make her fence to keep rabbits from eating her patch of thyme? Then she had brought gifts, a platter filled with fresh bread and potent new cheese from Adelie's goats, an armful of fragrant rushes for his floor. She had mended his boots, had brought him parchment so he could write down the words to the songs that were always dancing in his head.

He liked her near him, liked smelling the green earth tang of rosemary, sweet violets and lavender on her hands, seeing the tiny dimple appear at the corner of her mouth, the way her hair escaped whatever bonds she had placed on it to form floating spirals around her face. But this made his senses reel, and each time he tried to touch her, she slipped away. He did not know what he should do. It was easier when he watched her from afar.

Well, at least the hut was empty now. No Marc to jabber at him in Basque, no Maríana to make his loins ache. He placed the wool under his bed. Some of it he would give to Leila. She had promised to make a gown for Maríana if he supplied the wool. Maríana stubbornly clung to the old woolen robe she had taken from that chest in the tower. It hung in a shapeless bulge from her slender frame, and it was heavy. He lay down, stretched his legs, put his arms up, hands under his head.

He was tired of seeing Maríana swelter in that old robe. This gift was more for him than it was for her, although she probably would not see that. Well, if she would not take a gift from him, perhaps she would accept one from Leila. His jaw stretched in a yawn. Just as he closed his eyes, footsteps pattered up the path, pounded through the open door and into the hut. He opened one eye.

"The women are washing their clothing again." Marc stood hovering over him.

"So?" They went through this every day. Marc thought it was his duty to find a woman for him. Richard had tried to tell the young man that there was only one woman he wanted, but Marc would not listen. Now that spring had come, women seemed to be everywhere.

Last week, Richard had given in and gone down with Marc to the stream where women gathered to wash their gowns, their children's clothes, their husbands' or brothers' shirts and breeches. A ring of trees surrounded the shallow pool the stream formed before flowing out again to meet the river. Several young women from the village were there, barefoot in their chemises and underskirts, laughing and joking as they dunked their gowns into the water and stamped them clean. It was unseemly, seeing so many women practically unclothed. But when Richard had glanced aside, he had seen a line of young men and boys standing just beyond the boundary of the trees. They were all watching the women cavort in the pool. He had shaken his head and walked away, leaving Marc there.

"Maríana is with them this time."

"What?" Richard swung his legs over the side of the bed, hunted for the shoes he had kicked off. "How long ago did they go down there?" Maríana could not know that the men watched the women washing their gowns. He must go to her, see that no one accosted her.

"They are there now." Marc turned and walked out the door. He must have misunderstood Richard's question. This often happened. Neither French nor the langue d'oc was spoken here. Adelie could manage the langue d'oc, and Iranzu and Leila were fluent in both, but everyone else spoke Basque. And this, Richard still had not mastered. He did not believe he ever would.

Marc loped ahead down the path that led to the pool. Richard lengthened his stride, then halted when he looked down and saw his bare chest. "I forgot my shirt," he said, and turned to go back to the hut.

"You will not need it." Marc tugged on Richard's wrist.

Richard shrugged. The day was warm, after all.

He could hear them before he reached the ring of trees, the lilting voices, the music of women's laughter. The young men and boys had already formed a clump just behind the trees. When Richard and Marc arrived, a few glanced over at him, nodding their recognition. Several of his sheep-shearing companions grinned at him. Richard nodded back and then looked at the women in the pool. Maríana was there.

She leaned down, her hands in the water, wearing the nightgown she had torn off after she had lost her baby. The fall of yellowed silk clung to her form. Leila must have repaired it.

"He no longer troubles her." Marc's gaze slid over to him, then returned to the women.

"Who?" Richard must ask Iranzu for help. He could not master the inflections of this language. Marc often made statements that did not make any sense, yet Richard knew he was a sturdy, sober lad. It must be his own hearing or understanding that was at fault.

"The other one."

Richard waited for more, but Marc was silent. Should he ask Marc what he meant? Richard did this at least twenty times a day. It was fortunate Marc was patient.

The splashing grew louder, chattering voices turned to squeals. Leila had grabbed the sleeve of Mariana's woolen robe and was trying to wrest it from her. Good! Rip it to shreds. The old wool flopped and stretched. Several of the women looked over to where the men stood. The men froze, glanced at each other and their faces split into grins. Then a warbling cry started in the group of men. Its answer sounded from the women. Marc seized his arm.

"We are chasing today." With that, he was off, plunging through the trees and into the pool. All the men were.

Richard darted after them, headed for Mariana. He could not be sure that Marc had said "chasing" which was surely a harmless child's game. His grasp of Basque was so pitiful that Marc could have said "raping" and it would have sounded the same. This looked serious. The women were scattering, leaving their laundry on the banks. Whether their screams were prompted by delight or terror, he could not say. Canigou was a strange place.

Three men surrounded Mariana. She held up her hands to ward them off. They stopped an arm's length away, yet still circled around her.

Richard splashed across the pool. He would take the largest one first. His hands balled into fists; he flexed his arms. Mariana straightened, stared directly at him. The men stopped their circling. One looked at Richard, then nodded to the other two, and all three lumbered away, crossing the pool to the other side.

"What was that about?" It was good to speak the langue d'oc, to see Mariana without that dreadful wool robe. But Mariana did not answer. Her lips parted in a dazzling smile. Then she dashed into the trees, into the thickest part of the forest.

Damn! Richard lunged after her. Iranzu had told him there were wolves in this forest. What did she think she was doing? Three steps into the woods, the boughs of black pine swallowed the sun. He squinted into the green-black gloom. A flash of yellowed silk beckoned. He hurried after it, and the glimmer of nightgown and ivory skin vanished. Chasing, eh? Well, he would show her chasing. He looked down and threw his eyes out of focus. His mother had taught him this. When his eyes were not so busy seeing, he could catch more with his sight. Mariana's tracks appeared, bright glowing spots along the carpet of pine needles. He sped after her.

There she was, ducking around the massive trunk of a pine, darting ahead toward tall fine-leafed ferns. These ferns made a dense thicket. If she reached them, he would lose her. He leaped forward, reaching for her arm. She stumbled and fell, pulled him down with her onto the yielding floor of the forest.

The fall knocked the wind out of him. He lay with Maríana cradled in his arms, his legs tangled with hers, fighting for air. Lost in his battle to fill his lungs, he did not notice Maríana's hand until it settled firmly in the middle of his chest. He quivered, but could do nothing but wheeze. Then he felt her match his breath, quick, shallow pants in time with his attempts to bring air into his squeezed lungs. Slowly, her breaths lengthened and deepened, and his followed, until the roaring in his ears subsided. Until he could look into her face.

She was watching him with those green-fire eyes. When he met her gaze, she lifted her hand from where it had rested on his chest. His skin there prickled. "I did not use sorcery on you just now," she said, her voice constrained, defensive. "It was a trick to calm children. Ibrahim taught me this."

"Very well." He drew in a deep breath, released it. "Thank you." He did not want to move, but his left arm was wedged underneath her and starting to go numb. He could see the glimmer of her skin through the thin silk of her gown. The heat of his body rose. Everywhere they touched sent tremors all the way through him. If he did not move away now... .

"Are you cold?" She moved as if to touch his face, then stopped.

"No." He moved away and sat up. The steady thump of wet wool striking stone had started again. He rose to his feet, pushed ferns aside, reached his hand toward her. "It sounds like the women have returned to the pool. I will walk you back." This would give him time to cool his ardor.

For a moment, she did not move. Then in one fluid motion, she stood in front of him. He felt her regard delve into him, touch something that he did not even know was there, something that emerged in throbbing waves. His heart thudded, his whole body yearned. This was more than wanting, more than lust. He hurt. Even his fingertips carried the aching pulse. He reached for her shoulders.

"Richard." Her voice caught. "I cannot." She stepped back, eyes beset with remorse. "Adelie told me for the circle fire..."

He drew his hands from her grasp and turned away. The circle fire. Of course. She must be untouched the entire month before the circle fire. It was tomorrow, wasn't it? He waited for the bitter anger to fade. Yet it did not lessen his wanting, this anger. He had avoided the circle of wicker giants that stood in the field below Iranzu's stone house. Marc had asked for his help in making the lord, their Juanandim, but Richard had refused. He wanted no part of this ritual that would take Maríana even farther away from him. Just the thought of her in another man's arms drove him mad. It did not matter that what she would do in the circle was in service of the ritual. He drew in a deep, shuddering breath. Well, she had not asked him to be her consort, had she? He was not from

Canigou. His hands flexed. There, he could move them, unhook the fists he had made.

When he trusted his voice again, he said, "We must return, then." He extended his hand behind him without looking at her, felt the pressure of her fingers on his palm. Then he stepped out of the nest of ferns, pulling her with him, and marched off in the direction of the pool.

THE HEARTH fire painted golden patterns across her skin. Maríana stood quietly while Adelie braided the last of the vines into her gown.

Adelie stepped back, appraising the living fabric that hung from Maríana's neck to her toes. It was entirely made of newly sprouted vines with leaves and blossoms interlaced through the strands of ivy, of climbing bean and bindweed.

"Was there any more news about my father?" For the past two months stories from the outside had come to Canigou. One man who had kin in Reuilles-la-ville had risked the journey there, but Maríana could scarcely credit the tale he brought back. How could the Inquisitor have imprisoned Ysabel? It was Ysabel who had brought the Inquisition to Reuilles-le-château. No, she could not believe this. Yet every time she thought about it, she could not stop her lips from curving into a smile.

"Your father remains free." Adelie's voice was neutral, but her eyes were cold. She did not like Louis-Philippe, even though Maríana knew her aunt had never met him. "The two women are in the dungeon."

"Still?" But they had been taken before Christmas.

Adelie nodded, then grasped a trailing leaf and tugged it free. "The pope's men are waiting for someone to arrive," she said, "someone important."

"Who?"

Adelie shrugged. "Bauçais is there." She tilted her head. "He is with the church, yes? Perhaps he sent for someone."

Maríana had banished Henri from her heart, from her dreams. But the image of him standing in Ysabel's embrace still had the power to wound. She waited until the sting of memory washed through her and faded.

That life was gone. She would not see her father again, nor Johanna, nor Geneviéve. And Ibrahim... Maríana blinked her eyes, used her palms to wipe away the tiny droplets that coated her lashes. Once she had never cried, now she feared she would never stop. She made a half-turn, watched the leaves ripple around her as her tears dried. "I still do not know how I am to choose."

Adelie lifted her head. "Choose?"

Maríana stepped away from the hearth. She had nothing at all on underneath the leaf and vine gown. But the night was warm. Sweat was starting to bead between her lip and her nose. "Choose the one who will initiate me."

Adelie approached her, hands filled with a net covered with glittering shards of crystal. "I thought you had already chosen." She unbound Maríana's hair so it fell in undulating waves to her waist, then placed the crystal-encrusted net on top of her head, deftly fastening it to her hair.

"But you forbade me to tell him." Light flashed when she moved. The net framed her face, clear stones captured and threw the glow from the hearth across the walls. "You said I couldn't even touch him." Her last words died when she remembered yesterday, Richard's legs jammed against hers, the warm radiance from his bare skin as they lay there.

"You did not obey me, did you?"

Blast! Adelie always seemed to know everything she did.

"But don't worry," Adelie continued. "The call has gone out." She twitched a piece of the net so it hung in a straight line. "He will know."

How could he know? The last month had been pure torment. She had finally released all the anguish, the pain of her loss, of Henri's betrayal. Finally she could breathe, she could laugh, she could feel. And Richard was there.

He was there every morning next to Marc, eating the bread and cheese that was their morning meal, there every evening. Whenever she raised her head, Richard was there-his thoughtful, brown eyes, his stalwart and brave spirit that had thrown off all past bonds to bring her to safety.

She could not seem to find the courage to speak to him. She did not want to see him draw away when she spoke of her love, hear him try to shield her hurt with words of friendship. So she remained silent, stole glances at him when she thought he did not see, found reasons to walk by wherever he labored.

Then, one day she and Leila had been out in the field across the river gathering rushes. "Maríana," Leila had said, "You are an idiot." Her eyes had drifted from Maríana to where Richard worked, driving a post into the ground. Every thump of his mallet had sent a shivering wave through Maríana. "If you do not go to him soon," Leila had caught her Maríana's and leaned forward. "I will."

Maríana tried to shrug, but her body betrayed her, responded to Leila's challenge with a burst of wild longing. It was all she could do to bind her rushes, walk on wobbling legs back to the house. That afternoon, she had told Adelie she would ask for Richard's help with the fence she wanted to build around her patch of thyme. Adelie had nodded, then said, "Remember that you can touch no man until after the circle fire." Well, she had not. But to see the amber glow in his eyes as he spoke to her, to catch a glimpse of his fleeting grin when she made a jest-these were as important to her as air itself. It hurt to be so close to him, yet never touch him. Damn Adelie!

Now, Maríana looked up, saw her aunt watching her. No, she could not deny her aunt, her grandfather what they asked of her. They were family.

She had maintained her distance from Richard. Though her body clamored for his touch, she stayed just out of reach. Until yesterday.

Richard had been angry. He had walked her back to the pool, then left her there, stalking away, his back rigid. She had not seen him since.

So how could he know? Maríana turned away from her aunt. Light from the crystal shards danced across the table. "Maríana," Adelie started to speak, but a low thunder rumbled outside the house, shook the walls, sounded again in a broken beat.

"There were no clouds today." Maríana moved to the door. The night sky stretched above her, fine and clear; stars made a flashing arc. Yet the thunder continued, closer now.

The space just outside the house was filled with people, motionless, silent, their heads covered with the faces of animals. Now gray deer and owl, red fox and horse came forward, lifted her into the air. Behind them, three more held a drum taller than a man. Each had a mallet he played across the surface of the skin stretched over a large wooden frame, sending the beat of a colossal heart into the air.

Maríana twisted her head, scanned the crowd for a silky fall of raven hair. Would Richard be wearing a mask? But the people were carrying her now, all of them moving as one down the path that led to the circle of wicker giants. Adelie was just ahead, singing, her voice tugging them forward, the drum beat throbbing behind. The people surrounding Maríana joined her aunt's song. There were no words, just voices spiraling into the sky.

The four who held Maríana brought her forward to where Adelie stood at the edge of the circle and set her down. Her aunt backed away from them, into the center. The four guardians loomed around Maríana, each the height of three men, the width of five. Their arms and legs threw sharp-edged shadows across Adelie. Maríana did not like these giants made of sapling bough and vine, not even in daylight. There was something in the hollow eyes that made her jaw tighten, something observant that sat in judgment. She had helped make them, yet, in the moonlight they were alive. The bonfire in the center crackled, sent flickering radiance across the faces of the maiden and the mother, the grandmother and the lord. She was sure the one nearest her moved.

Adelie grasped her hand, pulled her forward toward the fire. Maríana trod upon layers of moss and rushes, brought into the circle just that morning. Behind her, the masked villagers crowded into the circle.

Adelie dropped Maríana's hand and went around the bonfire to stand on the opposite side. Now words emerged from the voices around her. "Juanandi," they breathed, "go underground." All of them were within the circle. "Wind-Hunter, go underground." Louder, now. They were moving in a coil, surrounding her.

Maríana stood five paces from the fire. She must leap over it, had prepared for this. But the flames were so high and her legs felt weak.

Eyes within the masks that swirled by her glittered. "Bring the Lady back to us." Their feet stirred the rushes and moss. Pollen and dust filtered into the air. She lifted her hands toward the flames, drew back when the fire kissed her fingertips. Her legs shook again. She locked her knees to still the quiver.

No choice. But there was a trick to this. Her gown of living greenery was moist with dew. Her feet were swift. Adelie had made her jump, again and again, over six women, all on top of one another. Much higher than the flames that licked up into the air in front of her.

Maríana dropped to the ground, balanced on her toes, then sprang forward, sent her body over the belly of the fire, felt its blast singe her bare feet. But she landed next to Adelie as she had been taught, knees slightly bent. She did not even stumble. Her knees straightened. She turned and extended her arms.

A roar now burst from the crowd, a cry that repeated their plea to the Wind-Hunter. Maríana stood, arms still raised, as the villagers whirled around her. She started when the first hands grabbed her sleeves, then closed her eyes and remained still while hands tore at her gown, shredded it, ripped it from her body until all that remained was the net handing in a straight line from her head. She had been prepared for this, too.

"You can open your eyes now." It was Leila's voice.

Maríana lowered her arms, squinted at the form in front of her. It was the red fox, but her half-sister's eyes glinted out at her. The bonfire was dying, only embers remained. The wicker giants encircled her.

"I am to tell you to create the sacred space." Leila was moving toward the edge of the circle.

"But how can he get through the barrier if I draw the circle?" Maríana looked at the wicker giants. No one else was there. The sound of the drum could be heard in the distance, fading toward the river. "Where is he?"

"Open the Door," Leila said, "and wait." She slipped out between the maiden and the mother.

RICHARD kept hitting the wrong notes. He plucked the harp strings, seeking the melody he had chased all day. A breeze curled around his arms and shivered the bells. He had been in the bell forest since sunrise. Now the black arc of night, full moon riding the heavens, made a canopy for his despair.

His music had never abandoned him before, but now he could not give voice to this melody that had been tormenting him, pleading with him, begging him to send it into the air. He dropped his hands from the air harp, lifted his flute. The song rang pure and clear in his mind, yet neither his fingers nor his breath could bring it to life. He could not even hum it.

At least the drums were silent now. Circle fire drums. The rise of cliff where the Guardian and the Beacon stood made a rippling curtain at the base of the sky. He could almost make out the features of the Guardian in the pool of cold light that poured from the moon.

At first, he thought he would join them, the circle dancers. He had his mask of wolf snout and gray fur. He had even started out of the bell forest when the deep pulsing cry of drumbeat sent its call. But, at the edge of the grove, his elbow had struck a trio of brass bells, bringing an angry pealing clamor that halted him. He could go no farther. That was when the shouting echoed along the mountainside. They were calling Juanandi.

He ran his fingers over the polished wood of his flute. In Brittany, they called to the Lord of the Forest to coax the Goddess from Her rest, to rise and claim Her portion of the year. He supposed this Juanandi was the same.

It was quiet now. The breeze touched his brow. He lifted his flute and breathed the first notes of the melody that haunted him. Still wrong. The moon had shifted now. His fingers were bleached in its light, bleached the color of bone. Perhaps he should return to Brittany and take his chances with the Inquisition. If even his music deserted him, what did he have left?

Maríana. She was down there, waiting for her consort. He ground his teeth. Maybe her consort was already there. Some man from the village, probably. Well, he would not go anywhere near that circle, would not risk seeing Maríana with some other man. A sharp twinge in his middle finger made his hand jerk. He held it before his eyes. Just a splinter.

He had nearly bitten the splinter out of his finger when the song spread everywhere in a liquid surge, circled his arms, faded to a whisper. The bells answered it; the wind harp moaned. Richard dropped his hand, retrieved his flute from the ground. He sent a few notes into the night, a question, then stopped and let his ears search for the answer. Only silence at first, then the wild and terrible entreaty, the yearning plea sounded again, farther away now.

It was the melody he had sought all day. There, just beyond the boundary of the bell forest. He moved toward it, held his flute to his lips. Notes flowed out. Three, no, four beckoned in a rising sigh, then seven fell and spread, till the last was no more than a deep rumble. The melody teased him, pleaded for more, dissolved into the distance. It was moving farther away. Richard stood at the edge of the bell forest. The full moon lay its silver fingers across pine bough and path. He could even see the far off glimmer of river flow. The song drifted toward him again, summoned, demanded his presence. His feet started moving. He would follow.

SHE WAS shivering. The bonfire was ashes, the guardians her jailers. Maríana stood at the center of the circle, in the same place she had stood after she drew the barrier, the sacred curtain. Its translucent swirls flowed just beyond the border of the wicker giants.

No one had come. She hugged her herself and shivered again. It was almost dawn and no one had come. The guardians seemed to lean toward her, hollow eyes shimmering in gleeful accusation. She had failed. Now there would be no one to go to the stone, to draw the barrier that would protect her mother's valley.

Would that be so bad? The thought startled her. She glanced up at the guardians, then straightened her back, glared at them. Iranzu had said this stone could send out a fatal radiance, a powerful, blighted wave that melted flesh and muscle. Surely, then, it could protect itself. She raised her chin. The people of this valley would just have to learn to be like everyone else in this world. What made them so special, that they could hide away here, deny the world outside their gifts, their healing? A rustling slither crept by her and she jumped. But the guardians looked farther away. Had they really drawn back?

No. Something was out there, poised at the edge of the boundary she had drawn. She widened her eyes, but could not capture its form. Bundles of flashing lights swirled in sparkling patterns. When she half-closed her eyes, she could see arms within the blinking lights, then legs. Tall. A man?

He seemed to be waiting for something, passing a long tube from hand to hand. Then he lifted it to his mouth. Four notes sent the promise of spring toward her. Just four notes, yet the hushed glow of a lover's voice, the whispered pledge of a lifetime reached out, engulfed her. The gleaming curtain of the Door parted.

Richard came toward her, flute still to his lips. His song took her breath. Moonlight crept around the limbs of the wicker giants, sought the rich black of his hair, kissed the bones of his cheeks. Then he stood in front of her, flute lowered, dark eyes grieving. "Is it over?" he said. "Is he gone?"

"What?" She could not seem to think. Her heart was making too much noise. Her limbs were melting in a golden fire. "Who?"

"What happened to your clothes?" A tiny muscle near his mouth jumped. "Where is your... consort?"

"He is standing in front of me." She grasped his fingers. "Here is his hand."

His mouth dropped open, eyes widened. "But, but, but..." He could not seem to form any words, stared down at his hand, at her hand holding his.

She could not stop the laughter that spilled out into the space between them. At first, he backed away. Then amber lights flared in his eyes, pure astonishment and simple joy moved across his face, and his own laughter rang out. The flute hit the ground.

Later, she could not remember when they stopped laughing, when the net dropped from her hair, when he caught her mouth with his. He was gentle, searching, but she pulled him into a fierce embrace and he followed, making shuttered moans that seemed to die in his chest as he caught his breath, only to start again when she moved beneath him, opened and drove him inside. Then a cry of shock and dismay tore from his throat, the pulse and spreading warmth filled her. She ran her hands across his back and smiled up at the guardians. It was done, and done well. She had not failed.

Richard raised up on his arms and tumbled off to the side, covering his face with his hands. "Maríana, I'm sorry! Forgive me, please!"

What was he mumbling? "Sorry?"

He took his hands away from his face. "I have wanted you for so long." His eyes were fixed on the sky. "I simply had no control. No control at all."

She smiled, reached out and traced the corner of his mouth with her finger. How long had she wanted to do that? "You did exactly what you were supposed to do. You were there. Weren't you listening when Iranzu and Adelie explained it to me?"

His amazement warred with delight, the amber in his eyes deepened.

"You really don't have any idea of what I am talking about, do you?" she asked.

"No."

The guardians were leaning toward them. She could barely see the stars through their wicker faces.

Richard lay on his back, muttering again. It sounded like "Bauçais was a dolt." But she could not be sure because his hand had captured her elbow and his fingers gently traced a line along the inside of her arm, a line that sent a flow of rich shudders that traveled to her toes.

"We're not through here yet, you know." He had rolled toward her. When had that happened? She could do nothing, see nothing with his hand roaming up her shoulder, lingering across her neck, teasing her ear.

"Through?" His lips replaced his hand, warm breath and moist kisses all along her chest, moving downward. No, his hand was still there, but it had moved to the other side, was making a path from her chin to her... .

"Look around us, the guardians are still waiting." He waved at the wicker and vine creatures, making a latticed shelter above her.

"What?" How could she think when his tongue now made lazy circles around her left breast, while his fingers teased the other into a singing peak?

"The Goddess wants to awaken and she has not been pleased enough to rise up from her slumber yet." He had raised his head and was gazing at her, amused, smug.

"Do not stop."

Again she felt his breath, tiny explosions against her skin as his lips moved down across her belly, felt his fingers still playing across her breasts. Was he laughing?

She did not care. A line of liquid fire erupted everywhere he touched, traveled to its center between her legs. But he moved to her feet now, his mouth progressing from her toes, to her ankles, calves, the inside of her thighs.

"No, no." She tried to pull him into her, to soothe the fluid ache he had called with his hands, his mouth.

"No?" His voice had deepened, was just a dark rumble. Yet amusement still quivered there. "I am not," lips moving upward, breath puffing against her skin, "through," warm tongue circling her navel, "here," and God!, he captured her swollen nipples again, "yet." He was finally above her. Each word brought a shivering answer from her core. His breath labored, lines of strain marked his face.

Her turn. She gripped him with her legs, drove him into her yet again. And after one exclamation, one ragged inhalation, he followed.

She could not seem to stop saying his name, but how could she say anything? Her breath, it kept eluding her. She could not fill her lungs. Yet there is was again, Richard. She thought he said her name also, but she was not sure. He was crying out something at the edge of pain.

Then they were still, unmoving. A last shudder caught her, spun out from her center in a fire-web. She burst in two; his cry and hers rent the night, twined in an echo that moved farther and farther into the depths of the earth.

He rolled to the side again. This time he took her with him and they lay pressed together. She looked up into his face. "I had no idea," she said, tracing the silver scar at the side of his mouth, the corners of his tilted eyes. "No idea at all."

Now a smile claimed his whole face. "Juanandi's gone underground," he said. "Goddess time is here."

Chapter 35

SHE WAS hungry. Ysabel leaned against the iron bars of her cell, felt their chill through the fabric of her gown. Surely it must be time to eat again, though they only came twice a day with food. How long had she been waiting? Without the sun to guide her, she never knew the hour. She placed her hand against the empty rumble in her belly. The skin puckered and fell in a loose fold to her women's cleft. No baby in there, not now. She had not seen her baby since that terrible day when she had awakened to find herself in this foul cellar, awakened to see Henri's pale face regarding her with horror. To see her baby cradled in that old woman's arms.

She looked across the dirt and straw-covered floor to the other cell where the bundle of bones and rags that was Utarilla lay unmoving. At least the old woman slept now. When Utarilla was awake, Ysabel had no peace. No peace at all.

Ysabel lifted her right hand, stared at the splinted fingers. They did not hurt so much now. She pressed her lips together. After she had awakened and seen Henri and Utarilla, their wide eyes staring at her, the creature Jean Becier had come into her cell. At first, she was confused. The last thing she remembered was laying down on the bed in her chamber. But her belly had flattened. And she was filthy.

The creature had marched right up to her, ordered two of his minions to grab her arms. She had straightened her back. How dare he? "I am the Baroness de Reuilles," she said in the tone Johanna always used. "Unhand me!"

It had almost worked. The pope's men fell back; even the creature paused. But a cold and hungry light had shone in the creature's eyes. The men reached out again, held her fast.

Such stupid questions they had asked her! Always it was something about two peasants from Reuilles-la-ville, some Antoine and Pierre. As if she would even speak to anyone from Reuilles-la-ville. She had sealed her lips and glared at them. But the first time they asked about these two men, the air trembled. She had looked over to see the blood fade from Henri's face.

And then, that creature, he made Henri leave! Henri had objected, but the baby was crying, long hungry wails that readied her breasts for feeding, brought milk spurting, staining the front of her gown. Henri had left with her baby, no, their baby cradled in his arms.

So she was left alone. Alone with the creature and his men.

Now Ysabel tried to move her smallest finger and stopped when it reached the limit of the splint Henri had placed upon it. She had refused to speak. Until she knew more, until her memory returned, she would say nothing. She was not stupid. They would take any words she uttered and twist them anyway. She had seen this happen in Gréves. A peasant, a frail slip of a girl, had answered questions. And had ended up on a pyre.

So Ysabel said nothing. The questions grew louder and larger. A vile spark flared in the creature's eyes. He was glad she would not answer; she was sure of this.

They broke her smallest finger first. She had wanted to scream but something crawled into her mouth, something that tasted of rose petals and honey. Tears had streamed down her cheeks when her finger snapped, but the sweetness in her mouth surprised her. She had kept her silence.

Henri came into the cell just as they broke her other finger. She could not suppress a whimper. This break filled her whole hand with fire, a fire that traveled to her elbow. Even the flow of honey and rose petals that filled her mouth and coated her throat, could not stop her tortured lament. Rose petals. How did rose petals get into her mouth? But she could not dwell on this. Henri had waved a parchment in front of the creature's face.

At first, the creature had turned on Henri, bared his teeth. That was when Ysabel noticed the hands. During the questioning, the creature's hands were clasped, like any priest. But when the Pope's men broke her fingers, one of the creature's hands moved to his groin, grasped and kneaded it. She was sure of this. When the creature turned to Henri, his hand was still there. Moving.

She shuddered. If it were not for the message on the parchment, they would have broken all of her fingers. The creature had taken the parchment, his eyes slid and darted across the page. Then he signaled his men to release her.

Ysabel had collapsed, cradled her hand in her lap. But even the agonizing fire that burned all the way up her arm could not stop her from leaning forward to catch the creature's words.

"Very well, Bauçais," he had breathed, his face nearly touching Henri's chin. "We will wait." He made a sharp motion and the two men who had come in with him filed out. "For now." The last was delivered in a low, menacing whisper.

Henri had splinted her broken fingers. She had tried to talk to him, but he would not answer. He had wrapped a dressing around her hand, then left the dungeon.

Soon after, Henri had sent Jeanne in with her baby. He was big, this boy. His eyes were blue, like his father's. She had taken off his swaddling, counted his fingers and toes. When he kept grunting and rooting, she had placed him at her breast where he latched on and gulped the flood of milk that leaked from her. He had barely started on her other breast when Jeanne came in and took him away.

They had not brought him back since then.

Now the door to the dungeon opened, bringing sweet air from the room above. Could it be spring already? She heard Henri's voice, there was no mistaking that guarded murmur. Yet the person on the stairs was not Henri. He was dressed in a splendid tunic, the white cross on a red background, a tunic of the pope's men. It was silk, though, as were his breeches; the movement and sheen of the cloth told her it was very fine silk. His hair was gray, but there were few lines on his face. He held a clove-studded orange to his long nose.

"Des Arcis." Henri spoke the name as he descended the stairs behind the man. "The women have been here since December." Her back stiffened. So this was Hughes des Arcis. The creature's superior.

"These are the two?" Hughes asked, his eyes moving from Ysabel's cell to where Utarilla slept.

Henri stood beside him. "Yes. The old woman is from the village and the other is Baroness Ysabel."

Hughes made a clucking sound. "Bad business, this," he murmured. "A few peasants, perhaps; but a baroness?" He shook his head. "This is not good after what has happened throughout Provence. What could Jean be thinking of?"

Henri favored Hughes with his withering stare, then replied, "Indeed. But it seems that she confessed to killing the gardener, although she denies this now."

She could not stop the yelp that jumped past her lips. Her two broken fingers throbbed. She had clutched the bars too tightly.

"Jean told me that." Hughes was looking at her.

Henri cleared his throat. "However..." Now Henri glanced her way. She looked away, then up at Hughes. Henri's eyes upon her hurt. There was no longer any fire in his gaze when he looked at her.

"Go on." Hughes turned away, held the orange to his nose again.

"I questioned the man who had led her to the belargusia, the belladoña."

Her breath caught and then spun into a swirling void. She had given Ibrahim a drink, hadn't she?

"And?" Hughes' voice floated toward her.

"He led me to the same plants." Henri again. "I will take you to them."

Footsteps on the stairs, then silence.

YSABEL shifted on the rickety stool, lifted her face to the soft fall of sunshine. She had almost forgotten its touch upon her skin. A sea of white crosses surrounded the long table in front of her. The creature's men were all there. Hughes was seated in a throne chair at the head of the table. The donjon loomed behind him. They had put Utarilla beside her. Henri paced around the periphery, whittling a small block of wood. The creature stood off to the side, hands clasped tightly in pious supplication, but his face was shiny with sweat.

Louis-Philippe and Johanna de Reuilles sat upon fine chairs to the left of the table. The old woman Utarilla kept staring at Louis-Philippe. Chuckling, she leaned close and whispered, "I would do anything to keep that one in my bed, too." Ysabel tried to catch Louis-Philippe's attention, but all he did was stare at Henri. When had the hair around his temples turned white?

She lowered her head. He had refused to come to see her in the dungeon. Well, she had killed his precious Ibrahim and now that might mean her own death. Or perhaps not. She looked at Henri, his hands making the black knife fly over the block of wood he carved. What image was he making? She pulled against the ropes that held her to her chair. No matter. Henri had told her that this would be a trial of sorts. Hughes des Arcis would be the judge. Henri had said that the man was fair... .

Hughes hit the table with a wooden mallet. "We are gathered here to examine a case of witchcraft." He raised his hands to still the murmur that rippled through the crowd. "You must remember that we are acting under the common law of St. Boniface and Charlemagne."

He unrolled a scroll and read: "St. Boniface has decreed that to believe in witches, or to hunt or to burn them, is unworthy of Christians." He met the eyes of every man at the table. "Until His Holiness decides otherwise, the only role for the Inquisition in these matters is to determine if actual harm has been done as a result of sorcery or witchcraft. If this is so, then the witches can be punished according to common law. As for heresy, we must give them to chance to recant. If they do not, then they will burn."

He gestured to the creature. "You may present the evidence."

The creature stood, made a tent with his hands. "I was sent here by His Holiness to look into some accusations of sorcery." He paused and stared at Ysabel, but fell back when she widened her eyes and glared at him. "These accusations were against a man named Ibrahim Al'Khaldun." The name rolled smoothly off his tongue. Well, of course. She had given them this name, hadn't she? "These accusations were made by this woman." He pointed a tapered finger at Ysabel.

The creature put his hands together again and paced. "My lords. Can you imagine my surprise when I arrived and found that not only was this man Ibrahim going under the false name of Jacques, but he was dead! Murdered. No one knew for certain how he was murdered, although the Baron of Bauçais," here he waved a negligent hand toward Henri, "suspected poison." He leaned his hands on the table and peered into the faces of the men gathered there. "But I have discovered how this man was murdered."

Now the creature stood and pulled out her cloth doll, untied the threads that closed the abdomen, saying, "This was found in the cabinet in the baroness's chamber." She leaned forward. The mannikin was silent. Sweat coated her brow. What would happen if it spoke? The creature handed the mannikin to Hughes, who examined it closely. "See the hair and the fingernails. With these the witch aims to hurt, or even to kill her victim."

Hughes fingered the lock of hair. "Or his victim," he said.

"What?" The creature seemed flustered. His tongue darted out to wet his lips and his eyelids fluttered over shiny hazel eyes.

Hughes looked up, then waved his hand. "Not important. Please continue."

"The other witch, Utarilla, admitted to instructing the baroness in the making of a dreadful poison." The creature paced around the table, coming to rest behind Utarilla. He pressed his hand on her shoulder. "Tell them what you told me."

Ysabel looked around the table. Some of the men were clearly bored, while others watched intently. The silence lengthened. The creature leaned harder on the old woman's shoulder.

"I don't remember," Utarilla finally said.

The creature thrust a document under the old woman's nose. Ysabel leaned forward. It looked like a confession. "Is this your mark?"

Utarilla glanced at it. "I suppose so," she muttered.

It was a description of the making of yellow water. The creature read it, every blasted word. Disgust and a terrible, avid curiosity shivered the air around Ysabel. The men closest to her drew back. When the creature read "You must dig up a child's corpse," the inhalation all around her split her ears.

When the creature finished reading, he placed the document in Hughes' hands and sat in a chair placed at the side of the table. At first, his face was impassive, but a muscle next to his left eye twitched, and his full red lips curved.

Ysabel heard a murmur at her side. "Looks like it be the stake for us, girl," Utarilla sighed. Ysabel looked into the faces of the men around the table. Maybe.

But now Henri stood and placed a goblet upon the table. What was this? Ysabel leaned as far as she could. The ropes holding her would not let her see more than a graceful curve of the silver cup.

"Potions!" Henri strode the length of the table, his ice and fire eyes catching the gaze of all the men who sat there. "Dolls! What are these?" His voice reached out, taunted. "Is there anyone here who has ever seen a man killed by a doll?" His shoulders lifted in an elegant shrug. "We have seen a blade strike down a man, yes. Axes and arrows, too." Now he leaned on the table. "But a doll?" His lip curled.

Bravo! Henri was always smart, always knew what to say. None of the men wanted to speak. They were all looking down at their hands. Henri had challenged their vanity. None could admit to the belief that a mere woman could injure him, Ysabel thought.

Henri looked from man to man. "As Hughes des Arcis has told you, what we have to determine is not that these women played such a foolish and unchristian game, even they do not deny that, but whether or not they were able to bring about harm as the result of their actions. The charge of heresy is the one that the bishop will decide upon." He appraised the men again, seemed satisfied by what he saw.

Hughes nodded. "Go on, Henri."

Henri lifted the goblet he had set upon the table. "I have prepared a draught of yellow water, using the same ingredients Ysabel used — with one exception — and the preparation of this draught was witnessed by Hughes des Arcis."

"No!" Ysabel strained at her ropes as an ugly muttering swept through the crowd. Some shouted, others were content to hiss. Henri stood in silence through it all, icy eyes assessing the crowd as the angry rumble dissipated. When all was still, he turned to Hughes. "My lord?"

Hughes leaned forward. "The Baron of Bauçais had the blessing of the church in this matter." He peered around at the men. "We used the bones of a cat in this draught, which Utarilla has said would be as effective."

Beside her, Utarilla was trying to make herself as small as possible, shrinking down into her chair. Henri approached her with the goblet. Holding it under her nose, he asked, "Is this yellow water?"

Utarilla shrank back even further. Henri did not look at Ysabel at all. Well, she had only made the wretched brew once. He could not possibly expect her to remember what it looked like.

Utarilla pulled against her ropes, but finally looked into the goblet, at the pale yellow scum on top, and nodded. "Yes, 'tis yellow water." She blinked as an angry murmur rippled through the village folk.

Now Henri's icy stare passed over Ysabel. She shivered. Where did he think to take this? She had indeed poisoned Ibrahim. He must know that. Did he want her to burn?

"And if I were to drink this I would die?" He held the cup toward Utarilla again. "Would I drop to the ground and die?"

"Yes." Utarilla held her head up, her corded neck straining. "Just a little bit would kill you, even if it were put in water or ale."

"What if I drink it as it is?" He held up the goblet and contemplated it in the morning light.

"You would die before your body hit the ground."

"Indeed!" Cup raised, Henri waited until all eyes were on him. Then he put the goblet to his lips and drained it to the bottom.

Every one of the men lifted up out of his seat. Some raised their arms to stop Henri, and a roaring groan could be heard from the throats of all in the bailey. Ysabel leaned forward. "No!" she screamed. He could not be doing this!

Henri placed the goblet down on the table and made a face, wiping his mouth. "Could use some honey." Then he spread his arms. "Well?" He walked around the table to Utarilla, arms still extended. "Shouldn't I be dead?"

Utarilla had drawn away from him, her wrinkled face contorted. "What have you done?" she whispered.

The creature jumped to his feet, shouted, "Trickery! You lie!"

Hughes turned slowly to his left side where the creature stood. The creature's whole body shook. His face twitched. "Sit down, Brother," Hughes said mildly.

The creature subsided after a long moment, but he was still shaking when he sat down.

"Made yourself an enemy there for sure, Bauçais," Utarilla whispered.

"Hush!" Ysabel said. She did not want to miss any of this.

Hughes nodded to Henri. "Continue."

Henri strode over to where Louis-Philippe and Johanna sat. A few servants stood in back of their chairs. He motioned to a slight young man with curling brown hair and a gentle face. Drat! It was the servant who had shown her to the poisonous plants. The man followed Henri to the table.

"This is Yves, second gardener of the château." Henri placed his hands upon the young man's shoulders. "It was he who showed the baroness to the belargusia used in the making of yellow water."

"I showed the baroness some plants when she asked me about belargusia," Yves stated. "But it was not belargusia I showed her."

Insolent pup! But if this was true, perhaps she did not kill Ibrahim. Ysabel lowered her head and listened.

The men around the table murmured to each other as Yves continued, "I showed her yellow gentian instead."

"Why is that?" Henri asked him, but his eyes were on Hughes.

Yves looked over at Ysabel. Blast the man. His eyes smoked with pity. "She seemed to be out of her head, Baron de Bauçais." He swung his eyes back to the men surrounding the table. "She had been acting very strangely for some time, so I thought it best to show her to something harmless, like gentian." Here he cleared his throat. "She did not seem to know the difference between rosemary and fennel, so I felt if I showed her the gentian she would be satisfied, and no harm would be done." He turned to Hughes. "Gentian is used in making a brew to reduce fever. It is quite harmless."

So. Her drink had not killed Ibrahim. Ysabel watched as the young man stepped down. Then what had killed the Moor?

The creature jumped to his feet as soon as Yves returned to his chair behind Louis-Philippe, and shouted, "He did not deny that they grow belladoña. Why do they grow such a plant in their gardens? Why grow such a poisonous plant at all?" He swung around to face Hughes. "You, of all people, know that the only healing approved by the church is prayer! Prayer and repentance! None of this makes any difference." He looked into the faces of the men surrounding the table. Spittle flew with his words. "If the mixture Ysabel gave Ibrahim was not real poison, then the mannikin killed him! They are both witches and they must burn!"

Hughes pounded the table with his mallet. The creature stood shivering as Hughes regarded him calmly. "Patience," Hughes breathed softly. "Patience." He stood up from his throne chair. "The church regards this matter as very serious, but we must proceed with proper procedure and caution."

The creature stepped back, face now composed as Hughes leaned forward and rested his fingertips on the table. "The women will be held in the dungeon while I consult with Bishop Durand."

Blast! The dungeon again.

"I will leave tomorrow to take this new evidence to him." Here Hughes's cold eyes fixed on the creature. "Until I return with his decision, no one will be burned." He made a gesture of dismissal.

Well. To the dungeon. But this was better. She had not really killed Ibrahim with her potion. Ysabel offered her arms to the men who came to take her back to the tower. A few penances, an act of contrition, and she would be free. She lifted her face and smiled.

JOHANNA'S chamber had the best light. Henri stood next to the broad window, looking out onto the inner bailey. Late afternoon sun warmed his face. "Can you stop this?"

Hughes des Arcis stood behind him, watching his squire stow his parchments in a black saddlebag. "I will do what I can," Hughes said. "But you must do something for me."

Henri waited, his eyes upon the older man.

"You must find Maríana de Reuilles."

That, he would not do. "We have been trying..."

Hughes held up his hand. "I know very well what you have and have not done." His lips drew together; the warmth in his face faded.

"Your men found a way up the mountain, but you stopped them from going further."

"It was impassable. There was a cavern that led nowhere." Henri's hand closed upon his carving knife. "They followed it several leagues into the mountain."

"Still, other ways could have been tried. I know of your relationship to the girl," Hughes said, watching Henri's face, "but Rome is convinced that she is the key to finding something, something of great value that came down from Montsegur last year."

"I could take up the search for Antoine and Pierre again..." An image leaped into his mind. The picture of Maríana, with Jean's hands upon her.

"It is too late now," Hughes said. "When you find the girl, bring her to me."

Henri tried to still the tremor that captured his hands. "To you?"

"I will not let anything happen to her. She is much too valuable."

"Will she be safe as the people of Montsegur were safe?" Henri shot at him. A mistake. But he could not stop it.

Hughes' mouth grew pinched at the corners. "Be careful, Henri. This is a dangerous game you play. Be sure you know which side you are favoring."

Henri remained standing, hand clutching the carving knife. "What came down the mountain that night?" And why was he not told what it was?

"Something of great value," Hughes said. "Something that will help us to regain the faith and devotion many have lost in the war against the Cathars." He moved to the door where his squire awaited him, then turned and smiled at Henri. "I will not tell you what we think it is. You must work this out for yourself."

JEAN PACED the dungeon's guard room, his back hunched, his arms hugging his middle. He had his men going over the donjon stone by stone now, searching for the torture chamber. "I will find a way," he muttered. "The burning will go forward." The old hag Johanna had told him Reuilles-le-château did not have a torture chamber. But he had seen the swift hooding of her eyes when he asked her. He would find it.

"Brother Becier."

Jean turned toward the guard. It was the same man Henri had wounded. His leg was slowly healing but he was useless for most tasks. When he had finally been able to walk, Jean assigned him to the guard room of the dungeon.

"These men are back from the mountain." The guard limped aside to allow three soldiers to enter.

"Well? What did you find?" Jean snarled. He had his men going over the entire mountain, cubit by cubit. They had combed the slopes for months now, but there was no sign of Maríana de Reuilles.

"We thought we should bring this back to you right away." One of the men stepped forward, handed Jean a small bundle of cloth, smears of moist earth clinging to the material.

Jean took the bundle gingerly. "What is this?" The cloth gave way under his probing fingers to reveal a tiny corpse no bigger that the palm of his hand.

"We found it buried between the roots of a huge oak tree," the man said. "One of de Reuilles' men led us there. He told us that they had found a footprint in that very place last year when the baron's daughter disappeared."

"So?" Jean asked, his finger gently tracing the skeleton's limbs. Only a little of the flesh remained. It resembled a wizened, miniature old woman. "A dead baby?"

The man's eyes went dark. "I was told," he said, "that the witch Maríana was with child when she disappeared."

Jean's heart skipped. All the usual noise around him, the clank of the guard coming down the staircase, the murmur of his men, faded and disappeared behind the roaring in his head. All Jean could see was his beloved Henri, pumping away between the thighs of a girl, planting a baby in her treacherous womb. But he could use this, couldn't he? A small pop sounded by his left ear and the noises of the donjon returned. "Was she?" he breathed, then carefully drew the cloth back around the corpse. "We will take it to Bauçais," he said. His voice trembled. Not good. He must not let his men see this. He drew in a breath. "Now." Better. His voice was strong and steady again.

Jean marched into the palais, six of his men surrounding him, the tiny corpse nestled in his hands. Bauçais and de Reuilles were both there, seated upon the dais, Louis-Philippe leaning toward Henri. Jean stopped in surprise. How curious. He had never noticed Baron de Reuilles' eyes before, thickly lashed blue-green. Well. The way Louis-Philippe inclined his head toward Henri, there was something familiar here. Were the two plotting? He shook himself and approached the dais. Henri saw him first. His frost blue eyes stabbed Jean. "What do you want?"

Jean allowed his gaze to sweep over Henri. Still beautiful, his Henri. What would the rack do to him? The thought brought a liquid fire to his loins. He extended his hands toward Henri, the small corpse hidden by folds of cloth.

Henri reached out, took the tiny package. Jean leaned closer, watched Henri's face as he unwrapped it. Puzzlement. Henri lifted his head. Jean sighed. Bauçais had no idea what this was.

"Jean?" Henri asked. For a moment, Henri's face was naked, vulnerable. Then his mouth twisted. "Thinking of making some yellow water?" His fingers covered the corpse.

"My men found this," Jean said, eyes watching Henri's face intently, "between the roots of an oak tree. Tell us exactly where you found it," he commanded a soldier, all the while never taking his eyes from Henri.

"At the top of a large slope, right before the climb steepens. There is only one tree at the top, a huge oak. Your men found a footprint there." The man turned toward de Reuilles.

Blood drained from Henri's face. He could not shutter his pain. Jean trembled. It had been so long since he had seen Henri's agony. He would remember this. But now Bauçais struggled to regain control, to close away the torment that washed over his features, shone from his eyes.

"I know the place," Henri said. "I remember." He gently folded the cloth in place around the tiny figure and handed it to Louis-Philippe. "This should be properly buried." Henri's face was under control again, impassive. Yet his voice deepened, caught.

An urgent longing swept through Jean's groin. He suppressed a shiver. "Did you know that witches sometimes use the bodies of their own babies to cast spells?" he asked, eyes pinned to Henri's face, then he leaned in closer, drew his mouth up into a leer. "This is yours, isn't it?" he hissed. "Your bastard."

Henri's eyes ignited and he lunged toward Jean. But Jean had already fallen back. His men closed in around him.

"Wait!" Louis-Philippe grabbed Henri's arm. Henri's muscles bulged against Louis-Philippe's hold.

De Reuilles must be strong to hold the younger man back. Jean now stood behind his men. "I will send word of this find to the bishop," he said, then turned, moved toward the door. He was not stupid. Henri would kill him if he could. His lips parted. He had won this round.

HENRI REMAINED at his seat, hands clenching and unclenching in a rhythmic spasm. Jean must be going mad. No one was safe now. "De Reuilles," he said. "I must go to the bishop myself. This changes things."

"How?" Louis-Philippe's eyes followed the departing party of men surrounding Jean.

"They want Maríana. This gives Jean even more reason to go after her. And after me, as well. Jean and I... well, there is bad blood between us." Henri looked at the older man. "I don't think I would be of any help here now. My presence might even harm you."

Louis-Philippe took Henri's arm. His eyes were shadowed, yet kind. "We do not know that what he had was your baby."

Henri could not look at him. "I know it is," he finally said. "I know."

JEAN'S HEART fluttered as he tried to keep a steady pace back to the donjon. The look in Henri's eyes before he lunged at him had started an inferno in Jean's loins. He was so aroused that he could barely speak, let alone play the outraged priest for his men. He was aware of them stealing quick glances at him from the side, and he strove to keep his face still.

Blessed Jesus, he would give all of them for one of Henri! He tried to keep his lips from curving at the thought of Henri de Bauçais and Jean Becier leading the Inquisition, of the thought of he, Jean Becier, initiating the Baron of Bauçais into the pleasures of torture.

When they entered the donjon he waved his men away. He only wanted to be alone so he could ease the hot ache that Henri had started in him. But as he climbed to his chamber, his man from the guard room called out.

"We have found something, Brother!"

Jean frowned down at him. "What?"

"Come, Brother!" The man motioned for Jean to follow him to the dungeon. "There is a door in the floor here."

Jean stepped carefully down the stairs. If he did not relieve the throbbing in his groin soon, he would burst. "Probably storage," he told the guard.

In their search for the torture chamber they had found several secret rooms filled with all sorts of dusty furniture, tapestries and even implements for tilling the soil. He looked at his men standing around a wooden door clearly visible in the floor between the two cells. Utarilla huddled in the far corner of her cell, but Ysabel was right next to the bars, straining to see.

"The door itself was buried in straw and several layers of dirt, but we dug it out." the man looked up expectantly at Jean.

Jean smiled at him. "Well, let us open it."

The man raised the trap door. Puffs of dust and clods of dirt swirled in the air.

Jean's pulse raced as the light from the man's torch swept across the angular form of the rack, the edge of the wheel. He descended into the chamber.

"Give me the torch," he commanded. When he had it in his hand, he looked around. "Close the door, and do not disturb me." The door closed with another puff of dirt, clumps of straw pattered down on the steps.

Jean lovingly stroked the rack, the wheel, the iron boot. They were all here, his favorite friends, including the thumb screw and a few gruesome implements that even he could not put a name to. He grimaced at the oily black dirt that came away on his hands when he touched the tools. Wiping his hands on his robe, he climbed on to the rack and stretched his arms out. Ah, Henri on the rack, face down, stretched to the limit of his endurance, biting back cries of pain... Jean's body shuddered with the force of the climax that finally allowed his hot and aching loins release.

Chapter 36

MIST FROM THE river rose in white streams into the gray half-light of dawn. Richard sat at the base of the path that led to the Lady's cave, his back against the trunk of a maple tree, arms wound around Maríana. His Maríana. She had not yet wakened. He had not slept at all.

He did not mind. He liked watching her sleep, liked seeing the brush of her lashes against her skin, the tremble of her eyelids. Whenever he shifted her in his arms, her lips curved in a smile. He buried his face in her hair and breathed in her fragrance; jasmine and powdered mugwort, violets and lavender. He could smell the aromatic woods Iranzu and Adelie had burned every day since the circle fire, pine-sap and ash, sticks of cedar from the holy land. He drew her closer.

Maríana had spent each day with Adelie and Iranzu, learning all they could teach her about drawing the web that would protect their valley from the world outside. He did not like to think about the danger she would face. But he could not avoid this, not now.

When the sun touched the mountain, Maríana must follow the track to the cave above, commune with the stone, somehow draw a net around Canigou. Iranzu had told him this stone radiated some sort of force. It was not fatal to the woman the stone accepted as the Lady, but it would kill anyone else. Richard nuzzled her hair and breathed deeply of her scent. She must go alone. He could not go with her.

He had accepted this. He did not like it, but he would obey. He did not understand how Maríana could enter the stone, how she could draw a net, speak with the Guardian. Yet, he accepted this, too. When he was a child, he had seen a wise woman go into the shadowed depths of a dolmen, a giant's tomb. When she came out into the sunlight, she was able to show her people how to fight the sickness that had swept through their village. He had asked the wise woman how this could happen, what she had done in the tomb. Now he lifted Maríana's hand, stared at the delicate trace of her veins, the pulse in her wrist. The wise woman had told him the tomb was a gateway to the drowned city of Ys. She had gone there, asked her questions, and had been given the answers that saved her people. He pulled Maríana's hand to his lips.

It was dangerous, this task. Iranzu had warned him, said that going into the stone would bring Maríana close to the Door to the Otherworld. The Door to Death. Adelie and Iranzu had spent days teaching her how to avoid the pull of the Otherworld, the lure to cross over. If she should cross the threshold of the Door, she could never return. Iranzu's own mother had passed through the Door and she had not come back.

Maríana was stirring, He looked at the twitch of her brows as she opened her eyes and looked into his face. Delight and wonder lifted the corners of her mouth. She grasped his head with her hands, drew his mouth to hers, traced his lips with her tongue. He groaned and deepened the kiss, pulled her up to his chest. A shaking plea escaped in a sigh with his breath. "There is no time before you must go."

"You should have wakened me earlier." Her words chided, but her voice was warm, indulgent.

Heat flashed through his groin, his breathing stopped. This was the fifth day since the circle fire. Four days of pacing, of knotted clumps in his belly, of watching smoke drift from the stone house, of trying not to think of what Maríana must do, trying not to worry. But five nights of her sweet skin pressed against him, of limbs tangled in honeyed abandon, of the dark, rich cries that poured from her throat when his hands roamed over her thighs, teased the swollen buds of her nipples, delved into the moist depths of her woman's cleft. Her breathless cries had always pushed him over the edge of his own need, had left him shaking until he could drive into her, join her in hot and shuddering release.

Fingers of sunlight touched her face. Richard held his hand over her forehead, blocked the soft fall of light. Not yet. He would not let her go yet. One more kiss. He took her mouth in his, tasted deeply of her lips, ran his tongue across her teeth, plunged into the depths of her mouth. She answered with her own wanting, pulled at his lower lip, captured, then caressed his tongue with hers.

Footsteps. Richard lifted his head. Maríana wound her arms around him in a brief hug before rising from the ground. "Grandfather, Aunt," she said.

Richard unlocked his legs and pushed up from the ground. Adelie and Iranzu stood there, faces solemn. Iranzu handed something to Maríana, something small wrapped in silk. "I want you to take this with you."

Maríana unwrapped the covering and held a gray and green chalice up in the sunlight. She traced a raised pattern that circled it. Puzzlement, then surprise chased across her face. She swiftly covered the sides of the cup with the silk, blew upon the fingers of her right hand. "What is this?"

Iranzu shrugged. "We do not know. A woman gave it to Antoine. She was from Montsegur." Maríana jumped. Iranzu paused, then continued, "Men from Rome are looking for it. They want it badly. Antoine brought it here. I want you to take it up to the cave with you."

"Of course, Grandfather." Maríana started to wind the silken cloth around it, but Richard reached toward her.

"May I see that?" He did not know why he wanted to touch it. When he saw it in her hands, a song trembled the air, then faded. Without hesitation, Maríana handed it to him.

It was heavy. This surprised him, that something so small could have such weight. He uncovered the chalice, grasped it firmly in his palm. He felt a stirring within his heart, a gladness that welcomed him, warmed his limbs. "What?" he breathed.

Iranzu's eyes were on him. The old man nodded toward Maríana. Richard covered the cup; the stirring within him dampened, but did not die. When he placed the cup back in Maríana's hands, a flare of wonder nestled in his chest.

"Once you enter the stone, you must remember to avoid the golden light of the Door," Iranzu reminded Maríana. "It will draw you, so be careful."

Too soon, Maríana was ready, her pack slung over her shoulder. She tucked the chalice into her bag while Adelie fussed at her, brushing her gown, smoothing the hair from her brow. Richard hung back. One more embrace. He could not let her leave without holding her once more.

"Sister-child," tears stood out in Adelie's eyes, "Lady's blessings always. And return to us!" She drew Maríana into her arms.

Iranzu put his arms around both of them while Richard stood apart. When they finally broke their embrace, Maríana turned to Richard, gave him that luminous gaze he loved so well.

He pulled her toward him, enveloped her. "I will be waiting for you right here," he whispered.

He watched her climb the path, Adelie and Iranzu at his side. When she could no longer be seen, the old man and Maríana's aunt turned, started down the track that went across the river, back to their stone house. Richard listened as their footsteps dwindled, then in silence he stood in the middle of the path looking up at the mountain. Until the shadows lengthened. Until stars began to show in the sky.

YSABEL SCREAMED again, a gurgling howl that cut off abruptly. Jean released the lever that moved the leather straps ahead each notch on the rack, easing the pull on her joints. She gasped and sobbed now, her voice dropping into a moaning plea.

He had been in the torture chamber with her all afternoon, yet he was getting nowhere. "You do not know where the witch Maríana has gone," he muttered. She had admitted to making a love charm to capture Henri. He had wrenched the tale of her jealousy of Maríana from her. But that was all. Oh, she had finally said that she wanted to kill Ibrahim. Yet she would not tell him why. He tapped the side of the rack a moment. This was the key, he was sure of it. "Why did you kill Ibrahim?" His hand moved to pull the lever again.

"No!" she screamed. "I will tell you."

"I am waiting."

Ysabel shuddered. Her mouth opened, then a string of sounds poured out. La il'aha il'allah.

Jean slumped down staring at her sweating, pleading face. This was as far as he could get. Whenever he asked this question, she spouted nonsense. It was almost as if she were being silenced. A shiver traveled from his chest to his feet. He leaned close to her face. How curious. He caught a whiff of honey. And roses. "A demon has stilled your tongue." A flash of desperate comprehension twisted her features, a quick nod turned into a shudder of pain. He must have pulled her shoulder out again.

"Then we will do this..." He grasped the lever, played with it. There was a slight stirring in his groin at the sight of her agony, her fear. Nothing more. Well, he had already soaked the front of his robe with his seed. It would take more than this to arouse him now.

He needed incriminating information to tell Durand. He had disobeyed des Arcis by putting the two women on the rack. Utarilla had lasted only a few moments, dying before he could ease the throbbing heat in his loins, but Ysabel had given him several stunning bursts of rapture. Perhaps he should be kinder. "I will give you the answers," he said. "All you must do is nod if what I say is right."

A mixture of grief and gratitude flowed from her eyes. Her lips trembled. He leaned forward again. "You wanted to kill Ibrahim because he was Maríana's friend." A swift shake of her head. "You wanted to kill Ibrahim because, because," his words broke off. She was struggling. He put his ear close to her lips.

"Lover." It sounded like a sigh, but he caught the word within it.

"Ibrahim was your lover?" No wonder her husband had never asked to see her in all this time. First her infatuation with his Henri, now the gardener?

He almost missed that rapid shake of her head. "Husband." The whispered word was clear, but was torn off as her teeth clicked in the air next to his ear. He jumped back. His hand moved to the lever, pulled it all the way. The bitch had nearly bitten him! He released it just before her eyes rolled up into their sockets.

Could she have been trying to tell him that Ibrahim was her husband? That she wanted to kill him so Louis-Philippe would never know? He frowned. This did not make any sense. From what he heard, this Ibrahim had been here long before she ever came to Reuilles-le-château. As he stared at her limp body, an unbidden image leaped before his eyes, that of Louis-Philippe, leaning toward Henri. Something in his face.

A roaring sounded in his ears. No, this could not be. He looked down at her again. But she had said it, hadn't she? Not her lover; her husband's lover. Jean shivered. "Louis-Philippe de Reuilles, the sodomite," he said, his lips stretching into a smile. "Perfect!"

Jean took the stairs two at a time and rapped loudly on the door. When his man lifted it he said, "I am through with this one at present. Put her back in her cell." He pushed past the man and climbed to his chamber, his chest trembling. He would send a man to the bishop today. If his man rode fast, Jean could have the bishop's approval to take the baron before anyone here knew his plan.

He would have all of them. Every last one. Henri would return from his flight to Durand, his desperate petition, to find the de Reuilles family beyond his reach. Beyond the reach of everyone. The rack, the iron boot and the Catherine Wheel would give Jean the answers he needed to secure a permanent place in the Inquisition against witches.

He entered his chamber, reached for his quill. Yes, he would find Maríana de Reuilles, deliver her to Durand himself. But perhaps, before he did, he would use her as barter. He had not missed the anguish in Henri's eyes whenever the girl's name was mentioned. Henri would do anything to save her, anything. Jean dipped his quill into the ink pot and scratched out his message to Durand.

MARÍANA patted loose clumps of earth over the shallow grave she had dug. Her great-grandmother's bones lay underneath her hands, under the blanket of dirt she had spread across the yellowed skull, the knobby spine. There was no flesh at all, just wisps of cloth that billowed out from the bones as Maríana lifted them from the stone. Teeth marks showed where rats had gnawed on the ribs.

She wiped her hands on her skirt. It had been thirty years, after all. She looked at the mouth of the cave. Iranzu had not told her she would find the bones of his mother here. When she found the cave, she had trudged inside, weary from her climb up the mountain. She'd dropped her pack to the floor, then suppressed her scream of fright when she saw the ghostly figure draped over the stone.

Why hadn't he told her? What other surprises waited? Maríana gave one last glance to the raw gash in the earth. "Good-bye Great-Grandmother," she murmured. She turned toward the cave. It was getting dark. She needed to light her lamp, to eat what Adelie had made for her. To ready herself for her task.

Her lamp filled the chamber with a soothing glow. A simple straw mattress, covered by a dusty blanket embroidered with a four-petaled flower pattern, rested in the far end of the cave. The colors of the blanket must have once been deep burgundy and royal blue, now faded into rose and pewter. The cave formed a large central chamber with the mattress and a small chest, and an alcove where the large, rough, dark gray stone brooded. It was waist-high and shaped like a table, with sharp edges.

She ran her fingers over its dirty surface, then sighed and looked around the chamber. In the alcove, she could see faint traces of paintings on the walls. The flickering lamp brought the dim paintings to life, the shapes and lines seemed to dance and sway. But staring at the stone did not set it in motion. There was nothing she could do until it awakened.

She lifted her pack and drew out the bread Adelie had sent, her fingers brushing the chalice that lay beside it. Pulling the cup out, she set it next to her. What was it? When she touched it, her hands burned. The chalice stood before her, glowing softly in the lamp light. So this was what Henri had sought. But why did the church want it? Some power lived within it, that much she knew. Was it a relic? She brushed crumbs off her hands and gown, took the chalice over to the stone, placed it on the floor and looked up at the walls.

Animals. It looked like someone had painted animals here. She traced the lines and her hands came away covered with black dirt. Johanna would never have let filth like this lay thick upon the walls.

The stone. It had a sullen presence, but was silent for now. She drew the blanket off the mattress, jumped when hundreds of bugs scampered out from the tightly-woven straw underneath. Taking the cleanest edge of the blanket, she scrubbed the wall.

A horse. Someone had captured it in flight, its legs raised and extended in a gallop. She hummed a weaving song as she rubbed at the dirt. Now a bull appeared. She ran the blanket along the lines of the horns and uncovered the powerful body. And a bird. She brushed enough of the dirt away to reveal a feathered creature that was drawn as large as the bull. The bird's wings were spread in a span that stretched across the east end of the alcove.

Now for the stone. She swiped at the powdery dust that covered it, then stepped back in amazement. The stone was black, not gray. Something on its top surface sparkled. She rubbed harder along the entire top, down across the sides. It was pitch black and shiny as mica, but its top surface was not even. The stone was pitted, as if thousands of hammers had struck it, chipping small indentations. The pebbled surface caught the lamp light, threw it in glittering strands across the cave. But the sides were smooth, silken. When she ran her hands along its surface, a thrilling shiver gripped her body, starting in her belly and spreading outward. At the same time, a dull green-gold light pulsed within the depths of the stone. She had the sensation of immense distances, as if she were gazing into a fathomless well instead of a large black stone. The light pulsed again and she felt another surge race through her body.

"Ah, God!" She trembled, her breath caught, and stilled. It had begun. She held her hands together, felt the sweat stand out in beads on her skin. Her heart raced, hands shook. Without thinking, she picked up the chalice and held it to her chest. Her heartbeat steadied, breathing deepened. She knelt before the stone, placed the chalice beside her, stretched her left arm out to rest across the top. The surface was warm now, and she could see the golden shapes that Iranzu had told her would appear.

"You must touch these shapes in this exact order," Iranzu had said, showing her the boat, the two upraised hands, the feather and the eye. "My mother told me that these are the signs of the Guardian and of the millions of years."

Maríana had frowned. "Millions of years?"

Iranzu had waved his hand. "You must not question what you are doing, there is no time. You must follow my directions."

Maríana saw them now-the boat, the upraised hands, the feather and the eye. She touched each in sequence, ignoring the other glowing forms that floated across the stone's surface. Then other symbols followed, curved lines and slashes, circles and six-sided boxes. She touched each of these in the sequence Iranzu had given her.

The stone hummed, as if some vast creature within had awakened angry. She held onto it with both arms, leaned her body against the side as she sank down next to it. The light within grew brighter with every pulse it made, going from deep green-gold to honey to bright sun-light. For a moment, she was poised on the edge of an abyss of swirling light. She closed her eyes, preparing herself for what would come next. She drew in a deep, ragged breath and the sounds she had practiced for the past five days tumbled from her lips.

Light within the stone flashed outward in the blue-white brilliance of ten thousand suns. The air shivered, congealed. Her head sank onto the stone.

HENRI GRITTED his teeth. He had been kept waiting outside of the Bishop Durand's chamber the entire morning. His stomach was complaining, hollow gurgles that sent sour froth into his mouth. The door to the Bishop's chamber opened and Hughes des Arcis emerged. Henri rose from his seat and started toward the door, but stopped when Hughes shook his head and motioned for Henri to follow him out.

Once they were outside, Hughes said, "It is no good, my friend. He will not see you."

Henri grabbed his arm. "Why?" He looked in surprise at the whiteness of his own knuckles.

Hughes shook his head again and stared at Henri's hand. Henri forced his fingers to release his grasp. "Follow me," Hughes whispered.

They walked together, up and down the narrow alleys of Carcasonne, talking of small things.

Henri's hands itched. Intrigue had used to amuse him with its double meanings and careful shading of words. He had also used to have more patience. Now all he wanted to do was wrap his hands around des

Arcis' neck, throttle the truth out of him.

Finally, Hughes glanced around and indicated that Henri should stop. Hughes drew a rolled parchment out of his robes and handed it over.

"You are to return to Reuilles-le-château with this."

Henri unrolled the scroll and read it, then stared at Hughes in disbelief. "Do you know what this says?"

"It is a lesson in obedience, my friend. I could not save the Baroness." Hughes's voice dropped. "I did the best I could."

"This document says that Jean can go after anyone he wants from the baron down. The only person safe from him is Johanna!"

"Obedience," Hughes repeated. His words were mild but his eyes carried a different message. "Your obedience has been questioned since Montsegur. I recommend that you do what we have asked of you: take this back to Reuilles-le-château."

He made a show of adjusting his robe, then spoke very softly. "Take men from Bauçais or Touraine with you, men you can trust. Decide for yourself how much you will tell them of what the contents of this document mean." Then Hughes backed away, inclining his head, and strolled in the direction of the cathedral.

Henri read the scroll again. He examined the seal and the ink and rolled it back up, tapping it against his hands. Then he placed it in his belt and strode off to locate his men. They would need to leave soon if they were to reach the château within a week.

In the late afternoon light, outside the walls of Carcassone, Henri stood before his men. "We will start our journey to Reuilles-le-château in the morning," he told them. "I have orders." He unrolled a scroll, holding his thumb over the seal to make sure it would still stick to the parchment. "Orders from the bishop," he continued, "to relieve Jean Becier of his position as Inquisitor in this investigation."

He looked up at his men. Blank faces, mostly, though three looked relieved. Not one of them seemed surprised or disturbed by such orders. Good. The scroll wound back into a tight cylinder. He had taken the bishop's seal off the scroll Hughes had given him and carefully fixed it to this one, after he'd written his own orders.

Henri knew the consequences if he were caught. His men were protected; none of them knew the original orders. He was fully prepared to take the blame, but he hoped he to find Maríana first and take her to Paris before the bishop discovered his duplicity. A petition to the king might save his skin and Maríana's. If Maríana did have this thing the church sought, it would be a valuable tool.

He looked out across the hills that surrounded Carcasonne. The green of the trees here was faded, tired. Not like the brooding black hills of Navarre. But the swell of earth that marched into the distance was touched with the gold and peach rays of the sun. He inhaled the fragrance of early blooming lilacs, surprised by how he enjoyed the simple pleasure. He had just thrown his entire life away, yet it felt good to breathe.

His men were waiting. Henri released the breath he had been holding. "We ride out at dawn tomorrow."

MARÍANA steadied herself, looking around in bewilderment. She appeared to be in a small room. White walls rose around her and blue-black tiles with tiny lights sparkling within them formed the floor. When she looked down, she saw the night sky spread out beneath her feet. All the constellations and worlds Ibrahim had spoken of were there in this floor.

A dusky voice spoke. "Oh, are you back, then?"

Maríana looked up. A woman with sun-bronzed skin sat at a table next to a window. The brilliant blue of a large body of water glimmered far below the window, and houses of a white so bright she could hardly do more than glance at them marched down to its shore. Maríana raised her hand to shield her eyes from the glare and studied the woman. It was odd. She was sure she had seen this woman before, but she could not remember where.

The woman stared at table's surface. Midnight hair fell in a straight line to her shoulders. Her eyes were outlined in black paint and her brows made perfect arches. Light played across the planes of her face, light that must have somehow come from within the table. "How could..." Maríana stopped.

The woman swept her hand across the surface of the table; the light disappeared. She stood and approached Maríana, hands held out in front of her. A violet gown with tiny pleats hung from a golden clasp on her right shoulder, straight to her ankles. Her left shoulder was bare.

"We do not have much time," the woman said as she took Maríana's hands. "If I am to get you back before the link is broken we must start now."

"May I ask your name?" There was strength in this woman's hands, great strength. "Is it allowed to ask?"

"You call me the Guardian, I believe."

"The statues!" This woman was the breathing likeness of the statue at the entrance to the hidden valley. "But where is the Beacon?"

The Guardian's lips lifted. It was not exactly a smile, but her impassive features warmed. "He will never stay here very long; he always goes back to your world." She pulled Maríana over to the table. "He is somewhere called 'Konya' now. It will not be too much longer before he returns, though."

The Guardian bent her head over the surface of the table again. "I

want you to look down here," she said, passing her hand across the table.
"What do you see?"

"A valley nestled within mountains." Maríana leaned forward.
"This is our valley as a bird would see it! How... ?" And it moved.
Clouds were tumbling across the peaks.

"No time." The Guardian put her arm around Maríana's shoulders.
"Do you remember when you first saw the Door?"

"Yes. It was in the circle. I was flying."

"So must we."

The room disappeared. Maríana was suspended far above the floor
of the valley, in a night sky among the clouds. She grabbed for the
Guardian's hand, found that the woman's arm was still around her
shoulders. "But, there was daylight where we were standing on the
room."

"I am sorry. None of you are ever truly prepared for this," the
Guardian said. "It is night time in your valley. I realize that this is your
first time, but don't worry," there was that lifting of her lips again,
"Jakintzas never forget how to do this." The Guardian pulled Maríana up
until they were both the height of a hundred men above the valley.
"Come, now!" she shouted, "Shape shifter!"

Something dark, with bones and stretched skin erupted above and
below Maríana's shoulder blades. Gigantic wings unfolded, spreading
out away from their imprisonment within her body. Wind passed over
and under her wings, lifting her in dizzying waves. Iridescent feathers,
still moist from captivity within her body, fanned out against the sky.
How she could move them? But with that thought, muscles that were
ready to obey her brought the wings first down, and then up in a graceful
arc.

"What did I tell you?" A real smile brightened the Guardian's face.
"You Jakintzas!" She had dropped her arm from Maríana's shoulders
when the wings started emerging. Now, she pointed to the mountain
peaks, where faint, pulsing lights very much like the lights within the
stone flickered. "We must re-draw the markers first," the Guardian said
as Maríana's wings beat against the air. She guided Maríana toward a
feeble yellow light. "I will act as the weaver, but you must draw the
energy through from the physical world in order to make this work."
They had reached the first marker.

"You have no wings." Maríana had just noticed this as they hovered
over the marker. She glided in a circle around the fragile light, but the
Guardian floated in the air.

"I have no body," the Guardian said, her smile radiant now. "It has
been thousands of years since I had a physical body. I no longer need to
return, since I have chosen the path of the Guardian." She floated to a
spot directly above the light and extended her fingers over it. "Now,

Maríana de Reuilles! Do what you were born to do! Bring your world through."

Maríana threw her head back and sang out the note that Iranzu had made her repeat hundreds of times. As she glided around and around the light, she sustained the note, until she felt a pull in her belly. Energy from the physical realm streamed through her. The Guardian's fingers wove a complex pattern, working the fine beams of light into a brilliant net. Maríana raised the note a half tone and sustained it to the limit of her breath.

They continued this way, Maríana bringing the light through her body and the Guardian plaiting it into thick strands, until they were up in the clouds again, well above the valley and the mountains. The net shone now, a fine web of light that rose up into a sphere, entirely covering the valley and anchored by the twelve markers that now burned brightly on top of the mountain peaks.

The Guardian grasped Maríana's hands. "Fine work! You should not have to do this again for some time. I think..." she broke off as the dark sky was suddenly flooded by a light that no words could describe. "Don't look at it!" she ordered Maríana. But it was too late.

Maríana's eyes filled with the light that was at once every color and no color, a light that lived and breathed and sang. A light that cried out in love and joy. *Come home.* She closed her eyes, but it bled through her lids, touched her everywhere.

"It is alive! It is calling to me," Maríana cried. "Iranzu! Why didn't you tell me it was alive?" She reached her hands into it, watched the trembling sparkle as it flowed through her fingers. "I am here," she said, then turned to the Guardian. But the Guardian was not there. There was only the living light, all around her.

She had gone through the Door.

Chapter 37

RICHARD turned his head to the side, felt the scratchy wool of the rolled blanket under his head. His eyes blinked open. He stared blankly at the tree trunks that surrounded him. What was he doing outside... ?

Maríana! He'd fallen asleep waiting for her to return from the mountain. He leaped up and ran to the path, looked eagerly up and down the length of the curving track that led from the river all the way up the mountain. No one was there.

He slapped his thigh and cursed. What a time to fall asleep! He bundled up his pack and slung it over his shoulder. Maríana must not have seen him when she came back down. He would find her at the stone house with Iranzu. Sprinting to the bridge over the river, he did not stop running until the stone house was within his sight.

The village was silent. He couldn't see any children playing outside and there were few people on the road. He nodded to the people he knew and marched up to the door of the stone house, bursting inside and slinging his pack on the floor.

"Where is she?" He glanced at the neatly-made box beds and the long oak table where Iranzu and Adelie sat. "I saw the lightning last night," he continued, marching up to the table. "I know she got inside all right. Now, where is she?" He stopped when he saw Adelie's reddened eyes.

"Sit down, Richard." Adelie reached out and grasped his arm. He allowed her to pull him onto the bench in front of the table.

"We all saw the light," Iranzu said. "The whole side of the mountain lit up when she entered the stone." He sighed and put his head in his hands. "We were following her until she completed her task of drawing the net. After that, we could not sense her any longer."

"Then where is she?" Richard's jaw locked as he stared into Adelie's face. It kept his teeth from clattering. He leaned forward, forced his mouth to open. "Where is my Maríana?"

"We think she is lost in the stone," Adelie said.

Richard slammed his fist on the table. "No! She is still alive. I would know if she had died." His voice broke. "I would know."

He turned and walked out the door.

RICHARD pounding the walls of his stone hut until his knuckles were raw and bleeding, yet he could not feel them. He looked at the jumble of clothes, his flute, the new gown Leila was making for Maríana. Then he drew in his breath and blinked his eyes hard. None of this was doing any good, none of this would help Maríana.

Marc entered the hut. "What are you doing?"

Marc looked wary. Well, no wonder. Richard hid his hands under his thighs. He must look mad.

"I am getting ready to climb up to your cave to get Maríana out of that damned stone." he said. "But I only have my sword here. There is nothing I can use to help her." He drew his hands out from under him, made fists. "I had to leave Reuilles-le-château with nothing. Nothing but the clothes on my back." Marc wavered in the doorway. Richard lowered his voice. There was no need to frighten the boy. "If only I could have brought my breast plate, or even my chain mail. Anything that would shield me from the force coming out of the stone."

Marc yelped. "Armor!" he squeaked.

Richard jumped off the bed and clutched Marc's tunic. "What did you say? Tell me!"

"You need armor?" Marc asked.

"You mean you have armor here? In this village?"

Marc nodded. "Yes, armor, very new armor."

Richard grabbed his sword. "Where is this armor?"

"I don't know what you have in mind, but Gorka has armor." Marc's face went impassive, but Richard could see the tremble of excitement in his limbs.

Now Richard grasped Marc's arms. "Take me to this Gorka," he said.

"I WAS ARMORER to Thibaut of Navarre. But I grew homesick for my valley." Gorka hefted the armor. It had a blue sheen to it. "This is what I was making before I left his court."

Amazed, Richard stared at the metal plates. "We have chain mail and breast plates, but nothing like this."

The suit formed an entire body-covering; chest and trunk, arms, hands, legs and feet. The helmet was made to cover the head, with a slitted visor that creaked when Richard lifted it.

"Can I try it on?" he asked, already pulling the metal gloves over his hands.

Gorka smiled and shrugged. "Anything for our Breton knight," he said.

Marc frowned, running his fingers along the joints. "It may be a little small."

Richard slipped into the arm-coverings. His hands stuck out and his wrists showed, but with a little adjustment to the gloves, his skin was covered. He looked at the leg plates and metal boots. "We can loosen these so I can wear it." He used his knife to pry the joints apart just enough to allow him to place his legs inside. He shrugged his body into the breast plate and back, donned the leg coverings.

Gorka made a small cry of amazement. "You really are a knight!" he said, eyes popping. As if Richard had just stepped out of a tale.

Richard frowned at the helmet. He had no time for their admiration. "Gorka," he said, "can you make a metal plate to fit over this part of the helmet." He pried the visor off, removed the gloves. "A plate that has no slits at all?"

"Of course! But why?" Gorka was puzzled. "Won't you want to be able to see?"

Richard looked at the helmet. This might work. Even if it did not, he would not give up, would not leave Maríana up there. "I will not wear it long, but it is important that nothing be able to penetrate it." How could he withstand a force that nobody understood?

"I will make it for you now," Gorka said, moving toward his forge.

Marc was grinning, his feet tapped the floor. "I knew you were a knight," he said. "But seeing you in this!" He waved his hands. "I always dreamed about being a knight, riding into battle in my armor!" He lifted Richard's sword and swung it around, knocking a flagon of ale and a bucket of pig's entrails onto the floor.

Richard flexed his arms and the armor creaked in protest. He rescued the sword. "I will keep this." Then he drew the metal gloves over his hands again, wiggled his fingers. "No one I know has armor like this. Gorka has made something quite new." He turned to Marc. "I may not have your magic, but at least I know what I can do with this armor, and this may be the only way I can bring my Maríana back."

MARÍANA was nestled next to something warm. Something that moved and sent tingling shivers through her. She opened her eyes. Someone's arms enveloped her, arms that held her gently. She stared at the hands that grasped her. Glowing, fine-grained skin. She stared at the line of the thumb, the square fingers, the transparent nails, then she jerked her head away. This was a trap, wasn't it? Earlier, she had followed the vibrant strands of a fern all the way to its roots and into the earth below. She must have wandered for days now, entranced by the landscape of this place. The gurgle of running water tickled her ears, yet she could not focus on anything but the arms that held her. Everything else was a soft blur of colors and light.

"Guardian?" she said, shaking her head. "I thought I went through the Door."

"Maríana!" This was a familiar voice, surely. But a voice she had not heard in months. "You have joined us so soon! How did you die?" The tones were low, pleased, with a dramatic rise at the end.

Maríana pulled away from the arms that held her, spun and rose up into the air, held the back of her hand against her mouth. "Oh, my God." Tears formed shards of crystals on her cheeks.

Ibrahim sat upon some kind of chair, one brow elevated. "Flying is fun, isn't it?" He beckoned to her. "But come down now." She curled her arms and legs inward, tried to drift toward him. "I want to talk to you."

"Are you real?" Nothing else seemed to be. Everything was always changing, even as she looked at it. After she had plunged into the earth to trace the roots of the fern, she had drawn in on herself, had somehow shut this world out. For a time.

Ibrahim took her hand and kissed it, tugged her to the ground. Or what felt like ground. She felt the pressure of his hand, saw the sparkle in his eyes as he regarded her. But his form shone and his skin was unlike anything she had ever known, firm and soft, yet more like a pliant statue than a human. Her fingers grew warm and prickled when she touched him.

He motioned for her to come closer. "How did you die? I had no idea..."

"She has not died, love." A voice that sounded very much like Adelie came from somewhere behind Maríana. "Not yet, anyway." Suddenly Ibrahim's face transformed, filled with so much light that his features disappeared in a luminous burst. Two strong, slender hands came into Maríana's view.

"See?" the voice continued and the hands grasped a translucent coil that seemed to be attached just above her navel. Maríana jumped as the hands tugged and she felt it all the way to her toes. "The cord is still there," the voice concluded and the woman who spoke moved next to Ibrahim, kissed his radiant face. Pitch black hair flowed around her shoulders, her eyes glowed emerald. "Maríana." She gave her greeting with a nod.

"Mama?" Maríana reached toward Thérèse, but she could not seem to stay on the ground. Her feet lifted and she started to spin again. Thérèse laughed and pulled Maríana into her embrace, anchoring her in between Ibrahim and herself.

"Now, now, petite." Thérèse stroked her hair as Maríana shook, stared at her mother's face. "It is wonderful to see you, but definitely too soon. Did you come through the stone?"

Maríana found she could not speak, but managed to nod.

Thérèse sighed. "I thought so."

Ibrahim touched Maríana's face. "Once you go through the Door," crystal pieces made tracks across his face, too, "you cannot return."

"Quiet, my love." Thérèse's fingers caressed Ibrahim's lips. "Not now." She pulled Maríana closer and rocked her back and forth. "I must think."

Maríana was sure centuries passed while she was rocked in her mother's arms. Yet no time at all had passed when Thérèse released her.

"Mama," Maríana said, rubbing at her eyes. "I am sorry that I turned away from you." What would have happened if she had embraced her mother by the pond, so long ago?

"What do you mean?"

"I saw you in the pool in your garden. I was young and I did not understand... I just saw a water creature with no eyes. I did not know it was you."

Thérèse became very still. "So." Her voice dragged; for a moment an image of her damaged face danced upon the radiant form Maríana saw before her. "I *was* there." She shook her head and sighed. "It is I who should be sorry, petite. I frightened you, didn't I?"

She pulled Maríana to her side again. "I never listened to Father when he told me what I must do after death. I think I wandered for a while in a dark dream." She turned to Ibrahim.

"You are fading again," she chided.

Ibrahim yelped, holding his transparent hands up to his face and glaring at them. As he stared at them, they became solid. First the palms, them the long fingers, finally the tips. He grinned. "I was thinking of the Mevlana," he said. "I have been visiting a man in Konya," he told Maríana as he floated off the ground. "I met him when he was a boy. Now I talk with him sometimes, when he dreams." He looked around at the light, shimmering in hues that were beyond color. "I think he is dreaming, now. That is why I was fading. He is calling me," he added.

"You can leave me here with my daughter," Thérèse said. "We will not be angry with you. Go now, Ibrahim. Go and see your Djalal-o-din." She dimpled at him as he lifted his hand in farewell, and vanished.

Thérèse shook her head. "It is better for him to leave now. It would be too hard for him to see you go back," she told Maríana.

"Then I can go back?" See Richard again?

Thérèse nodded. "I think so, but I must take you to someone first." She held Maríana's hands, drew her up where they floated in a lazy circle. Thérèse pulled her close at first, then held her at arm's length, looking into her face. "You do look like Louis-Philippe," she said, her voice wistful. "Maríana."

"Yes, Mama."

Thérèse hesitated. "I want you to know that Ibrahim and I will always be as close to you as your next breath. But I also want you to remember that there is a cost for all of this, for what we can do. We may not be able to see everything, but we can trust in the final result." She raised her arms in a graceful circle over her head.

MARÍANA swirled through a great distance. The changing landscape that had entranced her disappeared. She thought her mother was still next

to her; yet when she blinked, she was in the living light again and
Thérèse was gone.

But she was not alone. A body began to form out of the gleaming,
breathing light. It never formed completely, a limb reached out, a smooth
face emerged. Yet she knew it was a man. Tendrils of compassion,
strands of peace flowed toward her. She caught at it with her hands,
heard the voice within its shimmer.

"Why did you come through the Door?"

"Someone called to me," she answered.

Amusement sent ripples through the light all around her. "I do not
remember calling to you," he said. "Wait for a moment." The light
trembled again and a small boy appeared, ran toward her. "Here is the
one who called you."

Maríana opened her arms to the child. "You look like Richard when
he was a boy," she said. "But your hair is lighter." She ran her fingers
through his fall of chestnut hair. He turned his face up to her and smiled,
his brown-amber eyes sparkling. "How could this be? Is all that we were
still here?" she asked, "Is this Richard when he was little?"

"Mama," the boy said.

"What?" Maríana cried. The boy faded into smoke, leaving only a
memory of warmth in her arms.

"Even now you carry him within you," the form said.

"So you will let me return."

"If we are to send you back, you must do something."

Maríana inclined her head. Here was the cost. "And that is?"

"The cauldron cannot stay in your valley. It must return to its
source."

"The cauldron?" She knew of no cauldron.

Now she could see the shape of a tall man, legs stretched and trunk
expanded. His mouth moved as he spoke to her.

"The chalice Iranzu gave to you," he said. "The cauldron of life."

"Take it to its source?" How, where? She would need a disguise.
And a guide.

"You need not carry it that far," the form said. "But you must take it
to your home."

The light around her shivered, streams slipped away from her
fingers. "My home?"

"To Reuilles-le-château. You must take the cauldron there, give it
to the one who will carry it to its source."

"They will kill me." She had only just escaped. Even a disguise
would not serve her there. "Please," she whispered. "Do not ask this of
me!" The boy. She would never have him, never hold her son in her
arms. They had already taken her daughter. "How can you ask me to do
this?"

"I know you are afraid, but this is what you must do. What has been set in motion there is unfinished." The form drew back, receded.

"And if I do not?" She was already dead, wasn't she? No one had ever survived crossing over. Well, maybe Jesus. But she was not the Son of God. She was not even a very good daughter. Hadn't she left her father there to face the Inquisition?

The form came forward again, reached out to her, caressed her cheek. His touch set waves that spread out around her. "Then you must stay here."

"I see." This was the price. It meant death either way.

"We cannot guarantee the outcome, but it must be done," he said.

Maríana wrapped her arms around her, rocked back and forth. This was it, then. Perhaps she could survive it, perhaps not. She had no other choice. She was dead right now. If she agreed to do this thing, she would see Richard again. One more time. She straightened her back, lifted her chin. "Tell me exactly what you want me to do," she said.

RICHARD pulled the helmet over his head. "Perfect!" His voice was muffled, but he could be heard. Gorka beamed at him as Marc helped him remove it.

"Lady's blessings!" Gorka said, gripping Richard's gloved hands.

"Right." Richard tucked the helmet under his arm and turned to Marc. "I am going now," he said to the younger man.

"I will walk with you," Marc told him. "I can carry the helmet."

Richard hesitated, then shrugged, the armor clanking faintly with his movement. He handed the helmet over to Marc. Then he strode out the back of the smithy, into the fields. Along the way, people stared at him, mouths hanging open. Three girls walked beside them smiling up at Richard and stroking his armor. Finally, they came to the outlands where there were few people, and Richard increased his pace to make up for the time they had lost talking to villagers along the way.

"I still say you look like a hero!" Marc's eyes were glowing. "Can I wear this after you bring our Maríana back?"

Richard laughed. "Why not?" he said. "But I must warn you, my friend. This is heavy." He lifted his arm with difficulty and then let it swing back into Marc's side so that he felt some of the weight. "And it is hot." Sweat ran down his face and his hair was sodden.

"Maybe." Marc rubbed his side where the armor had hit him. "But when the women see me in this... Ahhhh!" He lifted his hands in jubilation.

The river was up ahead. "This is where I leave you." Richard reached for the helmet.

Marc solemnly handed it to him. "Come back, eh?" he said softly.

Richard set his teeth and looked up the path. "I will."

He had to stop several times on the way up. "It is the weight of this armor," he told himself. Each step toward the cave became more difficult. Soon he felt as though he were wading through deep water. Or honey, perhaps; something sticky and thick. He tried to move his arm against the pressure he felt pushing in on his body. Not only the armor was hindering him. Something was trying to prevent his reaching the cave.

He could see the cave's entrance now. It was late afternoon, but light emanated from the cave in bursts of brightness. An angry humming poured out, the sound wasps make when their nests are disturbed. He squared his shoulders and made his way over to the entrance, glanced quickly inside. A straw mattress and a chest stood at the back, over to the right of the chamber, he could see the corner of an alcove. Part of the train of Maríana's gown spilled into the main part of the cave from the alcove. He started, then leaned away. It would not be good to chance more exposure to the green-gold light radiating from the stone. Merely breathing was already difficult. Placing the helmet on his head, he stepped over the threshold and entered the cave.

"I CHOOSE to go back," Maríana told the glowing form, "and I will do as you ask." The form raised what must have been a hand, then his entire shape disintegrated in pieces, sending a spiral of currents through the light.

Maríana spread her arms, prepared for her return. "You will be dizzy and could feel ill for a few moments," the form had told her, "but if you concentrate upon something from your world — a tree, a room, anything — the transition will be easier for you."

She closed her eyes and the image of Richard's face appeared. She could see his brown-amber eyes, his shock of black hair, the curve of his smile. A pressure on her elbow chased the image away. Her eyes flew open. Ibrahim was there. His eyes darted from her to the living light. "A moment, please! Grant me this?"

He seemed satisfied by whatever answer he received and turned to Maríana. "We don't have long," he said, "and I did not want you to go without telling you that I am sorry." There were tears in his eyes again.

"What could you possibly have to be sorry about?"

"It was foolish of me — I did not want you to know that I was ill," he said. "I knew that I was dying, and I was afraid to see your grief."

"I understand."

"There is more." His speech became faster. The light was changing color from the deep glowing gold to a brighter yellow. "I tried to help Ysabel. But the pain..." Now a burst of white-gold brilliance sent Maríana spinning. Yet she could still feel Ibrahim's hands, hear his voice. "Maríana," he said, "tell your father, tell Louis-Philippe! I never told him this. I did not stay at the château just for you, just to honor my promise to Thérèse."

Spirals and labyrinths took her. Her stomach constricted in protest; the light pulsed. Ibrahim's grasp was weakening. "Have Iranzu translate the last pages of the red book. They are for your father! Maríana." His voice was cut off as everything around her shattered.

RICHARD shuffled to the right. He guided his feet, looking down through the space where the helmet did not quite meet the breastplate of his armor. One foot, then the other. He had no plan beyond taking Maríana away from the stone, refused to contemplate failure, could not think of what he would do if she was already dead. His foot touched her gown and he bent toward what he could see, his armor groaning with the motion. He reached out and fumbled until he grasped something soft, something that gave way under his fingers. He thought it was her arm. Grabbing it firmly, he set his feet apart and pulled. The light became slightly brighter and the humming grew louder.

Taking as deep a breath as he could manage, he pulled again. Damn! He was panting now, should be able to pull her off the stone. Why couldn't he? Squeezing his eyes shut, he put his back into it, pulled with all his strength. "Please, God, Goddess! Jesus and all the saints! Help me!"

Light flashed out in a brilliant arc. Whatever was holding Maríana released her. He fell backward into the cave, Maríana in his arms.

DARK NOW. No more flashing light, no more angry buzzing. Richard lay where he had fallen. How much time had passed since he pulled Maríana off the stone? He frantically pulled his gloves off.

His fingers found her hair, and he felt for the pulse in her neck. Not there. He took in a deep breath, felt again, this time following the curve of her jaw down to where her pulse should tremble in her neck. Still nothing. She felt cold. He grabbed one of her hands, began to chafe it.

No, no, no! She could not be dead. He blinked the moisture out of his eyes. "Jesus, Mary, Joseph, Juanandi, Allah," The moist warmth of his breath hit the cold metal of the helmet, curled back to his face. "Please." A shudder. Was that him? How could he shudder, encased in metal? Now Maríana's hand flopped across his chest. He could feel the push and sway of her motion. Thank you.

He tried to sit up, but something deadly had taken hold of his limbs and he could not move. "Maríana," he said, shaking her gently. "Maríana, we must get out of here and I cannot do this alone. I need your help."

Still no response. But she was breathing. Her mouth must be by his hand, warm streams flowed across his palm. Nothing had ever felt better.

He shook her again and tried to rise.

SHE WAS IN a dark space, lying on a hard surface. The cauldron was in her hand, her fingers locked around it. How had it gotten there? She had placed it beside the stone.

The surface she was lying upon, heaved. She could hear dampened sounds coming from beneath her.

She turned, ran her hands over something cold and slick. Metal? The blurred noises increased. She could see the outline of a man now, lying on his back on the floor. "Armor!" she exclaimed, then grasped the arms that were waving. She pulled the man to a sitting position and helped him remove the helmet.

"Maríana." His dark hair was plastered to his head. His voice shook, but its rich timbre filled the cave. "Thank God. We must get out of here before the stone awakens again." He struggled to get up.

"Richard!" She took his face in her hands, pressed her lips against his. "But how?"

Never mind. He was right. They must leave the cave. "Let's take off your armor first," she said. The dizziness the form had warned her about was washing over her now. "I cannot help you with all that armor weighing you down."

She helped him pry the metal plates off, and crawl out of the arm and leg coverings. Then, she drew his arm over her shoulder and hobbled out of the cave with him. He slid to the ground.

After a moment, Richard had revived enough to crawl back in the cave and dragged the armor out, piece by piece. "I promised Marc he could wear it," he said, collapsing next to her.

"Are we safe this close?" He looked anxiously at the mouth of the cave.

"We will have to be," she said. "I can go no farther." She curled up beside him and rested her head on his outstretched arm.

Chapter 38

JEAN BECIER extended his arms over his head and rolled onto his side in the bed. Voices of his guards below made a pleasant rumble and the fragrance of fresh-baked bread teased his nose. He yawned and rubbed at his eyes. Ysabel was nearly finished. He could get no more out of her. His last session with the thumb screw had sent blood pumping in a bright ribbon from her hand.

His first-in-command, Pierre, had bound her thumb in a tight dressing, but she was so pale Jean was sure she would not last more than two or three days. Before her hand had spurted so much blood, Ysabel had given him much to think on.

Jean dressed and climbed down the stairs to the guard room. Three of his men were there. One of them offered him some bread. He took a chunk of the warm bread, thoughtfully chewed upon it.

"Did you know," Jean asked them, "that the widow Geneviéve was married to a Cathar?" He looked around at the blank expressions and frowned. Weren't these idiots aware of anything? "Her dead husband was a heretic," he continued, and was pleased to see the surprise and anger on their faces now. "Oh yes," he said, chewing his bread with great enjoyment. "The de Reuilles family has many secrets."

Jean turned to Pierre. "We must bring Geneviéve in for questioning," he said. Geneviéve was fat. In his experience, fat women lasted a long time. And they suffered so beautifully, begged so piteously.

"We do not have orders to look for Cathars here."

Jean studied Pierre through slitted eyes. The man was becoming surly. After he bound Ysabel's hand, Pierre had reminded Jean that des Arcis had only ordered Jean to keep the women in the dungeon, not to torture them. And after Utarilla died, Pierre had insisted on a proper burial for her body.

Pierre had not gotten either of his requests. Jean had told him des Arcis merely said the women were not to be burned. And Jean refused to give a Christian burial to a witch. The old woman's body still lay in her cell. No, Jean was master here. They must do as he wished. He tore off another chunk of bread.

"There may be resistance, since she is the sister of the baron, and the people like her more than they do Ysabel. Perhaps you believe your men cannot take Geneviéve?" Jean raised his brow, let the last words slide into a sneer.

Pierre just sat regarding him for a long moment, eyes shadowed, face unreadable. Really! At the next assignment, Jean would ask for someone else as first in command. Indeed. When this was finished, Reuilles-le-château would be his. Baron Becier. Jean popped a piece of bread into his mouth, then nearly spit it out. Why not take Louis-Philippe, too? Surely his messenger was nearly to Carcasonne by now. Durand's approval was a mere formality.

"My men can take anyone," Pierre finally said. "But if we do, we must be prepared to hold the tower against de Reuilles' men." His eyes held Jean's. "Are you prepared to withstand a siege?"

"It would not be for long." The words tumbled out too quickly. Jean steadied his breath, said, "My man must have reached Durand by now." The men were worried, some even bit their lips. Pox! "Durand will send a company to take the château when he sees my message." And he would, wouldn't he?

Pierre kept chewing the bread. Would the blasted man keep him waiting? "Well?" Jean held his hands on the table. If he lifted them, they would shake. That would not do at all.

"We can take anyone." Pierre brushed crumbs off his hands.

"Excellent!" Jean jumped up from the table. "This is what we will do..."

RICHARD stood looking out the door, his back rigid. Maríana sat upon the bed, the chalice — the cauldron — between her hands. "I have no choice," she said, as she had been saying throughout the night.

Richard crossed his arms. "You are mad."

Maríana cradled the cauldron next to her belly, but there was no warmth in it for her now. She glanced at the tossed blankets, ran a hand across the surface of the bed. Even the bed was cold, though when they returned from the cave, it had burned with their desperate need to join, and join again, to crawl inside each other, to feel life beating in ancient rhythm within them and between them. She looked up at Richard, standing in stiff accusation in the doorway. He had stood there since she told him she must return to Reuilles-le-château.

"I have no choice," she said.

"No choice?" He whirled around, fists held in tight knots at his side. His eyes had gone silvery with rage. "You mean the glowing light man that told you to do this said you had no choice? Let me tell you something, Maríana. It was I who got you off the stone, me!" His fist thumped against his chest. "I saw no glowing light man there. It was I who saved you. No one else! Iranzu and Adelie-all of the people here-they would have left you up there to die."

His voice trailed off. There was something he was not saying, Maríana thought.

He continued, "I have seen some strange things here, yes. I know you can do things that are beyond anything I have ever seen, but I will not accept this!" He turned away again, hid his eyes from her. "You are not going back to the château."

"This is what I must do. This is why he let me return."

Richard's shoulders lifted, then deflated in a sigh. He turned toward her. "If all he asked is that this thing go back to Reuilles-le-château," his voice softened, "then let me take it back. I would be safer. They are not looking for me."

"You do not know this."

"No. But I refuse to let you go." His eyes went silver again. "Are you sure this is the only reason you want to go back there?"

"Do you think I want to do this?" She grabbed his arm, allowed the terror that lived in her to surface, to show on her face. "I do not want to go. But I must."

He placed his hand over hers; his eyes wavered. Some struggle shook him. He opened and closed his mouth several times; the line between his brow deepened. Then he drew in his breath, a long, shuddering inhalation. He pried her fingers from his arm, stood back.

"No," he said. "I gave up everything to come here with you, my family, my lands, my entire life. I can never go back to what I was before. And you are asking me," his voice broke, eyes squeezed shut for a moment, "you are asking me to watch you throw your life away for this?" He pointed to the cauldron. His face had stilled, eyes now remote. "I suppose Iranzu and Adelie agree to this?"

"They do not like it, but yes." She looked away from his face. Richard had always been open to her. To see his shuttered eyes hurt more than what she must face.

"And Leila?"

"She will never forgive me," she whispered, then lifted her head, forced her eyes to meet his. "But she understands."

Richard looked away. When he turned back, his eyes were once again distant. "I will not accept this." He turned and walked out the door.

MARÍANA sat huddled on the floor of the stone hut. Marc had come in and taken one long look at her, then dropped the large pack he carried and sat down beside her. He had said nothing, just sat next to her in silence. "What is that you have?" she asked.

Marc pulled the pack over to her. "I brought these for you. You could not hear me in your mind just now." His last words were desolate.

"No. Iranzu told me my powers may come back in time. His mother always lost her abilities for a time after she entered the stone."

He looked away, then gestured toward the pack which contained ropes, blankets, and food. "There are some things from Leila, too. Grandfather said we will need them."

"*We* will need them?"

"I am going with you." When she opened her mouth to protest, he quickly continued, "Only as far as the winter house — about a half-day's march from the château."

"Adelie will allow this?"

"Grandfather told her I must guide you." Marc's voice trailed off as she stared at him. "They do not know me, but Grandfather is well known. It is safer."

"Very well."

He took her hands. "What has happened to Richard? He ran past me as if he did not even know me."

"What do you think is wrong?" She squeezed his fingers.

"Maríana, this is hard for him. He does not know the things that we know. Please give him some time."

"I have no time to give him, Marc. We must go." She waited for him to precede her out the door.

The path wound south and started climbing. "This is a different way from the track we took to enter the valley. The bell forest is on the other side." Maríana pointed back toward the village.

"This is our usual path to the outside," Marc said, then he bit off an exclamation.

Maríana stopped, cried out, "Richard!"

Richard stood at the top of the rise they were climbing. He had his pack at his side, some rope wound around his shoulder. Maríana moved toward him, but he spoke to Marc. "I am coming with you," he said.

Marc nodded and climbed up to where Richard waited. The two of them walked on.

Maríana stood where she had been when she saw Richard. She waited until the joy, and then despair, had dwindled into a dull ache inside her. Then she continued up the rise behind them.

Chapter 39

MARÍANA could never seem to get warm anymore. She sat by the fire, her mantle pulled tightly around her shoulders, and studied Richard. His body was too rigid for someone who was asleep. She had not slept at all. Had Richard just awakened or had he been awake all night, too? He was turned away from her so she could not see his eyes.

During the entire journey, Richard refused to — could not — look at Maríana. But whenever she stumbled, his hand was always there to steady her. Whenever they approached a stretch of rough ground, he always moved to hold her arm. Her body sang at his touch, then shivered when he pulled away yet again.

Maríana felt the loss of him, a sharp ache that traveled through her limbs. She considered telling him about the child she carried, the little boy she had seen on the other side of the Door. But she could not. She cradled her head in her arms. If he knew about the baby, he would surely tie her up, imprison her to keep her from doing what she must do.

Richard stretched his arms and then hugged his body, trying to warm himself. They would not survive this journey. The Inquisition would kill them both; he was sure of this. He wanted to tell Maríana how much he loved her. But each time he resolved to tell her, an image of Henri de Bauçais appeared in his troubled mind.

Richard had seen Henri with Maríana in the great hall, before Maríana fled to his chamber in the tower that night, so many months ago.

The invitation to her wedding had caught him in Bourdeilles. He remembered this clearly. Beatrice had given it to him. She had said, "Oh, a wedding invitation from Reuilles-le-château! Maríana de Reuilles. Didn't you squire for her father?"

The next thing he knew, he was on his horse, his pack thrown across the saddle, harp bouncing against the horse's flanks. Beatrice and her family were there, he was sure. He seemed to remember her eyes were swollen and her father had shouted at him. But he had not stopped.

He had ridden day and night, until he reached Reuilles-le-château. If this was a match Johanna had made, perhaps he could convince her to break it. He wanted to see for himself. But he did not want Maríana to see him. If she really loved this Bauçais, then Richard would leave before she knew he was there.

So he had stood at the back of the great hall while Henri helped Maríana down the stairs. Bauçais had stayed at her side as they made their way along the family table, her hand tucked in his elbow. Protective and possessive, this man. Henri had murmured something, his voice a distant rumble. Richard had drawn in his breath. Henri's eyes rested upon Maríana, hot and filled with longing. A love match for Bauçais, then. But was it a love match for Maríana? Richard had not given up hope, not then.

Two things had finally driven Richard from the hall that night. He remembered Jean-Pierre speaking of Maríana. Something about Maríana carrying a burden, something about Bauçais not wanting to wait. Richard had turned to his friend, ready to hush him, when he had seen Maríana lift her face to Henri. A tender smile played over her lips. Henri bent toward her. Then the meaning of Jean-Pierre's words had broken through the shell that had encased Richard since he received the invitation.

Richard remembered Jean-Pierre turning to him, asking him if he was drunk, saying he was so pale that someone might come and sew him up in a shroud. Richard had not answered his friend. He had pushed past the crowd of guests, through the door and into the frigid night. He could never remember how he had gotten back to the room in the donjon. Maríana's old chamber. He had sat there unmoving on the bed until Jean-Pierre came in and told him he was going to visit one of the kitchen maids. By that time a numbness had seized Richard. He had undressed and slipped into the bed. Maríana was to have the child of Henri de Bauçais.

Too late.

But she had come to him, hadn't she? That night. She had told him she was leaving the château. But she had not known that Richard was there in the donjon. She was not coming to him at all; she had only come for the warm clothes that Alys had stored. Maríana had fled from the Inquisition.

Why was she going back there now? To return the chalice? No one would risk his life for a cup. The thoughts that had been torturing him all night whirled around and around in his head. All he could see was Maríana running into Henri's arms.

Marc shook Richard's shoulder. "We will eat now, then we must go on," he said.

LOUIS-PHILIPPE looked up from the papers he was studying. The soldier who stood before him was sweating profusely, the red silk of his tunic sticking to his chest. "B-Baron," the soldier stammered. "Brother Becier is asking that you come and witness the questioning of the baroness." He licked his lips and his eyes darted around the great hall.

Louis-Philippe frowned. "He has not asked for this before." What had happened?

The man cleared his throat, lowered his voice. "He has her on the rack."

Louis-Philippe watched his fingers grow white as he clutched a quill in his grasp. He jumped when the quill snapped. What game did Becier play now? He rose to his feet. Guillaume strode over to where he stood.

"Baron?" Guillaume said. "What has happened?"

"I want you to remain here," Louis-Philippe told Guillaume. "I will handle this." It might be nothing at all. Hadn't des Arcis told Jean he could not burn the two women? Jean was a worm, nothing more. He would not go against the orders of his superior.

Louis-Philippe motioned for Jean's soldier to precede him and followed them to the door. This would be the first time he had been inside the donjon since Jean had taken it. He glanced up at the ramparts, saw two of Jean's men peering down at him. His feet slowed. A stake and kindling stood just outside on the stones of the inner bailey next to the donjon. When had this happened? It had not been there this morning. Perhaps he should tell Guillaume where he was going first.

"We must hurry," the man grabbed his arm as the massive door opened, and pulled him inside.

The donjon's door shut behind Louis-Philippe. His eyes adjusted slowly to the dim light within. Jean Becier was there, flanked by four of the Inquisition's soldiers.

"Take him," Jean said, and two more of Jean's men came at Louis-Philippe from behind, grabbing his arms as the soldiers surrounding Jean moved forward with ropes, swiftly wound them around him.

"Jean!" Louis-Philippe shouted. "What are you doing? My men will flatten you!"

"I think not, Baron," Becier purred. "Remember I own the donjon. Soon I will own all of Reuilles-le-château." His eyes assessed Louis-Philippe's form, lingering upon his groin. "I sent a man to Durand with a request to take you."

"You do not wait for his reply?" Louis-Philippe relaxed his arms. How many steps to the door? Could he make it before one of them took him down?

"I need not wait." Jean moved closer. "You see, Ysabel told me," his voice dropped to a whisper, "about you and Ibrahim the sodomite."

Louis-Philippe bared his teeth and lunged; Jean jumped back before the baron could bite off his ear. "Now, now, Baron." Jean's eyes sparkled.

"Take the baron to the torture chamber." Jean waved his hand at his men. "When you have him secured to the rack," he turned to his first-in-command, "send the others out for Geneviéve, and take the two women in the dungeon to the pyre."

"No!" Louis-Philippe cried out as the men dragged him toward the dungeon.

"No?" Jean smiled and hugged his body. "Tie the women to the stake and burn them," he commanded his men.

JOHANNA looked up from her needlework. Two of the Inquisition's soldiers stood before her daughter. "I will take care of this, daughter," she said.

The two men shook their heads. "We are only here for Geneviéve," one said.

Johanna's heart skipped. They were far from Louis-Philippe and their own soldiers in the great hall. "But I am her mother," she argued. "At least let me go with her."

The soldiers looked at each other for a moment. Then one shoved Johanna down onto the floor, while the other clamped his hand over Geneviéve's mouth and pulled her to the door.

"Through the back halls," the first soldier whispered to the one who held Geneviéve. "Jean has had our men clear the back way, but we must hurry." He looked down to where Johanna lay crumpled on the floor. She could feel his eyes upon her, hear his words clearly. In fact, everything was very clear. The light seemed to be deepening, turning golden.

"Is she dead?" the man who held Geneviéve asked, then yelped. Johanna fought to stifle her giggle. Her daughter had bitten him! Johanna had never taught Geneviéve to do such things, but bravo, Geneviéve! Johanna could not seem to move, but saw the first soldier take a sash and pull the other's hand away from Geneviéve's mouth. Then he wound the sash tightly around her daughter's head, stifling her screams and gagging her.

"Who can say?" the first spoke again, prodding Johanna's still form with his foot. She could not even feel it, but she could see everything. It was most extraordinary. The man shrugged and motioned for the other to precede him out the door.

Light surrounded her. She seemed to lift up into it, bathe in its splendor. The two soldiers dragged Geneviéve down the halls, through the empty kitchens and out the back door. They encountered some château servants on their way to the donjon, but beyond a few gasps and puzzled exclamations, no one accosted them. Johanna paused in surprise. Where was Louis-Philippe? And how could she see these things? The answer seemed to elude her; she followed them to the donjon.

Jean had been busy. The old woman Utarilla was tied to a stake, body limp, head hanging down on her chest. Soldiers were tying Ysabel beside her. Johanna moved closer. Ysabel was gagged and her terrified eyes bulged. A bloody rag covered her right hand. Johanna tried to speak, to give her some comfort, but no sound would come out of her mouth. People streamed out of the stables and the palais, watching.

The two men dragged Geneviéve over the donjon's threshold. Shouts sounded from the palais. Good! Louis-Philippe would come. But one man yelled "Now!" and the men who had tied Ysabel and Utarilla to the stake dropped their torches into the kindling. They all retreated inside the donjon and pulled the door shut. Johanna heard the hollow thump of arrows hitting the outside of the door.

She should help, shouldn't she? It was her daughter in there. She looked around her at the men and women pouring out of the palais. But no one could see her. A flood of white gold burned, had she gotten too close to the pyre? But the space between the donjon and the palais fled by her in a dizzying rush. When she opened her eyes, she was on the floor in Geneviéve's chamber, looking at the pool of blood widen around her face, feeling her limbs slowly freeze.

"FASTEN IT!" Jean screamed. "Archers! To your posts. Let no one through!" The men clattered up the stairs, their bows tucked under their arms.

Jean climbed the stairs to the ramparts, rubbing his hands together. He could see his men at the edges, raining arrows down on Louis-Philippe's men below. "Have they been able to put out the fires?" he asked Pierre.

"Not that I can see," Pierre replied. "And if they do, it is already too late." He aimed and fired again.

Jean shivered. "Excellent," he said. He had been denied witnessing the burnings, but he had Baron Louis-Philippe de Reuilles in his torture chamber. The baron's own torture chamber. "De Reuilles, the sodomite," he breathed.

Pierre had everything else well in hand. Barrels of oil simmered over roaring fires, pitch for burning arrows smoked on the ramparts. Pierre was a soldier. He knew his job, if not his place.

Jean climbed back down the stairs and continued on to the dungeon. He glanced to the right. Geneviéve was there, already secure in her cell. The cell on the left was empty now. No more Ysabel. He lifted the door into the torture chamber.

"Oh, Louis-Philippe," Jean whispered. "We will have such fun!"

Chapter 40

IT SHOULD have been an easy climb. The sun had only peeked over the horizon when Maríana came to the cliff just above what Marc called the "winter house," where people from his valley would break their journey. Marc had fixed a rope to a sturdy tree, had Maríana and Richard tie themselves to each other so they could safely make their way down.

Richard was below her, almost to the bottom of the cliff. He had a distance of nearly the height of the donjon of Reuilles-le-château left to go. It was a sheer drop. She saw him look down, then he pulled his body out from the cliff and put his full weight on the rope.

One moment Richard was hanging onto the rope with his feet planted firmly against the side of the cliff. The next, he was plummeting down. She saw him drop, hit the ground and roll. His right leg snapped and whipped out at an angle just below his knee.

Maríana was already sliding recklessly down when Richard's scream reached her ears. He rolled over and grabbed his knee. She reached the place where his rope had broken, shouted to Marc, "Let out more rope," and waited while the boy gave her enough to climb down.

She hit the ground and raced to where Richard lay, still holding his knee, his knuckles white and his breath whistling through his teeth. Marc went to Richard's head and held his shoulders while Maríana slid her mantle under his injured leg. Richard's face was so pale that Maríana was sure he would faint any moment.

He looked at Marc and said, "I was not careful." He stopped, caught a breath. "It was not your fault."

"Keep him still," Maríana said, one hand underneath Richard's thigh just above the knee, the other poised to catch his broken calf.

Marc told Richard, "You will need to let go of your knee. We must have your leg flat, so that we can set it."

Richard gave a quick nod. Filling his lungs, he released his knee all at once, hissed through clenched teeth when Maríana took his injured calf and settled it on top of her mantle.

"It has not broken the skin," Maríana said, holding her hands inches above the break. At least she thought it had not. Her healing sense seemed to have left her, also. But there was no blood that she could see. "If we can set it, we should be able to move him to the winter house."

"Set it, then," Richard said through his teeth, eyes focused on the morning sky.

Marc scoured the brush for branches they could use as splints.

"Richard, I am not strong enough to set your leg by myself and Marc does not know how to do it well enough to ensure that your leg will grow back together straight," Maríana said. "To do this right, we will need someone to hold you still while we set your leg."

"I can hold still while you do it," he said, his body rigid, his lips pale. "What do you think I am, anyway? I am a knight." He shuddered. "I have broken bones before."

Maríana studied her hands in her lap. "Yes, you have." But they did not have Ibrahim to set it this time. "And you know that no one could hold completely still."

"But, what else can we do?" he whispered.

"There is another way," she said. "One of us could go into your mind to make you sleep..."

"No! You stay out of my mind!" His eyes met hers in a searing flash.

Maríana crumpled, bent around the hot flare in her belly. Then she drew herself up. He was hurt. Her feelings did not matter. If she did not survive her journey to the château, at least she would leave him with a straight limb. "I cannot go into your mind," she whispered.

"What?"

"I have lost the gift."

Puzzlement fought with pain, then his eyes widened. "You mean you are going back there with nothing to protect you?" His voice caught. "Nothing at all?"

She turned away, ran to Marc. "Marc," she said, looking back at Richard. He was struggling to sit, "can you force yourself into his mind?" Richard fell to the ground again, a low groan slid past his teeth.

"We are not supposed to..." he started, but after a glance at Richard, he strode over to where Richard struggled, hands held out before him.

Richard stopped moving, but his eyes were still open. Maríana watched Marc move around to Richard's head, then she rose slowly and picked up the branches Marc had gathered, using her knife to slice off the twigs and peel the bark. While she worked she stole glances at Marc as he smoothed the hair back from Richard's forehead. Richard's hands unclenched, then fell to his side. His lids closed over his eyes and his mouth fell open.

Maríana brought the splints she had carved over to where Marc sat with Richard. Marc's hair was damp and his hands were shaking. "Our knight has much pain held deep inside him," Marc said, getting up off his knees and stumbling over to where Maríana was measuring rope for the splints. "This pain is hurting him far more than his leg. It makes him say and do crazy things. I sent him into a dream for a long time." He touched Maríana's arm. "He should not wake until it is quite dark."

"As long as it keeps him still. We will only need a moment to set his leg." Maríana had finished measuring, and was now carefully arranging her mantle beneath his injured leg. His leg had swollen, pressed out against his breeches. Glancing up at Richard's face, she took her knife and split his breeches all the way to his groin. Beyond a short grunt, Richard did not react.

"We will need some time to get him settled in the winter house, but we must have even longer than that." Marc was looking at her. It was difficult to meet his eyes.

"Are you angry at me, too?" She peeled the cloth away from Richard's leg. The break was clean; it had not come through the skin.

"No. I will need time to convince him that it would be folly for him to try to crawl after you." Marc raised his eyes to her face. "You must have enough of a lead."

Maríana took Marc's hands in hers, raised them to her lips. "How can I thank you?" she whispered.

A ghost of his usual broad smile flitted across Marc's face. "Just come back, Maríana. He will be impossible if you do not."

"I will do my best, Marc," she said.

After they had set Richard's leg, Maríana wrapped it in her mantle to cushion it. Marc helped her tie the splints firmly to the leg, from the knee to the ankle. When they set his leg, Richard's arms had twitched, but he had remained unconscious. Marc had fashioned a travois out of larger branches he tied together, and the two dragged Richard to the winter house. They settled him in the one bed that was there and covered him with blankets.

"It is warm today, but the pain has drained his energy." Maríana tucked the blankets around Richard, kissed his forehead. "You will need to keep him warm and feed him only if he is hungry — do not make him eat."

Marc snorted. "As if I could make him do anything. It will be all I can do to keep him from following you." He drew his own mantle out of his pack. "You will need this."

Maríana sat gazing at Richard, holding the cauldron between her hands. She took the mantle from Marc and looked up at him. "Thank you, cousin," she said. "Keep him quiet." Tears stood out in her eyes. She dashed them away. Maríana de Reuilles does not cry. "Marc..."

"Yes, Maríana."

"If you feel anything from me that frightens you, anything at all, you must send out the call for your people to come and get you. Do not wait for me. Send out the call right away." She held his gaze with hers until she saw his reluctant agreement. Then she wound the mantle around her and opened her pack. "I will leave my pack here with you. There is willow bark and betony. Also the leaves of the purple flowers that Leila put in there. She said they are very strong, so be careful." She indicated the dose with her fingers, shaking a few of the leaves out into her palm. "This will keep him quiet and will send his pain away."

Marc's eyebrows raised. "Leila gave you some of those? She must have known." He bit his lips and looked at Richard, then at the leaves in her palm. "These will also cut him off from you. He will not be able to feel if anything happens to you..." His voice broke when he met her eyes.

"He has already cut himself off from me. I do not think Leila meant these for him. I knew this was a journey I was expected to make myself." Her voice trembled. "What has happened to him is my fault." She stood and went to the door.

Marc walked over to her and took her in his arms, holding her close. "You could not have kept him from coming with us," he said. "We will be here when you come back."

Could he feel the quiver that would not seem to stop? "Thank you, cousin," was all she said. Then she slipped out the door, started her final march to Reuilles-le-château.

Chapter 41

HENRI DREW back on the reins and shaded his eyes against the spear of sunlight that stabbed through oak and maple. They had made good time. He hoped to be back at the château by tomorrow morning at the latest. His horse fretted, then Henri heard pounding hooves sounded from around the bend, coming down the road.

One of Jean's soldiers rode toward him. He quickly urged his mount across the path to block the man's way, opening his mantle so the red silk and white cross would show.

The ploy worked. Jean's man pulled his horse to a stop. The horse was not even sweating. How long ago had the soldier left Reuilles-le-château?

"Are you on your way to the bishop?" Henri asked. "Where is Durand's livery?" The saddle was plain.

"I travel to Carcasonne." Jean's man lifted the reins. His horse pulled against the bit. "My first mount lamed. I got this one only this morning." He gestured toward the road. "I must be going."

So this man was late. Henri looked behind him where the road curved and disappeared into the forest. He had ridden ahead, leaving his men back at least half an hour's ride. Hiding his action with his mantle, he slipped his sword out of the scabbard and held it ready, shielding it with his body. He drew his horse back and smiled at the man, gestured for him to pass. Jean's man saluted Henri and urged his horse alongside him on the path.

Henri brought his sword around broadside, catching the man across the side of his head. The soldier plummeted to the ground beside his rearing horse.

"Sorry, soldier of Christ," Henri murmured as he bound and gagged the man. "I already did this to one of your compatriots, didn't I?" He touched the swelling lump on the man's head. The soldier had not come around yet, but would be furious when he did. "Someone should find you within a few days, eh? This road is well-traveled. You may be hungry by then, but otherwise unharmed." He stripped the saddle of the man's horse, sent it into the woods with a snap from his rope.

Henri slid his hand into the man's pouch for the message he was sure Jean had sent. His breath stilled when his fingers closed on it.

HENRI NODDED and smiled at his men when they rode past. He'd shredded the message written in Jean's tiny scribbling, which promised proof that Louis-Philippe was a sodomite.

No one at the château was safe anymore. Least of all Henri de Bauçais. Henri whistled through his teeth. He had burned all his bridges, would be a hunted man from now on; but he was finding this curiously enjoyable. The last of his men had ridden past and looked back at him in puzzlement.

"To Reuilles-le-château," Henri shouted, urging his horse to a gallop.

MARÍANA had to stop every few paces. She was shaking so hard that she could not stay on her feet. She kept stumbling, falling to the ground. She could hear shouts in the distance, and agonized screams. She knew Ibrahim's palace was near and that she would be at the château soon, if she could just keep walking. The shouting had ceased. Silence covered the mountain in a tattered shroud. She pushed off the ground again.

The palace was closed up, door bolted, windows shuttered. Maríana splashed her face at the fountain, then held her arms out in front of her, trying to will her hands to stop their endless shiver. Something was burning. The acrid odor floated on the wind. Using her teeth, she ripped off the left sleeve of her gown, dipped it in the water and tied it across her nose and mouth. There. Just a little farther.

The odor had weight. Its rancid breath wrung moisture from her skin. The walls of Reuilles-le-château finally reared in front of her. But no one paced the watchtower, no indigo and white standard crested the top. Where was the watch? Where were the guards? Maríana stumbled again, her feet caught on every stone that paved the open gate. This would not do. She needed a plan, needed to think, to do more than just trip and quiver. And she must find a place to hide the chalice. She slipped into the gardens and crept toward the pond. Silence commanded the château. Where there should be voices chattering, hooves stamping, there was nothing but a hungry void. Every sound she made was noted, swallowed, hoarded in some yawning chasm.

But the garden lay untouched. Flower beds drank in the sunlight. The manzanilla was ready for harvest. She touched the yellow-white blooms and her fingers came away bright with pollen. There was a new marker next to the rosemary. Maríana knelt before the tall stone. It was simple, just a square slab, crowned by a turban. A turban. She reached out, touched the elegant script that flowed across the surface. Arabic. *Ibrahim*. Had her father carved this?

She did not know how long she sat staring at the marker before a warmth against her left side bent her forward. The chalice. She took it out of the pouch on her belt. It would be safe here. She did not know who was to take it. Until she did, she must ensure its safety. Few would think to disturb a grave. She dug into the moist earth around the marker and buried the chalice. She bent her head. "Farewell, Ibrahim."

Then she wet the sash around her nose and mouth with water from the pond and made her way through the back of the gardens, using any cover she could find. As she came out by the stables, she saw the whole of the inner bailey. A smoldering pyre stood just outside the doors of the donjon; bodies were scattered all over the stones of the bailey. On the top of the donjon, the de Reuilles banner had been replaced with a red flag slashed by a white cross.

Who was strapped to the stake? She could not go closer to see. Two men with bows stood atop the ramparts of the donjon, looking down on the bailey. She crept down the side of the palais that faced away from the donjon. When she reached the door leading to the great hall, she stopped. She could not quit shivering. But this was what she must do; she could not stop now. She grasped the door to open it. Why was it bolted? She raised her hand and knocked.

"Who is there!" an angry voice inside challenged.

She took the sash off her face and pitched her voice so that she could be heard. "It is Maríana de Reuilles."

The door swung open and Arnaut stared blankly at her. She pushed him inside and scanned the interior, looking for her father and Johanna. "Where is my father?" she turned on Arnaut, her eyes impaling him.

"L-Lady Maríana," he stammered, then looked at her helplessly.

Alys came running toward her, face twisted in grief. "Ahhh, Maríana," she sobbed. "You should not have returned."

"Alys! Quickly, tell me what has happened." Now that she was actually there in the palais and the task she had been sent to complete had been set in motion, she found that her hands were steady and her mind clear.

"The Inquisitor and his soldiers have taken your father. They burned Ysabel and Utarilla and they took Geneviéve, too!" Alys wrung her hands. "Your grandmother is dead. They killed her when they came to take Geneviéve. And they killed my Jean-Claude!" She started to wail, shaking with the force of her tears. "He lies dead on the stones outside."

Bastards! They would not even hold their arrows so the de Reuilles could claim the bodies of their dead? Maríana sat holding Alys. She was dazed, yet a part of her was bathed in clarity. "What happened to the baby?" she asked.

"Baby?" Alys' face crumpled. "Oh, you mean Ysabel's baby? Your brother?"

"Brother..." Maríana sighed. "Where is he?"

"Jeanne has him." Alys' face twisted in anger. "Your father made sure he was safe from that devil over in the donjon. But now that the baron has been taken, what will become of us?"

"Enough!" Maríana shook Alys gently. "I want to see my

grandmother's body, Alys. Then there is something I must do."

Alys nodded. "We have her in her room."

Maríana climbed the stairs, watching upon the people huddled within the great hall. The younger knights argued about how they were going to free the baron. The rest of the people looked blank, as if the sun had suddenly refused to rise.

MARÍANA sat by Johanna in her grandmother's room. She did not know why, but she felt Johanna had answers for her, as if her grandmother was merely sleeping. "I have to try to help him," she whispered. "He is my father, and in some ways this is my fault."

She leaned over to kiss her grandmother's cheek, then stroked her hair. "I lost the baby, Grandmother." Her voice quavered, slipped into a sob. "I carry another now, but I do not believe we shall survive."

She was only here by the grace of God, or the Being who had let her return. He had promised her nothing. But she was a de Reuilles. Maybe the last de Reuilles. She would try to complete her task.

"I can use the cauldron to bargain for Father's life. Who can say who will be the one to take it from me? I was only told that I must return it here, give it to someone." If she must die, at least she might save her father... well, there was a small chance. She had no illusions about this. But whatever had sent her here would surely keep her alive long enough to complete her task. Johanna's body had already shrunk, her withered face appeared sunken and ancient. Maríana looked up as Jeanne entered the chamber holding a small bundle in her arms.

"Alys said you asked about Philippe," Jeanne said, placing the bundle in Maríana's arms.

Maríana bent toward the tiny sleeping face. "Philippe?" she asked.

"After his grandfather," Jeanne replied.

"Indeed." Maríana put her finger in the tiny hand, saw the features of Henri in the set of the chin and the shape of the eyebrows. She bent forward, nuzzled the soft skin of his cheek. Small fingers grasped her, milk bubbles blew out of the little mouth. Would the child she carried now ever be born? She handed the baby back to Jeanne.

"Jeanne, are my clothes still here?" she asked, rising.

"Of course! Everything in your room is as it was before you left! Henri would have it so."

"Indeed," Maríana said again. "I will need my very best gown, Jeanne."

IT WAS EARLY evening. The cool blue shadows had grown long, but golden sunlight still played over the stones of the bailey. Maríana walked toward the donjon, dressed in her dark gray gown of sendal silk. Across her arm, she carried the silk wrapping that had covered the cauldron. She paused over each still form she encountered on the ground before her, saying her farewells to the men who had given their lives in the attempt save her father. The archers above her held their bows ready, but did not loose their arrows.

As she came closer to the door, she forced herself to look upon the charred, twisted remains of the old woman from the village, and, finally, her enemy Ysabel. Ysabel's body was contorted, her hands curled into black claws, jaw hanging open. She had not died from the smoke.

Maríana raised her eyes to the thick oak door of the donjon, built and crafted hundreds of years before to withstand any force that may try to batter it down. She could see the scoring from the knights' attempt to gain entry by using the battering ram. Arnaut told her their rescue had failed when Jean ordered his soldiers to pour boiling oil onto the men below. Her father's seneschal, Guillaume, had died in this attempt. His burned body stretched just outside the door. She put her hand on his shoulder and said her farewell, then straightened her back and knocked on the door.

A low voice inside challenged her. For the second time that day she called out.

"It is Maríana de Reuilles."

Chapter 42

Kill them all; kill them all.
God will look after His Own.
Arnald-Amalric, Archbishop of Narbonne at the sacking of Béziers,
1209

JEAN DOWNED the ale. He wiped traces of foam from his lips and contemplated the glorious body stretched out on the rack. Though he had donned the thinnest robe he had, fingers of sweat trickled down from his temple. But the ale cooled the fire in his belly, and it satisfied.

Louis-Philippe had fainted again. It had taken a long time to get even a grunt out of the man, and Jean had gotten no information, but this body... Jean reached out and traced the smooth bulge of muscles that formed Louis-Philippe's arms, the swell of his chest. His breeches and his shirt were crumpled on the floor. Jean had wanted to see all of his glorious body.

The man would not bend or plea. When Jean had first moved the lever that pulled the leather straps attached to Louis-Philippe's wrists and ankles, the baron had laughed. "You cannot be serious!" he had scoffed. "You want to make me even taller?"

Well, Louis-Philippe was not laughing now. But he had only screamed once, when his left shoulder popped out of its socket. In a pique, Jean had yanked the lever to full force, giving de Reuilles a taste of the pain that was waiting for him. But since then, Louis-Philippe had stubbornly refused to make any sound at all. His eyes had quivered for a moment when Jean told him that his wife had accused him of sodomy with the "gardener," but his face became distant after that and he had kept his expression under rigid control.

Jean caressed the taut skin covering Louis-Philippe's ribs and shivered when he felt the puckered remains of a massive wound. Louis-Philippe had many such scars.

Jean wanted to break this man. But how? Louis-Philippe had given him nothing. Ysabel was dead; there was no one to make the accusations of sodomy. Jean should have gotten a written confession from her. Why hadn't he?

Because he had been certain Louis-Philippe would admit to it himself. Jean glanced again at the long legs, the splendid arms. He had not expected the baron's strength and determination. Most men would have given him anything he wanted by now, would have kissed his feet to stop the pain. But not this man. What would break him?

Jean stroked the juncture of Louis-Philippe's thighs, his groin, shivering when he touched the place where Louis-Philippe's manhood nestled. Glancing up at Louis-Philippe's face, he reached forward and gave a sharp squeeze. Air rushed into the Baron's lungs and his eyes flew open. Good. It was about time to get on with this. There was one more thing Jean wanted to try.

He climbed the steps and pounded on the trap door. When his man opened it, he said, "There is a leather bag on the table in my chamber." He turned to see Louis-Philippe, eyes open, body rigid. Good. He was listening. "Bring it to me" Jean added, "and send someone down to turn the baron on his stomach." Louis-Philippe's lips twitched, then stilled. Even better.

Jean held the leather bag in his hand, leaned over Louis-Philippe. "There is a way, Baron," he murmured, "to determine if a man is a sodomite." He unfolded the leather package and stroked the spikes inside the casing. "I have used this myself on boys in my abbey, to teach them to control their passions. I put it on Henri de Bauçais." Louis-Philippe's back jerked. Good. Let him think Henri was a sodomite, too. "Now, you shall have it."

Jean knelt and went underneath the rack. Reaching up, he fixed the restraint on Louis-Philippe and tied the belt to the slats of the rack. This would hold until he could get out and secure it around the baron's waist.

When Jean climbed out from under the rack, he looked at Louis-Philippe's face, then jumped away, his heart speeding. Hatred poured out of Louis-Philippe's eyes in a raw surge. Jean shivered, gave a shaky laugh. Louis-Philippe could do nothing to him. He moved to the rack to secure the belt. But he avoided Louis-Philippe's eyes.

"Now, Baron, we are ready." Jean removed his robe and mounted Louis-Philippe, caressing every part of the baron's helpless body. He could hear Louis-Philippe's teeth grinding. And the stifled catch in his breathing when Jean jostled his torn shoulder. Jean felt a brief stirring himself, yet he was not ready. This would not do.

Climbing down, he moved over to the table that held the thumb screw and the iron boot. There should be a rod here somewhere. The mere thought of impaling Louis-Philippe with the device sent a flash of heat through his loins.

He looked down. No, he would not need a rod. He had the implement between his legs.

The door. Someone was knocking on the door. Cursing, he left Louis-Philippe's body, jumping off the rack, grabbing his robe and throwing it around his shoulders. "What?" he shouted.

"We have someone from the château," he heard his guard say through the door. "I think you should see her."

Jean clenched his teeth and settled his robe about his body. "Very well," he said, then turned back. "I will not be long, my love."

He climbed the stairs, lifted the trap and saw a slight young woman with long auburn hair. Two of his men held her, but they seemed uncomfortable. Pierre stood behind them, holding a piece of silk in his hand. "Well?" Jean snapped, climbing the rest of the way to stand beside the woman.

"I am Maríana de Reuilles," the woman said. "I have come to bargain for my father."

"Are you?" His heart seemed to swell in his chest. "Are you truly?" No one else had been able to find Maríana, not even Henri. Now she was here and Jean would be the one to place her into Durand's hands. He breathed deeply, became aware his men watched him. "Put her in with her aunt," he said.

This would do it. He could become bishop some day. But he must be careful. Rome wanted this woman. He would let no harm come to her. Nothing that left too many marks, anyway. Durand would expect him to question her, wouldn't he? "Do not disturb me again," he ordered. He climbed back down into the torture chamber. The door shut behind him.

Ah, Louis-Philippe. The baron lay as he had left him, legs pried open. Well, Jean now had even more to break the man. "I told you I would not be long, Baron," he purred as he mounted Louis-Philippe. He felt Louis-Philippe's muscles stiffening, denying him entry. Try to block him, would he? Jean forced the length of himself into Louis-Philippe. His groin grew hotter at the baron's bitten off shout that rang along the walls.

"Oh, yes!" Jean cried. "Yes!" he hissed through his teeth, moving in and out freely.

Louis-Philippe was silent, but Jean could feel him tremble. If the baron was aroused, he would feel the bite of the spikes that encased him. As Henri had. Henri. It could be Henri here, underneath him. The ache in his loins grew; he could not stop the panting grunts that seemed to come from the root of his spine. What did it matter? He would burn this man, no one would ever know.

"And next," Jean whispered in Louis-Philippe's ear, then convulsed as his hot and aching loins exploded.

"Next, next." He pulled away from Louis-Philippe, slid over the edge of the rack, fell into a puddle on the floor. What was he about to tell the Baron? Ah, yes. Maríana. "Next, I will bring your daughter down here."

TWO MEN struggled to carry her father up the stairs from the torture chamber. One unlocked the door where Maríana and Geneviéve were held; then both men awkwardly shoved Louis-Philippe's unmoving form into the cell. Geneviéve crawled forward and took her brother's shoulders while Maríana grabbed his feet. They pulled him back to the pile of straw they had made.

Louis-Philippe started muttering. "Ibrahim, why don't we go to Roncesvalles. I hear they have a statue of the Black Madonna there." His eyes jerked behind his closed eyelids.

Maríana felt his forehead, his cheeks, his neck. The skin was clammy. "Draw my mantle over him."

They folded the mantle Marc had given her around Louis-Philippe's tall body as closely as they could. He had his shirt on, but no breeches.

Geneviéve's hands stilled. "What is this?" She moved the folds of Louis-Philippe's shirt to show a leather casing around his man's parts.

Maríana could barely see though the red haze that fogged her vision. Henri had told her of this, this device. No, he had not told her. She had taken the image from his mind. These animals. Worse than animals, much worse. They would seek to strangle the life force itself. She started when something wet dripped from her palms. Blood. She must have dug her nails in.

"See if you can get it off," she said. The God of Jesus and Mary would not condone this. Not the God that she had known. Ibrahim had said that there were many paths and all of them led to the same place. She watched while her aunt tugged at the straps. Then what was this? What place would this have in the church she known? Had she really known anything? She remembered saying her prayers, making her confession. But nothing had prepared her for this.

Geneviéve dropped her hands from the belt that attached it. "There is no fastener. It is tied in knots," she said, then tugged at the casing.

Louis-Philippe's eyes flew open. He caught both of Geneviéve's hands with his right hand. His left lay unmoving next by his side. "No, sister," a faint trace of amusement colored his voice, "there are spikes inside. Please do not disturb it."

Maríana reached for his left hand, stopped when he shook his head.

"The shoulder came apart."

Crimson spread before her eyes again. But she could not act on her rage. She could not draw a spiral that would send the donjon tumbling around their ears. "Barbarians!" Hot, salt tears flooded her eyes.

"Ah, girl," her father breathed. "So Jean did not lie to me. You really are here. When I heard you talking to Geneviéve, and when I saw you, I thought I was dreaming."

Maríana took his hand. "Yes — I mean, no. You are not dreaming." She blinked, felt the moist stream sliding down her cheeks. He must be in agony. But he just lay there looking at her. "Geneviéve and I can reset your shoulder."

He closed his eyes briefly. "So they can tear it out again?"

"It would ease you now, while you are here with us." She

uncovered his shoulder. "I do not think it is torn, just removed from its socket."

His right hand caught her arm. "You were safely away," he said. "Why did you return?"

"I did not want to, believe me." She stroked the hair from his forehead. "But I had to come. I really had no choice." She had died. They had let her come back, asked her to come here. Her father would not understand this, no more than Richard had. "There is something I must do."

"There is always a choice," he replied. "Ibrahim told me that."

"Even Ibrahim could be mistaken."

"What is happening out there? How long has it been since I was taken?" He turned to Geneviéve.

"They came for me right after you went over to the donjon yesterday," she said, placing her plump hand on his chest. "Mother tried to stop them, but she could not."

"What about my men?" His eyes gleamed in the dark. "What about Guillaume?" His voice dipped to a murmur. "He knows the other way into the donjon."

Geneviéve patted his arm. "I do not know."

"Maríana." His voice was barely a whisper. "Did you see Guillaume?"

She wanted to give him hope. How could she tell him what she had seen? But his eyes were a steady, blue green flame. If he could bear the pain of a shoulder torn from his body, he could bear this. "I saw Guillaume's body outside the door. They could not retrieve it — they told me they would bring the others in after night falls." She would not mention the red and black corpses still tied to the stake outside the door. She would not mention Johanna.

"What happened?" His eyes were blank.

"I am sorry, Father. Four men were killed trying to storm the donjon. Jean-Claude, Yves and Jean-Pierre, as well as Guillaume." She twisted the mantle in her fingers. "I came directly here after I spoke with Alys and Jeanne. I did not think to tell them of the other door." She had told no one what she planned to do. They would have stopped her.

Louis-Philippe let out a long sigh. "All those men gone." His eyes grew dark. "Except for you and I, Guillaume was the only one there who knew of the other door."

"There was no time for Mother to rouse your men when I was taken," Geneviéve said, wiping his forehead with the sleeve of her gown. Her lips stretched into a thin line. "Jean must have planned this carefully. Now, how badly are you hurt, beyond your shoulder?"

"I'll survive," a grim smile twisted his face. "He stretched me on the rack a bit and... did some other things." His gaze caught Maríana's, slid away. "But I am otherwise intact."

"Be still," Maríana motioned to her aunt and they turned him to his right side. "Hold his neck and chest with this hand, pin his hips with your leg." She positioned Geneviéve so Louis-Philippe was held still, immobilized. This should work. Geneviéve was heavy.

Maríana shut her eyes. Her mere touch could not heal now. But if there were enough strength in her arms, she could ease her father's pain. With her hands, she probed the joint that bulged out in an unnatural lump at the juncture of Louis-Philippe's shoulder. Ibrahim had taught her battlefield healing. Though he had never fought in any battle, he had taught her this.

Grasping Louis-Philippe's arm at the elbow, she felt for the proper balance, the correct angle. Shed pulled sharply, heard the swift intake of her father's breath, the hollow pop when the shoulder resettled, the long release of air from Louis-Philippe's throat. "You will not be able to use that arm for a while, but your strength will return. After a time." She smoothed the hair from his brow.

He lay looking up at her. His words surprised her. "What did you hope to achieve, coming here?"

"I came to barter for your lives."

"Whatever do you have to barter?" The gentle amusement was back. Ibrahim would have said something like this. Tears formed in her eyes again.

She wiped her eyes with the back of her hand. "You sound like Ibrahim."

"Do I?" he asked. "I miss him, too. But you have not answered me."

She took his hands. "I have knowledge of something they want. I know where it is. I will not tell them how to find it until they have let you go."

"And what is this thing they want?" He did not believe her, she could see that. She was looking upon the same shuttered mask that used to cloak his face when she was little.

"It came down from the fortress of Montsegur during the siege," she said. He would not understand the other pieces to this puzzle. Her mother's family had never seemed to interest him.

Geneviéve gasped. "Do you have it?" She grabbed Maríana's hands. "Is it safe?"

How did Geneviéve know of this thing? "What I have is a cup," she said, noting the spark that flared in her aunt's eyes. "I have been told it is the *cauldron of life*."

Her father's eyes widened. Her aunt's mouth dropped open. "I thought to trade it for you," Maríana said.

HENRI HALTED his men when the sun went down. He did not like to make them travel through the night in rough terrain, but he was restless and anxious when they stopped to camp.

Jean had moved so quickly. Henri paced before the fire, aware his men watched him uneasily. He needed to get back to see what was happening. His stomach roiled.

He reached inside his pouch and felt around for his wooden blocks. No more wood. He pulled out his carving knife and gripped it in his hand. "Maybe I should just discard you, or give you away," he said to the knife.

His men were watching him with alarm. "Henri is talking to that knife!" He heard their whispers, but could not summon the words to calm them.

THE SHAVEN priest snapped his fingers and two of his soldiers removed Maríana from the cell she shared with her father and aunt. She looked into her captors' faces. They would not meet her eyes.

Her father struggled to sit up. "Jean!" he shouted. "Take me!"

Maríana scrutinized the thin bald-headed priest before her. So this was Jean. She recognized the glittering eyes, the full lips. This was Henri's Jean.

Jean drew his lips back. "Ah, so soon? Later, perhaps." He made a gesture and his men pulled her into the torture chamber.

"Tie her to the chair." Jean stood back while the men wound ropes around her arms, her waist. They moved slowly. The chamber was not large, yet she heard the echo of their motion, the scrape of rope against flesh. The dungeon was damp; the walls were sweating. Despair lay in a thick coat across the floor.

She tried not to look at the table that stood against the far wall. Pieces of metal coated with blood were strewn across its surface.

Hands grabbed her hair, pulled her head around. She looked into the eyes of the bald priest, this Jean. "Maríana de Reuilles," he said. "Why did you flee?"

His men had already left. She was alone with him. Alone in this room that reeked of fear. "Why did you come back?" he was asking her.

There was something in his eyes. He wanted to hurt her, wanted it badly, but something was stopping him. "The bishop wants me unharmed," she said. She did not know this for sure; it might be a mistake to say it. The pits of his eyes darkened. He drew back.

"What is it, what is it?" He was muttering. "What are they after?"

She straightened in the chair. They had not told him what they sought? "You could have it for yourself," she said.

He moved in, the rank puff of his breath fouled her nostrils. "What is it?"

"First, you must let my father and aunt leave here," she said, when she saw the spark flare behind his eyes, adding, "alive and whole."

"You think I must do something?" He looked down his nose at her, then leaned in again. "No, you will tell me everything you know." He touched the ropes, but did not touch her skin.

He moved over to the table. "Tell me, Maríana de Reuilles," he approached her, carrying an iron box, a vise of some sort, "what was it like, having Henri de Bauçais between your thighs?"

She jumped. He placed the vise on the floor next to her left foot. He twisted the screw to open the vise, then wound a cloth around his hand before he touched her foot. "I want to know everything."

"You won't get anything from me this way." Was he afraid to touch her? No, that was not it. She saw the way his lip curled when he looked at her. She disgusted him.

Could she use this? Probably not. Jean knelt before her, his hands on the vise. Sweat spread in broad patches across the bodice of her gown, slipped down her thighs. "The Bishop will not like it if you hurt me."

"You think so?" His lips stretched in the parody of a smile. "You do not know Durand. But you will know me." He fit the vise over her foot and turned the screw. Once. Then another turn.

Two of her toes snapped. She heard the sound before the fire ran up her leg and made her gag. He was watching her face. She was sure she must have screamed, too. The sound still rang in her ears. He did not move now. One of his hands hovered over the screw. The other was pressed against his loins.

"You will tell me everything," he said.

HIS SQUIRE stood before him. "Baron de Bauçais," the boy said. "We know you want to get back to the château."

Henri nodded, his fingers playing over the hilt of his knife.

"We do not want to wait." The boy was watching his eyes. Did they all think he was mad? "So we were wondering if we could continue, go on to the château tonight." Here the boy made a gesture. It was a gesture Henri himself often made, a half shrug accompanied by a lifting of the left brow.

Henri leaned back. Robert had been his page first, then his squire, had been with him for years. Was this what would it be like to have a son? To have your own gestures cast back at you? "We must eat first, of course," the boy continued.

"Of course." Henri dampened his smile. Robert was so earnest, Henri did not want to show his amusement. It might belittle the boy. He tucked his knife into his belt, nestled it in the small pouch that rested there. "Very well," he said, rising and dusting off his breeches. "We shall ride out within the hour."

A COLD LIGHT shone on his face. Richard blinked, then turned his head. A boy sat next to a rough window, the shutters thrown wide open to the night. An owl hooted and the dark moistness of deep forest sent fetid and rank fragrance toward him. His mouth was filled with a bitter paste. When he moved his head, the room spun.   He tried to sit up, grunted in surprise as his hands pulled against ropes that bound him to the bed he lay upon. "What?" His right leg throbbed, but his left foot was on fire. He looked over to the window again. It was Marc who sat there, looking out into the darkness.

"Where is Maríana!" Richard struggled against his bonds again, stopped when the fire in his left foot crawled up his leg. "Why am I bound?" He strained, loosened the rope that held his left hand. "Marc!"

Marc turned toward him. The boy's face floated in the shadows, a pale skull with hollow eyes. "It is too late," he said. He turned back to the window.

"Marc! What is wrong?" He had broken his leg, hadn't he? They must have set it. It was splinted, and it looked straight. He remembered this pain, the deep fire-laced ache of a broken bone. It seemed duller than it should be, the paste in his mouth must be some plant Maríana had given him. But where was she?

His left foot went rigid. Something was crushing it. "Damn!" he cried, breath puffing through his teeth. "It was my right leg that broke, yes?" Marc turned to him, his large green eyes haunted.

"Yes, your right leg."

"Then why does my left foot hurt so much?"

Marc rose and came over to him. "You stubborn fool! You should have made your peace with her while you could," he said through his teeth. "You cut yourself off from her, but she is in your blood. You cannot shut out her pain." He held his hands over his ears. "Can't you hear her?"

Marc shivered, moved over to the window. "Maríana," he cried. "Leave your body, go away for a while! I cannot stand any more of this!" He slumped forward.

"Marc, what are you saying? Where is Maríana?" Richard worked stealthily at the knots.

"She was taken." Marc's voice was barely a whisper. "It started around sunset. They are torturing her." He turned around, stared in dismay at Richard standing before him. Richard swayed; the young man caught him and pushed back onto the bed. "I promised her I would see you safely back to the valley," he growled. "And that is what I will do. If I have to hit you over the head, I will."

Richard looked into the boy's eyes. Marc could not do this. The boy's face quivered. "I am going after her," Richard said. Using his arms, he heaved himself up off the bed, balanced on one leg. "Good splint." He turned to see the anguish in the boy's eyes. "I will need a staff." Marc lowered his head. "I could go get one myself," Richard patted the boy's shoulder, "but it would be faster if you got one for me." He looked away, gave Marc time to compose himself.

"I will cut one for you," Marc said.

Richard stood at the door of the wooden hut and watched Marc's gangling figure disappear into the forest. Maríana was not dead. She was not dead. The owl sent its call out across the treetops again, powerful wings beat in measured cadence. Not dead.

Chapter 43

MARÍANA was floating in darkness. A voice kept whispering, asking her questions. It grew louder, cracked and shattered. Somewhere someone screamed, then was silent. The silence pressed against her. Then, light — light that was all colors, and no color-drifted across her lids. She blinked. It was the singing light of the Door.

"Close your eyes, Mother," she heard a boy's voice say.

Maríana put her hands over her eyes, forced the lids down. "How can I see with no eyes, hear with no ears?" she sighed. "I have done as you asked. What eyes I have are closed now. I can no longer see the light."

"It will not be long," the boy's voice spoke again.

Shredded muscle and crushed bone sent their promise of agony to her now. No. She did not want this. But there was something she must do. Some task she must complete. The pain grew, cramped her belly. She fought against the bile that flooded her mouth.

"I know it hurts, Mother." The boy was speaking again. Why did he call her mother? "But you must go back. Your father needs you and Richard needs you." There was a short pause, then the voice continued, "I need you."

"Who are you?" Maríana asked. She did not want to go back. All she needed to do was open her eyes to the light and step into its welcoming beacon.

"I am to be your son. My name is Daniel," the boy whispered, then faded and disappeared.

Maríana opened her eyes briefly to see Jean's men around her. She closed her eyes again and shook when strong hands removed the vise from her foot. Someone lifted her. She held her sleeve against her mouth when someone grasped her foot. The pressure on it, the searing agony went on and on. Just when she had bitten all the way through the fabric of her sleeve, the pain stopped, slipped into a throbbing fire. But this, she could bear.

"Did you get what you were after from her?" The voice sounded northern. She opened her eyes again. It was the man who had taken the length of silk from her when she first entered the donjon. He was speaking to Jean, but his voice was nearly a sneer.

Maríana kept her eyes half-closed, glancing at the other men in the room. Something dangerous flared from their eyes. They were not looking at her. They were glaring at Jean. He was sweating. His robe was plastered to his skin. How long had she been in the torture chamber? Had she told him where the cup was?

"Never mind. This does not concern you." Jean waved his hands. "Just take her away." His shoulders were bent. Had she told him anything? He seemed to want to know about Henri. She remembered his questions, remembered telling him of her time with Henri, the feel of Henri's skin, the pressure of his thighs on her when he took her. When she told Jean that, a strangled growl had sounded in his throat. He had turned the screw three cruel twists. Blood had pumped in a scarlet river out of the vise, she remembered this. Mercifully, she had fainted.

The man who carried her held her gently. He climbed the stairs slowly, took her weight with his whole body, jostled her very little. Someone had carefully wrapped her foot; she could see the white cloth.

THE CELL DOOR creaked open. Louis-Philippe tried to crawl to where Jean's man was gently placing Maríana. Geneviéve held his arm, whispered, "Patience."

"Savages!" Louis-Philippe spit through his teeth when the man put her foot on the floor. Maríana knotted her fists and held them against her mouth. The man put a blanket over her. He had the length of silk that had covered the chalice tied around his arm.

When the men left, Louis-Philippe came to her and gripped her hands. "The iron boot," he said, tears filling in his eyes. "Ibrahim," he cried. "My daughter needs you now."

"Shhh." Geneviéve stilled his cries with her hand. "Let her remain unconscious."

"I am awake." Maríana looked up into her father's anguished face.

"Maríana," said Geneviéve, her voice steady, "we have nothing for you, no plants to take away your pain. Is there anything that we can do?"

"Talk to me." She could bear the pain. But she knew the foot was gone. It was crushed beyond all repair and would probably summon the green fever that would kill her. "Talk to me."

Louis-Philippe moved closer, settled her head in his lap. "I will stay with you. But you are an idiot, you know." His hand moved in her hair as he looked down at her. How many years had she wanted this, just to have her father know she was alive? "You should have stayed in your mother's valley." He stroked her forehead. "Now you will die."

"My mother survived worse than this. She only died when..."

"I know how she died," he said, his face smoothed of all expression. "Ibrahim told me he killed her before they could burn her." Maríana saw his chin, the way his throat was working. Yet all he said was, "Did you tell them where the cup is?"

"I don't know, I think not." I am sorry, Father. I cannot save us. It was foolish to think that I could." The fire in her foot pulsed. "Talk to me, please."

"What can I say?"

"Tell me about Ibrahim." Her teeth started to chatter. How much blood had she lost? "How long were you together?"

He seemed startled; she saw his eyes dart to the door of their cell. "We were not really together until years after your mother died." His voice was low; she had to strain to hear him.

"What?" Now it was her turn to be startled.

He shifted position, looked down at her. "Maríana, I left the château after you were born. Ibrahim and I did not join." He stopped, then continued, "It was four years after your mother died when we, when we..." His hand lifted, sketched an arc.

"But I thought..."

He shook his head. "You knew Ibrahim. Thérèse was his greatest love." Light from the single torch threw the planes of her father's face into a dance of shadows. "Thérèse wanted me to go away when you were born. I was happy to oblige. I was jealous, you see." He smoothed her hair. "I could not stand to see them together."

"See who together?" She pulled the blanket to her chin. Blood seeped from the bandage they had made. She could feel it pooling around her foot.

He was silent for a long moment. The rhythm of his breath shifted, grew shallow, then deepened again. "I would have thought he would tell you. Ibrahim and your mother were lovers. He often said he thought you could be his." His eyes closed. "I went away to Marseilles and stayed there for two years, but I was so lonely." The last was whispered. He would not look at her. "Many times I went out and tried to buy love from the young men who sold their bodies so that they could eat, so that they could live." His hand stilled. "It was not the same. Most of the time I just paid them to hold me so I could sleep." He opened his eyes now, looked down at her foot. "I wish Ibrahim was here now so that he could make your pain disappear!"

"Not even Ibrahim could do that," she said. "Father, you are telling me such things..." She reached up, touched his face.

"We are going to die, petite." He allowed her touch. "Ibrahim will be so angry with me. I have not kept you safe." His breath caught.

"Tell me more. Please."

At first, she thought he would not speak. But he continued, "I returned to the château after the two years had passed and asked Ibrahim to choose between us, between your mother and me. I wanted him to choose me, but he would not have me even then." He stroked her hair again. "I was mad with jealousy. Everywhere I turned I saw them together! Oh, they no longer shared the same bed as they had when I was gone, but they were always together in the gardens."

"What happened?"

"You mean, he did not tell you?" His hands froze, fingers tangled in her hair.

"Tell me what?"

He was silent for so long she thought he had decided to stop speaking altogether. Then his body shook with another long sigh, and he said, "I called the priests to come to the château. Called them to come for Thérèse."

"What?" She could hardly draw a breath, and shrank away from him. He lifted his hands, yet he did not let her slide off his lap.

"Maríana." Just her name, but spoken with such raw grief. She lifted her eyes to his face. He had not retreated. His face was naked, sorrowing.

"Tell me," she whispered.

"If I could not have what I wanted, then he would not, either." He leaned his head back again; she could not see his eyes. His voice was hard, bitter. "I did not name your mother as a witch, but that did not matter. The priests came and they told me they had heard of Ibrahim. He was a Saracen, yes? Well, at that time, they were looking for Saracens."

Now Geneviéve reached forward, grasped his shirt. "Brother," she said. "You do not have to do this."

Her father glanced at his sister. "I thought Ibrahim had told her."

"Ibrahim would not do such a thing." Geneviéve said.

Louis-Philippe closed his eyes. "No," he said. "I suppose not. He always pestered me to tell her. Ah, what does it matter?" He wiped at the wet tracks on Maríana's face. When had she started to cry?

"This will be my confession," he said. "I will not die unshriven."

"Father..."

He grabbed the fingers she held up, placed them against his lips.

"I had not expected them to want Ibrahim. And I thought Thérèse would leave, that she would run away when they came. But she stayed. She stayed." His voice grew faint; Maríana strained to listen. "I would not let them have my Ibrahim! Guillaume bound him and hid him in the tunnel. The priests were still there. They would have taken the château apart, stone by stone, to find him." He stopped speaking, but continued to stroke her hair. "Johanna had sent a message to the King, to ask for his help. But that would take time; I knew this." Maríana's father looked down at her. "So I gave them your mother."

She could not speak.

"I watched as they took Thérèse away. She was always stubborn!" Now the hint of a smile. "You are like her, I think. I begged her to recant her heresy and accept the cross, but she would not do this." His voice was growing ragged. He coughed. "Even Johanna could not convince her. They dragged your mother from the donjon in the middle of the night so that the town would not rise up against them."

His breath was catching in his throat now. "Oh, there were those who were afraid and those who sought to gain from the presence of the priests, but when it became known that they were really going to take her, that they would burn her, the people who had spoken against her changed their statements. She healed people in Reuilles-la-ville, you see." He looked down. "Much like you."

"And then?" She was surprised that her voice was so steady.

"My mother had Guillaume set Ibrahim free after Thérèse had been taken away." His lips twisted. "I started drinking after they took Thérèse and did not stop until I was nearly dead from it. My mother removed the wine from my room and cleaned me up. Then she told me what she had done, that Ibrahim had been set free. It was as much for our safety as it was for his. When the priests were through with your mother, they came back, looking for him."

Maríana could see his throat working, the steady clenching wave as he swallowed. "Ibrahim left without even saying good-bye. It was a year before he came back. He stood before me and told me that he wanted to kill me. I told him to go ahead, I would not stop him. But he had taken an oath, had promised your mother he would not harm me. I told him he already had hurt me more than anyone ever could. Since he could not have the satisfaction of killing me, I told him I would give him anything he wanted."

"Anything." She looked up at him. New lines marked his face, and the hair at his temples had turned white. "What did he want?"

"He wanted to study healing at Montpelier." Louis-Philippe's grimace was a shadow of the wide grin she remembered whenever he spoke of Ibrahim. "So I sent him there." He shook his head. "And he came back to me! Well, he came back as Jacques. A new name for a new person. A physician. I could not believe my eyes when I saw him. He could have gone anywhere, but he chose to come back here!" His eyes misted. "Well, you were here. He always loved you."

"Yes." Even death had not stopped him. Ibrahim had helped her escape. Now laughter trembled her throat. Here she was again. In the donjon.

"Is the pain worse?" His voice was sharp with alarm.

She looked up, saw her father's eyes search her face. "No. I was just remembering Ibrahim."

"I never stop remembering."

"What happened?"

"I sent him away to the palace I had built. I thought he would get lonely and come to me."

"Did he?"

"That very night." He stroked her forehead, smoothing the wrinkle pain had placed there. "He came to me and said that we were both to blame for what had happened, if he had not come to the château after I married Thérèse she might still be alive. So, he forgave me. He was lonely, too."

Silence now. And peace. The torch sputtered. Somewhere above angry voices warred. But the door to the dungeon remained shut. It would not always be so. They would return to inflict more pain. But the peace spread, settled over her.

Such a gift her father had given her, this gift of truth. They were to die, yes, but he had not needed to tell her this. Louis-Philippe de Reuilles did not fear death. Everyone knew that. She had known this all her life. Her father had gone to mass, but she did not believe he feared to die unshriven. Maríana looked up at his face, the proud, high brow, the shadow of whiskers along his cheeks. She had her own gift to give. "He loved you, Father."

Louis-Philippe jumped. "What?" He swallowed.

"It is true. I have his red book."

"Oh, that! I have seen that. Why do you say this about him? There is nothing in there that says anything like that." His voice cracked.

"It is in the back." She took his hand. "I am having Iranzu translate it. If we get out of here you must come to our valley." Now there were tears in her father's whiskers. "He did not stay at the château just for me, just for his promise to my mother."

Louis-Philippe took her hand and held it against his mouth. "Ibrahim," he whispered.

The door to the dungeon opened. Jean marched over to the bars of their cell. His robe no longer clung to his skin.

Louis-Philippe's hands tightened. "If he comes in here," he whispered, "I will try to take him."

Jean stood for a moment, watching them. His whole body trembled; Maríana could see his robe quivering.

"I have been speaking with my soldiers." His voice shook, too. "One of them was at Montsegur." He pointed at Maríana. "I know what it is you have, now. And you will give it to me!"

Chapter 44

THE SKY WAS still dark when he approached the gate. Henri held out his arm to stop his men. No guards here, at this hour? The gate was fully open. He hardly breathed as his men drew up behind him, their horses' hooves clattering upon the stone pavement under the arch. He held his arm up to signal for silence, and they all sat there on their steaming horses. No sounds, not even the scrabbling of fowl in their pens. He exhaled slowly, then turned back to his men.

"I will ride in," he whispered. "There may be an explanation for this, but I think it is best that we proceed with caution." He removed his mantle, his white silk cross glimmered in the starlight. If Jean's men had taken the château, this tunic might save his skin. He only hoped that Louis-Philippe's men would recognize him. An arrow in the chest, from either side, was not part of his plan. He urged his horse forward into the bailey.

The cloying, sticky scent of charred flesh assaulted him as he rode in. He knew the smell, but he could not believe this, that Jean would disobey des Arcis. His horse clattered to a stop in front of the donjon. He stared at two blackened forms hanging from a stake placed at the base of the steps.

"Who are you?" An angry exclamation sounded from above. Glancing up at the ramparts, Henri saw the red and white banner of the Inquisition and three of Jean's soldiers, their arrows aimed directly at his heart.

"I am the Baron of Bauçais," he answered, putting stern authority into his voice. "I have just come from Bishop Durand with orders to replace Jean Becier."

"Liar!" Henri heard the outraged retort and saw the arrow fly at the same time. He dropped to the far side of his mount when he saw the man's fingers release it, but the arrow caught his right arm below the shoulder as he slipped behind his horse. Hanging over the side, he urged his mount to a gallop. Two more arrows narrowly missed him as he sped toward the safety of the palais.

His men followed, galloping after him across the area of the bailey that was within shooting distance of the donjon. He held his breath again. Three arrows pierced two of the horses, one went down screaming, but the man on it rolled away, leaped to his feet and sprinted to the shelter of the palais. The other horse staggered, reared. "Give me cover!" Henri shouted, running toward the horse. It was Robert. The boy had done well, slipping over the far side of his steed. But the horse was in pain, Robert could not control it. Henri sped toward him, heard the whisper of his own men's arrows fly past him as he grabbed the bridle of Robert's horse, dragged the boy from the saddle. Tucking Robert under his arm, he dashed toward the palais. Another arrow struck his foot, glanced off the leather. He reached the wall that hid them from the tower, dropped Robert to the ground. "Are you all right, boy?" He saw Robert's shaky nod.

Henri turned, counted the men standing in front of the palais. All six of them made it. Cradling his arm, he nodded toward the door to the great hall. "I want three of you to stand close to the wall on the right side, and three on the left. Draw your swords." As the ring of metal against leather echoed in the bailey, Henri mounted the steps and raised his hand. "If I give this signal," he flexed his fingers, "go in swinging." He lifted his hand and knocked.

"Who is there?" It sounded like Arnaut.

"Henri de Bauçais," he answered. The door swung open at once, golden light from the hearth spilling out of the door and into the night.

"Baron de Bauçais! Thank God!" Then Arnaut fell silent when he saw the arrow in Henri's arm.

Henri set his teeth. "I could have been anyone claiming to be the Baron of Bauçais! You should have asked for proof before opening the door!"

Arnaut blanched. "Pardon!"

Henri waved at him. "Never mind." He moved through the door and into the palais, his men following behind. "Where is de Reuilles?"

His first-in-command, Marcel, pushed Henri into a chair, placed a cloth in his mouth. "Bite on this," Marcel said.

Henri nodded. He had felt the swift slicing of the arrow when it hit, then had nearly forgotten it was there. Now the pain radiated to his chest. Marcel was probing the flesh around it. Henri's teeth ground into the cloth. "What are you doing? Pushing it farther in?" His words were ignored, swallowed by the cloth in his mouth. Marcel took his chin, turned his head back, waved the bloody arrow in his hand. Robert was winding an ale-soaked bandage around his arm.

"Didn't hit the bone," Marcel said.

Henri spit the cloth out. "Where is Louis-Philippe?" he asked again.

"They took him." Arnaut gulped. "He is in the donjon with Geneviéve and Maríana."

He could not have heard right. "What did you say?" Then, "Blast! Robert." He turned to the boy. "Not so tight." He swung back to Arnaut.

"The baron and his sister and daughter are all in the donjon."

Sounds around Henri faded. All he could hear was a pounding. "Maríana came back. She came back." It was his heart he heard.

He looked up. Alys crouched in a corner, her nose and eyes red. Several squires and pages huddled by the hearth. A few of the younger knights stood over the long table. None of the older knights were in the hall.

"Maríana arrived just this afternoon," Arnaut said. "Alys told me that she changed into one of her gowns and went over to the donjon. We could not stop her. No one knew what she planned to do."

"Who are the two he burned?" *Maríana!* It could not be Maríana.

"Ysabel and the old woman."

Henri released his breath. "Where is Guillaume?" He scanned the hall, saw what was left of Louis-Philippe's men. All of them were very young, with pale faces and wide eyes. "Where is Bernart?"

"Bernart is in Bazas. He was not here," Arnaut said. "Guillaume is dead."

Henri rubbed the hand of his injured arm. "How many died?"

"Four, counting Guillaume. Jean's archers killed three out in the bailey when we tried to re-take the donjon."

"Didn't you use shields?" Henri rotated his arm. How could he storm the donjon with six men and these... children?

"Not at first." Arnaut's gaze dropped. "Guillaume had us approach the door covering our bodies with shields when we took a log across the bailey to ram the door, but Jean's men poured boiling oil on us. I don't know what he used, but it set the shields on fire. We had to retreat." He paused. "Guillaume was killed there."

"Probably shot burning arrows after the oil was poured," Henri murmured. "It's a trick I've used myself."

His nightmare was realized. Jean had Maríana. But he could not dwell on this, not now. They must get her out. He turned to Arnaut. "How long has he had her?"

Arnaut's face fell. "All night."

Henri seized Arnaut's arm, shook him. "I need you with me." He waited till Arnaut raised his head and set his jaw. Good. There might be some iron in this one. "What else have you tried?"

"That is all. We used shields and got most of the bodies out of the bailey after nightfall." His throat convulsed. "Not Guillaume. We could not risk having burning oil poured on us again."

Henri stood and motioned for all the knights to gather around him. Moving over to the long table, he swept everything on it off onto the floor. The clatter brought all eyes to him. "We will make an attempt on the donjon tonight." His voice rang out in the hall. He took a charred piece of wood out of the fire and drew a crude map on the surface of the table. The knights bent forward and watched.

"There is another way into the donjon," Henri said, watching their faces transform to show something that looked like hope. "There is a back door."

JEAN SAT OUTSIDE the bars of the cell. He had been there for some time. First he had only stared. Then he had eaten, an entire meal. The scent of beef and bread had started a rumbling in her belly. She had almost laughed then. Her left foot was gone, pulped by this man. She would probably not last through the next day. There were other implements in the torture chamber that would inflict even more pain than the iron boot and she had no doubt Jean would gleefully use them. She would not be able to withstand what he would do to her, was sure she would tell him where the cup lay buried. And yet her stomach was beseeching her, telling her to feed it.

Her father had felt the quiver in her arms. "What?" he whispered.

She had shaken her head. "Nothing."

When Jean stopped eating, he spoke. At first, she covered her ears. He spoke of things that her father had done, terrible things, painful things. He said Louis-Philippe had placed hot iron in the bottoms of small boys, had burned their testicles, had... cut them. She gave one, quick glance up at her father's face. He was looking down at her. Puzzlement and shock in equal measure shone from his eyes. He shook his head. She lowered her hands from her ears and listened.

It was the loving detail that brought tears. Every last act Jean described, he painted with sound and color and texture. The gulping sigh of one boy, the silken feel of another's buttocks, the bluish red of an anus stretched to its limit. She did not reach up to wipe her tears. They were all she had to give, to witness the pain and despair of these poor boys. How long did Henri say Fornault Abbey had suffered under the rule of this man? A sob escaped her. Jean noted it. She could almost feel his gloating. Yet he did not stop his tales.

Henri had been there, too, as a boy. Later, he had brought this man down. How could the church have let Jean continue to be a priest? She looked up at her father's face again. There were tears on his cheeks, too. She touched his chin. "I know he does not speak of you," she whispered, "this is his story."

"But I am a..." He could not say the word. "I loved Ibrahim."

"You are not like this man." She took his hand. "Neither you, nor Ibrahim."

Something clattered against the cell door. Jean stood there, shaking. The metal tray that had held his dinner canted to the side of the cell. One of his men stood by the upper door, watching him. It was the man who had greeted her when she first came to the tower yesterday. He still wore the silk tied to his arm.

"No talking!" Jean screamed. "Unless you want to talk to me!"

"Why doesn't he take me into the torture chamber again?" Maríana whispered.

"I am not sure," Louis-Philippe answered. "But I think it has something to do with that soldier over there, his first-in-command." He inclined his head toward the man who was leaning against the wall and watching Jean. "I do not know his name, but I believe he must answer directly to the pope, not just to Jean. I think he refuses to allow the other soldiers of the Inquisition to take you down there and Jean will not carry you there himself. Something has happened here, but I cannot tell what it is."

"He has the silk that wrapped the cup tied to his arm," she murmured. "He took it from me when I arrived."

"What did I tell you! No talking!" Spittle flew from Jean's mouth. He glared at the man up above, dropped his voice. "I could take Geneviéve," he purred. "Put her on the rack and make you watch." His eyes now fixed on Maríana.

Geneviéve paled, but her voice was steady. "Don't listen to him, Maríana. He has gone against what the bishop has ordered him to do and he is trying to find a way to save himself."

Jean bared his teeth and lunged at the cell, grabbing the bars. "Shut up!"

Now the upper door opened, then closed again. Two soldiers stood at the top, hesitating. "We heard shouting," one said.

Maríana whispered, "How many soldiers did Jean have?" Where were the others?

"He had twelve soldiers when he came here," Louis-Philippe murmured. "But Henri wounded one and Guillaume told me yesterday morning that another rode out the day before. That leaves ten."

"Where is Henri?"

"You be quiet! Unless you want to talk to me." Jean's voice was cracking.

Louis-Philippe straightened. His face went blank, stunned. But then a broad grin spread his lips. "Bauçais!" he said. "Of course! He..."

The crash of the cell door hitting the wall stopped Louis-Philippe. Jean marched into the cell and grabbed Maríana, tore her away from her father. Louis-Philippe grabbed for her, caught the edge of her gown, but the fabric ripped, and he was left with only a piece of silk clutched in his hand.

Her shattered foot hit the floor; the dungeon dipped and whirled as burning bile shot into her center. Jean was dragging her with one arm, fending off Geneviéve's blows with his other. He pushed Geneviéve; she fell back against the wall. Louis-Philippe was on his knees now. His left arm hung limp at his side. He launched himself up with his right hand, but Jean had already pulled Maríana out the cell door and slammed it shut. "Lock it!" Jean shouted.

He dropped Maríana on the floor just outside the cell. "Where is it?" he screamed. "What have you done with it?"

She was in the dark again, floating. Blackness spun around her. She focused on the sound she could hear in the distance. Someone was screaming.

Maríana raised her arms, opened her eyes. Jean's face hung inches from her own. "Tell me where it is!" he screamed.

"No!" she shouted. "It is not for you!" Her nails traced a crimson path up the side of his cheek and reached his eye. He grabbed her wrist and pulled it back, twisting it.

Jean's eyes bulged. He touched his cheek, came away with scarlet drops. He stared at his hand; shock momentarily freezing his face. But, with his other hand, he still held her in a punishing grip. He snarled at her. "You will pay."

He made a fist, swung his arm back. She watched the arc of his arm through the air and closed her eyes, waiting for the blow.

"What?" she heard Jean sputter. She opened her eyes and saw the soldier grab Jean's hand, pull him away from her. She dropped to the floor; her stomach heaved when her foot moved against the dirt.

"That is enough," the soldier said.

"Are you mad?" Jean breathed. "I could have you excommunicated! I could have you burned!" Jean yanked his hand away from the man's grasp and spit at him. "I don't care if you are Fouret's man!" He bared his teeth. "You! I will make you the first-in-command!" he shouted to another soldier, one who, with a comrade, stood back against the wall. "Put this man in the empty cell!"

The soldier obeyed Jean's order, taking his first-in-command's sword and pushing him into the other cell.

"Jean is the one who is mad," Louis-Philippe was shouting. The two soldiers wavered.

"You would listen to a sodomite?" Jean's voice roughened. "Help me take her down to the torture chamber."

The soldier moved forward to take Maríana's arms, but before he reached her, the door to the dungeon crashed open and banged into the wall. Louis-Philippe gave a loud whoop. "Bauçais!"

Henri stood at the top of the stairs. He met the blow Jean's soldier aimed at him, fell back against the door. But when Jean's man swung his arm back to strike again, Henri lunged forward and buried his sword in the man's stomach. The man fell, dropping his sword. Henri left his own sword in the man's gut and grabbed the unclaimed sword before the second man reached him. Their blades rang in a clashing burst of hot metal. The man's sword flew from his grasp. Henri swung the sword he held upward, opening the man's throat, and kicked the man down the stairs. Blood spurted in a fountain from the man's neck. Henri looked up.

Jean clutched Maríana's arm, his fingers digging so tightly that the blood had fled her fingers. Jean scrambled forward for the unattached sword, dragging Maríana with him.

Every time her foot touched the floor, a scarlet wave of agony climbed her leg, but she made her body go limp, made Jean work to drag her. Jean snatched at the sword, lifted it, held the blade against her throat.

Cold metal on her skin. Could she work her hands free, grab it? How strong was he?

"Bauçais!" Jean shouted. "Come any closer, and I take her head." He pressed the sword into her flesh. She felt a line of blood trickle down her neck.

Henri stood above the men he had killed. His eyes were stunned. "Jean," he said. "Jean, you don't have to do this." Henri stepped toward him.

"No farther!" Jean screamed. He grasped Maríana by the hair and drew her up to his chest.

Henri stopped, holding both his hands up, his sword dripping blood upon the stones.

"Throw down your sword!" Jean said. "Now!"

"No!" Maríana shouted. "Henri, don't!" Jean turned the blade so its flat side squeezed against her throat, cutting off her voice.

His gaze fixed on Jean, Henri lowered his sword and dropped it to the floor.

"Kick it away from you," Jean ordered. "Over here to me."

Henri pushed his sword along the floor toward Jean, then shoved it the rest of the way with his foot. The sword shot across the floor, clanked against the far wall.

"All right, Jean," Henri said, still holding his hands up. "I have done what you asked. Now let her go."

"You think I am stupid?" Jean laughed, his voice echoing. "No, I am not letting her go. You will let me go out of here with her. If anyone interferes with me, she will die!" He held the cutting edge of the sword close to her neck again.

The sword wobbled as he strove to keep it in position. Jean must be tiring. Maríana tried to shift her weight to the side and throw him off balance, but her foot dragged against the ground.

"Unnnhhh!" She could not halt the groan, but Jean glanced down briefly. If she made more sounds of pain, could she distract him? She looked down, then shuddered. The cloth they had wound around her foot was coming undone. Jean continued to drag her toward the door, his eyes on Henri again. "Back away!" Jean ordered as they got closer to Henri.

Maríana tried to shift her body again. No good. The cloth had unraveled; the raw flesh of her mangled foot touched the ground now. The walls spun. She would faint and his blade would open her throat for sure, then. Would her faint drag this creature to the ground?

She pulled air into her lungs; the walls steadied again.

Henri still held up his hands, but his gaze flickered to Maríana, passed over her, then dropped to the floor. She watched his face, understood he was assessing their situation, seeing how Jean had damaged her, searching for an opening, a way to save her. When he looked down at the ground, she saw his nostrils flare, his eyes widen. He raised his head.

The sword was drooping, the weight of it drawing Jean's arm down. He yanked at Maríana's hair, trying get past Henri and out of the dungeon.

HER FOOT, what had Jean done to Maríana's foot? A rough bandage had covered it once, Henri could see the remnants. Now mangled flesh and the crushed bones that showed a sickly white against the red of torn muscle, dragged against the dirt of the floor.

A mighty inhalation that seemed to go on forever drew his head up.

Jean saw Henri raise his head, look directly into his face, saw the deadly eyes, the flared nostrils. He tried to press the sword he held into Maríana's throat, but she was gone, had somehow slipped down beyond his grasp. When had this happened? He must get her back. She was crawling, he could feel the brush of her passage against his legs. He reached down to grab her, but could not tear his eyes away from Henri. He watched as Henri's shoulders lifted and Henri's hands reached toward him. He felt the steel of those fingers on his neck.

"I'll kill you!" Henri choked. Flecks of scarlet swam before his eyes, an ocean roared in his ears while he grabbed Jean's throat. Jean thrust the blade toward him. He released Jean's neck, and his fingers closed on the sword. With one hand, he grasped the hilt, with the other. He pushed, forcing Jean back against the bars of the cell behind him.

Jean struggled, breath puffing out in wheezing bursts as he turned the blade of the sword against Henri's hand. The edge sliced into Henri's skin. Blood spurted out of the wound and the sword slipped from his grasp. He fumbled to recapture his hold, but it was too late. Jean now held the sword by the hilt, his lips pulled in a snarl over his teeth, the point of the sword aimed at Henri's groin.

Jean's mouth spread in a sneering grin as Henri fell back, keeping his bloody arm between them.

"So you have finally come," Jean did not drop his grin as the sword plucked at Henri's breeches. "Too bad you chose the wrong side. Say good-bye, Henri," Jean whispered, then lunged forward.

Henri waited until the last possible moment. He feinted to the right. When Jean changed course to match Henri's movement, Henri snatched his carving knife from his belt. He thrust forward, catching Jean as the man moved toward him, and buried the blade to its hilt in Jean's belly.

At first, Jean did not react. The grin still spread his lips, he still held the blade ready. He tried to raise the sword, bring it around to slash Henri, but the muscles would not obey him. The sword clattered out of his hand. He stared down at the knife protruding from his abdomen and tried to pull it out.

"No, you don't," Henri said. "This," he drove the knife upward as a frantic gurgling emitted from Jean's throat, "is for my Maríana." He grabbed Jean's robe, kept him on his feet. "And this," he drove the knife further upward, "is for all the boys you raped, boys who had no one to speak for them." Jean was convulsing now, his body twitching as Henri fought to hold him steady. "But this," Henri breathed, bringing his face right next to Jean's eyes, "is for me!"

He drew the blade up, slicing through skin and muscle, through the sour reek of stomach and gut, all the way to Jean's breastbone. The stench and strands of gray intestine cascaded over his arms; both his hands were slippery with blood.

Henri released Jean, watched him hit the floor. Jean's arms jerked. He grabbed desperately at his belly, his breath now a keening whine. Henri reached down, picked up the sword Jean had held, then he paced to the far wall of the dungeon to retrieve the other he had relinquished. With both swords in his hands, crossed over his chest, he looked down at Jean.

Jean was still choking. His hands strove to push the snaking coils of his intestines back inside his abdomen. "For God's mercy, Bauçais," he gasped. "Finish it!"

Henri stared at Jean, at the glittering eyes, at the shaven head. Even beaten, Jean would try to wrest the power from Henri, to order him, tell him what he must do.

"Do it, Bauçais." Louis-Philippe stood, holding onto the bars of his cell. Geneviéve was next to him, his left arm angled over her shoulder. "You are not like this dog, eh?"

Henri drew in his breath.

In the other cell, Pierre stood, watching Henri in silence.

Maríana sat at the base of the dungeon steps. She was pale, but her eyes were steady. Those eyes... .

Henri turned to Jean. "I would not leave a dog to suffer this way."

Jean closed his eyes. Breath bubbled through his clenched teeth. "Be done with it, then."

Henri dropped one sword.

Jean cringed as the clang echoed from the stones.

Henri lifted the remaining sword, caressed the blade, and raised it high above his head. The sword whistled down across Jean's neck, sliced across and through, severing the head from his body.

Henri's arms shook. He stared at Jean, at the dismembered body on the ground. Then he lifted his head and his gaze settled upon Maríana. He stumbled toward her, went down on his knees.

Her foot was gone. Splintered bone and pulped flesh. Nothing could save it, but he could save her life. He must take her away, soon. The foot should be cleaned and bound. Maríana would know how to treat it. He would have his men do her bidding. She might not walk again, but what did that matter? He could make a special chamber for her in his château, in Bauçais. She would sit there all day, watch the sea from her window, listen to their children at play outside. He touched her face. "Maríana," he breathed. "Maríana."

"Henri." She took the sleeve of her gown, dabbed at the cut on his palm. "We thank you for our lives." Her hand dropped. "I thank you."

He took her right hand, held it between his. "We will bind your foot," he said. "And use a wagon."

"A wagon?"

"To Bauçais. You will not have to ride." He glanced up at the stairs. His men and the young knights of Reuilles-le-château were to follow him after they had taken the rest of Jean's soldiers. They would be here soon. "I have six men, and Robert, of course." He lifted her hand to his lips. "We will protect you." He looked into her face.

Her eyes held his, would not let his break away. "No, Henri." Was this his Maríana? The iron in her voice filled the dungeon. Her foot was nothing more than a piece of meat with bones poking through. Yet she sat with back straight, eyes level. "I will not go with you," she said.

Chapter 45

RICHARD'S right arm ached, from the pit of his shoulder all the way to his fingers. As for his leg, well, it was becoming more difficult to ignore the grinding spasm that flared in a splintered burst whenever he forgot and leaned on it. But Maríana and Marc's makeshift splint held his leg straight and took most of his weight. He was almost there.

Fingers of pearl and rose streaked the sky, chased away the night. Birds were starting their dawn chatter; finches and sparrows darted in the treetops around him. He could see the iron gray walls of Reuilles-le-château below.

Richard leaned against the trunk of a beech. He had made Marc wait at the winter hut, and hobbled alone through the dark down the track that led to Reuilles-le-château. Most of the way, he sat, grasping the splints that kept his leg straight, and slid down the path, inching along on his behind. If he struck a rock or large branch with his broken leg, he would not be able to continue. But he had made it; he was here. Richard glanced back at the mountain, at the slope he had come down. How he would get back up there was a puzzle that would have to wait.

Maríana was alive. He could feel her. Pulling his staff under his armpit, he limped away from the tree and toward the château.

The gate stood open and the inner bailey teemed with people. It looked like all of Reuilles-le-château: servants, knights, squires, pages; all of them stood or sat in front of the palais. Richard hobbled across the stones, looking from the stables to the garden, from the palais to the donjon. He froze at the sight of bodies upon the ground, counted four dressed in the livery of de Reuilles. The rest wore the red silk and white crosses of the church.

Where was she? He moved forward, oak staff tapping, right leg dragging against the stones, then stopped, drew in his breath. Bauçais stood there in front of the donjon. Men also dressed in the red silk and white crosses of the church huddled around him. Henri's right hand was bound in a bloody cloth. He was listening to one of the men.

Richard limped toward Henri. He did not notice the people in his way, did not hear their words of complaint as he shoved past them. He stopped in front of Henri. "Where is she?"

HENRI LOOKED up into brown-black eyes. Eyes that bored into him, that demanded. He was young, this man. A long face, good bones, a strong chin. The eyes were tilted, set in an almond slant above high cheekbones. There was the blood of a Saracen there, somewhere. The brows tipped as well, but were now drawn in a black line to the furrow between. Henri settled back on his heels. He knew this man. But how? "Whom do you seek?" Was he looking for his mother, or his sweetheart?

"Maríana."

Henri's heart stilled. Yes. He knew this man. His hands reached by themselves, made for the man's throat. Yet the man did not flinch, did not fall back.

Hands grabbed him and held him fast. Henri made a single sound of protest, then fell silent. Marcel and Georges held him. Marcel had thrown his right arm across Henri's chest. "Bauçais," Marcel said. "Who is this?"

Henri stared into the eyes. "Richard de la Guerche," he said.

"NIECE," GENEVIÉVE whispered to Maríana. "Where is it?" She nervously surveyed the crowd of people, the men who were removing the bodies of Utarilla and Ysabel for burial. "Where is the cup?"

"I have hidden it," Maríana said. She sat on the blanket Alys had placed in the sunlight and looked at her foot. They would never be able to get all of the dirt off it. It had dragged in the filth of the dungeon. "Boiling water," she whispered.

Geneviéve regarded her for a moment, her eyes wide, then laughed. "Why do you want boiling water?"

Maríana swallowed and hoped she could stand the pain. "It is the only thing we can do. The heat of the water will kill any of the evil left in my wound."

Geneviéve took her hands. "There is no need to do this," she said. "My husband was a Cathar..."

They heard angry voices. Henri's men were holding him. Geneviéve said, "Why, is that young de la Guerche?"

Richard heard Geneviéve call his name. He turned away from Henri and looked for Geneviéve. Beside her, seated on a blanket, was Maríana. He stumbled away from the knot of men, limped and hobbled in a lopsided run. A wordless shout behind him did not slow his pace. The oak staff fell from his hands, crashed down upon the stones. He hopped the final steps, sank to the ground and buried his head in Maríana's lap. He felt her fingers in his hair, her lips against the back of his neck.

HENRI LOOKED at Marcel, at Georges. "You can release me."

"He is unarmed." Marcel was uncertain. "And injured."

Henri let his arms fall. "I know." The two men freed him stepped back.

He watched as Maríana bent toward de la Guerche, laughing and crying at the same time, holding the young man's face between her hands. Then de la Guerche was looking at her foot, his face pale, his lips set in a furious line. Henri closed his eyes.

When he opened them, Richard sat behind her, holding her shoulders as her aunt probed the wound. Geneviéve was speaking intently to Maríana; her eyes darted to Henri. Geneviéve crossed the stones to where he stood in front of the donjon.

"Baron de Bauçais," she said. "My niece needs your help."

"I have already helped her, yes?" He wanted to look away, but could not. His gut twisted when Richard wound his arms around her, put his lips to her neck. Geneviéve snapped her fingers in front of his eyes.

"You are a knight, as well as a baron?" She waited.

He sighed. "What does Maríana want?"

A CUP. HENRI rested on his knees before the grave marker of the Moor. Maríana wanted a cup. He plunged his hands into the soil, let the dirt trickle through his fingers. She had buried the cup here, in the grave of her friend.

When Geneviéve made her request, Henri had turned to his men, to ask one of them to fetch this cup. They were no longer around him and could not be found. It was curious. He had given Geneviéve his best courtly bow, then strode to the garden. Here he was. Digging for a cup.

He had lost his love, his Maríana, to a Breton knight with a broken leg. The church would hunt him to the ends of the earth. Durand's men were no doubt on their way to Reuilles-le-château. Yet, here he was, rooting around in the soil for a cup.

He took a stick he had twisted off a bush nearby and dragged it through the earth. It snagged on something. Settling back on his heels, he stared at the lump he had uncovered. How far down had they buried Ibrahim? He did not want to disturb the man's final rest. He reached forward and grabbed the lump, wresting it from the ground.

It was a cup. He brushed the dirt away. A stone cup. But it could not be used for drinking. A rock was wedged inside. Now this was too much. Geneviéve had told him to put water from the pond in it and bring it to Maríana. He pulled at the rock, felt it give. Turning the cup upside down, he gave it three powerful shakes. The rock fell out onto the dirt. Where it disappeared.

"What?" Had he really seen the rock make a wiggling descent into the earth? His fingers had locked around the cup. He tried to pry them free as he rose to his feet and lifted his eyes. He saw the rearing mountain, the jagged walls of Montsegur, saw the cage of smoking embers at its base. Saw the blue-robed old man walking toward him.

HENRI KNELT before Maríana, looking as he had in the old days, before she had fled. His russet mantle and red silk tunic were the same, his beautiful, stern face was the same, but his words were different. He was uncertain.

"You could still come with me," he said, "I am the lord of Bauçais. I am a soldier of the king. I could make a petition to Louis for your safety." He held the cup in his hand. Water filled it to the top.

Richard stood several paces away; she felt his eyes on her. When she told Richard of Henri's rescue, of how he had fought the Inquisitor, something had flared deep in Richard's eyes: regret, envy, jealousy, shame. He had limped over to Geneviéve when Henri came out of the garden.

Now she sat back, looked up at Henri's face. "How long would it take, Henri? What would happen if a dear friend of yours fell ill, or a cousin, or even one of our children? Would you have me stand by and watch while someone died? Someone that I could have saved? Would you have me turn away? No, Henri. The Inquisition is right about me. It is me: I am the threat, and everything I represent." He held up his hands to stop her words, but she continued, "There is no place in your world for someone like me."

Henri took her hands in his. "You probably would not be safe there, anyway," he finally said. "Another baron or even a duke I could fight and vanquish, but, the church?" He shook his head.

"What will you do?"

"I am not sure," he replied. "Would you have me go with you to your valley?" He regarded her warily.

Maríana shook her head. "They may accept you there, but you must understand that I am with Richard. I..."

He placed his fingers upon her lips, stopping her words. "Please don't say anymore," he said, his face drawn. "I don't want to know." He looked away, trying to compose himself. "My life used to be simple. I had no ties to anything. I could serve whomever I chose. I had everything I thought I wanted, but I was dead inside."

He gave her his rare smile. "What can I tell you, Maríana? You brought me back to life. I will never go back to what I was." He studied his bandaged hand. "I don't believe in your powers, Maríana, I never did. You are an adept healer, I will grant you that, but magic? I cannot accept that, but I will always love you."

She stroked the palm of his injured hand. "You could go back to Bauçais, as you said."

"No." A shadowy grin. "I went against the direct orders of the bishop. I waylaid and trussed a Soldier of Christ. I killed an Inquisitor." His grin grew even wider. "I do not think that I will be going back there."

"You have not asked about our..." she stopped.

"About the baby?" He looked down. "Jean's men found her up on the mountain, by the oak tree at the top of the rise before the slope steepens." His cheek rippled as he clenched his teeth.

Her breath caught. "Henri, I am sorry!"

"So am I." He looked to where Richard stood. "I buried her next to Ibrahim."

"Henri." Tears welled in her eyes and she dashed them away with the back of her hand.

Geneviéve approached them. "Ah, very good Baron de Bauçais," she said. "You found it."

He looked down at the cup. "This is a strange piece. For a moment there, in the garden..." His eyes misted. "I think it set me dreaming."

Geneviéve took it and held it above her head. The disc of the sun rimmed the sides of the cup. "What are you doing?" Henri demanded.

"Only what needs to be done." Geneviéve flipped back the cloth that covered Maríana's foot and held the cup over it.

"Geneviéve!" Maríana snatched for the cup. She was not ready for the pain, the shock of cold water against her foot. She needed boiling water to cleanse her wound. She could not go through this twice.

Henri shouted, leaped to his feet, trying to grab the cup. "No!" he said. "You will hurt her."

Richard hobbled to her side and reached for Geneviéve's hand.

Too late. The water streamed down over Maríana's foot, covering it. Her head went back; her eyes squeezed shut. Breath whistled in through her teeth. But after the first shock, she felt no more pain. She opened her eyes and saw Henri glaring at Geneviéve.

"Why?" he asked. Geneviéve pointed at Maríana's foot.

Henri looked down, shouted, "My God!"

Richard dropped beside her, grabbing her arms as if he could draw her away from the writhing ferment that coiled from her ankle to her toes. She had toes again. She could see them, tiny bones dancing into place, knitting together, muscles around them weaving, growing, taking shape. Blue and red vessels whipped among the bone and muscle. Then a translucent pink veil, moist and soft, covered the muscle and bone. Now pale skin grew over the veil, clean and firm, until there was only a gaping wound the length of the foot. And it stopped.

Someone was choking. Maríana looked up to see Henri, arms jammed under his ribs, his eyes wild, mouth working. She feared he would fall, that some fit had taken him, but he looked into her eyes, reached forward and grabbed her hands.

"What? What?" His eyes were blank with shock.

"My husband was a Cathar." Geneviéve answered him. Henri flinched, then stared at the cup. "This is the sacred chalice that his people had at Montsegur." She wrapped her hands around it and smiled. "My husband told me it would heal all wounds and sickness," she said.

"Sickness of the body — and sickness of the soul."

It was painful to watch, this struggle. Henri was badly shaken, his face blanched, lips nearly white. Maríana wanted to help him, yet how could she? He had never accepted her magic, had never believed in anything beyond what his own senses told him. Now he was unraveling before her eyes.

Richard leaned to her ear. "Give him the cup," he whispered.

No. It could not be. She had planned to give the cup to her father. Louis-Philippe had no powers, yet he had respected Ibrahim's learning, her magic. Henri believed in nothing at all.

Except honor. She watched the color return to his face. Honor had led him to kick over the traces, to put his own life in danger.

"Take it, Henri." Maríana beckoned and her aunt placed the cup into her hands. Maríana offered it to Henri.

"Why am I afraid? It is only an old cup." He tried to reach for it, but his hands fell back. "I am not worthy." His voice was low and distraught. "My ignorance and the words I wrote sent more than two hundred people to the flames."

He backed away from Maríana. "I am afraid. If what I saw is real, then my whole life has been in error. Everything I believe, every battle I have fought. How can I start from the beginning?" He stared at the ground. "How can I remake my whole world?"

Richard took the cup from her and struggled to his feet. "You are a knight," he said. "This is your quest." He held the cup out to Henri.

Henri backed away. "Quest?"

"To remake your world." Richard remained where he stood, leaning on his oak staff, the cup proffered. "To take this back to where it belongs."

Maríana gasped. She had not told Richard that the cup must go back to its source. How had he known?

Henri was inching toward Richard. "How will I know where it belongs?"

"You must listen."

Henri received the cup in his hands. He stood in the shadow of the palais, yet light covered him, bathed him.

Maríana looked around the bailey. Everyone was still. Many were kneeling. Then Henri spoke. "I will take it."

"WELL, BAUÇAIS. Are you back among the living?" Louis-Philippe's voice jarred him.

Henri looked up. Louis-Philippe stood in front of him. Maríana was finishing a loose sling, winding it around her father's left arm. Over by the tower, Henri's men were wrapping shrouds around the bodies of the pope's soldiers they had killed. People gathered in small groups, talking and watching Henri's men. Henri had told them he had been acting under his own orders. They were free to return to Carcasonne. He had given the fake orders to Marcel. But none of them wanted to return to the bishop. They would all go back to their homes. Marcel agreed to free Pierre, but only after Henri had left the château.

Henri watched Louis-Philippe gather Maríana into his arms. "I am not going with you, petite," he whispered to her.

Maríana was startled. "But why? Iranzu has said you are welcome." Her lips made a stubborn line. "If you stay here, they will torture you again."

Louis-Philippe nodded. "I know and I am not staying here." He smoothed her hair away from her brow. "But I cannot go to your valley with you. You see, I cannot face Adelie yet. She knows that I was responsible for her sister's death. Perhaps later, when all this," he gestured around the courtyard at the bodies, "has passed, I will have the courage to face her." He hugged Maríana. "I plan to come back, in time. So I shall see you again."

"I had hoped to show you Ibrahim's book."

He shrugged. "Later for that, too." He grinned. "For now, it is enough to know of his feelings for me."

Henri stood rubbing his side. Their words confused him. Who was Adelie? The prickling in his ribs grew. He had tucked the cup into his belt so that it rested against his waist. Now he shifted it. Perhaps he should wrap something around it, more layers of cloth might mute its force.

"Henri." Maríana had come over to stand at his left side. He turned to her. "You must leave soon." She hesitated. "They want my father, of course, but they will really want to find you. You were one of them — they cannot forgive that."

"I know," Henri said. It was difficult to look at her, and he could see de la Guerche several paces away, watching him. Louis-Philippe had given them a small cart to take him up the mountain. Geneviéve and Jeanne stood beside it. Jeanne held baby Philippe in her arms.

"Maríana, they are leaving now," Louis-Philippe said. Moving forward to Henri, he grasped his hands and stared solemnly at him.

"They will be after you, too, Bauçais," he said.

Henri shrugged. "I have a disguise in mind."

"What about baby Philippe?" Louis-Philippe motioned to the infant in her arms. "Would you take him to Bauçais?"

His own son. But no, he could not. "It is better that he be taken to Maríana's people. A baby and nurse would slow me down. Nor do I think he would be safe here." Henri glanced up at the sky, then lifted a hand to Geneviéve. "I must be leaving before dark, if I am to outrun whoever Durand sends."

"Would you accept a traveling companion?" Louis-Philippe grinned.

To not go alone. And this man was worthy. He fought well; he did not flinch. Henri gripped Louis-Philippe's hand. "You would be welcome, Baron." He turned to Maríana, aching to draw her into his arms. But de la Guerche's dark gaze pinned him. "Farewell," he whispered, then raised his hand in salute to Richard.

Henri stood outside the walls beside Louis-Philippe and watched the wagon until he could no longer see it.

HIS SKIN itched. Henri rubbed the top of his head and looked at Louis-Philippe. He had done a good job with his knife. The Baron de Reuilles' tonsure looked quite authentic. But he bet it itched, too. Henri scratched at the round bald spot Louis-Philippe had shaved on the crown of his head. They had ridden hard and were far to the east of the château now.

Time to turn north. Henri drew up his reins, settling his black robe around him and waited for Louis-Philippe to catch up. Henri's years in the abbey would help him make this disguise believable. But de Reuilles!

"Louis-Philippe," he said as the baron pulled up beside him. "You must remember to round your shoulders more. Humility, my dear baron!"

"Yes, Brother Henri!" Louis-Philippe chuckled, slouching in his saddle and tugging at the black robe so it would fit better. Alys had stolen robes for both Louis-Philippe and Henri from Father Gregory's chapel. She had found it necessary to add several inches of cloth to the bottom of Louis-Philippe's robe so it would cover his long legs.

Henri touched the secret compartment Alys had sewn into the body of his robe. The cup rested there against his skin. Every time he touched it, a warmth radiated, spread out over his side and reached his heart. Listen, the Breton knight had said. Well, it did not exactly speak to him, this cup. He patted it.

He found he had an urge to go north. He had wanted to see where the Lionheart had reigned. Not Poitou, though. Not the Aquitaine. His eyes took in the rearing slopes of Navarre, the purple shadows, the brightness that dazzled the air. Across the sea. That was where he would go.

He turned to Louis-Philippe. "Well, we must get moving, Brother Louis-Philippe. North!" He dug his heels into the sides of his horse and rode on.

* * * *

Carol Lynn Stewart

Carol Lynn Stewart lives in Northern California with her 13-year-old son and a cat christened "Demonspawn." She has a doctorate in Social Psychology and works at a major university.

DOOR IN THE SKY is her first novel.